THE LOST DAUGHTER

THE LOST DAUGHTER

Lucretia Grindle

WINDSOR
PARAGON

First published 2011
by Mantle
This Large Print edition published 2012
by AudioGO Ltd
by arrangement with
Pan Macmillan Ltd

Hardcover   ISBN: 978 1 445 88184 3
Softcover   ISBN: 978 1 445 88185 0

British Library Cataloguing in Publication Data available

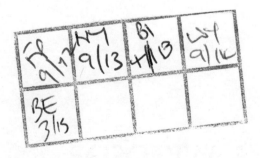

Printed and bound in Great Britain by
MPG Books Group Limited

This book is dedicated to the memory of Aldo Moro,

and to all of those who have met their deaths at the

hands of silence.

And for C;

In the everywhere

where you now are—

PROLOGUE

ROME

1978

THURSDAY 16 MARCH

The altar was washed in shadow. Behind it, a row of candles shimmered. Their flames caught the white disc of the host, then guttered and flared again.

Oreste Leonardi shifted against the back wall of the church. The gun was digging into his hip. He did not believe. Not deep in his heart the way you were supposed to—not with the 'soul and fibre of his being'. Still, he found it moving, this strange cannibalism. Eat of my body. Drink of my blood. Consume me, and you shall be saved.

He looked to the rear pew where his partner sat. Sensing his glance, Domenico Ricci glanced back and tapped his watch.

Their charge was at the front, on his knees. Candlelight licked the back of his dark suit, caught the silvered hair of his bowed head. There was, Oreste thought, no question about Aldo Moro's faith. He'd grown up with the Pope, for Christ's sake—pardon the pun, Father. They'd been little angels, boy servants of the Lord together half a century ago back on the hot white stones of the south. And now, who would have bet on it? One was the Father of his church, the other Father of his country.

Oreste had actually heard Moro called that yesterday, on the TV news, or the radio. By the end of today it would probably even be true. If they made him President. Which they would. Five times Prime Minister, and minister as many times again in everything from Justice to Foreign Affairs, what else were they going to do with him? He wondered if he would go to the Quirinale, too. If the family would even agree to move into the palace. Or if Moro would commute back and forth, *Pater Patrie* by day, *Pater Familias* by night. Now, that really would be a security nightmare.

Even as he thought it, it struck Oreste again how strange it was, that he should be thinking about keeping the next President of Italy alive. Him. A nobody. Nothing but a policeman, an ordinary cop doing his job. Which was all he'd ever set out to be. All he'd ever wanted, really. The job, and what came with it. A little dignity. A good pension. And look where it had landed him. Angels' wings, his mother would have said. Angels' wings feather our lips.

Domenico's eyes met his. Oreste shrugged. *Certo*, they were tight on time. But so what? It wasn't like Communion was something you could rush. *Hurry it along, could you, Father, this Redemption thing? We have an appointment at the Chigi Palace.* And what were they going to do, anyway, all those black suits and Andreotti, who looked like a gnome? Wait, that's what. They'd hardly start swearing in the government without Moro. After all, he'd put the damn thing together. Jury-rigged it with bits of goodwill and promises. It wasn't exactly elegant, but he'd hauled the Communists out of the cold, Grace of God, lured them into bed with the Christian Democrats. *And lo, the lambs shall lie down with the lions and the hand of peace shall be upon you.* Oreste smiled at himself. For a man who didn't believe in God, he'd come over all biblical. Must be the time of year. Easter was next week.

4

The tinny notes of a bell skittered down the aisle. Moro stood up. Oreste watched as he shook hands with the old woman in the pew behind him, exchanging the sign of peace. Holding her wrinkled paw in his, he smiled, his long horse face breaking into a softness, almost a joy, which Oreste found himself envying. When was the last time he'd smiled like that, felt it glowing from the bottom of his belly? Maybe he should try harder. Maybe every now and then—on Sunday mornings, say, or Easter—he should forget the world, just for a minute, and make an effort to believe. The idea fluttered in his head, feathered his lips, and left. *Get thee behind me.* Believing wasn't his job.

Pushing the church door open, Oreste Leonardi looked left then right, his eyes sweeping the street, the waiting car, the second group of bodyguards pulled up behind it. He felt Domenico Ricci slip past him, caught the signal from the escort and returned it. Then he heard the familiar intoning, *Go in peace, go in peace*, as Aldo Moro stepped from the shadow of God.

*   *   *

On Via Fani, the forsythia had begun to open, and the pink stars of the oleander that had been Monica Ghirri's favourite until she discovered how poisonous they were. She'd been just a little girl when a teacher had slapped her hand as she reached for the dusky spear of a leaf. At the time, Monica thought it was anger in the woman's voice. Now she understood it was fear.

That was what children did to you. The world looked ordinary, then you had them and it was filled with hazard. She wondered sometimes how any parents stayed sane, burdened with this love and its attendant terror. She could, for instance, perfectly well have let her son and daughter walk to school by themselves this morning. They were old enough, and it was all of three blocks, and what did she think was going to happen to them on a beautiful Thursday in the middle of Rome? It was one of the reasons they had moved to this neighbourhood—bought the flat she and Gio agreed they really couldn't afford—because it was safe. Patrician. An ordered, secure place.

Monica glanced at the bus stop. Two old ladies sat wearing headscarves and, despite the sun, fur-collared coats, each with a small dog on her lap. A group of Alitalia stewards lounged to the side, their travel cases at their feet. One, a tall guy with glasses and a moustache—and wasn't that a sign of the times—checked his watch, then looked down the road and shrugged.

Traffic was building. Furious honking erupted a few streets away. Something was niggling at her, like a stone in her shoe. She stopped, waiting to cross the street, and realized what it was. The flowers on the dining-room table were wilting. She needed another bouquet, something cheerful. But the flower-seller's van wasn't in its usual spot on the corner.

Monica was looking down the road, thinking he might have moved a block, when she heard the crunch of a bumper. A white Fiat had thrown on its brakes, causing the car behind to ram into it. Idiot, she thought. Then the shooting started.

*   *   *

6

To be honest, Oreste Leonardi hadn't been thinking about anything. His eyes scanned the familiar road, taking in the intersection ahead, the bus stop that seemed to be filled this morning with Alitalia crew, the woman who, he thought vaguely, was pretty in a too-soft kind of way, standing by the crossing, the opposite corner where . . . His brain clicked. Where the flower-seller's van was always parked.

But this morning, wasn't.

He frowned, suddenly completely aware of Moro behind him, lost as usual in his sheaf of papers. They joked that the back seat was his 'flying office'. The flower-seller's van. Not there. Without even being aware of it, Oreste reached for the holster on his hip. He opened his mouth to say something to Domenico, was just forming the words when the car in front of them threw on its brakes, and Oreste thought, This is it, and flung himself into the back seat.

When the first shot hit him, Oreste Leonardi was looking into Aldo Moro's startled face. He felt the impact, then the unexpected frailness of Moro's body as he shoved the man down, covering him as the rattle of semi-automatic fire and shatter of glass ripped the car.

The second shot hit Oreste in the back, and suddenly he was aware of words.

They came whole. Filled his head. Rising, white and perfect, from somewhere deep in his memory, when, holding his mother's hand in the shadow of another church, he had believed.

'Deus in adjutorium meum intende.'

Oreste Leonardi didn't know if he said it, or if

7

Aldo Moro said it, or if, in the brief moment before his life ended, they said it together.

'Domine ad adjuvandum me festina.'

God, come to my assistance. Lord, make haste to help me.

PART ONE

FLORENCE

2010

WEDNESDAY 27 JANUARY

Kristen Carson folded the sweater and placed it in the suitcase. She ran her hand across the soft wool, lavender, her favourite colour, and glanced in the mirror again. The woman in the salon had talked her into it. Promised the copper highlights would make her look really different. Liven up everything, especially her eyes. She knew some people called her eyes her best feature, but she'd always thought they were kind of dull. Ordinary mid-sky blue. Now, they seemed darker, deeper, sparked with mystery. Or something.

She fingered the new fringe, cautiously, as if the curls were spun glass and might break. It had taken her about an hour to style it this way. She hoped he'd like it. Kristen twisted her neck to look at the sides and back. Putting it up definitely made her look older. Now, when people saw them together, maybe they wouldn't just assume she was his daughter.

The memory of his voice ran across her, rippled her skin the way wind fingered grass. She'd been waiting for this day, knowing it was what she'd wanted since they'd first 'met'. Since the first time she'd read his words.

She took a breath, smoothed the sweater again, and closed the suitcase. Then she turned and lifted the coat off the bed, peeling back the plastic bag that covered it like a skin. Slipping it on, she admired the final result in the mirror. The idea of introducing him to her parents—well, to be accurate to her father and stepmother, her father

11

and Anna—flitted through her head. And why not? After all, her dad was always talking about how they wanted to meet her friends. The thought made her laugh out loud. Walking into their hotel with him, bringing him to dinner—just the idea of it filled her with a sort of queasy glee, a high as bright and sharp as jagged glass.

Which was weird because it wasn't like they were bad people. It wasn't like she blamed her father, or Anna—whom he hadn't even met until a year after the accident—for what had happened. Or as if they'd been in any way mean to her. Or even unfair. On the contrary, they'd been pretty much close to perfect. Considerate. Generous. They hadn't batted an eye, for instance, when it came to paying for this year and all the extras—this apartment instead of a grungy dorm. In fact, they'd been thrilled. That she'd developed an interest in art. That she'd wanted to learn Italian, do something ambitious for once. Kristen glanced at her watch. Five minutes to five. She had to get going. If there was one thing he hated, it was being kept waiting.

She lifted the suitcase off the bed, then looked around the room one more time, and came face to face with Mr Ted. The little white bear was losing his fur. A thread on his nose had come loose and his paws were ragged. She should get him a new ribbon. The red one around his neck was grubby and frayed. Kristen picked him up. He felt familiar, warm and moulded, like silly putty or one of those old rubber super balls she used to love. Mr Ted was her Better Half. He'd gone everywhere with her—camp, vacations, boarding school. Overnight to the hospital when she had her tonsils out. She'd even taken him on sleepovers. For a split-second she hesitated, then she placed him back on the pillow.

'Sorry, Buddy.' She winked. 'You stay here and watch out for things. If Miss Goody-Goody asks, tell her it's none of her business.'

Even as she said the words, Kristen felt a pang of guilt. It was true that Marie Louise was vomitously good, and also true that Kristen owed her money. And that, having lent it—without batting an eye—Marie Louise had never mentioned it. Had never even asked when Kristen would pay it back.

'That's what people like her were put on this earth for,' she muttered. 'To be so fucking perfect they make everyone else feel bad.'

Mr Ted frowned.

'OK, OK,' she said. 'I'll leave a note.'

Five minutes later, Kristen Carson passed under San Frediano Gate, and paused. It was colder than she'd thought. Dark was coming down fast, folding the last light in a curtain of mist. From where she stood, she could just make out the apartment window, the one at the end of the hall. It was glassy and black. She'd forgotten to leave a light on. Neither of them would admit it, but both Marie Louise and Kristen were afraid of the dark.

WEDNESDAY 3 FEBRUARY

'So, what do we know about the girl?' Enzo Saenz asked.

Pallioti glanced at him and shrugged. It was nothing more than a slight lift and fall of his

13

shoulders—and spoke volumes. Of impatience. Annoyance. And something more than a tinge of disdain for the schools who could not keep track of their students, especially when those students were wealthy and American and had parents who were making a fuss. They stopped for a stream of traffic that spilled down off the Lungarno towards the Ognissanti.

'Kristen.' The unfamiliar name came awkwardly off Pallioti's tongue. 'Kristen Carson,' he said.

It was just after nine o'clock in the morning of the first Wednesday in February, and still freezing. Tyres spat last night's snow, causing both men to step backwards.

'Seventeen years old. Well, actually, she'll be eighteen on Friday.' Pallioti's nose wrinkled—at the dirty snow and the leaden sky that promised more. 'American citizen,' he added. 'Arrived here in September with a group from a Sherbrooke College. Post-graduate year abroad.'

The tone in which he spoke the last four words suggested that, in his opinion at least, this particular rite of passage—common throughout the world but especially in America and England—was of dubious merit. Academically and otherwise.

That, Enzo thought, was debatable. Some minds would never broaden, no matter how many stamps their passport had. Others flowered in a local library. What could not be argued, however, was that the post-graduate year, the gap year, the junior year abroad, the self-discovery sabbatical—whatever you wanted to call it—contributed considerably to the city's coffers. Flats were rented. Language schools bulged. Visits to the Uffizi and the Accademia tripled. And of course,

14

the students bought things. Gelati. Beer. Shoes. Gloves. Anything with Prada written on it. And postcards. They bought lots of postcards.

The Grand Tour wasn't dead. It had simply shifted gears. Moved with the times. Or not. Basically, it still meant the same thing. *I came, I saw, I shopped.* Sometimes Enzo thought it should be the city's motto. Other times, he realized it was.

The traffic stopped as suddenly as it had begun, the tap turned off at some unseen light blocks away.

'I'll make a guess,' Enzo said as they stepped into the street. 'She's studying Art History?'

'Her parents landed in Rome on Sunday morning.' Pallioti sighed, as if the mere idea of a transatlantic flight exhausted him. 'Flew up here in the afternoon. She was supposed to meet them for dinner at their hotel. When she didn't turn up, they figured she'd appear in the morning. She didn't, and didn't answer her messages. On Monday night they contacted the school. Yesterday they went to the Consulate. Her father knows people in Washington. Replaced part of the Vice-President's brother.'

Enzo looked at him as if he'd lost his marbles.

'He's a surgeon. Knees.' Pallioti waved his hand vaguely, as if that explained everything. 'They're visiting for a week,' he added. 'The parents. For her birthday. They have a party planned, for Friday night.

'The girl shares a flat, with another student on the programme. She hasn't been seen there, and there's no record of her leaving Italy,' Pallioti went on. 'Or of her flying, down to Sicily or Sardinia, wherever they go. No airline booking. No car

15

rental or train booking made online, either.' He spoke abruptly now, the clip of his words matching their pace, which quickened as they shouldered past a few cold-looking tourists and scurrying locals.

'Any chance they're together, this Kristen and the other girl, the flatmate?'

Pallioti shook his head.

'None. Unless she's hiding under the bed. I've arranged for the flatmate to meet us, with the parents and the teacher in charge.' Pallioti clapped his gloved hands together. 'I also called the school that runs the course. This morning,' he added. 'She, Kristen, didn't attend it, for high school or whatever they call it, so they don't know all that much about her. She signed up for this programme more or less at the last minute. When I pushed, they admitted that the recommendations from her own school weren't good. Apparently she's done this kind of thing before.'

'What kind of thing?' Enzo asked.

Pallioti shrugged without breaking stride.

'Pulled vanishing acts. Disappeared. Her record suggests she likes to get people in a stew. Especially if they're her parents. The school wasn't going to accept her because of it, for this course, but . . .' He rubbed his thumb and forefinger together in the universal sign for cash. 'They were having a hard time filling places. And *papà* was persuasive. They said they haven't had a problem with her. Until now.'

'Until her parents arrived.' Enzo stopped in the street, planting his feet like a mule's. 'So, this is a complete waste of time? Another wind-up?'

Pallioti stopped and looked at him. 'Does it

16

matter?'

It didn't, and both of them knew it. What mattered was that the girl's father knew 'people in Washington'. What mattered was that foreign students equalled cash, and Florence wasn't the only beautiful city in Italy, and February was a dull time for the press, and wealthy blonde American girls were like bait to sharks.

Pallioti shook his head, and walked on.

'As of now,' he said a moment later, 'that's all Guillermo's dug up.'

Guillermo, whose very sharp brain was housed in a head as bald and polished as a billiard ball, was Pallioti's secretary, and notorious for his efficiency. And speed. The joke in the office was that if Guillermo called you in the middle of the night he'd tell you what you were dreaming.

Even so, Enzo was surprised he'd had time to find out this much. He'd only heard of the girl himself half an hour ago when Pallioti had barked down the phone, clearly in no good temper, that 'the Americans had gone and lost one of their students'. He hadn't added, *ancora*. Again. But Enzo had heard it, loud and clear.

It happened every so often. Like keys, passports, and train tickets, students got misplaced. Among the police and Carabinieri it was commonly acknowledged that the Japanese kept the best track. The French and Germans were OK. The English and Scandinavians were indifferent, and the Americans were hopeless. Usually these fragments of wandering youth, who were almost always girls and almost always found in the arms of some local Lothario, were none of Pallioti and Enzo's business. Usually they had bigger fish to fry.

17

But then again, usually the kid's father hadn't replaced the Vice-President's brother's knee.

They turned the corner. Wind hit them in the face, splintered with cold. Even Enzo, who was normally impervious to weather and seasons, hated February. He began to turn up his collar, then thought better of it. They were only steps from the American Consulate, and it was arguably bad enough that he was wearing one of his habitual leather jackets. He kept several changes of clothes in his locker, and had offered at least to shave, and even to change into a suit and tie for this meeting with the girl's parents, but Pallioti had snapped that he didn't have time. Which was nonsense. Enzo Saenz was a shape-changer. He could go from Unshaven Street Punk to Suited Ponytailed Five O'clock Shadow faster than most magicians could blink. But that wasn't the point. The point was that it was bad enough that they'd been called out on 'babysitting duty' in the first place, and Pallioti was damned if he'd compound the insult by having his officers tart themselves up for the American Consul who, just for the record, he considered to be a bore and a halfwit.

All of which Enzo knew without a word being spoken because he had worked for Pallioti for the better part of a decade now, ever since Pallioti had first come to Florence and talent-spotted him for the undercover unit he had set up and run—an anarchic and surprisingly effective group that came to be known informally as the Angels. When Pallioti had been promoted and asked to form his new department—an elite squad designed to deal with especially complex, or unpleasant, or simply politically suicidal cases that no one else could be

18

arm-twisted into taking—the first person he had asked for was Enzo Saenz.

Since then Enzo had become Pallioti's shadow. His fixer. The occasional Sancho Panza to his Quixote. And once or twice, his bodyguard. If a decade ago they had been master and pupil, now they were something more equal, and more ill-defined.

*   *   *

Pallioti swore under his breath at the sight of the new security wall that had been erected outside the Consulate. A legacy of the latest terrorist threat, it was see-through, bulletproof, presumably bomb-proof and, to be fair, not altogether unsightly. It was also, Enzo knew, nothing to do with his boss's current fit of ill temper. Alessandro Pallioti was not annoyed about boring Consuls or bulletproof panels, but simply because he was here. Because, despite the fact that he was one of Florence's most senior policemen, he had been more or less ordered to drop what he was doing and proceed post-haste to what was commonly known as Uncle Sam sul Lungarno to personally express his deep interest and concern over the fact that a wayward teenager had run off for a few days.

'The father's name is Kenneth Carson,' Pallioti murmured to Enzo as they were waved through the Consulate's security barrier. 'Doctor, as I said. Surgeon. Famous. Wealthy. From the East Coast. Boston.'

Enzo knew Boston, as much as you could know anywhere in forty-eight hours. He had visited there once from New York. It was cold.

19

'And the mother?' He tucked his identity wallet back into his inner pocket and fell into step beside Pallioti.

'Anna. No other children. She's his second wife.'

'So, not the girl's mother?'

Pallioti shook his head. 'No. According to the school, the mother was killed in a car accident when the girl was small. The headmistress suggested, strongly, that that's one of the reasons she gets away with behaving the way she does.'

Pallioti's own mother had died when he was a child. Somehow Enzo doubted that Kristen Carson or anyone else getting a free pass because of a similar tragedy would hold much water with him.

'As I said,' Pallioti went on, 'the parents arrived Sunday. It's Freedom Day, or some president's birthday. One of those American holidays. In any case, the school's on break. There aren't any classes. Which probably explains why they didn't notice she was missing. About half of the girls live in independent flats and apparently a lot of them have gone off.'

Carnival was coming up. If they were anything like most teenagers, Enzo thought, they'd have scattered to the four winds.

'So, what do we actually know?' he asked. 'I mean, in terms of facts?' *Do we have anything more solid*, he wanted to ask, *than a vanishing act*?

They had reached the landing. A woman came towards them, glassy-eyed and nodding, mobile phone jammed to her ear. Pallioti paused to let her pass. A not especially handsome man whose restless soul was betrayed only by the habitual drumming of his fingers, he was both loved and feared by those who worked for him. They were

20

inclined, somewhat to their surprise, to stand up when he came into a room, and were silent when he spoke. Many of them had asked specifically to be assigned to his new unit. He was so immaculately dressed that behind his back they called him 'Lorenzo', after Lorenzo de' Medici, known as The Magnificent. Now the smile that flitted across his face turned his rather ordinary features sharp and fox-like.

'That,' he said, 'is what I am counting on you to find out.'

*   *   *

James MacCready, the Deputy to the American Consul in Florence, looked and sounded like an advertisement for America's elite Ivy League colleges.

The fact that he actually came from Indiana, and had not gone to one of the fancy East Coast schools like Harvard, Princeton, or Yale didn't matter. As far as Enzo was concerned, the whole obsession with schools and universities—subjects that often seemed issues of life and death to his English-speaking friends—bored him stupid. He suspected it bored James MacCready, too. James was a little too good at playing the part to take it seriously. More than once Enzo had wondered if he really was just a junior diplomat or something more murky.

They'd met a couple of years earlier when they'd both ended up at the same gym, running side by side on treadmills late into the night, and later in the spring, playing football—or, according to James, soccer—on the same Sunday afternoon

21

pick-up team. In a more official capacity, Enzo and James came across each other from time to time, usually in the city jail where James had been despatched to explain that, contrary to popular wisdom, the Consulate offered no protection from Italy's, or any other sovereign nation's, laws.

Now, MacCready caught Enzo's eye. *All this hoo-ha over yet another kid who'll probably stroll back in the next hour, unsuitable boyfriend in tow.* The message flickered between them. Trying not to smile, Enzo pulled out a chair. There had been two cases like this in spring last year, both handled by the Carabinieri, and both involving well-groomed American girls from nice homes. In each, they had gone AWOL with newly acquired heart-throbs. The first had come back in two days, after a row. The second in four, when her money ran out.

Enzo knew that at least half of the people gathered in the conference room—certainly himself, Pallioti and James MacCready, and probably the art teacher and Kristen's flatmate as well—would put money on the fact that that's what would happen in this case, too. But, on the other hand, there was the infinitesimally small chance the girl was in serious trouble. Or about to be in serious trouble. Or dead. Which more or less summed up what he hated about cases like these. They didn't require policemen; they required seers.

Kristen Carson's father had the kind of fifty-year-old good looks—at once handsome and completely nondescript—that reminded Enzo of advertisements for luxury goods. Cars with a lot of walnut veneer. Flight cabins with seats that turned into beds. Credit cards named after rare metals.

22

On first glance, his wife was a perfect match. Good-looking but not showy, blonde and conservatively dressed, Anna Carson was sitting beside her husband. And across the table from Pallioti, who she was not looking at. Which was interesting. Because, while everyone else in the room was at least pretending to be intent on what Pallioti was saying—to be listening closely to his expressions of concern for her stepdaughter's well-being, and to his reassurance that she had probably not gone far and that the police, even as he spoke, were doing everything humanly possible to find her—Kristen's stepmother was studying her hands.

Her profile was classic, her nose so perfect that Enzo wondered if its shape was entirely due to nature. Her skin was slightly bronzed, but not out of a bottle. From playing tennis probably, or golf. No fake tan, Enzo decided, probably meant no fake nose either. Which made it odd that her hair was dyed. In his experience people went one way or the other—all fake or all real.

It was done well, of course. Expertly. There was no darkness at the roots, and doubtless it had cost a fortune. But it was dyed. Enzo had seen enough people trying, for one reason or another, to be someone else, to be sure. Maybe, he thought, her husband had a thing for blondes. He gave a mental shrug, made a doodle on his pad, and surveyed the rest of the table.

Apart from Pallioti and himself, the Deputy Consul and Kristen Carson's parents, the only other people present were Clarissa Hines, the Sherbrooke College Junior Professor of Art unfortunate enough to be in charge of the programme when Kristen decided to go AWOL,

23

and Kristen's flatmate, Marie Louise Tennyson.

One look at Marie Louise was enough to make Enzo realize he owed her an apology. He'd assumed she'd been living with Kristen because they were two of a kind, which was clearly wrong. If Marie Louise Tennyson had chosen to share a flat with Kristen Carson—something he was now willing to bet she hadn't—it was definitely not because like attracted like. Even without the school's 2 a.m. assessment, the picture of his daughter that Kenneth Carson was passing around the table made it clear she was blonde walking trouble. Half confrontation, half come-hither, with blue eyes and a smile that virtually telegraphed *I Dare You*, Kristen Carson was every parent's teenaged nightmare.

One glance told Enzo that Marie Louise, on the other hand, was the one who did not lose tickets and keys. The one who could be relied on to make friends with the fat and the shy. A keeper of secrets, and always on time, she was loyal, generous, and safe—largely because she wasn't desired. Yet. Marie Louise's bright eyes, dark curly hair and round cheeks all suggested that one of these days she'd turn into a bombshell and break hearts left, right, and centre. But that was still on the other side of the dimples and baby fat she hadn't quite lost. For now, she was round and reliable. In short, every teacher's dream. And every bad girl's stooge. Which was why she was sitting here.

He made another doodle on the pad in front of him and wondered how much money Kristen Carson owed her. Then he glanced up and wondered, when it came to it, if Marie Louise would lie out of some kind of tribal loyalty, or because she was afraid. And if so, of what.

Pallioti stopped talking. He had removed his black overcoat and sat, impervious, in his black suit. His tie was a deep crimson. Gold cufflinks winked at his wrists. He steepled his fingers and let silence fall over the room.

'What I don't understand—I mean, what I think we should try to get a handle on here,' Kenneth Carson said finally, 'is, when was the last time anyone actually saw Kristen?'

He looked around the table, his face full of expectation. Enzo wondered if the man had heard a single word Pallioti had said, or if he'd simply been sitting there waiting until he could talk.

'I mean—' Dr Carson raised his eyebrows—'when, exactly, is the last time we can verify that?'

Enzo stifled a sigh. This was the beginning of the requisite 'This could never happen at home, how stupid are the foreign police' lecture. Most parents, usually fathers, felt compelled to give it at some point. It did exactly nothing to help find their child, but it made them feel better.

As a rule, Enzo let it pass. Caught unaware, the art teacher, Clarissa Hines, took the bait. She shook her head, something close to panic passing over her face, as if she had looked into the missing seer's crystal ball and seen her career vanishing. She was, Enzo guessed, probably in her early thirties. A perfectly nice woman, not overly forceful, but not stupid. According to the brief information they had, she'd done a post-graduate year in Florence, so knew the city well and spoke passably fluent Italian. None of which meant she was necessarily suited to riding herd on a bunch of

25

teenage girls whose monthly credit-card bills were probably about the same as her yearly salary.

Clarissa Hines sank in her chair. She opened her mouth like a fish gasping for breath.

'Wednesday,' she said finally. 'Wednesday afternoon. At about two o'clock. That was when I last saw her. At the end of the last class.'

'A week ago?' The tone of Dr Carson's voice suggested he had just looked at a diagnosis and realized it was far worse than he thought. 'Is that right?' He looked around the table, raising his eyebrows as if he expected to be contradicted, by James MacCready, or Enzo, or possibly Pallioti himself. 'How can that be?'

Pallioti said nothing, but Enzo knew what he was thinking. *Let him play it out. Let him get it off his chest. It may tell us something, and even if it doesn't, the faster he gets it over with, the faster we can get on.*

'How can no one have seen Kristen for a week? How can no one have realized anything was wrong until we couldn't find her on Monday?'

The words were met with thick, unhappy silence.

'How can that be?' Kenneth Carson asked again. He turned on Clarissa Hines, his voice rising. 'How,' he demanded, 'can the whole weekend have passed and no one have realized my daughter was missing?'

'Because she wasn't.'

It was Marie Louise Tennyson who spoke. She had an accent. Southern, Enzo thought, if he had his films right. *Mississippi Burning. Sweet Home Alabama.*

'I beg your pardon?' Dr Carson looked at her as if she was a stuffed toy that had just uttered a full sentence. 'What did you say?'

26

Marie Louise scowled. 'She wasn't missing.'

'Don't be ridiculous,' Kristen's father snapped. 'Of course she was missing.'

Enzo couldn't decide if Dr Carson was more annoyed by being contradicted or by being interrupted. Either would probably be unwelcome. The combination was obviously toxic.

'No she wasn't.' The girl shook her head. 'At least, not on the weekend.'

'What do you mean? She disappeared on Wednesday and—'

'I mean,' Marie Louise tightened her arms across her chest, fixed her gaze on Kenneth Carson and spoke slowly and clearly, 'I mean that Kristen wasn't missing because she didn't expect to be back.'

Kenneth Carson began to splutter. Before he could get anything out, Pallioti cut him off.

'I don't understand, Signorina,' he said quietly. 'When you say she didn't expect to be back, do you know where from? Did you speak with her? Did Kristen call you?'

Marie Louise shook her head. 'No,' she said. 'She left me a note.'

'A note?'

Unless Kristen's father was as good an actor as he was a surgeon, Enzo thought this really was news to him. News his daughter's flatmate had apparently decided to keep to herself, until now. Which made him look like an ass. Enzo reconsidered Marie Louise. Maybe she wasn't as nice as he'd thought.

'Why didn't you tell us this?' Kenneth Carson's voice began to rise again. 'Yesterday. Yesterday morning, you told us you had no idea where

27

Kristen was.'

'I don't.' The girl bristled visibly. 'I don't know where she is,' Marie Louise Tennyson said. 'I don't have any idea.'

She turned away from Kristen's father and spoke directly to Pallioti, pointedly ignoring the rest of the room.

'Kristen didn't tell me where she was going. She just said she was gone. Which I kind of figured out anyway, since the apartment was empty. She said she'd be back Sunday or Monday. I assumed she'd called them.' The girl glanced at Kristen's parents. 'When they told me she hadn't, I called her cell. Yesterday, last night, a bunch of times. I left messages saying her Mom and Dad were here, and that they were worried and she should call. It didn't say anything anyway,' Marie Louise added. 'The note. It didn't say anything,' she repeated. 'Just that she'd left.'

Dr Carson's face coloured. He didn't seem like a particularly nice man, but for a moment Enzo felt a pang of sympathy. Someone should have reminded him that teenagers were not for the faint-hearted.

'This note,' Pallioti asked quickly, before the situation could deteriorate further. 'You received it when, Signorina Tennyson?'

'Wednesday,' Marie Louise said. 'Wednesday night. I didn't get back till around nine, so I guess I found it around then. A few of us went to a movie,' she added, 'in the afternoon, after the last class. Then out to dinner. To, you know, start the break. I asked Kris, the night before, if she wanted to come. But she didn't.'

'Was that unusual?'

28

'Not really,' Marie Louise said after a moment. 'Kris didn't do things with us much. You know, movies and stuff.'

There was something in the words that Enzo couldn't quite put his finger on. Hostility? Disapproval? Hurt feelings? Pallioti leaned forward.

'Do you still have the note, Signorina?' he asked. 'Or did you throw it away?'

'I have it.'

Marie Louise reached into the small bag slung over her shoulder and produced a folded slip of pink paper. Dr Carson's hand stretched out. She ignored it and passed the note to Pallioti.

Slipping his gloves on, Pallioti took the paper by the corner. He unfolded it, glanced at it, then handed it to Enzo who slipped it into a plastic evidence bag he'd produced from the inner pocket of his jacket.

Dr Carson sat back in his chair.

'Is that really necessary?' He nodded at the plastic bag, his voice petulant. For the first time Enzo saw fear in his eyes.

Pallioti saw it too. 'I'm sure it isn't,' he said. 'But we like to be careful.'

Kristen's father opened his mouth. Then he closed it, saying nothing.

Enzo ran his eyes over the brief message that had been penned in bright purple ink. *Hi. Decided to go away for a few days. Back Sun or Mon. Have fun, K.*

The letters were girlish, loopy and flourished. There was a smiley face after the words *Have fun.* Enzo stood up and handed the evidence bag to Kristen's stepmother.

'Could you confirm,' he asked, 'that this is your

stepdaughter's handwriting?'

She glanced up at him. Her eyes were wide-set, a dark greenish-brown. The wrong colour. Her skin tone didn't match her hair, either. Definitely bottle blonde, Enzo thought, not sure why this interested him as much as it did.

Anna Carson took the bag, laid it in front of her and looked at it, one hand fingering a small gold locket that swung from a chain around her neck.

'Yes,' she murmured, sliding it towards her husband. 'Yes, that's Kristen's writing.'

Close as he was, Enzo had to strain to catch the words.

The note had a numbing effect on the room, suggesting as it did that they had been brought together in fraudulent circumstances. Set up. Duped.

James MacCready concentrated on his fountain pen. Clarissa Hines sank further into her chair. Dr Carson sat eyeing Marie Louise's tiny bag as if he expected his daughter to hop out of it. Kristen's stepmother returned to the study of her hands.

It was Pallioti who finally spoke.

'Is there anything else, Signorina Tennyson,' he asked, 'that you might be able to tell us? Did she, for instance, have a boyfriend?'

'The girls aren't allowed to have men in their dorms or apartments,' Clarissa Hines said, as if she believed this might actually mean something.

Marie Louise shook her head.

'No. No,' she said again. 'Honestly. She didn't have a boyfriend. I swear. I last saw Kris, Kristen, in class on Wednesday. Like everyone else,' she added.

Enzo smiled and drew a small devil on his pad. It

had a forked tongue and horns.

*　　*　　*

Once the routine list of questions had been asked and answered, and Kristen's passport and laptop computer—both of which had been taken by her parents from her flat—had been handed over and signed for, along with information on her mobile phone and credit-card accounts, the meeting broke up. Kristen's parents and Clarissa Hines stayed behind to talk with James MacCready, and possibly with the Consul himself, who was threatening to make an appearance. Marie Louise took one of the cards Enzo handed her without meeting his eye, mumbled something, and fled.

Enzo planned on giving her an hour before he appeared at the flat in San Frediano. In the event, he didn't have to wait that long. He and Pallioti were on the last flight of the stairs on their way out when they saw Marie Louise standing to one side of the lobby, watching for them.

*　　*　　*

The American base in Lucca was the Consulate's primary reason for being, and a steady trickle of people, many of them obviously military, came and went. None paid any attention as the three of them moved to a corner.

The doors behind the security gate opened and closed, letting in a gush of cold air. Enzo suspected that, like spies on foreign territory, all of them would rather talk outside the enemy gates. But the idea of standing on the pavement in spitting snow

31

wasn't inviting and Marie Louise obviously felt that whatever she had to say was urgent. Where upstairs she had looked defiant and more than a little annoyed, now she looked scared.

'I'm sorry.' Despite the fact that there was no sign of the Carsons, and no indication that anyone near them seemed to be the least bit interested in what they were saying, the girl was barely whispering. 'Look,' she went on, 'Clarissa—Ms Hines—she's in enough trouble already because of this. And, well, I didn't want to drop Kristen in it, either. I mean, more than she is, with her dad and all.'

She looked from Pallioti to Enzo and back again.

'Ah.' Pallioti nodded. 'So, you are telling us that Kristen does have a boyfriend?'

Marie Louise blinked. Her large dark eyes were glassy with exhaustion. And probably shock. She'd probably lain awake for the last week, and possibly for God knows how long before, carrying the burden of this particular secret. It occurred to Enzo, not for the first time, that secrets sucked blood every bit as efficiently as vampires.

'I take it,' Pallioti muttered, 'that you think she's gone off with him?'

'I don't know.' Marie Louise shook her head. 'Honestly,' she said. 'I really don't know. I didn't tell her parents about the note so I'd have a chance to call her. Give her a heads-up. You know, so she could get back here. Or at least call them, stop them freaking out like this.'

The loyalty between kids, even if they didn't particularly like each other, never ceased to amaze Enzo. Inconvenient as it almost always was, it filled him with admiration. And sometimes more than a

32

twinge of jealousy.

'I don't get it, really,' Marie Louise was saying. 'I mean, don't get me wrong,' she added quickly. 'Kristen isn't my favourite person. But she's not stupid, and she wants to go to college. She gets thrown out of here, out of this programme, she's nixed. And,' she added, wiping her eyes with the back of her hand, 'I mean, with what happened to her mom, you know, her getting killed when she was little and all . . . I mean . . . I guess, everybody's got stuff, you know?'

She looked at Enzo and Pallioti for a moment, presumably trying to judge whether people their age could understand.

'I really did think . . .' she continued, apparently deciding they could, 'I mean she was excited about her birthday. So I thought she'd be back. For this party. I mean, maybe she still will be. She had her dad invite all of us, like she wanted to show off. She was looking forward to it. At least I thought so.' She shrugged. 'But maybe it was an act. I don't know her that well. I guess I could be wrong.'

Enzo felt something like a string being plucked.

'Do you really believe that?' he asked. 'That you were wrong?'

Marie Louise studied his face. Then she shook her head.

'No,' she whispered. 'No, I don't.'

'Tell me,' Pallioti asked, 'about the boyfriend. Let's start with his name.'

'I don't know it.'

'You don't know his name?' The question was sharper than Enzo intended. 'I'm sorry,' he added quickly, seeing the look on the girl's face. 'It just seems—'

33

'I know.' Marie Louise deflated as quickly as she had bristled. 'I know. It seems weird. It is weird. But honest to God, it's true. I swear. That's why I'm telling you. Because it is so weird. Usually, you know, girls, like, talk about this stuff. And Kristen did, kind of, at first. I mean, like when we first moved in. Then she totally shut up. And the last few months, I don't know, since before Christmas, she's been really careful.'

'Careful?'

Marie Louise looked at Enzo and nodded. 'Yeah,' she said. 'Like, really. I mean, I never even met him. If she brought him to the apartment— and I don't know if she did—she made sure it was when I wasn't around. All I really know about him is he's older.'

'Older?' Enzo heard the alarm in Pallioti's voice.

Marie Louise nodded again. 'A lot older,' she said, looking at Enzo. 'Older than you.' She turned to Pallioti. 'Maybe more like your age. I mean, he's like—my dad. In his, I don't know, fifties, I guess.'

'If you've never met him, Signorina,' Pallioti asked quietly, 'how do you know?'

'Because I took his picture,' Marie Louise Tennyson said.

*   *   *

The photo had been taken with a mobile phone, from above, and through a window. The image showed a large car, probably black, possibly a BMW or a Mercedes, parked in the street. A blonde girl, presumably Kristen Carson, was ducking into the passenger seat. A man was opening the driver's door. Marie Louise had

34

caught him as he looked up, straight at her. She was right. He was older.

It had been a bright day, and the definition was good. Enzo made out what looked to be a strong-featured, clean-shaven face. Of medium height, broad-shouldered but not fat, even on the little phone screen it was clear the guy was handsome. And knew it. He wore a dark, high-necked sweater under what appeared to be a suede jacket. His sunglasses were pushed up on his forehead, nestling in still abundant and curly dark hair. One gloved hand rested on the top of the car door.

There was nothing overt, but the immediate impression was unsavoury. The girl, the car, the sunglasses. Enzo felt another twinge of unease.

He handed the phone to Pallioti and asked Marie Louise, 'How long did you say this had been going on? This man and Kristen?'

Marie Louise shook her head.

'I don't know. Exactly. I thought at first—well, you know I didn't know Kristen until we got here, until we got put in the same apartment. But I thought at first, they'd been together before. But now I don't think that's right.' She ran her hand over her eyes. 'I don't know,' she said. 'I've been thinking and thinking about it. Kris was, she was so excited, way back when we first arrived. All like, you know, fizzed up. Like when you've just met somebody you really like. But . . .'

Marie Louise looked at Enzo and shrugged.

'But?'

'But that isn't right either. Because she was like that on the plane. On the way over. You know, we all met and flew over together in a group, and when we got here, I mean the second we landed,

35

she started texting and she said some stuff. Back when she said anything about him—some stuff that sounded like she knew him before.'

'Before she got here? Before she arrived in Florence?'

Marie Louise nodded. Enzo felt the weight of Kristen's laptop in the bag her father had handed them upstairs. His eyes met Pallioti's over the girl's head.

'Why did you take it?'

Marie Louise looked at him, her eyes welling.

'His picture.' Enzo tried again. 'Why did you take his picture?'

'My mom,' she said. 'My mom always told me if you feel like there's something wrong, you should do something about it. You know, not just sit there. That afternoon, it was a Sunday, I don't know, like just after Thanksgiving, and Kris had spent hours hogging the bathroom, getting ready. Washing her hair, blow-drying it. The whole deal. When I asked her where she was going, she said "nowhere". Which was obviously a lie. Finally, I heard her answer the intercom. I was in my room. After she went out, I went to the window, at the end of the hall, it looks over the street, and I had my phone in my hand, and . . .'

Tears began to run down Marie Louise's cheeks.

'I couldn't think of anything else to do,' she said. 'I couldn't think of anything else.'

She groped in her bag for a tissue. Enzo wondered if she was still staying in the flat, if anyone from the school had thought to move her, or if this poor girl had simply been left carrying the whole weight of whatever had or hadn't happened to Kristen Carson. She might be old enough to drive, to go overseas for a year, or to volunteer to get killed for her country or elect its government, or in some places even buy a drink, but dabbing the mascara smudges that she knew were there even if she couldn't see them, Marie Louise Tennyson looked very much like a child. So much so that Enzo was half-tempted to ask for her parents' telephone number and call to suggest they come and take their little girl home.

Pallioti put his hand on her shoulder.

'Signorina Tennyson,' he asked, 'where are you staying?'

Marie Louise made an effort to smile.

'I'm OK,' she said, sniffing. 'Really. For the last few nights—well, I didn't want to stay there any more, so I moved into one of the other apartments. With some of my friends.' Her eyes widened, mistaking Pallioti's concern. 'I left a note,' she added. 'In an envelope on the door. And another one on the table, where Kris couldn't miss it. So if she came back she wouldn't think—'

'That's exactly the right thing.' Pallioti's smile didn't reach his eyes. 'You don't need to worry about this any more,' he said. 'You let us worry about it now.'

Marie Louise looked at him for a moment, then she said, 'There is something else.'

'Go on.'

'Up there, in front of her parents.' She twisted the sodden tissue. 'I wasn't telling the truth. I couldn't.'

Enzo thought of the devil on his pad.

'About two weeks ago,' Marie Louise began. Then she stopped. When she started speaking again, the words came quickly, as if she could no longer contain them.

'Kristen borrowed some money from me. Kind of a lot, actually. She said she needed cash, and she didn't want to get an advance on her credit card because her dad would see it. So, I used mine.' She looked from Pallioti to Enzo. 'It was seven hundred dollars.'

'Did she tell you what it was for?'

She dropped her eyes. A blush crept from under the collar of her jacket.

'Well, no,' she said. 'And I didn't ask. I was waiting for her to tell me. I thought she might be, you know ...'

'Pregnant?'

Marie Louise nodded.

'That's where I thought she went, actually.' She looked up. 'That's why I was so careful, about what I said, around her folks.'

Pallioti nodded. 'So you think she needed the money for an abortion, and that's what she's gone to do?'

'She could have told me,' Marie Louise said after a second. 'I guess I'm mad she didn't. I mean—' she dug her hands into her pockets—'I know Kris doesn't like me that much. But I would have helped. I wouldn't have said anything.' Hurt etched across her pretty face.

'You did the right thing. Absolutely the right thing.'

Pallioti pulled out his own phone. He asked Marie Louise for the address of the flat where she was staying, confirmed that there was someone there so she would not be alone, and called Guillermo to arrange for a car to come to the Consulate and take her home.

38

'My phone?' she asked.

Pallioti handed Marie Louise's phone to Enzo.

'I have to take it now,' Enzo said. 'But I'll get it back to you as soon as we download this picture of Kristen and—'

'What picture?'

Between their own conversation and the to-ing and fro-ing in the lobby, none of them had noticed James MacCready escorting the Carsons and the art teacher down the stairs. Now they stood barely a metre away. Enzo didn't think they could possibly have heard what Marie Louise had been saying, but she blanched nonetheless, her dark eyes turning shiny with tears.

'What picture?' Dr Carson asked again.

'This picture.' Pallioti closed his own phone and reached for Marie Louise's. 'Miss Tennyson,' he said, 'very kindly agreed to wait and answer some more questions for us. She remembered that she'd taken a photo of Kristen and a friend.'

'A friend?' Kristen's father was extracting a pair of glasses from his jacket.

'He may have nothing to do with Kristen's disappearance.' Pallioti smiled. He handed Kenneth Carson the mobile phone. 'Do you recognize him?'

Enzo and Pallioti watched as Kristen's father studied the screen. He frowned, then shook his head.

'No,' he said. 'No, I've never seen him before in my life. Is he a professor or something? How does Kris know him?'

Pallioti ignored the question, retrieved the phone, and handed it to Clarissa Hines. She took it gingerly, as if it might explode, studied it for a

39

moment, then shook her head. Enzo caught James MacCready's eye as he looked over her shoulder. He shook his head, too.

'No,' Clarissa Hines said to Pallioti. 'No. I've never seen him before.'

Kenneth Carson was saying something to Pallioti, asking some question about what they were going to do next, but Enzo didn't hear what it was. He was too busy watching Kristen's stepmother.

In the harsh lights of the lobby, Anna Carson looked exhausted. As if she was about to fall over. It was jet lag, probably. Or maybe just years of worrying about Kristen. Enzo looked around to see if there was a chair he could offer her.

'Let me find you somewhere to sit.'

The words came out before he remembered to translate them into English. She looked at him, then frowned and shook her head.

'I'm sorry,' she said. 'I'm the original ugly American. I don't speak a word of Italian, or . . .'

Clarissa Hines was handing her the phone. Kristen's stepmother took it the way someone takes a newspaper or a magazine they aren't interested in. She started to hand it to Enzo, then glanced at the screen. Their fingers were touching when he felt her freeze.

'Signora?'

Anna Carson blinked. Her face had the confused look of someone surfacing from deep water.

'Signora?' Enzo touched her elbow, his fingers grazing the soft cloth of her coat.

She shook her head. A frown webbed her face.

'Where?' she asked. 'I mean, I'm sorry, when was this taken?'

'Outside Kristen's flat.'

40

'No.' She shook her head again.

Enzo looked at her.

'No?'

Anna Carson forced a bright, cheerful, and very fake smile. 'No.' She dropped the phone into Enzo's hand. 'I have no idea who this man is. I've never seen him before in my life,' she said, answering the question he hadn't asked.

*   *   *

The Excelsior Hotel stood on the Piazza Ognissanti looking down its nose at its rival, the Grand, which sat almost directly across from it. Enzo suspected that since both of them were now owned by the same American chain the rivalry was, like more and more of the city, as much marketing gimmick as reality.

Now, as he came through the door, he was forced to admit that the much-trumpeted refurbishment was indeed impressive. The inlaid marble floors with their clashing circles and squares, the blue insets of the coffered ceiling, and the chandeliers that hung from them were undeniably brighter. The Persian carpets were no longer threadbare. The mahogany and brass glowed, and the potted palms had been banished. Denied their dusty corners, their shadows to hide behind, the place had been cleared of its ghosts.

At the reception desk, Enzo slipped his identification out of his pocket. The doorman, who had not been replaced in the frenzy of updating, had recognized him. The young woman on duty did not. All she saw were jeans and trainers topped by a leather jacket and ponytail. She was about to say that deliveries went to the service door, or possibly to ring for security, when he placed his credentials in front of her. She looked at them. Then she looked at Enzo, who smiled and told her what he needed.

According to the concierge, Mrs Carson had asked about the best places to run in the city. The concierge had steered her away from the Cascine and suggested instead that she head for the Lungarno Torrigiani and, if she didn't mind hills, the Costa San Giorgio. He'd marked the route on a map. She'd come down ten minutes later, in running gear, and gone out. That had been over an hour ago. No, she had not yet returned. But, he murmured after a moment's hesitation, it had come to his attention that the Carsons had a reservation for lunch. In the restaurant at one o'clock. A table for three. They were being joined by the American Consul.

Enzo glanced at his watch, then wandered into a corner where he settled on an uncomfortable settee that had a clear view of the entrance. The old revolving doors had survived along with the doorman. They swung at regular intervals like some kind of circus show, spitting the wealthy and well-heeled into the lobby or spinning them out into the grey, cold morning. Watching them, Enzo resisted the impulse to take out his phone and check with the computer lab, see if they had found anything on Kristen Carson's laptop.

It wouldn't do any good in any case. The police geek squad was impervious to harassment. They nested in the heart of the labyrinth of the building's basement, breathing their own air, running on their own time, and no one had yet

42

discovered the threat or bribe that could disrupt them. If there was something to find, they'd find it, and when they did, and not before, they'd text him. Enzo leaned back on the uncomfortable settee and concentrated on the revolving doors. He had the patience of a born predator, the ability to forget himself and concentrate entirely on what he was watching for. In this case, Kristen Carson's stepmother, who his instinct told him was not going to be delighted to see him.

*   *   *

It was almost an hour later when Anna Carson finally came into the hotel lobby behind a family with two teenagers. Half-shielded by them, she looked so different from the woman Enzo had seen at the Consulate a few hours earlier that he almost didn't recognize her.

'Signora Carson?'

She looked up, startled, then, almost too late, remembered to smile. It was nothing more than a slight upturn of her lips.

'I'm sorry. From the Consulate this morning— I've forgotten your name.' She shook her head in a 'silly me' gesture that Enzo found entirely unconvincing. 'I'm not very good with names.'

'Saenz.' Enzo held out his hand. 'Enzo Saenz.'

Her skin was cold from the outdoors, her fingers hard and lean. The rings were gone, consigned, doubtless, to the safe in the suite her husband had reserved for the week. She dropped his hand.

'You'll have to excuse me, I've just come in from a run.' She looked down at her leggings and shoes. Made an effort to laugh. 'Stupid, isn't it?' she said.

'But it helps me relax. All this with Kristen, it's so
. . . My husband is up in the room,' she added. 'So,
if you've found something I should call him.'

Enzo shook his head. 'I'm not here about
Kristen,' he said. 'Not exactly.'

'Then—'

'As a matter of fact, I came to see you.' He
nodded towards the uncomfortable sofa where
he'd been sitting. 'I wondered if we could talk a
minute?'

Anna Carson opened her mouth. Then she shook
her head and smiled again, if anything more stiffly.

'I'm sorry,' she said. 'But I'm rather damp. If I
don't get out of these things, I'm going to get cold.
And we have a lunch reservation. With the
Consul,' she added. 'So, I'm late already. Really,
Mr Saenz, if this isn't urgent, it would be better if
my husband—'

'Signora Carson.'

She stopped talking.

'It's about the man. In the photograph.'

'The man?'

Enzo nodded. 'The man Kristen was getting into
the car with.'

'Oh,' she said. 'Yes.' As if she remembered, but
only vaguely.

She was fiddling with her sunglasses, turning
them over and over, her fingers running like a rat
on a wheel. Enzo resisted the impulse to reach out
and cover her hand with his own.

'I wondered,' he said, 'if there was anything you
could tell me. About him?'

'Tell you?' Her hands stopped moving. 'Me?' She
shook her head, the smile widening. 'Why would I
be able to tell you anything about him?'

44

'Because you recognized him.'

She tried and almost succeeded in denying it, but Enzo saw the arrow hit home.

'You recognized him,' he said again. 'The man in the picture, on the phone. I was standing beside you. I saw your reaction.'

'That's ridiculous.' The smile froze. 'Ridiculous,' she insisted.

'I don't think so.' Enzo waited a moment, then, when she said nothing, he added, 'I think you know who he is.'

'Why on earth would I know who he is?'

'I don't know.' Enzo didn't take his eyes off hers. 'I was hoping,' he said, 'that you'd tell me.'

Voices and footsteps clattered around them. Enzo could sense the concierge and the young woman at the reception desk making an effort not to watch.

'Signora Carson.' He dropped his voice, wishing now that he had found somewhere else, somewhere more private to talk to her. 'If you're in trouble . . .' He reached out, his fingers brushing her arm. 'I can help you. And I will. But only if you talk to me.'

Anna Carson's eyes seemed to darken, to turn the colour of moss and earth. She stared at him, still as an animal caught in a beam of light.

Enzo let a heartbeat go by. Then two, then three. He was about to open his mouth when she put the sunglasses on.

'I'm sorry,' she said. 'But I really have no idea what you're talking about. Now,' she moved her arm deliberately out of his reach, 'if there's nothing else, Mr Saenz, I really do have to get going.'

'If there's anything you need to tell me. Anything at all,' Enzo said quickly, 'now is the time.'

Anna Carson stared at him for a moment. Then she smiled, turned on her heel, and walked away.

*   *   *

'I can't do that! For Christ's sake, Enzo.'

James MacCready leaned back in his chair. Gingerly. In the last few days the wheels had taken on a life of their own. He'd asked for maintenance, or a new chair, but neither had been forthcoming. He shook his head. 'I can't just go around digging up dirt on American citizens.'

'Yes, you can.'

Enzo was standing in the doorway of MacCready's office where he'd appeared without warning, like something conjured out of a lamp.

James MacCready looked at him and sighed.

'All right,' he said. 'All right, yes. Strictly speaking, I can. I'm the Federal Government. I'm the State Department. I can do whatever the fuck I want. Or at least find out whatever the fuck I want. You're right. You. Are. Right. Score one for you.' James laced his hands behind his head. 'Why do you want to know anyway?'

Enzo shrugged.

'A hunch.'

'A hunch?' MacCready laughed. 'Oh, come on. Drop the enigmatic cop routine. You don't have hunches, Enzo. I know you.'

You don't know me, Enzo wanted to say. *We've drunk beer together, it isn't the same thing.* Then he wondered if it was. He stepped into the room and closed the door.

'She knows him.'

The Deputy Consul frowned.

'What do you mean, she knows him? Who knows who?'

'The man her stepdaughter was getting into the car with. Anna Carson knows him.'

'Uh huh. And how do you figure that?'

Enzo looked at him.

MacCready rolled his eyes.

'Oh, I see. She told you, did she?'

'No.' Enzo shook his head. 'No. She didn't tell me. That's why I want you to run a background check on her.'

James MacCready made a face. 'Run one yourself.'

'I will,' Enzo said. 'But it could take weeks.'

James sighed. It was true. As far as 'official channels' in the United States went, background checks from foreign law enforcement might be dealt with in a day, or a week, or two months, or not at all. Plainly speaking, it was a crap-shoot.

James swung his feet onto his desk and crossed his ankles.

'So,' he said. 'You're saying you really think Mrs Perfect Doctor Wife knows this guy? The fifty-year-old Lothario in the phone picture?'

Enzo nodded.

'So, why wouldn't she tell you who he was?'

'I don't know.' Enzo crossed to the window and looked out through the venetian blind. 'I can think of a number of reasons,' he said, moving the slats aside and looking down at the street. 'But all they'd be is guesses.'

'What if you're wrong, and she doesn't know anyone?'

'Then I'm wrong and she doesn't know anyone.' Enzo dropped the blind. He glanced back at James MacCready. 'I'm not asking you to dig for dirt, Jim,' he said. 'I'm just asking you to run her details, a routine check, see if anything comes up. Any criminal record other than a parking ticket.'

'Oh, well. I'm glad you don't want those. I take it this hunch tells you something will? Come up?'

'When a kid disappears family members are the number one choice.'

'The woman was four thousand miles away. What do you think she is?' he asked. 'A time traveller?'

Enzo shrugged. With the light behind him, James MacCready couldn't see his eyes, but he remembered they were an odd colour: a brown so light it was almost golden. Very weird. Kind of like Enzo. Whom, despite the fact that he had the irritating habit of being right all the time, James liked. He swung his feet off the desk.

'How long has she been seeing him?' he asked. 'The girl? Kristen Carson, I mean. This guy? Do we know how long she's been with him?'

'Not really.' Enzo turned round. 'Certainly the whole time she's been here. The other girl, the flatmate, thinks Kristen might even have known him before. It's hard to tell because she didn't talk about him.'

MacCready's eyebrows jumped, disappearing momentarily under his thatch of blonde hair.

'I thought seventeen-year-old girls talked about everything.'

Enzo nodded. 'Exactly.'

James picked up an elastic band, pinged it at the mug that held his pens and said, 'So what do you think this is? I mean, what are you suggesting? The

48

guy has a thing with the stepmother? You think we're talking kidnapping, extortion? Some weird sex thing? What?'

'I don't know.' Enzo smiled. 'That,' he said, 'is what I'm hoping you can get a line on.'

James sighed. Personally, what he was hoping was that this stupid girl would walk back into her parents' swanky hotel room so everybody could scream and yell and call each other names and then go off to their fancy birthday party like one big happy family and let him go back to doing his job. At least the part that didn't include babysitting.

'OK,' he said after a minute. 'So, we have a seventeen-year-old girl missing. Potentially. Personally, for the record—I think that's horse shit, especially since she's done it before. But I guess you're right, we can't dick around with it. If I do this officially . . .' MacCready jerked his head in the vague direction of the upper floor where the Consul had his offices. 'Put in a request to run a criminal background check on the stepmother, he'll hear about it.'

'Which means the Carsons will hear about it.'

'Bingo,' James agreed. 'They're tight as ticks. Not only that—if he gets a bee up his ass, he'll start screaming about privacy and sovereignty and due process. He's really into due process these days.'

Enzo started to point out that that was ironic, given extraordinary rendition and all. But in the interest of Transatlantic Co-operation—and getting what he wanted—he decided to leave it alone. Instead he asked, 'Can you call someone?'

'I have some favours I could call in.' James MacCready's handsome face creased into a frown.

'Do you really think this is something? I mean, something more than a teenage girl running off with somebody old enough to be her father because, well, she wants to freak out her father?'

Enzo looked at him.

'Right,' MacCready said. 'Right. OK.' He looked at his watch. 'Give me a couple of hours. I'll see what I can do. I'll call you. Who knows?' He shook his head. 'Maybe Mrs Perfect Doctor Wife is one of those low fliers with ten warrants out on her.'

Enzo smiled, but neither man laughed.

*   *   *

Enzo listened for the soft thud of the bolts dropping into place. When he was satisfied that the combination lock had reset itself, he turned and surveyed the room. Performed the nightly little ritual of taking inventory, listing the objects that summed up his life.

A pair of brown leather sofas faced one another, their arms creased and dented from supporting either his head or his feet. There was no television and no sound system, just piles of books, stacked more or less neatly on the bare chestnut floor. In the kitchen area, stainless steel and marble glowed faintly. A blue plate sat on the glass dining table. At the far end of the room, the futon bed—the closest he could come to a bare board—was covered in a red spread.

The spidery arms of a pair of reading lights threw a web of shadows across a collection of framed photographs, most of them landscapes, that hung on the far wall. Several were by the same photographer, Seraphina Benvoglio, and several

50

others by friends of hers. One, a study she had called *The Winter Line*, took pride of place above the bed. In it a gravel road, headed by gate posts, stretched away between the snow-crusted ridges of ploughed fields.

The print had cost Enzo more than he had wanted to spend, but he hadn't hesitated for a second, knowing the moment he saw it that he needed it. Much as he had felt, from the first moment he saw her, that he needed Saffy herself. Which was stupid, and pointless, and therefore entirely safe. A coward's passion if ever there was one. Because Seraphina Benvoglio was not only happily married with a young son, she was also Pallioti's sister.

He slid out of his jacket, hung it up, and flipped on the lights. The loft took up the top floor of what had once been some kind of medieval warehouse at the edge of the Oltrarno. Now it was a block of flats, one of several in the city owned by his grandparents. When he joined the police, Enzo had told them that he intended to live, not off their generosity, but off his salary. They had bridled a bit, then accepted his terms. With one exception. His grandmother had convinced him, finally, to let her give him a home. He would, she had insisted, be doing them a favour—save them the fuss of converting, dealing with a management company, leasing to potentially awkward tenants. She'd had the good grace to attempt sincerity, but both she and Enzo knew that was rubbish. His mother had drifted, bumping up against Florence and floating off again, all her life. His grandmother was simply trying to give him an anchor. Ultimately it had seemed not only unkind, but stupid and churlish

51

not to accept the gift.

It was past 10 p.m. Enzo crossed the room and raised the blinds. The night roofs of the city stretched beyond the glass that made up the east wall. On the opposite bank of the river, the Duomo and Santa Croce glowed like spaceships fallen to earth. An outdoor table sat on the terrace, icicles hanging from its rim, surrounded by a skeletal set of metal chairs. The cat sat on one, looking cross. She jumped down as Enzo slid open the door and came pattering in, making her bird noise, demanding to know where he'd been, and when, exactly, he was planning on feeding her.

'I told you,' he said. 'You wanted to stay out. It snows, don't blame me.'

She swished her tail. He'd left food in her hutch on the terrace, but she considered it downmarket. A dosshouse of last resort. Which Enzo thought a little unfair. The thing had cost him a small fortune. He'd even had it insulated. She stalked into the kitchen, throwing him an evil look. Her eyes, a palish golden brown, were almost the same colour as his. Sometimes he wondered if they were twins.

The cat had arrived almost a year ago. She had come over the roofs, dropped down onto his terrace, and informed him she was home. He really should, he thought as he went to the refrigerator, give her a name. He couldn't just go on calling her 'the cat' forever. Or perhaps, actually, he could.

Enzo spooned her some rabbit, apologizing that it was not something more interesting, put the bowl on her mat, and poured her some milk. Then he retrieved a beer. As he reached for the cold bottle, he registered the fact that there were

52

several things alongside it that could be turned into something enticing. He wasn't entirely undomesticated, and in the ordinary course of things found cooking—the chopping and measuring as well as the eating—a pleasant punctuation, a sort of formal end to the day. But tonight, the idea wasn't even tempting. He wasn't hungry. He was worried about Kristen Carson.

She hadn't turned up—at her parents' hotel, or at her flat or, as far as the police could tell, anywhere else. Hospitals, clinics, jails, and now morgues were being checked. As the hours had ticked by with no sign of her, Enzo had sensed Pallioti becoming as uneasy as he was. When, having finally decided he'd done all he could, Enzo dropped in to announce that he was on his way home, he'd found Pallioti standing at his window, staring morosely down onto the snow-sodden piazza. Leaning on the door, he'd actually opened his mouth, started to say something about the girl's stepmother, then decided against it. What he had—or rather didn't have—was so vague that it would just be a distraction, make him sound as if he was clutching at straws. Besides, it was Pallioti who believed in hunches, who seemed sometimes to stare into thin air and pluck solutions out of it, not Enzo. Enzo believed in evidence. Facts. All the boring little concrete bits and pieces. And as far as Kristen Carson's stepmother was concerned, he had none.

'She's only a little girl,' Pallioti had said finally, not turning round. 'She's really not more than a child.'

The statement hadn't required an answer, so Enzo hadn't offered one. He'd just watched his

53

own reflection nod in the glass. Now, he opened the beer and slid a copy of the photo Ken Carson had provided of his daughter out of the file he'd brought home. Pallioti was right, she was a child. A very pretty one and, from the looks of her, one drifting in that dangerous place—a girl inhabiting a woman's body and all too eager to put it to use.

The photo had gone out to all police stations and customs points across Italy. For good measure, it had also been circulated to Europol. The geek squad was taking its sweet time with her computer—Enzo had got nothing but a grunt when he'd finally broken down and called an hour ago. The police didn't have Kristen Carson's mobile phone records yet, either. They'd done better with the banks. Getting her credit-card history had felt like a major triumph, but the story they told offered little reassurance.

Enzo dropped the file on the counter and pulled a copy of the printouts from the wad of papers. Kristen's parents had thoughtfully provided her with both Master and Visa cards, neither of which had been used since Tuesday 26 January. That afternoon, however, she had, as the Americans would say, gone hog-wild. Basically, as soon as she'd finished her morning of conjugating Italian verbs and listening to a lecture on the symbolism in Piero della Francesca's late works, Kristen Carson had gone out and spent close to fifteen hundred euros. It seemed like a lot for a girl worried about getting a cash advance.

Kristen's first charge had been made in the department store Coin, where she had purchased a black cashmere coat, a pair of leather boots, and a large amount of lingerie. Then she had come back across the river to a boutique in the Borgo San Jacopo. There, she had bought a black dress, a pair of black wool trousers, a black sweater, and two pairs of very expensive and very high-heeled shoes. The final charge, made just after 5 p.m., had been from somewhere called Carlo Bay Diffusion, which turned out not to be a surf shop or music emporium as the name might suggest, but a hairdresser where she had a cut, a 'deep pampering conditioner', and something called 'double-depth highlights'. All of which took the better part of three hours and had been booked by telephone, ten days before.

A can of stale nuts sat at the back of the counter. Enzo opened it and ate a handful. In his humble opinion, Kristen Carson's purchases read like the checklist for a dirty weekend. All that was missing was a stop at one of the sex-shops behind Santa Maria Novella. Certainly none of the purchases sounded like they'd been chosen by a girl about to slink off and terminate a pregnancy. Who took a black lace garter belt and three pairs of black stockings to have an abortion?

No. The seven hundred dollars in cash was never intended as a doctor's fee. The sex-shop was, of course, a possibility, but he thought it more likely that the cash was intended to pay for whatever she might otherwise have put on her cards after she left. In other words, to ensure that she couldn't be traced exactly the way he had traced her that afternoon. To guarantee that once she walked out of the flat in San Frediano, she would leave no trail.

Enzo laid out a line of nuts, and ate them one by one, tossing them into his mouth like a trained seal. As he did, he wondered if Kristen had thought of that herself. Or if someone else—someone older and more experienced—had suggested it to her. Enzo flipped open a second file and spread the papers in a fan.

On top were a handful of printouts Guillermo had put together from a routine web search. Most of them concerned Kenneth Carson's general fame as an orthopaedic surgeon who had worked miracles for a number of well-known athletes. One, a profile that had appeared some four years earlier in a publication called *Runner's World*, showed several pictures of him. One with his first wife, Karen, who, it noted, had been tragically killed in a car accident, and their then seven-year-old daughter, Kristen. There was another of him with his second wife, Anna, a 'web-design executive' who, the caption said, had met him when he miraculously healed her knee, thus allowing her to resume her 'passion for the marathon'. Enzo rolled his eyes. He seriously doubted anyone had a 'passion' for running twenty-six point two miles, although it probably explained why she looked as good as she did. He put the pile of clippings aside and reached for an enlargement of the photograph Marie Louise Tennyson had taken with her mobile phone.

Blown up, the picture was a little muzzy, but good enough. The time and date stamp confirmed that it had been taken on Saturday 28 November at eleven forty-two in the morning. Enzo smoothed it on the counter, reached into the refrigerator, and opened another beer.

There was no question that the girl getting into the car was Kristen. Her head was bent, but now, in larger resolution, her profile was visible through the windscreen. Thanks to the shadow of the building, there was no glare on the glass. Kristen's hair, then plain blonde, was tucked behind one ear and fell to her shoulders. She was wearing sunglasses, a blue denim jacket, and jeans. Entirely different from the clothes she'd purchased a week ago.

The car itself was a big black four-door BMW that appeared to be in good condition. He'd get somebody to check, but he thought it looked new. The angle was such that Enzo couldn't see into the back seat, or make out whether or not anything was sitting on the rear shelf. He could, however, see the roof, the bonnet, the blue and white disc of the BMW badge, and part of the front number plate. It had not been obvious on the phone's screen, and was not crystal clear in the enlargement. But it was there—the first two letters, the three number sequence, and possibly part of the third letter. Enzo squinted. He could make out a B or an R. The following numbers were obscure. He'd ask the photo technician to see if he could improve the resolution, but it probably wouldn't yield much.

Earlier in the afternoon, after finishing his tour of boutiques and hairdressers, Enzo had paid a visit to Kristen and Marie Louise's building. There was a *lavanderia* two doors down on the opposite side. Going in and gazing between the chipped blue letters that read 'Wash'N'Dri' he'd had an excellent view of the window where Marie Louise had to have been standing when she took the picture. It was almost directly above the street door.

Most of the buildings on the block were residential: flats or small townhouses. But there was a *salumeria* a few doors up. There was also a bank with an ATM around the corner. And, of course, the *lavanderia* itself. It was not a busy area, but it wasn't a dead one either. If Kristen's suitor called often enough, someone might have noticed him, and the car. The flat wasn't in a wealthy part of town. And what else did people in a Wash'N'Dri have to do but look out of the window?

Pallioti's officers were all busy, but Enzo had arranged to borrow two of the Angels. The sort of people they kept in contact with tended to have good memories. If they got lucky and asked the right questions in the right places they might just get another letter or digit off the licence plate. It was a lot to wish for, but wishing never hurt. He smoothed the enlargement with his thumb, as if he could polish it like murky glass, and turned his attention from the car to the man.

Closer inspection did nothing to change Enzo's initial impression. The guy was handsome and knew it. His suede jacket still looked expensive. His black high-necked sweater, his sunglasses, and what Enzo could now see were driving gloves—complete with open backs and snaps at the wrists—still smacked of the self-consciously slick. The haircut looked expensive, too. It was not quite 'styled', but it wasn't a barbershop chop. Square, even features topped a generous mouth. He had white teeth. And was smiling. Definitely smiling. In fact, he was almost grinning. And suddenly Enzo knew why. It was not because he was about to drive off with the blonde seventeen-year-old. It was because he was having his picture taken driving off with the blonde seventeen-year-old.

Enzo stared and sipped his beer. He could almost see the gloved hand lifting off the car door and sketching a wave.

*   *   *

On the other side of the river, Anna Carson stood in the shower of her suite's master bedroom on the sixth floor of the Excelsior Hotel. She could hear her husband in the sitting room. He was talking to somebody in the States, giving them hell in fast, agitated clips.

Bracing her hands against the marble wall, she let the water beat down her back. It didn't work. She couldn't get the policeman's face out of her head. Policeboy, she thought. Policepunk. No, Policechild. That was even better. He was young enough to be her son, for God's sake. She closed her eyes and made him very small and very inconsequential.

Anna bent one knee, then the other. She stretched her calves and bounced on her toes. Her legs ached, from tension mostly. It was the only thing about hitting fifty she'd really minded. Her muscles seemed to be on some kind of vendetta. Going running this morning had probably been stupid, or at least going as fast as she had, but it was the only thing she'd been able to think of that would get her out of the hotel and allow her some time alone. She hadn't followed the concierge's advice. Too late, it had occurred to her that asking him at all might have been a mistake. She was rusty, no question about it. Like an abandoned engine, her brain had seized up, wilful neglect making sure certain parts no longer worked. She'd had the wit, at least, to stay away from the Cascine. *Never do the opposite, it's too obvious.* The words came back like an unwelcome prayer.

She'd decided on the Piazzale Michelangelo, and by the time she hit the stairs beyond San Niccolò she'd been going a good forty minutes, fast all the way, and her calves were screaming. Driving up the long flights of stone steps, she hadn't slowed but pushed hard, then harder, as if the pain might mean something. As if she could run away, or at least outpace it—the picture on that girl's phone.

When she'd finally slowed at the top of the steps, she was shaking, and had actually wondered if she ought to be afraid. If her heart was out of control and her body was about to follow it. If right there she would start to spasm and twitch. Jig and writhe until she died like some poor medieval peasant, racked with St Vitus' Dance.

Catching her breath, Anna had crossed the road beside the dumpy cafe, climbed the last few yards to the Piazzale Michelangelo, and seen the city laid out below her. She didn't really know Florence all that well. She'd only visited once or twice, a long time ago, and always, it seemed, in the winter. Maybe in spring, or summer, or autumn, it was beautiful. Standing up there this morning it had looked like nothing more than a jumble of roofs with an inky green ribbon threading through it, a broken maze with no centre. She'd closed her eyes, felt her body still trembling, and wondered if she was making a wish, and if so, what it was. Finally she'd unzipped the pocket of her windbreaker and pulled out her mobile phone.

Anna turned off the shower and stepped out. Ken's voice had stopped. She heard him rustling in the bedroom, then a *whump* as he threw himself down on the bed. In a matter of minutes, if not seconds, there would be snoring. She stood on the mat, digging her toes into the deep nap then, instead of reaching for a towel, she stepped, naked and dripping, across the floor. Steam rose from her pinked skin. She sat down on the edge of the tub, holding on as if she might fall off.

*   *   *

'*Ciao*,' Kristen's message had said after barely one ring. 'Wait for the tone,' she'd added, her voice faux-sexy and terribly young. 'Then, tell me everything.'

As if she could know what that meant. Another time, Anna might have laughed.

The beep had sounded. She'd taken a deep breath, and did it again now. Then she looked up into the fogged mirror and whispered the words she'd left on her stepdaughter's voicemail.

'*Sono io*,' she'd said. It's me. '*Ho visto la foto.*' I've seen the photo.

THURSDAY 4 FEBRUARY

Enzo Saenz looked at his watch. Just after 8 a.m. Perfect.

Kristen and Marie Louise's flat was no more

than a ten-minute walk from his building. He had been sorely tempted to come straight here last night, but only inexperienced burglars broke in when any thump, scrape, or flash of light was sure to be noticed. The hours when people were getting ready for work, or coming home from it, were infinitely preferable. Contrary to popular wisdom, true wickedness, Enzo thought, did not always, or even often, happen after dark.

He slipped inside as a couple came out, dressed for work in almost matching suits. The young woman held the door for him, smiling, somehow getting the impression that he was something to do with maintenance, or possibly one of those guys who always seemed to be reading meters.

Actually getting into the flat took perhaps another two minutes. Enzo could have been quicker, but he waited to make sure there was no one in the stairwell, then waited again outside the door. Marie Louise's envelope was still pinned below the tarnished brass knocker. Even so, he stood still as a cat on the landing, reassuring himself that Kristen had not ignored it and come home overnight, that he was not about to come face to face with her.

He needn't have worried. The flat was empty. So much so that when he stepped inside he paused, reluctant to disturb the stillness. There was a confusion of smells. Dry burnt dust from the heating system, stale food, and something else that made Enzo's skin prickle. Footsteps and the sound of a radio echoed from upstairs.

Enzo circled the main room, a combination of kitchen and lounge, slowly, sticking to the perimeter, careful not to step on the rug. Two windows looked out over the back of the building. The shutters were open, revealing silver sky, part of a wall, and a cracked mosaic of roofs. To his right, a corridor stretched down to another small window, the one where Marie Louise must have been standing when she took her picture. Three doors opened off it. Enzo pulled on a pair of gloves and pushed the first one.

The room was obviously Marie Louise's. It was little more than a white-walled box, but she had done her best to make it habitable. A pink and green spread was smoothed across the bed, two matching pillows at its head. On the far wall, a string of fairy lights framed a poster of one of Duccio's madonnas. Another string of lights wound around the shade of the lamp that sat on her chest of drawers. He flipped a switch. The tiny bulbs glittered and winked, catching a display of jewellery—bracelets, a bowl of earrings, and a necklace—arranged next to three small picture frames. One held a close-up of a small terrier of some kind. The next showed Marie Louise standing between two people who were obviously her parents. In the third picture she had her arm around a girl who looked so like her that she had to be her sister. Wearing bikinis, they posed on a long white beach. Notes on heart-shaped pieces of pink paper were stuck to the mirror. One read, *M L, we LOVE you!!! Have-a good-a time-a in Italia! Mom and Dad.* Another, written in a boy's dark block print over a phone number, said, *Hey, Girl, Don't forget this number—Kisses, B.*

Enzo saw himself smile in the glass.

He made a quick survey of the desk on the far side of the bed, then switched off the lights and closed the door. The bathroom was next. He lingered there long enough to examine the cupboards, the shower, and the space under the sink. None held what he was looking for. He hadn't expected them to. He stepped back out into the corridor. He had known somehow that the third door, the one at the end of the hall, would be Kristen's, and found himself surprised that the knob turned easily under his hand. For some reason he'd assumed he'd have to pick it. He waited for a second before he stepped inside.

The air in the room felt thick and slightly chilly. A stale scent of flowery perfume mingled with something that might have been hairspray. Dull grey light fell from the small window on the far wall. The bed was a double, the spread rumpled and pulled haphazardly over two pillows.

Enzo turned on the light. A couple of books were piled on top of the chest of drawers. There were no notes on heart-shaped paper stuck to the mirror or anywhere else. No posters. No fairy lights. The only thing that suggested the room might be inhabited by anyone with any character at all was a small moth-eaten white bear that sat on a pillow at the head of the bed. Its chest had been rubbed bald from years of being held close. The red ribbon tied around its neck was frayed. Enzo leaned down and picked it up. The stitching on the little bear's nose was coming loose. The brass Steiff button in its ear was dull. Its glass eyes winked up at him from a face so serious it appeared to be frowning. Enzo heard Pallioti's voice—*She's only a little girl. She's really not more than a child*—and felt a wave of sadness wash over him.

In the next ten minutes, he went through the

room methodically. With hands every bit as quick and delicate as a surgeon's, he examined the contents of the chest of drawers and bedside table, the papers piled on the desk, the pockets of the jackets and trousers that were hung in the wardrobe and strewn over and around the straight-backed chair in the corner. He unfolded the glossy stiff shopping bags that had been shoved in the back of the cupboard and shook them out. He reached inside the scuffed cowboy boots and looked under the bed, then went carefully through the waste bin. After that, he stopped and stood, trying to think like a seventeen-year-old in love.

Further exploration yielded no slits in the mattress, and nothing beneath it. Enzo circled the room, aware of the bear's eyes following him. He slid out the chest of drawers, then tested the ceiling of the cupboard for loose tiles. Then he looked again at the room. The few pieces of furniture were arranged exactly the same way as Marie Louise's. With one exception. The desk. Where Marie Louise's had been in the obvious place, under the small window that looked out onto the wall of the neighbouring building, Kristen's had been pushed into the corner so the window was to her left and she was staring at the wall. Enzo stepped across the room, slid it sideways, and revealed the heating duct.

He squatted to look closer. The slats of the grille were rimed with dust, but not the edges of the frame. Scratch marks laced the screws that held it in place.

*   *   *

65

Fifteen minutes later, Enzo Saenz turned off the Borgo San Frediano and headed for the river with a spring in his step. Being a policeman in no way diminished his pleasure in being right. Within seconds of removing the grille and reaching into the heating duct in Kristen Carson's bedroom his fingers had encountered what could only be a shoe box. He'd pulled it out gingerly and set it carefully on the floor before he opened it.

The box was heavier than it should have been, and it had briefly occurred to Enzo that perhaps he shouldn't take the lid off without the assistance of a bomb-disposal unit. Then he'd told himself not to be melodramatic. The chances of Kristen Carson secreting supplies of plastique in her bedroom were minimal. Still, he'd held his breath. Then smiled in satisfaction. The box held a dried long-stemmed red rose, two paper cocktail napkins, and a brand new Toshiba netbook.

The rose and the cocktail napkins he'd set carefully aside. The netbook he'd opened and switched on. He got the password on the second try. It was '*Amore*'.

Enzo had been sorely tempted to take the time to scroll through the files, most of which, on first glance, were saved emails. But by that time he'd been in the flat for over a quarter of an hour. The building was beginning to quieten down. Soon it would be tomb-like, every squeak of a door and footstep noticeable. He'd considered simply taking the box, but decided instead to leave it in place. He didn't have a warrant, and for now—on the off-chance anyone else knew where it was, or that Kristen came back—he'd rather no one realized he'd been there. Reaching into his pocket, he'd pulled out a memory stick. It had taken only a couple of minutes to copy the entire hard drive.

While the computer did its work, Enzo made a note of the names and addresses of the bars the cocktail napkins had come from. He knew both. They were large, ritzy in a bland kind of way, and expensive. The sort of place frequented by the kind of tourists who prided themselves on being 'stylish'. In short, a great location if you didn't want to be remembered. He'd try, of course. But unless Kristen and her date had tipped over a table or got into a knock-down, drag-out fight that involved the police being called—in which case she probably wouldn't have kept the napkins—he doubted he'd strike it lucky.

The rose told more or less the same story. Carefully wrapped in a piece of tissue paper, its leaves brittle and cracking, its dried petals puckered in a bud, there had been no point in lifting it to his nose. As a token of love, it was tawdry—the sort of thing that would impress only a starry-eyed seventeen-year-old.

As he'd repacked the box, replacing the contents exactly, Enzo had found himself developing a strong dislike for the man in the photograph. Enzo had slid the pathetic little treasure back into its hiding place, then screwed the grille back over the duct and finally replaced the desk against the wall. After that, he'd taken one last look around the room. Then he'd left the flat. Fingering the memory stick in his pocket, he'd slipped down the stairs and let himself out onto the street.

*   *   *

67

Hi, the first message said. *Has anyone ever told you you have the most beautiful eyes in the world?*

Enzo looked at the date. 20 April 2009. Ten months ago. If Kristen had replied, she hadn't saved the message. Which suggested she hadn't— because she'd certainly saved everything else. There were almost six hundred emails in the folder. 'Giorgio', if that was his real name, which it probably wasn't, might have started off a bit rocky with the Internet equivalent of 'What's a nice girl like you doing in a place like this?' but he'd hit his stride fast enough. By late May there were as many as five emails a day, assuming all of them had been saved. Maybe more. Enzo clicked on another at random, this one in early June, from Kristen.

I miss you so much. Things have really sucked recently. If it wasn't for you, I don't know what I'd do. See? You're bringing out the poet in my soul :)

He scrolled back to the second mail in the list, sent on 22 April.

I am sorry to bother you. I'm not harassing you or trying to stalk you, but I wanted to contact you again because I read the poems you posted on your page, and I was so moved. Your words touched me deeply. I would like to read more.

Your page. Facebook. Enzo hadn't seen it, he'd only heard it referred to by the computer geeks when they'd phoned last night. They'd said there was nothing unusual on it, but he'd bet some of that 'nothing unusual' included an email link, and poetry. Which 'Giorgio' had spotted, and fastened on when the *you have beautiful eyes* line hadn't worked, even on a seventeen-year-old. So, he'd tried again. Appealed to artistic vanity, the old inner hidden soul. Did it every time.

68

Enzo clicked on the next mail. 23 April. This was from Kristen. She'd waited a day, but she'd taken the bait.

Thank you so much for your kind words about my poetry. I will be posting some more poems soon. I hope you'll enjoy them.

A day later, she'd asked him where he was from.

Florence, the home of Dante.

Before they ran him out of town.

I love Dante! Kristen had replied.

Then I will call you Beatrice :)

Enzo felt a wave of depression and pushed back his chair. Was this really all it took, to net a lonely teenager? Yes. He already knew that. He'd seen it a billion times before. Social networking sites were a mecca, a happy hunting ground for every horny, lying sleazebag on the face of the earth. The last statistics he'd read suggested that as many as forty or fifty per cent of the postings were made under false identities. You could talk all right. You could even fall in love. In your own head. Because the truth was, you had no idea who you were talking to or falling in love with.

He scrolled through a few more of the emails quickly, then came to one that stopped his heart.

I am so sorry to hear about your mother. I know what it is like to grow up alone. I feel as if I can reach out and touch your loneliness.

It was possible, of course, that Giorgio was the guy's real name. That somewhere in this dismal correspondence he had told her that he was, what? At least a good twenty, and Enzo would bet it was closer to thirty, years older than she was. It was possible that all of this was, if not innocent, at least not illegal. There was no law that said two lonely

69

people of whatever age couldn't talk to each other over the Internet.

But nothing about it felt right. Enzo doubted it would have felt right even if the girl wasn't missing. Dismissing what now seemed to be his slightly deranged fantasy about Signora Carson, Enzo thought again of the scentless rose and closed the file. He ejected the memory stick. He needed to get it down to the basement, to get the geek squad to take the hard drive copy apart and see if they could at least trace the server paths back and try to get some line on who this guy was.

Maybe when they found him, he'd answer the phone. Maybe he'd hand it to Kristen who'd explain where the two of them were and why she was torturing her parents. Maybe there were unicorns in the Apennines and mermaids in the Arno.

*   *   *

There was no smoking in the fancy new police building, a fact which was much lamented, and probably just as well, because anyone lighting a match in the outer room of Pallioti's office would have blown up.

Pausing in the doorway, Enzo felt a pang of alarm, then relief. An import/export case they had been tracking had flared. Between putting out that fire and visiting the computer labs—where he'd called in every chip he had to get them to put a 'rush' on looking at the netbook's hard drive, something they'd promised to get to sooner rather than never—he'd lost track of time. His stomach told him it was well past lunch, but he had no idea

70

what was going on 'in the real world'. If they'd found Kristen's body, the atmosphere would be altogether different. Low, sober, and morose. This was electric.

Guillermo, whose head had been bent far too industriously over his keyboard, looked up and widened his eyes which were round, very blue, and generously lashed. His eyebrows rose in a pantomime gesture of alarm.

'Warning,' he muttered. 'All personnel to battle stations.'

The comment was amusing but not very helpful. Enzo was about to ask what on earth had happened, when the office door flew open.

'For Christ's sake, will you get a hold of—' Pallioti stopped in mid-sentence, glaring first at Guillermo, then at Enzo. His reading glasses had slipped on his nose and he was holding one of his fountain pens, which was as likely to mean he had been beating it against the edge of his desk as writing down great thoughts.

'Where the hell have you been?'

Enzo had turned his mobile phone to mute before going into Kristen's building. On going down to the labs, he'd turned it off. The computer geeks couldn't actually insist that all pagers and phones were killed in their presence, but they could give strong hints.

Now he slid it out of his pocket and saw that there were a slew of messages. The first three were from Guillermo. The last two were from Pallioti.

'Never mind that now,' Pallioti snapped. 'You'd better have a look at this.'

Before Enzo could ask what 'this' was, Pallioti disappeared back into his office. By the time Enzo joined him he was brandishing a copy of the enlarged photograph from Marie Louise Tennyson's phone.

'I don't know how I could have been so stupid. I should have seen it immediately.'

Enzo was inclined to be sympathetic, but he had no idea what Pallioti was talking about. The photograph didn't seem to have changed since last night. Kristen was still getting into the car, part of the licence plate was still visible, the man was still smiling.

Pallioti sank into his desk chair, reached for his pen and began beating his little tattoo. The taps were so sharp and so measured that Enzo sometimes wondered if they were Morse, or some other secret code known only to Pallioti.

'Well, don't you recognize him? No,' Pallioti muttered, staring towards the window. 'Why would you? You were hardly even born.'

Looking at his boss, Enzo began to wonder if it was him, or something in the water. The computer techs barely grunted at the best of times, and both Guillermo and Pallioti seemed to be speaking gibberish. The most intelligent conversation he'd had so far today had been with the cat. He looked at the enlargement again, and shook his head.

'Should I?' he asked. 'Recognize him?'

Pallioti dropped the pen abruptly, took off his glasses and rubbed the bridge of his nose. Today's cufflinks were lapis, and matched his tie.

'No,' he said quietly, when he finally looked up. 'No, you shouldn't. But I should have. Before I did.'

'Why? Who is he?'

The prickling Enzo had felt on entering Kristen

72

Carson's flat ran down his neck again.

'Antonio Tomaselli.'

Enzo frowned. The name sounded familiar, but he couldn't put his finger on why.

'1978.' Pallioti stood up and went to the window. He dug his hands into his pockets. '16 March 1978.'

Pallioti was not quite right—Enzo had been born, but he'd only been two. Not that that made much difference. He knew about it, all the same. There wasn't an Italian of a certain age—and certainly not a European policeman of any age— who didn't. It was the day Aldo Moro, leader of the Christian Democrats, the man known as the 'Father of Italian Politics', had been kidnapped by the Red Brigades.

Italy's answer to the Baader-Meinhof Group, ETA, and *Action Directe*—their own home-grown version of the left-wing terrorist groups that had swept across Western Europe in the 1970s—the *Brigate Rosse*, or simply BR as they preferred to be known, had been almost single-handedly responsible for the *Anni di Piombo*, the Years of Lead. A decade during which so many bullets had been fired, banks robbed, judges and union leaders and policemen kidnapped and kneecapped and just plain killed, that the numbers were still squabbled over to this day. Fourteen thousand, fifteen thousand, or ten thousand 'acts of violence'. Seventy-five, sixty-five, or a hundred and fifty dead. Not that it mattered. The net result was the same. A failed reign of terror that resulted not in some dreamed-of Utopia of the Proletariat, but in deaths and maimings and arrests and ransom demands. Ironically, it had been the BR's *pièce de*

73

résistance, the kidnapping of Aldo Moro, that had finally turned the country against them. And achieved, however briefly, what Moro himself had been trying to for most of his long career—the uniting of the political jigsaw that was Italy.

Pallioti's back was stiff. He appeared to be staring down into the piazza, but Enzo didn't think he was seeing the fountain, or the fogged windows of the restaurant on the far side of the square, or the glassy damp paving stones. There was not a policeman in Italy who did not remember exactly where he had been when Moro was kidnapped. Or what he had been doing when, fifty-four days later, after the biggest manhunt in Italian history, his body was found and their failure broadcast to the world.

The prickling on Enzo's neck was replaced by a cold feeling. When Pallioti finally turned round, his face was drawn.

'I recognized it last night,' he said. 'Or thought I did. I called someone, a friend. In Rome. Emailed him a copy.' He gestured towards the picture in Enzo's hand. 'He confirmed an hour ago. He's sure. It's Tomaselli. Antonio. Fifty-four years old last August. Born Ravenna. Educated at Padua. Father deceased, mother in a home outside Mestre. No other known family. He was convicted in the Moro kidnapping, as being part of the group that carried it out—ran the flat, engineered "The People's Trial". They were never able to prove,' he went on, 'in court at least, exactly who killed Aldo Moro. There were conflicting reports, confessions.' He nodded at the enlargement. 'Tomaselli was certainly one of the candidates. Not that it matters,' he added, smiling sourly, 'who actually

74

pulled the trigger.'

Enzo shook his head. 'I don't . . .' Then he remembered. There had been an amnesty of sorts.

Pallioti nodded.

'Antonio Tomaselli was caught, in 1978. In 1981 he was convicted. He served twenty-eight years. His behaviour inside was exemplary. He was released ten months ago.'

Pallioti crossed to his desk, sat down again, picked up his pen and began to tap it.

'None of which,' he said, 'necessarily means anything. He may be entirely innocent. Have done nothing wrong. All we know for sure is that the girl knows him. Well enough,' he added, 'to get into a car with him a few months ago. We don't even know if she's with him now. Or if she is, what the hell he's doing with the seventeen-year-old daughter of a surgeon from Boston, Massachusetts.' Pallioti looked up and smiled. There was no warmth in his face. 'Maybe,' he said, 'Signor Tomaselli just likes little girls.'

And maybe, Enzo thought, 'Giorgio from Florence' was someone else altogether. And pigs with wings fluttered above the unicorns and the mermaids.

*　　　*　　　*

Anna came round the corner without breaking her stride. When she had been here two days ago with Ken and the terrified art teacher, she had not taken much in. They had been in a taxi and she had been exhausted. Now she glanced up and down the street and registered the lights in the *salumeria*, and the launderette, and the tall rows of the

75

houses.

It was late afternoon, and foggy. A grey mist drifted across the city. Already the street lights glowed in dull orbs, highlighting the sleet that ran down the chipped plaster facades and the tracks of rust that dribbled from the shutters. It was a typical student neighbourhood, the sort of place friends back in the States would rave about as 'authentic'.

For which read 'grubby', Anna thought sourly. For a moment, she felt a longing for the safe, comfortable, boring, suburban street she had called home for the eight years she had been married. For the spreading trees and lumpy pavement, the manicured lawns and wooden houses. It was almost a physical pain. She pushed it away. Blocked it with the memory of his voice.

The call had come at breakfast. She'd come down before Ken, which was lucky, because she wasn't sure how she would have explained it otherwise. Even without him there, she'd stood up and stepped away from the table, turned her back on the room.

The number had shown on her BlackBerry's screen as *unknown*. Of course.

It would be a land line, in a bar or a phone box, if they still had them. Or, in this day and age, a pay-as-you-go disposable. They'd all read about Al Quaeda using those—about how death could be neatly arranged with anonymous numbers.

The chatter of conversation, the clink of cutlery and china rose behind her, and for a split-second she had contemplated not answering, pressing the red symbol, dropping the phone on the over-patterned carpet and standing on it. Grinding the black lozenge with her heel until it cracked, and

76

broke, and was silenced to nothing. Then she thought of Kristen. And pushed the green button.

At first she'd heard only the empty buzz of miles, and wondered if it was better, or worse, this hovering silence. Then his voice, like a remembered touch.

'*Ciao, carina,*' he'd said. '*Da quanto non ci si vede.*'

Hey, sweetheart. Long time.

*   *   *

Anna glanced at her watch. She crossed the street, reached into her pocket, and pulled out the spare set of keys. It was half past three.

It had been pathetically easy. All she'd had to do when they visited the school this morning was wait until Ken was grilling someone before she sidled up to Clarissa Hines and mumbled some nonsense about Kristen's dress for the party. The poor woman had given her the building's security code and handed over a set of keys to the flat so fast she seemed almost grateful—almost as eager as Ken himself to buy the idea that Kristen might actually show up for her birthday bash tomorrow night. It was, Anna reflected, and not for the first time, amazing what people could believe when they really wanted to. People like her, for instance.

She punched the code and pushed open the door. Standing in the dingy stairwell, she fumbled for the light, then stood blinking in the sudden glare, breathing in the damp smells of mildew and cooking. The girls' flat was on the third floor. Anna had passed the second landing when she heard the street door open. Two women came in, discussing the shocking cost of children's clothing, their words bouncing and echoing in the hollow space. Keys in hand, Anna stepped inside Kristen's flat before they even suspected she was there.

Opening the door to her stepdaughter's bedroom, Anna Carson felt a pang of something like shame. Long years of habit made it hard to ignore the barrier of privacy, the fact that she had never snooped on Kristen, and rarely gone into her room uninvited, even when she was a little girl. Maybe I should have, Anna thought. Maybe she didn't want to be left alone as much as she insisted. Maybe if I hadn't 'respected her privacy' so much—and what was that anyway, except an excuse for fear, or laziness? Maybe if I'd inserted myself into her life, like it or not. Maybe if. *If ifs and ands were pots and pans there wouldn't be trade for tinkers.* The words popped up from her childhood like bubbles released from mud. Anna took a deep breath and stepped inside. The single window looked out onto a wall. She flipped on the light.

A wave of sadness washed over her. This was hardly the den of a teenage girl away from home and having the time of her life. It looked like a cell. Or a cheap motel room. It looked like one of the loneliest places she'd ever seen. Then she noticed Mr Ted, and felt a sudden, heart-thumping panic.

The little Steiff bear had been Karen's last present to her daughter and for as long as Anna had known her, Kristen had never gone anywhere without him. She even used to take him to school in her backpack, his little head sticking out of the top where the zippers met. Now, meeting his black glass eyes, Anna Carson wondered for the first

78

time if her stepdaughter was dead.

'No!' she said out loud.

If she stepped too close to that whirlpool, fell down that rabbit hole, she'd never come back. Anna pushed herself away from the door, forced herself across the room, and opened the cupboard.

As usual, Kristen's clothes were a mess. Things hung every which way. Shoes were piled on the floor, boots shoved to the side. Anna had to get down on her hands and knees to find what she was looking for—the bright red backpack with Kristen's initials embroidered on it. It was part of the luggage set they'd given her for this trip. She wished it wasn't so new, or so red. A single Alitalia tag, from the flight Kristen had taken to get here in September, dangled from the back strap. She pulled it off, then laid the pack on the bed, unzipped it, and turned to the chest of drawers. Opening the drawers felt like another violation, and again she told herself not to be stupid.

Anna Carson had seen her fiftieth birthday come and go. Still, she was not much bigger than her stepdaughter. That was, she supposed, partly thanks to genetics, and partly thanks to the running that Ken joked was her 'addiction'. More than a dozen marathons in as many years had kept her leaner than she had any right to be. Kristen was as tall, and a little thinner through the hips and chest than she was, but Anna didn't think she'd have a problem finding things that would fit.

Winter helped. Kristen favoured bulky sweaters, ethnic stuff. Anna chose two and laid them on the bed. Then she pulled out a pair of fashionably slouchy 'boyfriend' jeans, and a second pair of combat trousers. Socks and underwear came next.

After she'd made her selections, Anna untied her trainers and peeled off her leggings and thermal top. She folded her own clothes into the bottom of the rucksack, packed the things she'd chosen on top of them, then pulled on a pair of trousers, found a black turtleneck in Kristen's middle drawer, and put one of the sweaters on over it.

She found a belt and chose a scarf. Shoes were more difficult. Her feet were bigger than Kristen's. Anna was about to give up, dig her own trainers out and put them back on, when she noticed the cowboy boots. Kris had complained after buying them online that they were too big. Anna grabbed one and stepped into it. Perfect. When she looked at herself in the mirror on the back of the bedroom door, she almost smiled. She looked like an ageing, boho graduate student. She pulled her hair out of the ponytail, braided it quickly, then tucked it under the grey woolly hat she'd found in the top drawer.

Satisfied with the overall effect, she went down the hall to the bathroom. In the cabinet that was a complete mess, and therefore obviously Kristen's, she found several lipsticks, some grey eye shadow, and a too-black mascara. Anna daubed her eyes, then painted her mouth a purple-pink that didn't suit her, or Kristen—or anyone who wasn't a corpse, for that matter. Now all she needed was a jacket. She had noticed Kris's new parka—goose down and, if she remembered correctly, costing a small fortune at Barney's—still hanging in her closet, obviously abandoned, like the rucksack, for something more chic and Italian. Back in the bedroom, Anna slid it off the hanger. The fabric was beautiful, dark olive green and satiny. She stood holding it, her hand fastened on the collar, suddenly paralysed by the memory of another jacket, much smaller, but also expensive. Also smooth and shiny. The first gift she had ever bought Kristen, almost exactly eight years ago.

It was pink. With silver piping and a hood trimmed with white rabbit fur, and personally, Anna thought it was hideous. Not Kristen, though. The minute she saw it, the little girl had fallen in love. Hanging on Anna's hand in Sak's Fifth Avenue, she had pleaded and whined and reminded Anna that she had promised, absolutely promised, that this stepmother, stepdaughter shopping trip was all about her, all about whatever special treat she wanted to pick out for her birthday.

Even as Anna had handed over her credit card, knowing it was absolutely against her better judgement, and that she was falling for the oldest trick in the book—that she was a new wife being manipulated into buying her stepdaughter's favour—even then, it had seemed worth it. And when Kristen threw her arms around her, squealing, and when afterwards at their special lunch she had kept peeking into the bag, stroking the fur as if it was a pet, Anna had known it was worth it. If only for Kristen's smile. Which was radiant, but too rare, and almost never bestowed on Anna.

She'd been a fool, of course, and even half-realized it at the time. But for a few days she'd actually deluded herself that somehow the gift had sealed something between them, and that maybe, just for a minute, it had taken away some of the hurt that had hovered like a storm cloud over the little girl since her mother's death.

So, a week later, when Ken was away at an overnight conference leaving them alone together for the first time and the school called to report that Kristen had asked for a bathroom pass and vanished, Anna had not only panicked, she had defended her. Determined to stand up for her stepdaughter even as the headmistress pointed out that this had happened before, Anna had insisted that the police be called, and that they organize a search team. Lunchtime that winter afternoon had found her wading through the bog along the Concord River, certain the next thing she would see would not be more golden bullrushes or a flight of green-backed mallards, but the shiny satin and muddied fur of the pink jacket.

Which was in fact found, and at about the same time. In a dumpster, smeared with you wouldn't want to know what, behind a mall two towns away.

Kristen herself was found inside the mall. In an outlet of Gap Kids, where she was nabbed for shoplifting. By the time the dots were joined and her parents notified, she was being held in juvenile detention by a social worker and a cop.

Ken came roaring back from New York, calling his lawyer on the way, who made the whole thing go away and charged them the better part of a thousand dollars for it. Anna, having given righteous lectures to both the school and the police, apologized profusely, and went home with her tail between her legs feeling like a hysterical idiot. Which was nothing compared to how she felt that night, when Ken—after reassuring his daughter that they loved her, and that they really, truly wanted to understand—had asked Kristen

82

why on earth she had done something like that?

Sitting at the kitchen table drinking hot chocolate, Kristen had looked at her father, her beautiful blue eyes welling with tears, and had replied, sadly, that she was sorry but she'd 'really, really needed a new jacket'.

At the sound of the words, Anna, who had been standing at the stove making Kristen's favourite dinner, cheeseburgers, had felt something inside of her stop.

'I mean, Daddy, I couldn't wear that gross pink thing Anna made me buy,' she'd heard her stepdaughter say. 'I know she liked it. But it was so ugly! She made me wear it, and everyone laughed.'

$$* \qquad * \qquad *$$

Standing in the dim light of the bedroom, Anna blinked, amazed that after all this time the pain was still there. She put Kristen's jacket on, trying not to notice that her hands were shaking. Then she picked up the rucksack, fitted it over her shoulders and adjusted the belt. The last thing she did before she left the room was grab the little white bear and stuff him into her pocket.

$$* \qquad * \qquad *$$

'So, yeah. I saw her.' The big man's face split into a wide grin. 'A fox,' he said. 'Blonde hair. Fake blonde, but pretty. You know, with those stripes. Street lights, whatever they call 'em. Sometimes they're pink, green, whatever. Hers wasn't like that, though. She looked like that actress, you know? All in black, and her hair twisted up.'

Enzo did not know which actress Benny was talking about and he didn't care. All that mattered was that it really did sound like he'd seen Kristen Carson.

Benny Ibrahim, which was almost certainly not his name, was well known to the police, and particularly to the Angels. He was harmless enough, a big north African guy who sold counterfeit sunglasses and cheap gloves with *Made in Italy* tags that came from Morocco. For a while, Benny had lived in the Cascine, which was where Enzo had met him. They'd got talking and found they had a few things in common. Benny, for instance, didn't like drugs and he didn't like men who hit women. A few years ago, he'd tipped off Enzo about a particularly unpleasant Bulgarian trafficker. The information had been good and the bust that followed significant.

He sometimes worked the area around the Carmine. It was worth seeing if he'd been around a week ago Wednesday. As it turned out, Enzo and the Angels got lucky. Benny'd folded up his pitch and had been wandering down towards Piazza Gaddi when he'd noticed a big black car pulled up on the opposite side of the Lungarno Santa Rosa. It had struck him as strange because it was too early and the wrong part of town anyway for kerb crawlers, and there was no real reason to stop there. Then he'd seen the girl. The fox. All dressed in black, hauling a suitcase on wheels.

*   *   *

Sleet splatted against the plate-glass window of the cafe. Tiny ice crystals twinkled briefly in the pink

84

neon light of the sign, then slid away. The Angel who had found Benny had already bought him a sandwich and a coffee while they waited for Enzo. Now, she got up and went to the bar again.

'OK,' Enzo said. 'So, what else?'

Benny shrugged, his big shoulders hunching in the matted black woollen jacket that matched the watch cap pulled down almost to his eyes. He knew the routine. Details were what you got paid for.

'Well, if I'd known I was looking for her . . .'

Enzo waved his hand in an 'OK, come on' gesture.

'All right, all right,' Benny smiled. 'Like the man said, hindsight is a beautiful thing.'

Enzo resisted the impulse to roll his eyes. Benny occasionally waxed poetic. Putting up with it was the price of admission.

'She didn't look forced,' the big man said suddenly. He shook his head. 'She didn't look like, you know, she was scared. If she had a been . . .' One of Benny's more endearing fantasies was that he was some sort of superhero, drifting through the Oltrarno protecting young women in peril.

'The car?' Enzo asked.

He really wasn't in the mood for one of Benny's soliloquies on the evils of men and the vulnerability of young girls. After telling Pallioti about his discovery of the heating duct and the netbook, he'd spent the better part of the last few hours back in the computer labs watching the geeks re-create Kristen Carson's hard drive then prise it apart again. Wheedling their way into her life. Plucking her secrets one by one, until he felt he could have written the story himself.

So much for his half-baked theories about the

stepmother. She'd probably done nothing more than think Antonio Tomaselli reminded her of somebody else. Happened all the time. Enzo felt an unaccustomed punch of embarrassment. He no longer had a shred of doubt that 'Giorgio' and Antonio Tomaselli were one and the same. Which made him all the more eager to catch this slimeball.

The emails pretty much told the whole story. Tomaselli had noticed Kristen on Facebook where, stupidly but not uncommonly, she'd posted a Hotmail address for use by new 'friends'. That was one of the things Enzo really hated about Facebook—what it had done to the word 'friend'. That from now on one of the most beautiful words in any language would carry, at best, the hollow ring of false intimacy. At worst, the stink of outright lies.

By May, Antonio was sending her presents. One of the first had been the netbook, which had been delivered, not to her home, but to an address at somewhere called Mailboxes Etc., where he had thoughtfully suggested she acquire a mail drop. The emails suggested he'd taken care to do this by 'snail mail'—still the best untraceable method of all—sent to her boarding school. There would be a little cache of letters and cards somewhere, Enzo thought, under a drawer liner or in another heating duct, probably tied with a ribbon. All of which explained why they hadn't picked up anything on the original laptop. No history of connections. No Hansel and Gretel trail of cookies. The netbook, along with a new email address and Skype connection, had taken care of that. Assured that they could 'talk freely'. Have, as 'Giorgio' put it,

86

'some real privacy'.

By July, he'd mentioned the gap-year course in Florence. Shortly afterwards, he sent her the link. Parsing the emails had made Enzo feel like he was watching a snake slithering through tall grass.

A very well-prepared snake. Because it was clear, at least to Enzo, that, even before he contacted her, Antonio Tomaselli knew an awful lot about Kristen Carson. He knew where she lived, and went to school, and what she looked like, all of which he could have figured out from her Facebook page. What was more puzzling was how he had known about her mother. Because he had.

It was skilfully done, Enzo had to hand it to him. He'd let Kristen actually tell him about her mother's death. But reading the emails it was easy to see he'd been priming her. Fishing for it the whole time, lacing his comments with sympathy and understanding that were so pointed that eventually she'd poured out the whole story. All the details of the night when Kenneth Carson, chairing a panel in Cape Town, had left his seven-year-old daughter at home with his wife, Karen, who had proceeded to drink the better part of a bottle of vodka before locking their only child in the basement—leaving her with her new teddy bear, a six-pack of Coke, and a packet of cookies—and picking up the car keys.

Reading it left Enzo queasy. Kristen's description of how she'd felt, waiting for her mommy to come home and unlock the door, had made him feel like a peeping Tom, the worst kind of voyeur. The queasiness had turned rapidly to rage when Antonio had responded with his own confession. He had never told anyone else, he wrote, but his mother drank, too. And she too had died young. When he was only eight. It was a sign.

*   *   *

Seeing the look on Enzo's face, Benny nodded. He stirred the cappuccino that had just been placed in front of him.

'The car,' Benny said. 'Right, man. The car was Big Ass. A Beamer. Black. You know, fancy. When he saw her coming, before she got there, he popped the boot. Opened it up like a smile. That's what I remembered.' He laughed and sipped the coffee. 'That Big Ass car looking like it was grinning.'

Enzo tried not to think of jaws, and what they did when they closed.

'You don't remember any of the numbers on the plates? Or anything like that?'

The tech squad had promised they would start running possible combinations as soon as they had time, but another digit would help. The province seal would be a ten-strike. Even Enzo had to admit it was asking for pennies from heaven.

Benny shook his head.

'What about the driver?' Enzo asked. 'Did he get out? Did you see him? Any idea if there was more than one person in the car?'

'Yeah,' Benny nodded. 'He got out. Real gentleman. Gave her a kiss. Put the bag in the boot, held the door. Like I said, it wasn't like he forced her or anything.'

'What did he look like? What was he wearing?'

'Tall. Dark hair. Some kind of jacket. I wasn't really paying that much attention, you know? And it was getting dark. He was definitely waiting for her, though. Lifted the case in, closed the boot. Then they hopped in front and *sayonara*. The whole thing didn't take more than a second or two.'

'OK.' Enzo stood. 'Thanks.' He clapped Benny on the shoulder, and slipped a twenty-euro note under the edge of the sandwich plate. 'By the way,' he asked, as he turned towards the door. 'I know it was getting dark. But the suitcase, you didn't get a chance to see what colour it was?'

If Benny said black, or leather, or canvas, they'd have to think again.

His face broke into its familiar grin.

'Red, man,' he said. 'I told you. She was a fox. That case.' Benny Ibrahim shook his head and laughed. 'That suitcase was red as a cherry.'

*   *   *

'So, *bambino mio*, how was your day?'

Giulia Saenz rolled her eyes as she spoke, laughing at the American TV show greeting. Enzo smiled in reply, plucked an olive out of the bowl in the centre of the long table and bit it in half, watching his mother as she stood at the stove. She had been no more than a girl, seventeen, younger than Kristen Carson was now, when she got pregnant. Eighteen when she had him. Barely twenty when she left her marriage—and essentially everything else she'd ever been—pausing only to hand her son over to the safe keeping of her parents.

There was no denying that three decades later, Giulia Saenz was still a woman who turned heads.

89

But despite her cloud of dark curly hair, despite her smile, and her wide-set eyes, which unlike his own were a conventional brown, Enzo doubted she'd ever been what was conventionally thought of as 'beautiful'. His mother was tall and moved with a faint trace of awkwardness, as if her own body was somehow unfamiliar. For as long as he could remember, Giulia had lived a life best termed 'alternative'. She'd dabbled in every trend the counter-culture had to offer, whatever it had been at the time. But for all that, there was nothing of the ethereal hippy about her. Enzo wondered if youth had suited her, and suspected not. He guessed her restlessness had been less rebellion than an effort to survive—a way of marking time until she finally grew into herself. He wasn't sure, at fifty-two, if she'd done that yet, and chose not to think too closely about what that might mean. For either of them. Upbringing could only do so much; traits travelled in blood and bone. Enzo had been aware of various men in the past, but none lasted long, and there had been no one in the last few years. Giulia had never remarried, and although she rarely mentioned him, she had never given up his father's name. She looked up.

'What do you think?' she asked, nodding towards the far wall.

Like Enzo, Giulia had been given her house by her parents. She was their only child, and they had never made her a black sheep. Never cut her off or cast her out, even when she had disappeared for years at a time. His grandparents knitted what ties they could. One was this farmhouse outside Greve. His mother had gutted and remodelled it over the years, when she was around. She leased the small

90

vineyard and the several acres of olive groves, and had stripped one of the barns and turned it into a studio where she periodically made increasingly large, and to Enzo's eye increasingly bizarre, pieces of what she called 'fabric art'.

Her latest creation took up most of the far wall. He suspected it might be some sort of seascape. Bits of the blue and green felt she made and dyed herself undulated in waves, interspersed with scraps of livid pink and slices of something metallic that looked suspiciously like pieces of old tin cans.

She was smiling when he looked back at her.

'Never mind,' she said, reaching for a bottle from the wine rack, 'tell me instead about your day. Week. Month.'

After a lifetime of sporadic contact and sometimes outright absence, Enzo had found himself visiting Giulia, when she chose to be in Greve, more or less regularly. Occasionally he brought one or both of his grandparents, but usually he came alone, sometimes announced, sometimes not. Often they cooked and ate together. From time to time he simply stood in her studio and watched her work.

He reached for the corkscrew. Giulia put two glasses on the table. Enzo poured, the sound of the wine lost in a rattle of wind. It was a filthy night. Taking his glass, he went to the fireplace, picked up the poker and jabbed at the big log. A flame jumped and died, falling back into the embers.

'Tell me about the Red Brigades.'

He said it without turning round, and heard rather than saw her pull out a chair to sit down at the table.

'What about them?'

91

Enzo glanced over his shoulder. His mother was wearing her habitual jeans, red high-topped trainers and one of her own sweaters. In the shadowed light, with her long boy's legs and half-pinned-up nest of hair, she might have been any age. Or no age at all. As eternal as the Medusa.

'Did you know any of them?'

She picked up her glass, took a sip, and shook her head.

'Not personally, really. If you mean did I know anyone who was running around toting machine guns, no. But, yes, of course.' She glanced at him. 'I mean, back then, everyone knew someone who knew someone. Or said they did.' She shrugged and pushed up the sleeve of her sweater. A set of silver bangles clinked. 'It was the times,' she added. 'What it was like. If you were young. And like-minded.'

'And were you? Like-minded?'

Giulia smiled. Her mouth was wide and generous. It was the one physical feature they shared.

'Of course,' she said. 'Everyone was. Well, everyone I knew. Everyone on the Left, more or less. At least at first.'

She stopped talking. Something passed behind her eyes, and for a moment Enzo wondered who she saw when she looked at him.

'You have to understand,' she said finally. 'It was different. Everything was different then. Italy was different. Europe was different. We were different. The war hadn't been over very long, really. What? Twenty-five, thirty years? And a lot of people felt, well, that promises had been betrayed.'

'Had they been?'

'That depends what you thought you'd been promised.'

She looked into her glass, studying the dark inky liquid.

'The university system was collapsing,' she said a moment later. 'There had been so much hope, and then there was so much anger. We were educating people so fast, promising them a different life. But there was no different life because there weren't enough jobs. The country didn't grow as fast as the promises did. So, yes. Some people, young people mostly, thought they'd been betrayed—been promised a better life then had it snatched away, when in fact it couldn't be promised because it wasn't there to be offered. It had to be built and that takes time. But . . .' She reached for an olive and shook her head. 'When you're young,' she went on, 'you don't want to hear that. You just want everything. Now. "*Vogliamo tutto e subito!* We want everything and right now!" That was actually the Red Brigades' motto.'

'You're kidding?'

'No.' She laughed. 'Looking back, it seems so childish. A sort of tantrum by spoilt infants.'

Spoilt infants with guns, Enzo thought. He wondered if that was what Aldo Moro had tried to explain to them—that 'Everything Now!' is nothing but the outraged wail of children and martyrs. In itself, the message would probably have been unwelcome, more so since it was delivered from the sullied state of adulthood. No wonder they'd killed him.

'Some people—well, a lot of people really,' his mother was saying, 'blamed the State. And, of course, NATO. And the Americans.' She sipped her wine. 'Thank God we have the Americans to blame. I don't know what Europe would do without them.'

Enzo had a quick vision of James MacCready, who would undoubtedly agree.

'Anyway.' Giulia tucked her hair behind her ear and smiled. 'We all quite enjoyed feeling betrayed and hard done by and righteous. Imagining we were just like Che, spouting Marx and frantically understanding the proletariat. But of course, Italy wasn't Cuba, and the proletariat didn't want to be understood. They just wanted stability and jobs. So . . .' Her shoulders jumped under the russet wool. 'A lot of shouting went on, especially in the universities. About Mao and Lenin and Marx. The usual, really. Then some people decided to take it a bit more seriously.' She lifted her glass again. 'They modelled themselves on the Partisans, the *Brigate Rosse*. Did you know that?'

Enzo shook his head.

'I don't know,' his mother added, 'what the Partisans made of it. I should think people were careful not to ask them.'

She stood up and went to the stove, adjusted the gas and took a lid off a pot. A warm, garlicky smell flooded the room. Enzo relinquished the poker and reached for his own glass. There was nothing counter-culture about his mother's taste in wine. She kept a very good cellar.

'It was a nice idea,' she said, reaching for a wooden spoon. 'To play at being heroes. Don't get me wrong, some of them, the *Brigate Rosse*—the BR, as we called them—some of them, a lot of them, probably most of them, wanted, believed in, a better, fairer, more just society. They just

94

misunderstood how to go about getting it.'

Enzo watched his mother drop the spoon in the sink and put the lid back on the pot. He remembered the wool her sweater was made of. Remembered the day he had watched her lift it out of the dyeing vat, limp and dark and dripping like something drowned.

'The BR. They made the mistake,' she said, turning round and looking at him, 'of thinking that just because you happen to have a conviction it's a good idea to act on it.' A smile flickered across her face. Enzo couldn't see if it reached her eyes. 'That's the problem with convictions. You have to test-drive them to know if they're any good. If they're not, well, it can be a bit late.'

'Certainly when they involve things like guns.'

'A hazard of youth. Believing.'

Giulia folded herself into one of the kitchen chairs, a leg tucked under her.

'That, and having the courage to act,' she continued, reaching for her glass. 'A lot of the BR were very young. Most of them. That was part of the tragedy of it. Noble ideals. Courage of convictions. Living the word. I think sometimes about the university professors, who did all the preaching, and . . .'

She shook her head. Enzo thought she was going to add, *Who should have known better*, but she didn't. Instead she said, 'There's something childish about those kinds of notions of purity. Don't you think? That's what makes them so dangerous.'

Enzo prodded the log with his toe. It rolled backwards, sending up a fizz of sparks.

'Where were you?' he asked.

'When Moro was killed or when he was kidnapped?'

He realized he hadn't even had to tell her what he was talking about. It was like JFK's assassination in the States. Before 9/11, all you had to say to people of a certain age was, 'Where were you?' And they knew you were talking about Dallas. Now he supposed that, at least for his generation, it would mean the Twin Towers.

'In Paris. I saw the footage on the news, walking past a shop that sold televisions. The cars in the road. That body lying there with its arms flung out—the driver or one of the guards, I can't remember. They killed them all,' his mother said. 'All the police who were guarding him. Gunned them down. The others were still in the cars. Only that one poor man fell into the road. I didn't know what had happened, just then, standing in the street. But I knew it was Rome. There wasn't a sign or a caption or anything. I just knew. And oddly,' she added, 'I wanted to come home.'

She glanced at him, and Enzo felt himself returning her smile.

'Did you?' he asked.

Giulia stood up and lifted a set of plates down from a cupboard.

'Yes,' she said. 'As a matter of fact I did. It's strange, but at times like that, when something horrible happens, it's what you want to do.'

Enzo watched as she laid the table, aligning the cutlery. Reaching for the pepper grinder and the salt dish. Fetching linen napkins out of a drawer and folding them on the bread plates. The kitchen of the farmhouse bore no resemblance at all to the rather formal dining room of his grandparents'

96

flat, but the gestures were familiar.

He went to the oven, opened it, and lifted out the leg of lamb that was spitting and hissing. Giulia was slicing a loaf. Enzo set the meat to rest, then reached for the carving knife and the whetstone, and began stropping the blade.

'Some of them are out now, aren't they?' She didn't look at him as she asked.

Enzo turned to the meat. Browned slices, pink at the core, peeled away from the bone.

'That's why you want to know, isn't it?'

*   *   *

By the time Enzo left, the sleet and snow had stopped. Clouds chased by a strong, gusting wind shredded themselves above the twisted branches of the olive trees. A smattering of stars appeared, cold and far away.

Giulia stood in the doorway, the big sweater rolled up to her elbows, the silver bangles catching the light. She kissed him, then laid her hand against his cheek, studying his features as if she was memorizing him.

'Be careful,' she said. 'Of the *Brigate Rosse*.' She looked at him for a moment, then added, 'Not all of them were dangerous, even then. But some were, the True Believers.' Enzo felt his mother's palm, the brush of her fingers like a memory against his skin.

'You won't understand them,' she said. 'It's not that you're not clever—but your generation doesn't have those kind of idealists. Not any more. So, you won't know them. You won't recognize them. But the real ones, even after all this time,

97

they won't have changed.'

He leaned down and kissed the smooth, bronzed skin of her forehead.

'Goodnight, *mamma*,' Enzo said. 'Sleep well.'

She dropped her hand and smiled.

'*Sogni d'oro.*' Golden dreams.

He was halfway down the path, had reached for his keys, was pushing the automatic lock and hearing the answering ping from the car, when she called to him.

'Enzo.'

Her voice sounded like a bird's trill, a nightjar in the dark. He stopped and looked back.

'Your father,' she said. 'He sends his regards.'

FRIDAY 5 FEBRUARY

Enzo Saenz knew that somewhere deep inside he harboured the suspicion that, having been abandoned by his mother, he probably shouldn't love, much less like her. And almost certainly shouldn't care what she thought. The fact that he felt all three—and that he had forgiven, and even understood, her—was more worrisome than he cared to admit. If only because it was one more piece of evidence, along with the shape of their mouths, that they were, in fact, the same. And suggested he was capable of doing what she had done. Abandoning. Running. Disappearing. He thought of it as a genetic flaw, or hereditary disease. A tiny fragment buried deep inside him that might one day become unmoored and drift into his blood. His organs, his liver. His heart.

He made himself a pot of coffee and a plate of eggs. The cat, having devoured her own breakfast, rubbed against his legs, then invited herself onto his lap. He sat, stroking her and sipping the hot black liquid. A second later when the phone chirped and jumped on the table, he was so certain it was Pallioti that he didn't even bother looking at it before answering.

James MacCready's voice came as a surprise.

'Hey, my man. How about a cup'a joe?'

Despite being well into his thirties, James had the uniquely American ability to say things like this without even a trace of embarrassment. Even more amazing, when he did it he didn't sound like an idiot. James habitually called coffee 'joe' and in the locker room after football matches slapped backs and called people 'bro'. In bars, he asked who wanted a 'brewski'. Enzo wondered if he was even the tiniest bit jealous of this bonhomie, and decided probably not.

'Seriously, where are you?' MacCready asked, before he could answer.

Enzo looked at the phone. Where did he expect him to be at six forty-five in the morning? Out making Florence safe for humanity? Pursuing drug runners and low-lifes? Running laps? Doing a hundred push-ups? Knowing James—and for that matter, himself—he had to admit any of the above were possible.

'Seriously,' James said, 'you on your way in? How 'bout we meet, have a little chat?'

*   *   *

The cafe was crowded. Bankers and businessmen

99

milled at the bar. Every time the door opened, several thousand dollars'-worth of leather briefcases swooshed in and out. Enzo was probably the only person in the place, at least on the far side of the counter, who wasn't wearing a black suit.

He ordered two espressos, staked out a table, and waited. It was nearly half past seven when James MacCready wove his way through the crowd, his camel overcoat flapping, his height and blonde hair making him a stalk of corn in a field of crows.

'Hey,' he said by way of greeting. 'Sorry about the early hour, but I needed to talk to you. And I didn't want Dickhead dropping in.'

Enzo assumed Dickhead was the American Consul. James had a variety of names for him, depending on his mood. Or on the Consul's recent behaviour.

'So,' James said, biting the top off a sugar packet and emptying it into his cup. 'About our little problem.'

Enzo started to say he'd made a mistake, that James had been right and the idea of Kristen Carson's stepmother being involved in her disappearance was desperate. Or just plain silly. Then he changed his mind. Who knew what had turned up? One of the clippings had said Anna Carson worked in computers, design. Maybe she did have a link to Tomaselli, had designed a web page for him or something. Maybe that was how he'd fastened on Kristen. You never knew.

'Is she?' he asked. 'A problem?'

A smile twitched James's lip, making him look almost sinister.

'Like I said, or maybe I didn't,' he added. 'Sorry.

100

I have this friend. A good guy, in New Jersey.' James reached for a second sugar packet. 'Anyway, I thought it was better, you know, than calling DC. Would look more run of the mill—and my guy was happy to do it. So, he ran a routine check on Anna Carson of Monument Street, Concord, Massachusetts. White female, born Manhattan, 11 May 1960. Social Security number, blah, blah, blah. No problemo.'

Enzo waited. James picked up the tiny silver spoon on the edge of his saucer and began to stir the dark inky coffee in his cup.

'And?' Enzo asked finally. 'That was it? No problemo?'

James shrugged, his overcoat falling back to reveal a tiny American flag pinned to his suit lapel.

'More or less,' he said.

'Nothing?'

Enzo scowled. Which made James MacCready smile.

'Hold your horses,' he said. He took a sip of espresso. 'So my friend, he does this check, and she comes back clean as a whistle. Right? Anyway,' James went on. 'No outstanding warrants. No previous arrest record. Not so much as a goddamn parking ticket. My friend calls me and tells me our Mrs Blonde Perfect is indeed perfect. That's at about 6 p.m. last night. Our time.' He put the cup down. 'So, that's all fine and dandy, right? Until midnight, one o'clock—my cell goes. Hauls me out of lala land where I'm having a really nice time with some hot girl I last saw in high school. So, I jump up, and there I am in my underwear thinking, shit, they've found the Carson kid in pieces in a garbage can. Or Dickhead has gone and started

World War Three. Or there are riots out at the base because of God knows what, or—'

'But, no?'

James shook his head.

'But, no, indeed,' he agreed. 'Guess what? Or rather who? It's my friend from Jersey. And he wants to know what the fuck I'm doing, because he's just had one weird phone call.' James pushed the espresso cup away. 'He's leaving the office, right?' He leaned forward, dropping his voice. 'Closing up for the day, and the phone goes, so he grabs it, thinking, OK, it's probably his wife telling him what to get for dinner or something, and, well . . .' James MacCready leaned back. 'All I have to say,' he continued, pointing at Enzo, 'is, You Are The Man. You don't just hit the jackpot, you win the whole freakin' lottery.'

Enzo frowned. James MacCready glanced over his shoulder. Then he lowered his voice again and said, 'The call came from some guy from the Federal Marshals' office.'

'The Federal Marshals?'

James nodded. 'Uh huh. Wanting to know why my friend wanted to know about Anna Carson.'

Enzo thought for a moment. James MacCready was watching him.

'Like I said,' James said, finally. 'It looks like you hit the sweet spot, my friend. Because this guy was real interested. Within hours of filing an ordinary background search from a police station in Jersey, the Federal Marshals know about it. And they want to know what he wants to know about Anna Carson, and why he wants to know it.'

'So, what the hell does that mean?'

'Well,' James said. 'That was the very question I

102

asked myself.'

Before Enzo could ask if his self had come up with an answer, James smiled his twitch of a smile.

'Think about it,' he said. 'For a start, it means the search is flagged. Right? Anybody anywhere runs a routine check on Anna Carson's background, the Feds know about it. I wondered if it was some kind of mistake, you know, like the Do Not Fly lists, or some screwed-up Terrorist Watch thing. But that's Homeland Security.'

'And this was definitely the Federal Marshals?'

Enzo was scrolling back through his head, trying to sort through the tangle of US Federal Agencies. There was the FBI, the Treasury, the behemoth of Homeland Security and a host of others. As far as he could remember, the Federal Marshals were responsible for court security, for arresting federal fugitives, moving high profile prisoners and . . .

James MacCready nodded.

'Look,' he said, 'I don't know about you, but unless you think Mrs Blonde Perfect is a high-value prisoner they've misplaced, in which case I think they would have mentioned it, or a federal fugitive from justice, in which case I think they would also have mentioned it—apart from the fact that a warrant as long as my arm would have turned up. Or unless you think she's done a runner before giving evidence in a mob trial, which is possible, but personally, I think they might also have said something. Then that only leaves one thing.'

He leaned back, looking pleased with himself.

'It's what the Federal Marshals are famous for,' he said. 'Sort of like the Mounties. They claim they've never lost a man. Or in this case, I guess, a woman. My friend calmed them down,' he added. 'Made them dry up and blow away. Told them he was doing background checks for a local charity that works with children.' James shrugged. 'It's a federal law—easiest thing to say. For women. Some after-school programme or something. If it's a guy, go for a gun licence. Doesn't ring any alarms, you know? Anyway,' he went on. 'My friend thinks it was a babysitting call. You know, just making sure their little Bundle of Joy is A-OK.'

Enzo stared at him. 'Let me just get this straight,' he said finally. 'What you're telling me is, you think Kristen Carson's stepmother is in the Federal Witness Protection Program?'

James looked back at him.

'Hey,' he said, raising his hands, 'I'm not telling you anything.'

'So, who the hell is she?'

James MacCready laughed. 'Well, if she's in Witness Protection, not who she says she is. That's kind of the point. My friend didn't ask,' he added. 'Not that they'd have told him.' James looked at Enzo. 'You sure you don't know?'

Enzo was already zipping his jacket.

'Why would I know?'

'Just a hunch.' James MacCready's blue eyes were suddenly shrewder than his thatch of blonde hair and All-American Boy talk suggested. 'Same hunch that tells me you think this thing is a little more complicated than a roaming Sweet Seventeen. The girl, Kristen,' he asked. 'You think she's dead?'

Enzo shook his head. 'The odds would say so, but I don't know. Honest to God.' He looked at James.

'I don't. I don't know.'

'So, what have you found out?'

'Nothing good.'

'This is about the guy. The guy in the picture, right? The guy Mrs Blonde Not So Perfect After All recognized. You going to tell me who he is?'

Enzo hesitated.

Before he could answer, James smiled. 'You owe me dinner,' he said, and turned towards the door.

*   *   *

Enzo Saenz stepped out onto the street feeling like a fool. He had started to call Pallioti, tell him about Anna Carson, or whoever she was, then thought better of it. Eating humble pie, particularly when you might choke on it, was best done in person.

Enzo didn't need to be told that he'd behaved like the worst kind of cowboy. Gone off 'half-cocked'—assumed he knew what he was dealing with before making any serious effort to find out. Then he'd compounded the mistake by breaking Pallioti's cardinal rule, the one he liked to think he didn't believe in. Namely, ignoring his instincts. Which had told him, loud and clear, that he ought to separate Anna Carson from her husband, bring her in, and make her sweat.

Well, there was no time like the present to start making amends.

Enzo broke into a half trot, shouldering his way through a flood of office workers who spilled across the street and swarmed onto the pavement chattering so loudly he didn't hear his mobile phone, just felt it start to jump like a demented

105

cricket in his pocket. Feet still moving, he pulled it out, saw it was Guillermo, and put it to his ear.

'Get to the Excelsior,' Guillermo barked. 'Now. Lorenzo's already on his way.'

Good morning to you too, Enzo thought. If he'd been in a different mood, he might have smiled, marvelled at Guillermo's mind-reading. Again. Or paused to wonder how on earth Pallioti could have got ahead of him so quickly.

'Is he bringing her in?'

Enzo could imagine this scene, exactly how thrilled Kenneth Carson would be to be informed that his wife was 'being escorted' to the Questura for questioning. He was probably bellowing down the phone to the Consul right this second. Demanding that the Marines be deployed from the base to protect his family from the depredations of the Italian police. MacCready must have known. He was probably there already.

'Bringing who in?' Guillermo asked.

Enzo's feet slowed.

'Anna Carson. Bringing her in for questioning. Isn't that why Pallioti's—' Enzo didn't get to finish.

'I'm sure he'd love to,' Guillermo snapped, cutting him off. 'In fact, I can almost guarantee you nothing would thrill him more. If he could find her.'

Enzo stopped dead. A woman ran into him from behind, shook her head and stepped down into the street, picking her way through a crust of slush.

'What?'

'You heard me. Dr Carson's having trouble keeping track of his women. He ought to put those chip things in them.'

'What do you mean?' Enzo asked.

106

'I mean,' said Guillermo, 'that he called here in hysterics fifteen minutes ago because his wife is missing.'

*　　　*　　　*

'How did this happen?'

White lines pinching the edge of Pallioti's nose were the only visible sign he was angry. Enzo, who had just relayed the bare bones of his conversation with James MacCready, took a breath. Pallioti dismissed whatever he'd been about to say with a wave of his hand.

'It doesn't matter,' he murmured. 'We don't have time.'

They were standing in the sitting room of the Carsons' suite. Behind the half-open doors of the bedroom they could hear the sound of running taps. Kenneth Carson had excused himself, said he needed a glass of water. Enzo wondered what he was taking with it. Some kind of sedative, probably. Not that he blamed him. His teenage daughter had driven off with a man old enough to be her father—and who had just served the better part of thirty years in jail for being a terrorist and possibly a murderer, not that they'd shared this piece of joy with him, yet—and now his wife had disappeared as well. In Kenneth Carson's place, Enzo'd probably take something, too.

He glanced at the sitting room's unmade sofa bed, the rumpled pillows, sheets, and blankets spilling onto the rug, and wondered if it was a one-off or a regular occurrence.

'I snore. At least I do when I've been drinking.'

The answer came from the bedroom door where

107

Kenneth Carson stood running his hand through his hair. The man at the head of the table, the head of the surgical team who had been so visible at the Consulate forty-eight hours ago, was gone. Now Dr Carson just looked scared. And hungover.

'Why don't you start at the beginning? By telling us,' Pallioti said gently, 'everything you can remember. When was the last time you saw your wife?'

Coffee had been delivered. Enzo crossed to the tray and poured a large cup, black, and added extra sugar.

'We were going to dinner.' Kenneth Carson shook his head as Pallioti shepherded him to a chair. 'With the Consul and his wife,' he said. 'Or at least we were supposed to. I mean, I did.'

Kristen's father took the cup Enzo handed him, tasted the coffee, and made a face. Then he drank it down. The winter sunlight falling through the suite's window was unkind. Kenneth Carson's skin looked grey and was bristled with a night's growth of whiskers.

'Annie insisted on going running. She does that.' Kenneth Carson shrugged. 'She's, well, obsessed. Like a lot of these people. Runners. That's how we met, actually.' He glanced up and smiled. 'I operated on her knee.'

Enzo remembered the magazine article and nodded.

'Or actually, I didn't,' Kenneth Carson said. 'Not really. I went in and did the minimal then oversaw her physio. Can't do that with most of my patients, or I'd be out of business.' He put the cup down. 'Worked for Anna, though. She qualified for Boston this year. You know, the marathon. It's a

108

big deal. That's why she went out yesterday.'

'To go running?'

It was Enzo who asked. Kenneth Carson took a moment to nod, and Enzo wondered again how many pills he'd popped.

'She didn't even want to come. I mean on this trip.' Kenneth Carson looked down at the cup and saucer and seemed mildly surprised to find himself holding them. 'I only convinced her,' he said, 'finally, because it's Kris's birthday. And because it was only eight days. She said she couldn't leave the company . . .' He glanced at Pallioti. 'She consults on web design. Builds pages and stuff. For corporations. Although that was bullshit,' he added abruptly. 'About the company. She didn't want to come because of Boston. The marathon. Training. Distance runs, all that shit. I promised her I wouldn't bug her about it—she could run wherever the hell she wanted. Jesus!' He started suddenly. 'What if she's been hit by a car? What if—'

'There's no record of her being admitted,' Pallioti said. 'But we're checking the hospitals again, to be certain. She wore an ID?'

'Yeah. One of those wristband things. And yeah, she had it on. It's missing.' Kenneth Carson leaned back in his chair and sighed. 'I don't know if that's worse or not. About the hospital. To be honest, she was so mad, at Kristen. And at me, because of Kristen. And just because. We haven't been getting along that well. For a while. So, I thought she might have just gone back to the States. But her passport, her purse, everything's here.'

'Would that have been like her?' Pallioti leaned forward. 'Just to leave without telling you?'

Kenneth Carson shook his head.

109

'No. Not really.' He made a face. 'Anna's nothing if not responsible. Even when she's mad.'

'But you argued? About Kristen?'

Enzo remembered the way Anna Carson had sat at the meeting in the Consulate. Studied her hands, barely whispered. He'd thought then that she was just tired. Now he wondered what she had been tamping down inside.

'Yeah, we argued. Sure we argued.' Kenneth Carson made an attempt to smile. 'We're married. And like I said, we've been going through sort of a rough patch. Couples do. But Annie's had it rough. Kristen never gave her a break, not one. Her patience is pretty much worn out. She didn't want me to pay for this year thing to start with. At least not here. There was another programme she thought Kristen ought to go to, in Paris. Or to a crammer. Then this.' He shrugged. 'Yeah, we argued about it. So when she didn't show up—I mean, I wasn't that surprised.'

'When your wife didn't show up?' Pallioti had unbuttoned his overcoat. He leaned forward on the stiff brocade chair. 'When your wife didn't show up where, Dr Carson?'

'At the restaurant. Some fancy place in town where we were supposed to be meeting Edward, the American Consul, you know. And his wife. They thought it would make us feel better. It was nice of them. Anyway, Annie didn't go out running until late, and I knew she was going a long way— she does these distance things. And I was mad at her because I thought she did it on purpose. She said if she wasn't back that I should go ahead, apologize for her, and she'd meet us there. Come on over as soon as she could.'

110

'But she didn't?'

'No. No.' Kenneth Carson shook his head. He reached up and tugged at the collar of his shirt as if it was making him hot. 'No,' he said. 'She called me. At about seven. Said she'd just got in. She'd slipped on some steps somewhere and she was afraid she'd twisted her knee. She was going to put ice on it, put it up and stay off it. So she wouldn't be coming.' He glanced from Pallioti to Enzo. 'I wasn't really surprised,' he added. 'She doesn't like the Consul, Edward, much. And, like I said, we'd been arguing.'

'So you thought she was lying. About her knee?'

Kenneth Carson opened his mouth and closed it. He appeared to have been about to snap at Pallioti, rise like a fish to the bait of defending his wife, then decided against it.

'No,' he said. 'No, not exactly. I mean, not necessarily. It might have been true,' he continued finally. 'I mean, I know how much running Boston means to her, if . . .' His voice fizzled out. 'I went to the bar,' he added a moment later. 'Here in the hotel, when I got back. I drank—I don't know how much. Too much. A lot. When I got back up here, the bedroom doors were closed and the sofa bed was made up. Annie'd left a note. On the pillow. She said her knee was OK, but she needed the sleep. She'd taken a pill and didn't want to be disturbed. She'd see me in the morning.'

'Do you still have it, the note?'

Kenneth Carson nodded wearily and pulled a folded piece of paper out of his pocket.

'You're getting quite a collection of those,' he said, as he watched Pallioti read it. 'Do you have any idea where she might be?'

111

'I'm sure we'll find her.' Pallioti glanced up. Someone who didn't know him might have found his smile reassuring.

As Pallioti began asking Kenneth Carson about his wife's background, trying to feel out what, if anything, he actually knew about the woman he was married to, Enzo stood up and slipped through the double doors into the bedroom. A bottle of Ativan, the prescription made out to Anna Carson by Dr K. Carson, sat on the bedside table. Good, Enzo thought. They'd relax him, but they shouldn't make him dopey. Or worse, irrational or weepy.

Kenneth Carson had opened the safe. He had already told them there was nothing missing from it, and Enzo found nothing in it except their passports and some jewellery. A double string of pearls, a couple of bracelets. The rings he'd noticed, Anna Carson's wedding band, the diamond, and the large emerald, were safely nestled in a velvet box. Only the small gold locket she'd been toying with was missing. He'd get a description out on the database, in case it turned up in one of the city's less reputable 'antique shops'. Or as a marker on a corpse. He took a quick look around, noticing that her trainers were gone. Retrieving Anna Carson's handbag from the chair where it had been abandoned, he decided there was nothing else the room could tell him.

A moment later, as he let himself out of the suite, Enzo heard Kenneth Carson describing his wife. And came to the conclusion that the poor man had no more idea who he was married to than he and Pallioti did. He wondered if the US Federal Marshals, who were notoriously tight, would ever care to share that information with any of them.

112

Or if they'd all die wondering. Kristen first. Today was her eighteenth birthday.

*   *   *

Riding down in the lift, Enzo was neither surprised nor reassured to see that Anna Carson had left her credit cards and driver's licence in her wallet. Wherever she was, and wherever she was going, she didn't intend to be Anna Carson any more. He made a mental note to keep an eye open for the ID wristband, but doubted it would turn up. If she was doing what he thought she was doing, it would be in the Arno by now.

On reaching the lobby, he pushed through the revolving door and spoke for a moment with the doorman. Then he set off to the larger banks within a couple of blocks of the hotel. At the third bank he visited, Enzo found what he was looking for. Shortly after 9 a.m. yesterday morning, Anna Carson had used the card registered to her business to withdraw a total of two thousand euros in cash. There had been no sign of it in the suite. The money and her BlackBerry had gone with her.

The spare keys to Kristen's flat, however, had not. When he got to the building in San Frediano, Enzo found them in the mailbox, thoughtfully wrapped in a flyer from the laundry across the street.

*   *   *

Standing in the doorway of Kristen Carson's room, Enzo Saenz saw immediately what had happened. And knew he was to blame for it. After he had

113

tipped her off, set her running by ham-fistedly sidling up to her in the hotel lobby like some sleazy private eye, Anna Carson had come here and rifled through Kristen's things, cherry-picking a disguise so she would not leave a credit trail shopping, the way her less experienced stepdaughter had.

The wardrobe door was still open. There was a hanger on the bed, and an indent on the ugly orange spread. Enzo stepped forward carefully, as if wary of disturbing the chilly, stale air.

A gap in the clothes hanging every which way on the rail suggested that something large had been on the hanger. He closed his eyes, summoning the pictures stored in his head. He thought it might be a jacket, a bulky winter thing in a dark colour, possibly blue or green. The cowboy boots were easier. He'd tipped them up and checked inside them. A quick look at the drawers showed gaps there, too. He fished the Alitalia tag that had not been there yesterday morning out of the waste-paper bin. There was a small red duffel bag at the back of the closet. They knew Kristen had taken the matching suitcase, but there had been something else with it. A backpack, also red, part of a set, now gone.

Enzo ducked into the bathroom. The cabinet that was obviously Kristen's was emptier than before. Sitting on the smeared glass shelf, dead centre, the metal bar with her name, age, and telephone number inscribed on it, was Anna Carson's ID wristband. She might as well be standing in the doorway raising her middle finger at him.

'Fuck you, too,' he muttered.

Tamping down a flash of rage, Enzo fished a

plastic evidence bag out of a pocket and swept the contents of the shelf into it. Then he returned to the bedroom. Crossing the floor in two quick strides, he slid the desk aside and got out his penknife. The shoe box was exactly where he had left it. This time he didn't bother to replace the grate.

He was so angry that it was not until he was leaving the room that he realized what was wrong. The pillow. The place where the little white bear had sat looked like a thumbprint. Enzo stopped and stood staring at it. Then twisted the fact—the grubby red ribbon, the little bear's worn chest and bright black eyes—trying to make its absence fit.

*   *   *

The church was dark, lit only by dull electric orbs that were supposed to look like censers and tall candles that guttered on either side of the altar. Which was why Anna had chosen it. Evening Mass could always be counted on for shadows. Shadows and women.

She'd lingered outside first, sitting on a bench across the street for the better part of an hour. Forgetting to search for mittens or gloves in Kristen's flat had been a mistake. She'd kept her hands in her pockets, flexing her fingers back and forth, although it hadn't done much good, and had been wondering what she would do if her luck failed—how long she could last sleeping rough in this cold—when she saw the woman.

Dark, with shoulder-length hair, athletic, probably in her early forties, she'd walked quickly along the opposite pavement, passing directly under the street light opposite Anna's bench as she hurried up the steps to the church. Like a prayer answered, Anna thought. A kiss blown by her guardian angel. She'd reached inside her sweater, fingering the gold locket that hung around her neck, thinking she'd have to remember sometime to ask if the angels still looked out for you when you no longer believed in heaven.

Light sliced the steps as the woman opened the church doors. After they closed, Anna counted three minutes—three times sixty with a breath in between—enough to make sure the woman was not coming out again. Then she stood up and crossed the street.

As soon as she stepped inside the smell came rushing back. Darting up and touching her like a child playing tag. Burnt spices. Offerings. Incense and myrrh. Her eyes were already adjusted to the dark from sitting outside. Even so, Anna blinked, and felt something inside her shift. When she finally stepped forward, her feet were hesitant, as if she was stepping on black ice.

It took her a moment to spot the woman, pick her out from the handful of bowed heads. She was in the third pew from the back, which was probably where she always sat. People who came to evening Mass rarely came on a whim. From her perch across the street, Anna had noted that some of them carried grocery bags from the supermarket two blocks away. The dark-haired woman had one. And a white box from the bakery two doors down. She'd been juggling them with her fashionable short-handled handbag. Another kiss from the guardian angel. Anna slipped the rucksack off, moved quietly up the aisle and slid into the same

116

pew.

Anna arranged the rucksack, taking up as much space as possible on the far side to discourage anyone else from joining them, then folded her own hands and bent her knees. Instead of praying, she peered through her laced fingers at the lights over the confessional boxes, the banal little yellow bulbs that lit up, announcing that the priest was behind his curtain, ready and waiting to take away the sins of the world.

Ten minutes before Mass was due to begin, the woman lifted herself back onto the pew. Anna waited a moment, then did the same. The woman looked at her, asking silently if Anna would watch her things while she went and did her bargaining with God. Anna nodded. The woman smiled her appreciation, then slid to the far end of the pew. The high heels of her boots clicked on the ochre tiles as she approached the confessional.

Anna watched her kneel. She saw the black beetle toes of the priest's shoes shift slightly as the woman began to whisper. Then she reached out and folded her fingers over the shiny tortoiseshell handle of the handbag.

The expensive leather whispered across the worn pew. The zip made almost no noise. Her eyes still on the woman's head, which was bent even closer now to the confessional's curtain, Anna reached inside, her fingers groping past the familiar shapes of a lipstick, a compact, a phone and set of keys. The wallet was at the bottom. Anna resisted the temptation to look at it as she slid it into the deep inner pocket of her jacket. Then she stood up, lifted the rucksack, and walked quietly to the doors.

*   *   *

Now, almost three hours later, Anna Carson leaned against the padded headboard of the hotel's double bed and unwrapped a sandwich. Prosciutto and pecorino, the original ham and cheese. Just smelling it made her realize she was hungry.

The Catholic Church in Italy might not have moved with the times, but retail had. Both the chemist and the supermarket had been open until 9 p.m. Anna had bought the scissors, comb, tweezers and hair dye first. It wasn't the woman's money she'd been after, it was her face.

Graziella Farelli's identity card lay on the bedside table. Anna had studied the photo carefully, forcing herself to stand in the mouth of an alley under a light before she'd done her shopping. In the ID picture Graziella was a little fairer than she'd looked in the church. It had taken some time, but Anna thought she'd made the colour match pretty well. She put down the sandwich, hopped off the bed, scooped up the card, and padded into the bathroom. Several of the hotel towels were ruined, but her eyebrows were about the right shape and colour and her hair looked good. She studied the photo for a moment, then indulged in a few more minutes of careful snipping.

When she was done, reddish-brown curls hung to her shoulders. She'd left the length deliberately because when the police came looking for her they'd look for a woman with dark, short hair. The opposite of long and blonde.

Don't do the opposite, it's too predictable.

118

Always sidestep, never turn.

The litany came back, popping into her head as if it had never left. As if thirty years had never happened.

*　　　*　　　*

'Before she was Anna, she was Angela.'

'Angela.'

Enzo turned the name over, fingering it like a coin. Pallioti nodded and glanced up.

'They keep the names as close as possible,' he said. 'Try not to change the initials. Or so I'm told.'

Enzo knew better than to ask how he had come by this information. Rome. A Ministry. A friend. Someone who knows someone who knows someone. All reasons why it had been both more efficient and faster to turn the riddle of Anna Carson's identity—or rather, Enzo thought sourly, the lack of it—over to his boss. Lorenzo had not only been the most elegant of the de' Medicis. He had been the most powerful.

Pallioti laid his hands on the open pages of the thick file that had appeared as if by magic, not to mention in record time, on his otherwise bare desk.

'Angela Vari,' he said. 'Born Ferrara, 11 May 1958.'

Enzo looked up. Pallioti nodded.

'Yes,' he said. 'She's Italian. Or at least, she was. We need to find her,' he went on quietly. 'If we find her, the chances are good we find the girl.'

Enzo nodded. They both knew the chances were also good, even statistically probable, that Kristen Carson was dead. If by some chance she wasn't, the odds on her surviving got worse every day. That was the golden rule in abduction cases. It came right after the golden rule that said family members were the number one suspects.

'Do we have any idea?' Pallioti asked. 'Any idea at all, where Anna Carson is?'

*   *   *

It was just after 9 p.m. Looking out at the city lights, Enzo realized that since returning from Kristen's flat he had all but lost track of time. Most of the rooms in the new police building had no windows. This was supposedly a gesture towards security but Enzo suspected it really had more to do with the Black Arts. Architectural design in the service of police efficiency. Deprived of dawn and dusk, humans could stay awake and immersed in whatever they were doing for days. You could work an investigative team to death and they wouldn't even be aware of it.

He, for instance, had no idea how long he had spent with the photo technician. They had agreed about the clothes Anna Carson was likely to be wearing, and thanks to the samples from Kristen's bathroom, how she might have made herself up. But they had argued about her hair, the tech insisting that Anna's hair would now be short and black. Enzo had given in at first, then realized it was a mistake and made her change it. He'd been sure she wouldn't do anything that obvious. In the end, they had compromised and produced several composites, all different.

Enzo had them despatched to the bus stations and the train stations, and at the same time had

120

requested the tapes from all of their CCTV cameras. He'd done the same at the airport and car-rental companies, but with considerably less optimism since using them required photo ID. The tech could think what she liked, but he'd learned his lesson. Instinct told him that unless Anna Carson already had one ready and waiting for her somewhere—in which case they were screwed—she'd get well clear of the city before dealing with the problem of a new identity.

With that in mind, he'd posted an urgent notice concerning pick-pocketing and purse snatching on the nationwide database. The victim would be between thirty and sixty, likely female, but possibly a clean-shaven male, and would definitely be Caucasian, no more than one metre seventy in height, and probably of lithe, athletic build. He or she might or might not be Italian, would probably not be blonde, and would have had identity documents stolen within the last twenty-eight hours while in a public space where he or she might have noticed someone carrying a red backpack.

Combined with the composites, it might be enough for them to get lucky. Not that Enzo was optimistic. He had a bad feeling about Anna Carson, or Angela Vari, or whoever the hell she was now. Maybe, he thought ruefully, that was what had alerted him, what he had recognized in her. The chameleon gene. The blank space of a fellow shape-changer.

'No.' Enzo leaned back on the appallingly uncomfortable but very stylish black leather sofa that had come as part of Pallioti's new office. 'No,' he said again. 'We have no idea where she is.' He

121

felt his foot begin to tap and looked out of the window. 'She could be anywhere.'

* * *

Pallioti watched him. 'Well,' he said at last, 'you're correct, of course. She could be. Angela Vari could indeed be anywhere. But officially, she's dead.'

'What?' Enzo's head snapped around.

Pallioti leafed through several of the file's pages until he found the one he wanted. He held it up and nodded.

'She died in an accident. In prison. A fall down stairs, I believe. In December 1980.' He peered at the paper. 'Yes, that's right. While being escorted from the physical recreation area in the isolation block on Tuesday 9 December. It says here that she slipped.'

'How very convenient.'

Pallioti smiled. The expression was not full of warmth.

'Oh, yes. Very,' he agreed. 'So much so, in fact, that other than the guard who was with her, there were no witnesses.'

'Really?'

'Absolutely. And by that time, Angela Vari had no family, either. Her mother died when she was born. Her father, who raised her, was also gone. No aunts, uncles, and cousins to speak of. So there wasn't exactly an outcry. A brief piece appeared in the papers and the body was cremated.'

'Convenient again.'

'*Certo.*'

Pallioti took off his glasses, picked up his pen, and tapped it on the edge of his blotter.

'They probably called it Operation Lazarus,' he said. 'Or something like that. It's expensive,' he added a second later. 'That kind of magic trick. But I gather that in this case, enough of the right people thought it necessary. Have the fingerprints come back?'

Enzo shook his head. Given the ID bracelet it hardly mattered, but they had dusted all the make-up samples and sent a team to the flat anyway. Pallioti shrugged.

'They will. The only thing that might be interesting is if there's anyone else.'

'There won't be.'

'No,' Pallioti said. 'I don't think so, either.'

He stood up and walked to the window. He had rolled up his shirt sleeves. With bare forearms and without his cufflinks, he looked strangely naked. The thin gold face of the watch his sister had given to him glinted on his wrist. Pallioti complained frequently that it was finicky and Swiss and hard to read, but Enzo had never seen him without it.

'Angela Vari's mother was an American. She worked here, in repatriation, for the Red Cross, after the war. Fell in love, got married, stayed. It was enough, apparently, to convince the Americans to take Angela—the fact that her mother was a citizen. And they owed us some favours.'

Pallioti spoke without turning round, still staring down at the piazza.

'Angela spoke fluent English. Her father kept it going at home after her mother died and she studied it at school. So that made it easier.' He glanced over his shoulder. 'Our friend at the Consulate was right. After she was cremated in

123

December 1980, she was enrolled in the American Federal Witness Protection Program. She arrived in the United States in January 1981. So, *voilà!*'

He turned round.

'Her accent is brushed up, a few years are peeled off her age, and Angela Vari becomes Anna Vanetti. They gave her an Italian family background, got her a place in a college in Boston, and well . . .' Pallioti spread his elegant hands. 'Really, she never looked back. I suppose you could say, death became her. Arguably better than her previous life.' He smiled at his own little joke.

'Anna Vanetti was an excellent student,' he went on. 'She got a scholarship to graduate school, worked for a consultancy in small-business development and eventually started her own company. AV Design. Which became AVC design when she married Dr Kenneth Carson in June 2001. First marriage for her, second for him. No natural children, one stepdaughter, Kristen. Anna has an emergency number, but has never called it. Not once in thirty years. In fact,' he continued, leaning against the window ledge and crossing his ankles, 'I'm almost surprised she's still on their radar. But that's one of the strengths of their programme.' He regarded his shoes for a moment. 'It's one of the reasons the Americans are so successful with this. The rules are draconian, but once you agree to go into the Witness Protection Program, they agree to protect you. Forever. In Anna Vanetti's case it hasn't been necessary. She never put a foot wrong.' He looked at Enzo. 'Until now. Or not,' he added. 'As the case may be. It's worth remembering that all we know is she's taken some of her own money and disappeared.' He

124

shrugged. 'She's upset her husband, naturally. But that's not against the law. Yet. That I know of.'

Enzo opened his mouth to point out that neither of them believed that for one second. Then thought better of it. 'You haven't told me why,' he said instead. 'You haven't told me why they went to all that trouble. All that expense. To make Angela Vari disappear. You haven't told me why she was so important.'

For a moment, Pallioti said nothing. Then he smiled one of his non-smiles.

'She was a high-value witness,' he said. 'It was 1980.'

Enzo felt the unpleasant prickling again, as if someone was rubbing sandpaper down his arm, and realized he knew the answer. He wondered if he'd known it since the second Pallioti had told him who Antonio Tomaselli was. Wondered if that was who he had really been asking his mother about last night—not Tomaselli at all, but the woman he had faced, touched, stood so close to that he had seen the flecks in her eyes and smelled the faint woody scent of her perfume.

You won't recognize them, his mother had said. And she had been right. He hadn't.

'That was the thing that was so difficult about the Red Brigades.' Pallioti pushed himself off the window ledge and returned to his chair. 'You have to understand this, because it's important. And because we didn't, at the time. You see, the BR weren't like the other left-wing groups. They weren't a personality cult like the Baader-Meinhofs. They were disciplined. Their security was very, very good. Excellent. They were very professional.' He shook his head. 'If we'd really

125

understood that, if we'd really known . . .'

Pallioti ran a hand over his brow. He'd been junior, only beginning his career in the police. Even so, the weight was personal. Enzo could see it. And hear the unspoken words that hung in the room. *If we'd really understood that, if we'd really known, Aldo Moro might still be alive.*

'So, this wasn't some long-haired bunch of left-wing junkies.' Pallioti picked up his pen, stared at it, and put it down again. 'They understood keeping cover. They fitted in. They looked normal and they behaved normally, and yes, some of them did have girlfriends, boyfriends, lovers, whatever, who had no idea what the hell they were doing. They even published a manual. How to keep their houses. How to leave at eight and come back at five. Keep their cars registered. Not throw parties. Stop for red lights. They worked in cells,' he added. 'Strictly on a need-to-know basis. It was one of the reasons they were virtually impossible to infiltrate.' Pallioti shrugged. 'It's so simple and so few people actually have the discipline to do it. If you never tell . . .'

It was one of the acknowledged wonders of policing, that most people simply had to spill, sooner or later, to someone. Forget forensics and clues and evidence. The human ego needed to talk. Confess. Yet another universal truth the Catholic Church had cottoned on to a long time ago. The rare ones who didn't were almost impossible to crack.

'There was one effort, early on,' Pallioti went on. 'But after that, the security services got nowhere. They could never put anyone inside the BR. And that,' he said, looking at Enzo, 'was what made

126

Angela Vari so valuable.'

'She was an informant?'

'Not quite. Although some people did think she was a hero. Others thought she was nothing but a duplicitous liar, playing the system when it was most vulnerable.'

'Why?'

'Because she didn't come forward until after Moro was dead. And . . .' He stopped talking and stared out of the window. Light spangled the dark glass.

'And?'

'Well,' Pallioti said finally, 'the upside was that when she did, she gave them Tomaselli. Without Angela Vari, they wouldn't have got him. And that led to others. And to the flat where they'd kept Moro, the People's Prison. The whole thing. It all unravelled very fast after that.'

'And the downside?'

Enzo wasn't sure if he asked the question or thought it. It didn't matter because he already knew the answer. Pallioti turned to him.

'Angela claimed she wasn't one of them. She claimed she didn't know, had no idea, to begin with anyway, what Tomaselli was doing. What, or who, he was. But . . .'

He swung back towards the window. The pen beat a sharp little tattoo on the edge of his blotter, then stopped.

'But?'

'But some people just didn't buy it, because what made Angela Vari so valuable also made her suspect. She was Tomaselli's girlfriend. More than that.' Pallioti looked back at Enzo. 'They were living together,' he said. 'They were lovers. They

127

had been for a long time. I gather since they were very young. She was, I suppose you might say, the Juliet to his Romeo.'

Or, Enzo thought, the Lady to his Macbeth. He stood up.

'So, has she gone to look for him? Or to join him?'

Pallioti shook his head.

'I don't know. But I find it hard to believe that out of all the teenagers in America, Antonio Tomaselli happened to pick her stepdaughter by coincidence.'

He placed his hands flat on the pile of papers that covered his desk, as if he could hold them down, stop the past from leaking back into the present.

'What I do know,' he said, 'is that there were people who blamed her, personally, for Moro's death. Who never trusted her—magistrates, police, even some of the psychiatrists thought she was playing a double hand. So, not prosecuting her was controversial. But the doubters lost the argument. I suppose it was a judgement call. They needed her. Then the Red Brigades started killing witnesses. Even the jails weren't safe. So they had to make Angela Vari disappear.' Pallioti shrugged. 'They had a code name for her, by the way.' He began to push the papers together. 'They called her the Butcher's Daughter. I don't know why,' he added. 'I haven't had time to read this. But I'm assured it's all here. Everything. Her past. This,' he said, sliding the file towards Enzo, 'is how you'll find her.'

PART TWO

FERRARA

1965

The first time Angela sees Antonio she is seven years old and thinks he is a leopard.

'Are you hiding?'

His voice comes out of nowhere, like the Cheshire Cat's. Angela opens her eyes. He is standing above her, the long grass coming almost to his knees.

She knows, of course, who he is. Ferrara is a small place so everyone knows everyone. And Antonio is new, which makes him an object of special interest. Angela knows that he is two years older than her, and that he has a brother who is two years older than that, and that his family has moved from the country so his father can work in one of the new factories. She knows too that they live in one of the buildings that have been put up specially for people like them on the far side of the Darsena, the old port where the Po used to run before it changed its mind and meandered away like a senile relative.

Those buildings are taller than any in the old city, except for its bell tower, and even though they're not supposed to, Angela and her friends have gone to see them. They've stood clutching each other's sleeves and giggling because they're forbidden to wander outside their neighbourhood, much less outside the city walls. The buildings are ugly: grey, and made of dirty-coloured concrete and glass; the flats in them are stacked one above the other like giant shoe boxes. Each has a tiny balcony where laundry loops from metal railings and flaps in the wind.

131

Angela blinks at the memory. She can feel spots of sun and shade on her face, and the prickle of grass through the thin material of her summer dress.

'No,' she replies. Although it isn't true, because of course she is hiding.

*   *   *

It's a Sunday, one of the last August afternoons before school starts again and autumn brings the first whisper of winter—foggy mornings and sharp nights and early reports of frost in the hills—and they've come out to the orchard, a group of children and an assortment of aunts and uncles and fathers and mothers and someone's grandfather in the back of Signor Pirotti's truck, to help with the picking. Trestle tables have been set up between the avenues of trees and all the other girls have gone off to pick flowers to make into necklaces, or hold under your chin to see if you like butter.

Angela thinks that's stupid, so she's rambled off and lain down in the spangled shade. Closed her eyes and listened to the shouts of the boys' ball game, and the rise and fall of the adults' voices as they unpack the food. And she's half-asleep. Drifting on the smell of the fruit trees and the low throbbing hum of Signor Pirotti's bees that live in the hives by the gate, when she hears his voice.

'What's your name?' Antonio asks.

He looks at her as if she's something he's found. His eyes are dark as wet stones. Leopard light falls through the leaves and toys with his black hair.

'Angela,' she says, and he nods.

132

'You're the butcher's daughter.'

Since it really isn't a question, Angela doesn't answer. Although she does wonder what he's heard, because it's strange to have only a father and have your mother be dead. It hangs around you like a smell. And there is always the suspicion you might pass it on, like the flu, and make other mothers die. Angela knows some of her friends whisper. They say her mother touched her going out of the world as she came in to it. Left a thumbprint in some private place. She's heard there are bets. About lifting up her dress.

But Antonio doesn't ask to look, or lean down and grab at her hem. Instead, he says, 'the butcher's daughter', again, as if he likes the sound of it. Then he whips his hand from behind his back and gives her an apple.

It's not a big one. In fact, it's tiny and there's something wrong with it because it's fallen off the tree too soon and has little black spots on it, and Angela knows if she bites it, it will feel like chalk on her teeth. But she keeps it anyway. It rides home in her pocket, jumping against her thigh, and when she gets to her bedroom, she puts it on the windowsill.

When, after three weeks, the apple begins to grow soft and wizen and look like the face of the old man who sells newspapers in the kiosk by the cathedral, Angela refuses to throw it away. It spawns a halo of fruit flies, and still she won't get rid of it. Her father indulges her. But not Nonna Franchi, who is not really her grandmother at all, but the old lady who comes to clean the flat, to sweep the floors and bang the rugs and polish the heavy brown furniture with beeswax and linseed oil. Nonna Franchi survived the Nazis. The apple doesn't have a chance. So Angela is not surprised when she comes home from school one day and finds the sill empty.

Even so, she stands for a moment, looking at the spot where it sat, where the stickiness has been rubbed away, and feels a kind of hollow in her stomach. Then she closes her eyes, and under the sharp tang of the vinegar and lemon juice Nonna Franchi uses to clean the windows, she can smell the memory of August.

*   *   *

The flat where Angela lives with her father has five rooms and is on the second floor of a house in Via Vittoria, which is in the ghetto and only a few steps from the Spanish synagogue that was built for the Jews when Duke Ercole d'Este, who was good and kind, invited them to come to Ferrara after they had been expelled from Spain by King Ferdinand and Queen Isabella, who were not good and kind.

Angela knows this because she learns about it in school. Where she also learns how the Nazis ruined the synagogue. How everyone was too afraid of them to say anything to stop them, so they destroyed everything inside and put chains across the door. This story makes her worry about the ghosts of the Jews. Sometimes she stands putting her key in her own door, and looks over her shoulder at the padlock and at the synagogue's shuttered windows, and thinks that they are locked out and have nowhere to go. Other times, she's sure she sees them. Gathered at the corner. Or walking just ahead as she comes down the street,

134

their soft leather shoes shuffling on the cobbles.

One day, her teacher reads, as part of the lesson, the most important Jewish prayer. She explains that it is said first thing in the morning and last thing at night. And that it is the prayer of beseeching. And of martyrs. And is always on the lips of the dying.

Angela is not sure what beseeching is but from then on, the prayer echoes in her head like bells. The words call her at sunset, and again at dawn. Sometimes she hears them in the rustling of the birds in the eaves. Or in the clack and rattle of shutters opening and closing down the street. Or in the low muttering of the wind as it kicks lost paper along the pavements.

'*Papà*, are we Jewish?'

Angela asks this one night, knowing full well the answer is 'No' but still half-hoping it will be 'Yes', although she is not quite sure why. Perhaps because they never go to Mass. She is taken sometimes by the Ravallis downstairs, or by Nonna Franchi, who fears for her soul. But she does not go with her father. They never lean duck-toed clutching a rosary, or have their foreheads smudged with ashes. So at least if they were Jewish, it would explain why they live where they do. And mean they are something.

But as she knows he will, her father shakes his head. Confirming their nothingness, he runs his hand across the top of her hair the way he always does, and says, 'No, Kitten.'

'Then why do we have this flat?'

From where she lies on the knobbly carpet, a book open in front of her, her father looks huge. Sitting in his armchair, he looks like a giant in a

135

story.

'Why do we live in the ghetto?'

Angela knows that for some reason she shouldn't persist with this, but she does anyway, and for a moment she thinks her father's answering smile, which takes longer than usual to come, is sad.

'Because lots of people live in the ghetto now, Kitten,' he says, finally. 'Not just Jews. This flat belonged to your grandpa.'

'But why? If we're not Jewish?'

Her father regards her for a moment.

'It was the war,' he says finally. 'People needed places to live. They just needed a place to live.'

Angela nods. This seems reasonable enough. But in some way she does not quite understand, it doesn't answer her question.

Her father got the flat with the brown furniture and the knobbly rugs and the blue brocade sofa no one ever sits on after her grandparents died and before she was born and at the same time he inherited the butcher's shop on Via Mayr. Angela knows all about it. And knows too that he and her mother never intended to stay. Because they had Big Plans.

After they got married, Angela's mother, Annabeth Who was Good with Numbers, kept the books and started setting aside money to open a second butcher's shop, one with what she called a 'Deli Counter', for sandwiches and cheeses and salamis. Then, after they had taken Ferrara by storm, conquered it with American-style corned beef and pastrami, her parents planned to open a third, and even a fourth shop in other towns. And after that, they would have so much money that they would rent the flat in the ghetto and move

136

outside the city walls, or up to one of the newer houses near the Angels' Gate, where the street is lined with trees.

Angela's mother came from America and missed trees. As he tucked Angela in, plumping the pillow with his chapped hands and squaring the edge of the blanket, her father told her that on the street where her mother was born, the trees were huge. That they grew high as houses, and spread like giant umbrellas. And that in the autumn, their leaves turned as red as rubies.

Angela didn't really believe him, at least about the rubies. But as she grew older and was allowed to go on errands alone, she found herself drawn towards the Angels' Gate. Like all children in Ferrara, she knew that it was one of five gates in the city walls, and the only one whose doors were closed, and that they had been that way for almost three hundred years. Because when the last Este dukes were banished by the Pope, when their carriage—windows curtained so they could look no more upon their city—had trundled down the Corso d'Este for the last time, the doors of the Angels' Gate swung shut behind it. And the townspeople locked them. And vowed never to open them again, and sealed them with tears, because their dukes were gone.

Walking towards it, Angela felt herself grow smaller and smaller. The noise of the ghetto and the crowds in the piazzas fell away as she left the Castello behind her, and passed the Questura and the palazzo opposite where the little fat boys sat, their dimpled legs dangling in the air. Beyond the Diamanti with its strange triangular stones, and the Parco Massari where adults rubbed the nose of

137

Verdi's statue and children were not supposed to run, the silence deepened. Until finally all she could hear was the slap and click of her shoes on the pavement that had begun to buckle and become slippery with leaves.

The gate itself was crumbling, but the houses below it were new. Or at least new compared to the houses in the ghetto. Some sat in gardens ringed by fences. If no one was around—and it seemed no one ever was—Angela would cross the road and peer through the iron railings and tell herself that her mother lived there, and that if she looked closely enough or waited long enough, she would see her coming down the steps with a handbag on her arm. Or moving like a shadow behind the glass of an upstairs window.

She understood, of course, that this was not really possible. Because, like the old Jewish men in their soft leather shoes, her mother was dead. Angela knew that. And knew that what was left of her, if anything at all, was not behind a newly painted door or a silvery pane of glass, but lying under the feet of the stone angel in the cemetery where once a year she and her father left a bouquet of flowers. Not that it mattered. Because she could no more stop herself from walking up the Corso d'Este and looking through the railings, than she could stop herself hearing the prayer in the rustle of birds' wings and clack of the shutters.

Neither of which she ever told anyone about. Not Nonna Franchi, nor Signora Ravalli from downstairs who sometimes braided her hair. Not even her father, whose face always seemed on the edge of smiling and whose plans grew less and less ambitious, until by the time Angela was twelve and

138

went to what she thought of as 'the grown-up school' he could barely bring himself to open the shop on Saturdays, much less imagine an empire built on corned beef and prosciutto.

*   *   *

It was more than six years before Angela spoke to Antonio again. She saw him, though, from time to time. Once, she spotted him in a group of boys who hung about the Piazza Trieste at weekends, loitering near the record store, trying to look dangerous. Another time, she found herself standing almost next to him waiting to cross the street, but was too afraid to catch his eye or say anything. And one Saturday afternoon, as she walked home with her father after he had closed the butcher's shop, Antonio appeared ahead of them in Via Volte.

It was winter and very cold. White ice stippled the eaves of the buildings and lined the brackets of the street lights. Antonio came out of nowhere like a ghost, pushing a bicycle with one hand and carrying a bag of groceries with the other, and Angela noticed that he was wearing only plimsolls and not boots like everyone else, and that his coat hung from his shoulders.

She didn't dare call his name. But she wanted him to look back and see her. To reach into the shopping bag and hand her an apple. He didn't. Head bent, he seemed intent on the spinning wheel of his bike. It had a loose mudguard, and when he turned off into an alley, she heard the click and rattle as he crossed the broken cobblestones.

139

Listening to the sound grow smaller and smaller, Angela remembered the flats that looked like so many shoe boxes, all stacked one on top of the other. She reached for her father's hand, which was warm and broad as a bear's paw, and as they walked on, she scuffed the toes of her new boots and felt sad for Antonio, wheeling his bike out beyond the walls into what the TV called 'the New Italy', with its cross-hatching of railway tracks and highways, depots and factories, that popped up overnight like mushrooms.

*   *   *

It is almost a year after that, late one afternoon in early October, when she sees him again. Summer has stayed too long. It makes the air thick and turns the sky mauve and everyone knows it will leave any day now and all at once, like an embarrassed party guest. So, while it is still warm, Angela dawdles.

She has already made one loop around the castle on her way home. Now she stops to stare down into the moat and wonder if Lucrezia Borgia—whom her class is studying—was really as beautiful as everyone said, and what will happen if she drops her school bag into the still green water. If it will sink or float. She's lifting it up, resting it on the warm stone of the balustrade and toying with the idea in a way that is tempting but guarantees she'll never do it, when she hears someone call her name. Well, not exactly her name.

'Butcher's Daughter.'

Angela looks round. A man walks by, head bent, following his dog which strains at its lead. A police

140

car rumbles over the cobbles and disappears around the corner into Via Frizzi. She pulls the bag back, snagging her skirt on the wall, and is beginning to think she imagined the voice, when he appears beside her.

At sixteen, Antonio is now almost as tall as her father. His black hair is still curly, but wilder. If Nonna Franchi saw it she would come after him with scissors the way she came after Angela when she was little, stalking her through the flat brandishing the blades that glinted, bright and sharp as the knives that hang along the back wall of the butcher's shop.

'What are you doing?'

Angela shrugs. A dark fuzz shadows Antonio's chin and cheeks, but his eyes and smile are exactly the same, and she's suddenly flustered with the idea that he can look straight in and read her mind.

'Nothing.'

Antonio looks at the sky. Then he looks back at her.

'I got a place,' he says, 'at the Liceo Classico.'

Angela notices he is wearing smart clothes. A pair of dark trousers, leather shoes, a long-sleeved white shirt. Nothing like the plimsolls and thin coat she saw him in last winter. The exams for the Liceo are difficult. Already, the threat of them sits like a big ugly bird perched on the windowsill of her class. It caws. When the teacher's back is turned, it cackles, and whispers that the weak and the stupid will be sacrificed, plucked off the path that leads to university and everything that goes with it. When the bird looks at Angela, she sees in its yellow eye the scrubbed counters of the butcher's shop and feels the meaty breath of the cold room.

'I didn't thank you,' she says suddenly, pushing the bird away. 'I never thanked you. For the apple.'

For a moment Antonio looks confused. Then he laughs.

'Come on,' he says. 'I'll walk you home.'

*　　　*　　　*

Although Angela has been told how her mother chose her name before she was born because she already knew Angela would be her beautiful angel, and although her father assures her she is prettier than any princess in a book, she knows it isn't true. But she is not too tall, or too fat, or scrawny either. Nor is she loud, or stupid. Her greatest achievement, in fact, is that she isn't anything. She understands when to be quiet and when to laugh and how to get along without drawing much attention to herself, the same way a chameleon understands when to turn brown or green.

This shell of ordinariness has been a project. She has built its layers carefully, sealing one on after the other. But now, walking next to Antonio, who is carrying her bag, who has remembered, if not exactly her name, at least who she is, and who is actually talking to her, telling her about the Liceo and his friends and the football club he's joined, she feels her shell melting. It's perilous and terrifying, this dissolving of her protective layer, and part of her wants to turn and run. The part of her that does not feel him burning around her like a halo.

Dusk slides down. They turn towards the Duomo. Pink-grey light feathers the roofs and chimneys of the old town. One by one, the windows of the municipal offices turn yellow. As they drift across the wide lozenge of the Piazza Trieste, Antonio tells her that he has an 'exception' that waives some of his book fees, but that it won't be renewed if he fails to live up to his promise.

'It's hard,' he says.

They pause before the brightly lit window of a shop, and Angela notices that his cheeks are thin. His nose is sharper than she remembered.

'But do you like it?'

Antonio shrugs, as if liking it or not liking it has little to do with anything, and Angela's suddenly afraid the question was so dumb that he'll give her bag back and walk away.

'My father thinks it's stupid,' he says. Antonio's studying a jacket in the window. 'He says I'll end up in the factory anyway. So, what's the point? He says I'm trying to be too good for what I am. Not like him and my brother. My mother's happy though.' He stops studying the jacket and looks down at Angela. 'You don't have a mother,' he says.

She shakes her head.

'Do you like your father?'

Angela nods. Although 'like' does not seem to be a possible word when it comes to her father. Like is a small word. Everything about her father is too big for it.

'You're lucky,' Antonio says. Then he adds, 'I'm going to university. I don't care what my father says. I'm not going into the factory. I'm not going to be him. Or my brother. Work like that, so you can lose everything. Like my *nonno*'s farm. I'm not doing that. I'm going to university.'

The words are clipped and angry, like a

143

challenge, and before she can stop herself Angela reaches out and touches the back of his hand.

'Me too.'

She has never said this before, not even to herself, but the minute she does, she knows it's true. She's not going to be plucked off by the bird. Antonio looks down at her fingers. Then he twines his own in hers. She doesn't know how she expects his skin to feel, but she isn't surprised that it's as smooth and cool as the skin of the apple.

*   *   *

It was not long after that, after the night Angela watched the street lamps pick out Antonio's white shirt as he walked away, standing on her front step for so long after he turned the corner, that Signora Ravalli finally poked her head out of her kitchen window and asked if she'd lost her key again, that she was adopted by Barbara Barelli.

She always thought of it that way because Barbara's choice of her as a friend seemed as arbitrary as picking out a stray cat or dog from the animal shelter. And because the dedication Barbara applied seemed, even to Angela at the time, more suited to something like a new pet or a cause than a friendship.

Barbara was a year older. Her family had moved to Ferrara at the end of the summer because her father was teaching at the university and her mother taught at the Music Conservatory. She was tall for her age and very good at sports, which, Angela thought, made the fact that she was Barbara's chosen friend even more unlikely. Still, Barbara began to wait for her. She sought Angela

144

out from the throng that poured through the school gates into the freedom of the afternoons, and they started to walk home together. By the time winter arrived, Angela often found Barbara leaning against the wall of the Spanish synagogue in the mornings holding a bag from the bakery on the corner, jam melting through the thin paper onto her gloves, powdered sugar sprinkling the cuff of her coat. They ate the pastries on the way to school, talking between mouthfuls, brushing crumbs from one another's sleeves and chins like monkeys picking lice.

In the evenings, after they finished their homework, Barbara dragged Angela off to Corso Martiri. Striding past the lit walls of the castle and statue of Savonarola that Angela had been afraid of when she was little, Barbara would push open the door of a cafe and herd Angela before her into the fug of cigarette smoke and tongue-curling sweetness. They sat in the corner on spindly chairs and sipped hot chocolate bought with Barbara's pocket money while Barbara dispensed beauty advice.

The secrets they shared as they ate, and window-shopped, and lay across each other's beds on Sunday afternoons, were mainly Barbara's. Things her two older sisters had done, or that she had overheard them saying. Rows her parents had had. Graphic descriptions of the rustles and small cries that emanated from their bedroom afterwards.

In return, Angela told her about being chased at infant school, and about the bets that were made, and even about the time she saw her father standing under the street light kissing Signora Ravalli. But she never told Barbara about the ghosts. Or about the fact that she still sometimes heard the *Sh'ma Yisrael* in the autumn rains. She never told her about walking up the Corso d'Este to peer through iron railings. She did once mention something about trees with ruby leaves, and was pleased when Barbara's father, who had recently lectured in America, confirmed that this was, in fact, true. But she said nothing about being her mother's angel. Or about the apple. And she never once mentioned Antonio.

*   *   *

For a while, after the night he walked her home and carried her bag and lifted her hair from her forehead leaving behind nothing but the brush of his fingertips, she had thought he would come back. She'd looked for him on the street, and in crowds at the market. Had scanned the faces of the boys who hung around Piazza Trieste on Saturday afternoons. But Antonio was no longer amongst them. From time to time, when she could slip away from Barbara, Angela had even gone home exactly the same way and at the same time as she had on the day when he had appeared beside her. She would be sure to stop and look over the wall and down into the moat. To stand in exactly the same spot and ask herself exactly the same questions, about Lucrezia Borgia and the books. It became a small ritual, like staring through the railings of the houses on the Corso d'Este. A sort of prayer. As if in holding faith with that afternoon, she could wind back time. Re-create chance. Summon him from out of the ordinary evening air the way an alchemist summoned gold from lead.

146

But it never happened. And finally, all she could think of was to wander along the city walls on Sunday afternoons while Barbara was at one of her mother's recitals or having lunch with her family. Then Angela would stand in the line of trees and pick out Antonio, his wild curls bobbing in the afternoon light, and listen to the raucous shouts and shrill burst of the whistle as the boys played football, racing up and down the ragged pitch beyond the Angels' Gate.

*   *   *

Summer came and went. The football games stopped. Barbara's family rented a villa on the coast below Rimini for the month of August. Angela was invited for a week, and found it hot and sandy and rather boring, and was more glad than she would have thought possible when it was time for her to return to Ferrara, where she helped her father in the evenings as he scrubbed the marble tops of the counters in the butcher's shop and washed the floor and sprinkled it with sawdust. On Sundays, she sometimes went with him to his cousin's farm where the veal calves were raised, driving in the butcher's van, her father's big hand beating time to the radio, dry wind blowing through the open windows of the cab.

In September, Angela started at a new school where, increasingly, she found herself wandering happily in lines of equations. Angles and spheres and cubes floated through her dreams. She marked the anniversary of the night Antonio had walked her home by slipping out after supper and walking up to the Castello, as if her presence could

147

summon him. The weather was colder and the big square empty. When she stopped in Via Mazzini to stare in the window of the same shop, she thought for a moment that she saw him in the reflection, hovering at her shoulder. But when she spun around, it was not Antonio at all, just some other boy with curly hair and bad acne who looked at her, then smirked and slunk away.

Christmas arrived. On New Year's Eve bells rang and fireworks exploded. Angela had forced herself to stop going to watch the football games. She had told herself it didn't matter if she ever saw Antonio again or not. And mostly, she believed it. Mostly, he felt like a dream. But occasionally she would remember the warm indolent smell of August. Or see a smattering of speckled light. Or spot someone in the street, walking just ahead of her, who might be him. Then she would climb up onto the city walls and stand in the line of the trees and allow herself a guilty look down at the football pitch, just to prove that he was real.

*   *   *

It is on a Sunday like this, in February, that, without quite meaning to, Angela takes Barbara with her. The fog of the previous week has finally given way to a limpid blue sky. But even with the sun out, ice silvers the trees, turning even the tiniest twigs into frozen fingers that grasp at nothingness. Bushes glitter in the old Hebrew cemetery. A thin bright skin forms across mud-churned puddles.

For Christmas, Barbara's parents increased her pocket money and opened a bank account for her,

148

saying that she has to get used to independence. Barbara's parents talk a lot about 'independence' and rarely ask where the girls are going or what they are doing. On this afternoon, Barbara telephones and suggests they take the train to Bologna and go to a film. But Angela is feeling a tugging in her stomach, the sort of thing she imagines stitches straining over a wound must feel like. The night before, she dreamed of Antonio. Woke up in the dark with a hot-hand feeling on the back of her neck, sure his fingers were lifting the hair off her forehead. So, when Barbara reels off a list of what's playing, Angela says nothing. She mutters, finally, about 'getting some exercise'. To her surprise, after a small silence, Barbara announces that the films are all meant to be stupid anyway. Angela is right, she says. They should get some exercise. Angela puts the phone down feeling as if she's been shoved from behind in a crowd.

When she arrives at the Barellis' house and rings the bell, Barbara is waiting.

'Come on.' Before Angela can even step inside, Barbara grabs her by the arm and spins her round, barely giving her time to hear the rising voices that are coming from the dining room. 'Let's go,' Barbara hisses. 'Let's get out of here.'

She almost runs down the steps.

'They're arguing,' she says, as they reach the pavement. '*Papà* and all his friends. It's supposed to be a lunch party, but all they ever do is argue. Every weekend. I can't stand it. Talk. Talk. Talk.' Barbara's hair, which is pulled back in a long dark braid, swings like a pendulum. 'All they ever do is talk about politics. They don't do anything, just talk. They never shut up.'

149

It's a conversation Angela and Barbara have had before. More than once. Well, not really a conversation, Angela thinks, since she doesn't say much. Barbara's father teaches politics and economics, and since the oil crisis of the autumn before and the general strikes that followed, the Barelli house seems, especially on Sunday afternoons, to be full of cigarette smoke and shouting. As a result, it's not uncommon for Barbara to seek sanctuary at the flat, where the girls work at the kitchen table or watch television undisturbed because Angela's father does not care about politics.

Since the supermarket opened down by the train station, Angela's father has been forced to keep the butcher's shop open on Saturdays, which means he spends Sunday afternoons getting ready for the week ahead, doing the books and working in the cold store. Running the mincer. Invoking the recipes his father taught him as if they are a magic shield that will protect against polystyrene-backed shrink-wrapped chops and pellucid watery chicken breasts.

Her father's heavy hands are nimble as he lays breadcrumbs and sage along fillets that he rolls and ties with bright white string and places in long pans to be set out garnished with parsley or watercress as Monday's 'Special of the Day'—a gimmick he previously snorted at, but now resorts to like everyone else. When he is done, he cleans his knives and scrubs the counters. Then sometimes he drives out to his cousin's farm, which is barren and muddy with winter, and stays there into the evening, joining a card game, coming home smelling of cheap cigars and grappa and

150

kissing Angela on the top of the head. Mussing her hair as he has since she was a little girl, squinting at the numbers and shapes on the bright white page of her exercise book and asking her how her schoolwork is and not really listening to the answer.

As well as mathematics, and everything else, Angela is studying English. Her mother taught her father, and when she was little, he taught her. Sometimes, she still speaks it with him. But not as often as before. During the week, he still does the cooking, but after supper as often as not now, he falls asleep in his chair while the television talks to itself, its eerie shadows flicking across the newspaper spread on his knees. When Angela comes in to switch it off, she sees the pages of newsprint spelling out yet another strike, or the collapse of yet another government and its replacement by one so similar no one notices the difference. As her father begins to snore, they slither onto the rug and rest in a black and white blanket of mayhem on the worn toes of his slippers.

*　　　*　　　*

'I can't wait to get out of here.'

Barbara pulls her new jacket tighter around her as they turn the corner and pass the high, dark walls of the Casa Romei. 'I hate it,' she says suddenly. She stops in the street and turns on Angela. 'Don't you?' Barbara's cheeks are pinched with cold and unhappiness. 'It's like a prison, this place,' she says. 'It's even got walls like a prison. I can't wait until we go to university.'

Barbara shakes her head and starts walking again.

'We had a fight about it,' she says. '*Papà* wants me to go here. But I'm not going to. I won't. I told *mamma*. I swear. Laura didn't, and I don't have to.' Laura is Barbara's middle sister. She left in September to begin university in Padua. 'He's only picking on me,' Barbara adds, 'because I'm the last one left. Because there isn't anyone else he can boss around.'

Angela nods. She might suggest that perhaps Professor Barelli wants Barbara to stay because he will be lonely with no daughters in the house. But she isn't sure if this is true, or even if it is, if there is any point in saying it, or in doing anything but nodding, which is probably all Barbara wants her to do. Certainly, she does not want Angela to say that she could not imagine leaving her own father. Or, for that matter, Ferrara. That to her, the walls are not a prison, but an embrace. She remembers how sad she felt for Antonio that winter night when she thought of him living outside them. Her father's newspapers, the ones he falls asleep reading in his chair, skitter through her mind. The pictures of striking workers, and of the men who were kidnapped in Milan, their faces staring out after they'd had their heads shaved and their photos taken and been left chained to the rails of the Fiat factory with placards hanging around their necks because the Red Brigades say they are 'Enemies of the People' and Fascists. She thinks of the photos of demonstrators throwing stones. And of police with guns. And knows she does not want to go out there. Ever.

They pass the wire-topped walls of the hospital,

cross the roundabout, which is quiet on a Sunday afternoon, and climb up the steep bank onto the ramparts.

'Come on.' Barbara bangs her hands together as they reach the packed gravel path. 'I'll race you.'

These races take place frequently and are pointless. Barbara runs in the girls' team at school, and is taller and faster, and stride for stride can beat not only Angela, but almost anyone else most of the time. Angela laughs and chases her anyway. Through white huffs of breath, she sees her friend's long gangly body transformed as her black braid flies out behind her catching the half-hearted sun.

As they reach the section above the football pitch, Angela slows. Shouts, cut by the blade of a whistle, rise in the chilly air. A group of parents and girlfriends stand at the top of the bank, stamping their feet, digging their hands in their pockets, calling encouragement and clapping. As Barbara runs on down the avenue of trees, her figure growing smaller and smaller, Angela stops, hovering at the edge of the supporters, and scans the game. She has become expert at spotting his shape, picking out the way he moves. And of course, his hair. But today she doesn't see Antonio.

Something in her chest deflates as she watches the pack of boys hurtle down the muddy pitch. Damp rises through the soles of her shoes. Then the ball flies, and a clump of arms and legs and jerseys tangle and collapse as the whistle blows. The referee shouts and waves his arms. The players line up for a penalty kick, jostling and pushing, and suddenly Angela sees him. He is standing in the wall, in front of the goal. After the

153

kick comes and is successfully fended off, Antonio runs up the field, his arms above his head.

'Who is he?'

It's not until Barbara speaks that Angela realizes she has turned and come back, is standing so close, her chest rising and falling, her face flushed and eyes bright, that Angela can feel the hot huff of her breath. Angela opens her mouth, then closes it.

'Who's who?' she says finally, and feels the telltale pink flush burning up her neck and into her cheeks.

Barbara grins, watching her as if this is the single most interesting thing Angela has ever done. Then she looks back at the pitch, shoves her mittened hands into her pockets and says, 'He comes from the factories, doesn't he?'

Angela shrugs.

'What's his name?'

'I don't know.'

Angela turns and begins to walk away. She's making for the path that cuts down towards the Certosa, suddenly anxious to be off the walls. 'Come on,' she calls. 'I'm cold.'

But Barbara doesn't move. Instead, she stands looking down on the football pitch, hands still dug in her pockets, braid hanging over her shoulder. She is leaning forward, frowning, and for a moment Angela thinks she looks exactly like she does when she's spotted something in a shop window but can't quite make out what's written on the price tag.

It is exactly two months to the day after that, on 18 April 1974, when the Red Brigades kidnap Mario Sossi.

Angela saw it first on the television news. It was an hour or two after supper, which had been spring lamb, chunks so pale they were almost white, braised with peas, tiny and bright green.

After eating, Angela and her father had stood side by side at the deep sink, passing dishes, forks, knives, from hand to hand, washing and drying. Angela would never have told Barbara, or anyone else for that matter, but it was her favourite time of the day—these few minutes she and her father spent, moving around the stove and sink and table, clearing away, wiping, scrubbing and drying, no words necessary between them, the warm smell of the meal they had just shared still hanging in the room.

When they finished, her father placed his hand on her head, as he had done every night since she could remember, the weight of his palm resting gently on her hair. Then he sighed, a smile lighting his broad round face, and ambled into the sitting room where he turned on the television and picked up his paper, sinking into his sagging brown chair, the pages across his knees.

Angela knew it would not be long before he fell asleep. And sure enough not half an hour later, from the kitchen table where she sat, her exercise books spread across the scarred wooden surface, she heard the muffled grunts and little gasps that meant she could turn off the television. Cut dead the aimless mumble that wandered through the flat like a senile aunt muttering about strikes and weather reports.

She stood, pushing the chair back. The nights

had grown warmer. Before dinner she had opened the window. Now she closed it, fastening the latch, then went across the hall to the sitting room. From where she stood in the doorway, Angela saw her father's mouth open, his head lolled back, resting against the worn cushion. It occurred to her that his hair, although still abundant, was now almost white. She found herself wondering when that had happened, and why she hadn't noticed it before.

His blue eyes were closed, the lashes dark against his cheeks, which had bright red patches on them and had sagged slightly in sleep. Her father's hand twitched, fingers jumping on the newspaper as if he was trying to point something out. Angela turned towards the TV. She was about to switch it off, when the picture shifted abruptly to a street, to an ordinary-looking house. The announcer said it was in Genoa. Then a picture of a man in the white and black outfit of a prosecutor appeared and was rapidly replaced by a policeman who announced that someone called Mario Sossi had been kidnapped. Witnesses saw him shoved into a van. Five thousand police and Carabinieri had been called into the city. The picture switched to a line of traffic. Carabinieri officers moved from car to car, opening boots and doors. Some carried sub-machine guns cradled in their arms like babies.

Angela stood staring. She had never been to Genoa. She had never been anywhere larger than Bologna. She leaned down and turned off the television, driving the pictures away, sending them back where they belonged, outside the walls.

But Mario Sossi did not go away so easily.

By the next morning, his face looked out from every kiosk. It stared from the racks of the corner

156

shops that sold magazines and gazed from the rumpled pages of newspapers being read in cafes. In the electrical shop it filled every screen of a whole row of televisions.

Then a new photo was released. In this one, Assistant Prosecutor Sossi no longer wore his black robes and milk-white collar. Instead, he sat with his hands folded between his knees and looked small and sad and unimportant. Hardly someone worth kidnapping. Being shoved into a van. Called an 'Enemy of the People'. Behind him hung a banner. On it were printed the words *'Brigate Rosse'*. Below them was a five-pointed star.

The star bothered Angela. The two bottom points were longer than the others, so it looked as if it was leaning backwards, like something propped unevenly against a wall. Its angles, she thought, were not correct. It wouldn't be possible to work out an equation for that star, and if you did, the sums would not come out the right way. Looking at it made her feel queasy, the way the glasses of wine Barbara's parents sometimes pressed on her or the cigar smoke and grappa of her father's Sunday breath made her feel.

Sossi Sparito Nel Nulla. Sossi Disappears into Thin Air, the newspaper headlines cried.

But it wasn't true. Because no matter what the newspapers or the politicians or the Carabinieri said, Mario Sossi was everywhere. Even Ferrara's walls and ramparts couldn't keep him out. His face stared out, replicated on pages and screens again and again. And as the days passed and Mario Sossi's family—his wife and his children—begged and pleaded for his safe return, Angela began to dream of him. He slithered under the rusted iron

157

footings and wriggled through the padlocks on the Angels' Gate and slid like rain through the alleys of the ghetto, and the shadow he threw as he passed under the street lamps was not his own. It was not even human. Instead, it was a long, sharp shape scratched against the dark walls and closed shutters. A five-pointed star that swayed in time to Mario Sossi's footsteps as they whispered across the cobbles like a prayer.

*   *   *

'My father says he's a political prisoner.'

Barbara announces this as they are walking home from school seventeen days after Assistant Prosecutor Sossi has vanished into nothingness and become everywhere at once.

Summer has arrived abruptly, bursting into the city, rushing the trees into leaf and turning the mud on the paths that run along the top of the walls to dust. The cafes have doubled their outdoor tables and the old men walking their dogs have shed their scarves and jackets and unbuttoned the tops of their collars. In a week, Angela will be sixteen.

She starts to reply that it is not Barbara's father at all who has said that Mario Sossi is a political prisoner but the Red Brigades themselves, who have just sent another of their 'communiqués' to the newspapers. In this one they have announced that Mario Sossi is being put on trial for his crimes against the workers, and that after that, because he is a political prisoner, he can be 'exchanged'. For four terrorists he was prosecuting, whom the Red Brigades would like flown to Cuba or Algeria. Or

158

possibly North Korea.

'Criminals!' Angela's father had shouted at the television the night before. 'Anarchist scum!'

But Angela can't be bothered to point any of this out. It's too hot and she wants to get out of her school clothes and Barbara won't pay any attention anyway.

'They got in a big fight about it last night.' Barbara slides her eyes sideways like a cartoon cat.

'My mother and father,' she says, in case Angela thinks she is talking about someone else. 'My mother says they're nothing but spoilt children, the Red Brigades. My father says they're fighting capitalism. They don't do anything any more but argue,' Barbara adds. 'My mother says she's taking me on holiday alone this year. She doesn't want my father to come.'

Angela looks at her. Barbara is watching her feet now, concentrating on them as they fall one after the other onto the pavement.

'We're going to Positano.' Barbara shakes her head and tugs her braid. 'To stay with my aunt. Her new husband has a villa. And a boat.'

'But do you want to?'

As far as Angela knows, for the last few years it has been Barbara and her mother who do nothing but argue. Signora Barelli is neat and very precise. She has long-fingered hands that she flexes and rubs cream into, and is, in Angela's opinion, rather mean. She calls Angela Barbara's 'little friend'. As if she's a hamster. Or a mouse that talks.

Angela stops. Behind them a woman on a bicycle swerves and rings her bell. The girls step into the shadows at the entrance of the theatre. Barbara shrugs.

159

'My cousins are OK,' she says.

Angela has no idea if this is true, or if it is wishful thinking, since until that moment she has never heard Barbara mention her cousins.

'I've never met the husband,' Barbara admits. 'Neither has my mother. My aunt only married him last month.' Barbara fingers the edge of her book bag. 'We're leaving right after school.' Her cheeks colour. '*Mamma*'s already bought the tickets.'

She does not need to add that there will be no invitation for Angela this summer. Unlike Rimini, Positano is too far away. And there are the cousins, and the new husband, and the boat.

'But what about your father?'

The idea of Professor Barelli rambling through the house alone, smoking his cigarettes in an empty sitting room and cooking his meals in the big fancy kitchen while he makes pronouncements to himself and laughs at nothing, seems impossible to Angela. Barbara shrugs again.

'He's teaching at a summer school in America.' She smiles and drops her braid. 'I might get to visit him,' she adds. 'In August. Come on.' She grabs Angela's arm and steps out of the shadows. 'Let's go and get something to eat. Let's eat lots.'

They have hamburgers. And French fries, and *gelati*, and by the time they part on the corner of Via Mazzini, Angela feels sick. As she turns into her street, she looks at her watch. It's just before six, but her father won't be home yet. He keeps the shop open until seven on week nights, although he grumbles frequently that there isn't much point because more and more people go to the supermarket where they can buy everything at once. It's only the old ladies, her father says, who

160

come to peer through the glass of the display case and ask questions about the cut of the fillets and how long the beef has been hung. And they always come in the morning, early and dressed in black. So what is the point of leaving the doors open until seven so he can stand behind the counter all by himself?

Angela doesn't know what to say to that. She doesn't know the equation that would make the supermarket go away. As much as she would like to, she doesn't know how to reduce it to zero—cancel it out with *involtini*, and veal *piccata*, and the soft, fat *manicotti* her father still sometimes makes on Saturday night.

The flat is empty when Angela gets home. She goes to her room and tries not to think of her father standing by himself in the shop. Or of the picture on the front of the day's newspaper which, for once, had not been of Mario Sossi, but of his wife, who had tears running down her face because she did not want to go away from her husband, to Positano or anywhere else, but wanted him back. And who, when she was not allowed to go on television any more, had written letters to the Pope and to the President. Pleading with them to somehow do what five thousand police and Carabinieri have so far failed to do—reach down and fish her husband out of the nothingness he has vanished into. Finally, Angela lies down on her bed and closes her eyes and sees the summer stretching out ahead of her like a long, hot, empty road.

*　　　*　　　*

For Angela's sixteenth birthday, Barbara gives her

161

a silver bracelet. Her father gives her a record player and a locket with the letter 'A' engraved on it that once stood for Annabeth, because it was her mother's, but now it stands for Angela because it's hers.

He puts the gold chain around her neck, but his fingers are too big and too callused to fasten the tiny clasp, so Angela does it herself. Then she hugs him, and feels his arms huge around her and breathes in the smell of him—the carbolic soap he uses to scrub down the counters of the shop, and the detergent from the launderette that lingers in his shirts, and the sweet woodiness of the cheap cigars he buys with his newspaper every morning and thinks Angela does not know about because he smokes them after work while he helps Signor Pirotti, the two of them side by side puffing like steam engines as they pull the metal grates down across the front of the Pirottis' fruit stall and the butcher's shop and fasten them with the same padlocks their fathers used.

A week later, on 18 May, the Red Brigades announce that they have decided to execute Mario Sossi. They say he has been 'tried in a Revolutionary Court' and found guilty. That he is an enemy of the people, a cohort of the Fascists and the capitalists who keep the proletariat enslaved, and that therefore he must die. Then they change their minds and free him. On the thirty-fifth day, Mario Sossi comes back from nowhere.

Once he is free, once everyone knows where he is—home again with his wife and children—Mario Sossi vanishes again. He disappears from the television and the magazines and the front pages

162

of the newspapers as if he had never been. And after that, school ends, and Barbara leaves for Positano, and Angela goes to work in the butcher's shop.

*   *   *

At first, her father argued. He did not, he said, spend his days up to his elbows in sausage meat so his beautiful daughter, who was so clever at maths and English and was going to be the first person in their family to go to university, could learn to pull the guts out of chickens. If her mother knew, he insisted, she would reach up from the grave, grab him by the shirt tails, pull him down in with her and slam the lid.

Angela, however, pointed out that she intended to work for someone, not only because she had nothing better to do, but also because she wanted to make some money of her own, so it might as well be him. And, she pointed out, it would only be for the summer. Then she suggested that if he did not want her slicing liver and arranging beef tongues, he could at least let her run the till and keep the books, which was, after all, what her mother had done.

Faced with this, her father agreed. Grudgingly. So, as the days grew hotter and the nights grew shorter, Angela began to walk in the footsteps of her parents and grandparents. Every morning she threaded her way down Via Vittoria and along Via Ragno and into Via Carbone, which had once been the haunt of the charcoal sellers. She passed under the dark, cool arches of Via Volte, where she had seen Antonio that night, and stepped finally into

163

Via Mayr with its traffic and potholed pavements and brick-fronted buildings rimed with soot.

The butcher's shop was on the corner. A few years earlier, before the new supermarket had opened, her father had, in a fit of optimism, invested in a new sign and a new front window. Their name, VARI, marched across the plate glass, which was kept spotless. But the red and black letters that hovered above, spelling out *MACELLERIA*, had been made grubby with winter rain and the exhaust fumes from the trucks that rattled by on their way to Via Ripagrande.

Angela doubted that the outside looked much like the place her mother knew: the family shop where she had gone out of her way to stop every evening after her work of rehousing the bombed-out, homeless, and just plain lost, to buy her supper and practise her bad Italian and fall in love with the butcher's son. That shopfront, which Angela had only seen in photographs, was gone forever. But the inside had not changed much at all. The big glass case still ran down the centre. Marble counters still hugged the walls, stretching above rolls of waxed paper and string and seals for wrapping. Knives and cleavers still dangled from ceiling racks like bizarre Christmas decorations. A small service hatch that led to the store room and was never used sat halfway up the wall, its shutter permanently closed. Her grandfather's mincer gleamed on its stand, while on the wall above it, beside the heavy white door that led to the cold room, a picture of a cow, its body neatly divided up and labelled—flank steak, sirloin, rump roast, brisket—smiled happily. A pig, similarly carved up, faced it, also grinning, as if it could think of

164

nothing better than to have its head cut off and be turned into trotters and hams and slabs of bacon.

Angela's father told her with some pride that her grandmother had painted the animals, drawing in the cuts of meat. Then, he said, they had been whimsy—something for decoration, to make the shop cheery. Now they were necessary, since half of the people who came in seemed only dimly aware that steaks and veal knuckles came from animals at all.

Angela didn't know if the white coat she wore had actually been her mother's, but she liked to imagine it was. After putting it on, she braided her hair and stuffed it under a cap. Then she sat behind the cash register and tried to imagine that in this white-walled room surrounded by knives and lumps of flesh, it would be possible not only to fall in love, but to build dreams, of a house with trees that had spreading branches and leaves made of rubies. Tried. And failed.

She did not do much better with the books. The long and the short of it was, her father was in debt. Several years earlier, he had borrowed to pay for the new sign and the window and the butcher's van. All of which had probably seemed reasonable at the time, when the choice people had was which butcher to use rather than whether to use one at all. Now all that had changed.

As she watched him, his large hands unexpectedly graceful as he teased out gristle or brought a cleaver down, she understood why he had not wanted her to see the accounts. The more he fell behind, the greater risk the bank considered him, and the higher they raised the rates on his loan. It was like a silly nursery rhyme about

165

running round and round in circles. Or worse, the mushroom clouds they were shown in films in school. Sometimes Angela feared the debt would blossom and spread forever, the interest growing and growing, until it turned the sky black and blotted out the sun. In the quiet of the afternoons while he worked in the cold room after the morning rush—when there was one—she took to easing open the till. Holding her hand over the bell so he wouldn't hear it ping, she slid half the lire notes he paid her back into their little plastic slots.

*   *   *

It's a Sunday at the end of July when she decides to wash the sign. Her father has taken the van and gone with Signor Pirotti, whose own van has broken down, to collect an order of cherries from somewhere near Imola. They rattle off just as the bells start ringing for Mass. Standing in the street, Angela waves. Then she takes the keys to the store room in the alley that they share with the fruit stall and fetches the ladder and a bucket and sponges and a bottle of the detergent they use to mop the floors.

The only ladder they have is old and very long and heavier than she thought it would be and it takes her some time to manoeuvre it out of the narrow side door. Then she has to drag it round the corner and into Via Mayr. She's relieved the street's empty, closed up tight for Sunday, so there's no one to witness her first ham-fisted attempt at getting it up against the front of the shop. Afraid of resting it on the glass, she props the ladder against the grimy brick so she can lean over and wash the first letters.

When Angela puts her foot on it and begins to climb, the ladder feels flimsier than its weight suggests. A rung is broken, and the bucket is heavier and more unwieldy than she counted on. There's a hook at the top, but hanging the bucket from it makes the ladder tilt, which frightens her. Down feels like a long way. Finally, she's reduced to leaving the bucket on the pavement, soaking the sponge, going back up the ladder and leaning over to swipe inefficiently at the M and the A and eventually the edge of the C. The E is out of reach.

Sweat mingles with the dirty, soapy water on her hands and arms. It dribbles down her side, soaking the thin cotton shirt she is wearing until it clings like a damp second skin. Angela rubs the hair from her eyes with the back of her arm, and wonders how she's going to clean the Ls and the E and R in the middle. She feels the sun beating down on her back and on the top of her head and thinks suddenly of Barbara on her uncle's boat in Positano. Which makes her think of Barbara's mother, of her smiling her smile which is not a smile at all, and saying, *'Now, what about you and your little friend?'*, or *'Would your little friend like to stay for lunch?'* and how she wanted to turn and shout, *'My name is Angela!'* She thinks about that, and about the columns of numbers in her father's books that get larger and larger in the wrong way, multiplying, no matter how many lire she slides back into the plastic trays. Then she begins to cry.

The M and the A and the C are dripping down onto what was the clean plate-glass window. The ladder has given her a splinter that catches and rips at her thumb. From behind the glass, the pig and the cow laugh at her. She decides she hates them, and has no idea how long she has been standing there, crying and sniffing and feeling the damp squelch in her shoes, when she hears his voice.

'That looks better,' Antonio says.

'No, it doesn't.'

Angela doesn't even turn round to look at him. She shakes her head, suddenly beyond caring about anything—what she looks like, or what Barbara's mother thinks, or even about the fact that Antonio has appeared like magic and is standing less than a metre away and speaking to her.

'It's a mess. It's just a huge, big mess.'

Antonio steps round in front of her. He is wearing jeans and a white shirt and carrying a gym bag. A pair of football boots are tied by their laces and dangle from the handle. He looks at her for a moment. Then he looks back at the sign.

'I can't reach.' Angela wipes her nose on the back of her hand and knows she's sounding like a baby, but she can't help it. 'I wanted to surprise *papà*.' Her voice is perilously close to a wail. 'And now I've gone and messed up the window, too.'

Antonio laughs. Then his face sobers.

'Hey,' he says. He reaches out and touches her cheek with the tip of his finger. 'It's only soap and water.'

He steps into the shop doorway and puts the gym bag down, and before she realizes what he's doing, he's taken the ladder and jiggled it around, releasing a latch she hadn't even noticed and somehow opening the rungs so the top feet will reach well above the sign. He steadies it against the wall.

168

'You hold it.' He turns to her. 'Like this.'

Antonio grabs the ladder on either side and braces his foot against the bottom rung. Angela stares at him.

'What are you doing?'

He cocks his head and smiles at her, rolling up the sleeves of his shirt.

'I'm washing the sign, Butcher's Daughter.'

Before she can say anything—protest that he will be late for wherever he's going, football practice, obviously, or that he will get wet—Antonio grabs the bucket, throws the sponge into it and starts to climb. Angela darts forward, grabbing the ladder, bracing her foot as he'd shown her, feeling his weight as he moves upwards as if she's holding him in her hands.

'I'm going,' he says a moment later, without looking down at her.

Angela has no idea what he's talking about. Balancing, he holds the bucket with one hand and wrings out the sponge with the other. Water plops and foams, splatting beside her shoes.

'To the university, at Padua.'

He begins to clean the middle E she had not been able to reach.

'Remember?'

She nods. Of course she remembers. The old wooden ladder is digging another splinter into the heel of her hand, but she doesn't feel it. Instead, she feels the strong hard bones of Antonio's fingers. She feels his skin, smooth and tight as an apple's.

He switches the bucket to his other hand, washing the first, then the second L.

'Philosophy.' He shakes his head, making the

169

ladder wobble. Laughter bounces down to her. 'In a few weeks. I can't really believe it.'

'Is your father still angry?'

Antonio shrugs, a rapid jump of his shoulders under the white shirt. He leans out to clean the second E, then starts climbing back down. The long stretch of his leg is above her. Then the small of his back. When his foot hits the pavement, she lets go of the ladder. Still, his arms brush hers as he turns round. He smiles, hands her the bucket and grabs the rungs, shifting the ladder sideways.

'Yes,' he says. 'But not as much as he pretends to be.' He takes the bucket and starts to climb again. 'They've been out on strike,' he adds without looking down. 'So he has plenty of time to sit at home and tell me that nothing but "a day's hard, honest work" will get me anywhere in this world. Needless to say,' he adds, 'he doesn't consider university "a day's hard, honest work".'

Antonio laughs again as he says this, but this time it doesn't sound as though he thinks anything is funny. Suds stream across the black and red letters and down onto the window. The smiling pig vanishes behind a cloud of foam. The soapy water slides onto the hot pavement and rises like breath around Angela's ankles.

'*Miserabilismo*,' Antonio says. 'It's stupid. They strike and strike, but they don't even ask for anything. Just enough to survive. Lousy little scraps, as if they work all their lives and that's all they deserve. Me,' he glances down at her and smiles, 'I told my brother, I told Piero, he deserves more than bread. He deserves roses, too.'

Bread and roses. Angela sees them, a round loaf beside blooms, swollen and warm in the sun.

'Piero wants me to go,' Antonio is saying. 'He can't tell *papà*, but he wishes he'd gone. Or at least tried. I keep telling him it's not too late, but he won't listen. What about you?' he asks, and although he is not looking at her now, but back at the letter he is washing, Angela nods.

'Here,' she says, telling him what she cannot tell Barbara. 'I want to get a place here.'

'Why?' He glances down at her over his shoulder. 'There's the whole world.'

Angela wants to say, *Because I can't leave my father. Because I'm worried about the books and the cloud. Because without me, he would vanish into nothingness.* But Antonio's concentrating on the sign again. As he finishes the last block of shiny black beyond the A and begins to climb back down the ladder, she says instead, 'I've been watching you. I mean,' she adds quickly, 'playing football. I've seen you.'

Antonio jumps down the last rung. He stands facing her, so close she can see where he's nicked himself shaving above his upper lip. It's everything she can do not to reach out and touch the tiny cut.

'I know,' he says. 'I've seen you, too.'

The air is hot and close and his eyes on her face are like fingers on her skin. Angela realizes she is holding her breath. Antonio smiles. He puts down the bucket. His hand reaches out. The pad of his thumb brushes her chin.

'We should change the water,' he says. 'Or it will just make the window dirty.'

Later, when Angela looks back on that day, it feels like it's trapped in glass. Preserved. Perfect and sparkling, like something hidden in the back of a drawer.

171

Antonio helped her wash the big front window.

Then, while they rinsed the sponges, he told her about the farm north of Ravenna where he had been born and that his grandparents and their parents and their parents before them had owned. He talked about living there before his *nonno* died, before it had been lost and his father moved them to Ferrara. He told her about the flatness of the fields and the herons that stood in the irrigation ditches, still and white as flags on a windless day. And about his grandfather's dog that slept by the well, its yellow coat fluffed with heat, its paws scrabbling a dream his *nonno* said was of rabbits because all dogs dream of rabbits, although this dog had rarely seen one and was used only for hunting ducks. He told her about the wind at night, and how he and Piero had lain in their room at the top of the house listening to it snickering through the reed grass.

The words unspooled like threads stored in the dark because they are too fragile to bear the light of day. Angela rode the rhythm of his voice and said nothing, because what flowed out of him was not something you would interrupt or reply to any more than you would interrupt or reply to music.

'Some people think it's ugly.' Antonio shrugged as he emptied the dirty water into the gutter. 'They say it's empty. That there's nothing out there any more. But I think it's the most beautiful place in the world.' He'd taken Angela's sponge from her, dropped it into the empty bucket. 'It's not far from Pomposa,' he'd added. 'You could see the tower from my *nonno*'s farm. Hear the bells. There were still monks there, then. They'd give us things. Honey, sometimes. Teas they made. Herb stuff.

172

Have you ever been?' he'd asked. 'To Pomposa?'

Angela had shaken her head. She had almost been there once, to the great abbey that sat on the edge of the marshes, a place of pilgrimage hung between land and sea. A school trip had been scheduled, then cancelled because of snow.

'So,' Antonio had said a minute later as he'd collapsed the ladder. 'I'll take you.'

He'd helped her put the things away, carrying the ladder round the corner one-handed and propping it against the wall of the store room. Then he'd stepped back into Via Mayr, and picked up his gym bag, which was spattered with drips, and slung it over his shoulder.

'To Pomposa,' he'd said. 'I'll take you some day. It's beautiful.'

*　　*　　*

After he'd walked away, Angela stood outside the shop. She watched the wet prints of his shoes on the pavement as they dried in the sun and the last plume of the soap as it caught in the drain, the bubbles popping one by one. Then, finally, she went inside and sat at her place behind the till, and unlocked the big drawer, and took out the accounts and order books she was supposed to be working on. But the numbers made no sense. They kept shifting, rearranging themselves into pictures of Antonio's face. And of the span of his back under the white shirt. Of his arms, brown below the rolled-up sleeves. His foot on the rung of the ladder.

The street was almost empty because it was a Sunday in mid-summer, but every time a car went

173

by the roll of the tyres sounded like his voice. *'I'll take you . . . To Pomposa.'* And she wished, more than anything, wished with a desire so deep it made her stomach hurt, that she had run after him. That she had grabbed his arm, and made him tell her, *'When?'*

*   *   *

It's barely two weeks later, on *Ferragosto*, when she sees him again.

The holiday falls on a Thursday, and by Wednesday afternoon there's barely a car on Via Mayr. Everyone who is leaving town has left, and everyone else has already stocked up for the weekend. The shop has done better than expected. For once, they were so busy that Angela had to serve behind the counter. At two o'clock, when her father decides to close the shop for the weekend, he takes an envelope out of his pocket and hands it to her.

'Here, Kitten,' he says. 'For all your hard work.'

He reaches out and tousles her hair, his big hand resting, momentarily heavy, on the top of her head. 'Buy yourself something pretty. For Saturday night.'

On Saturday night there will be fireworks at the castle and a dance in the piazza. A band from Bologna is playing, and flyers plastered over the city promise a street fair. No one knows exactly what this means, since Ferrara has never had one before, at least in living memory, but there's a general air of excitement.

As her father shoves the envelope towards her, Angela begins to protest. With Barbara gone, she

174

has no one to go with. Some of the other girls from school will be there of course. But that isn't the same. She starts to hand the envelope back, but her father presses it into her hand.

'Buy yourself a dress,' he says. 'Go dancing. Have some fun.' He nods at the interior of the store, at the scrubbed marble and newly mopped and sawdust-sprinkled floor. 'There's not much point in all this, if I can't buy my daughter a dress.'

The dress is blue and green, blotched with huge flowers. Angela spends half the money on it and puts the other half in her savings account, and even then she almost doesn't go to the dance.

Standing in front of her mirror on Saturday night, her dark hair corkscrewing in the heat, the material already sticking to the backs of her legs, she feels a burst of shame. The dress is a halter top. In the store it looked pretty. Now, her small breasts feel like they barely fill the cups. She picks up the pink lipstick she's bought and rims the edge of her lips. Then she fills in the space with gloss, rolling it back and forth across the faintly chapped skin the way Barbara has shown her.

Even with the make-up and a cardigan on, which makes her look like an old lady, she feels scrawny and exposed at the same time, as though she's about to go out in her underwear, and she'd take the dress off, put it back in the box and slide like a snail back into the shell of her jeans and old flowered blouse, spend the night curled up with her book, except for the fact that her father is in the sitting room pretending not to, but waiting for her all the same. Waiting to see her step out of her bedroom door, not his slightly bedraggled, pale-skinned 'Kitten', but a princess. A Cinderella transformed by a wad of lire. By an envelope of notes worn soft as chamois, each earned with the chop and slice of a butcher's knife.

*　　*　　*

A handicrafts fair has been set up in the courtyard of the Palazzo Ducale. All the women keeping the stalls have long hair and headbands and gypsy dresses. The men wear leather jerkins. *Peace* medallions wink from tangles of chest hair. Someone has hung a banner that says *No to NATO* on the side of the Municipio stairs. Angela glances at her watch. It's barely half past nine. Her father is having supper with the Ravallis and if she comes home now he'll hear, and worry that her dress wasn't expensive enough, or that she's not popular and no one wanted to dance with her. One more hour, she thinks, and the men will go to the taverna. Get to their feet hiking up their trousers and wander out in jovial packs, puffing their cigars while their wives and sisters—and in some cases still, mothers—watch them leave with a mixture of hurt and relief before congregating in the Ravallis' kitchen to boast and complain about them. Then Angela will be able to slip through the door. Swim under the current of gossip and clatter of dishes, and make her way upstairs and into the flat without anyone noticing. Until then, she has time to waste.

The air is heavy with the smell of grilling sausages and patchouli oil. Angela sneezes and stops for a string of people who dance by waving their arms and shouting 'Where Have All the Flowers Gone?', the English rolling awkwardly off

176

their tongues. Out by the Castello, the band begin to play 'Stairway to Heaven'.

'Are you hiding?'

She is standing beside a jewellery stall, fingering a blue beaded bracelet when she hears his voice. This time, she laughs.

'Good,' Antonio says. 'So am I.'

He is wearing the same white shirt, the same jeans. His sleeves are even rolled up again. He nods at the bracelet.

'That's pretty,' he says, and before Angela realizes what he's doing, he digs into his pocket, pulls out some notes, and hands them to the thin girl who sits behind her display of chokers and earrings threading beads onto fishing line. A baby lies at her feet in what looks like an old dresser drawer. It squirms, lets out a red-faced cry, and lapses into silence as Antonio takes the bracelet out of Angela's hand and slips it onto her wrist.

'Happy birthday,' he says.

'It's not my birthday.'

Angela closes her free hand over the beads as if she's afraid that, once he knows this, he'll take them back.

'Well, you have a birthday don't you?'

He's smiling at her as she nods and wonders why, exactly, she's finding it so difficult to speak, why her tongue feels thick in her mouth.

'In May,' she manages, finally.

'May what?' He reaches out and touches her hair as if he's touching a leaf or a flower petal, lifting one sweat-damp curl off her forehead.

'May the eleventh.'

'So, how old are you, now?'

'Sixteen.'

In the last hour the light has faded and the crowd has thickened. Antonio takes her arm. They dodge a juggler and another line of dancers whose shadows twist and writhe. One of them staggers, then falls in slow motion and lies laughing on the floodlit cobbles.

'I'm going to the university,' he says. 'To Padua. Tomorrow, on the nine o'clock bus. So you have to dance with me.' Angela is aware of his fingers kneading her arm through the silky cheap nylon of the cardigan. She shakes her head.

'I'm a terrible dancer.'

'So what?' Antonio grins. 'I helped you wash your window. You have to. That's the price.'

Her tongue is cottony again, reluctant to make words. She nods as Antonio guides her across the piazza. When they reach the mouth of Via Garibaldi, a figure jumps in front of them. As tall as Antonio, his hair is wild. Crimson face paint streaks his cheeks.

'Surrender!' he shouts. 'Surrender the princess!'

Angela starts backwards, but Antonio laughs. He lets go of her arm and punches the boy in the shoulder.

'Shut up, you drunk!'

For a moment they wrestle, their arms twining around each other, heads butting. Then they stop. Antonio grabs the boy's ear and, still laughing, orders, 'Apologize to the lady.'

To her surprise, the boy does. He makes a low, swishing bow.

'At your service,' he says, still grinning.

'Angela,' Antonio supplies.

'At your service, Angela.'

The boy takes her hand and kisses it.

'Don't be an ass.'

Antonio cuffs him round the head, then they both start to laugh and suddenly, seeing them side by side, with the same wild hair, same black eyes and sharp noses, Angela realizes who this is.

'Piero.' Antonio puts his arm around his brother's shoulder. 'You'll have to forgive him,' he says. 'This is my stupid older brother, Piero.'

'And this,' Piero says, 'is my clever little twerp of a brother, Antoni-on-io.'

They stand there, in front of her, so alike they might be reflections of each other. Piero's face paint has smudged on the arm of Antonio's white shirt. The lines on his cheeks are smeared from wrestling. They look at each other, and laugh. Then Piero reaches into his back pocket and pulls out a silver hip flask. He hands it to Antonio and punches him on the arm.

'Have fun, Little Brother,' he says, then bows again to Angela, and spins away, whirling into a stream of people who are running around the corner towards the castle.

'Sorry.' Antonio looks faintly sheepish, but the grin doesn't leave his face. 'So that's my brother.' He takes her arm again, laughing and shaking his head, and Angela realizes she is laughing too, and that she had expected Piero to be older. Older and stern and worn down by working in the factory instead of a lithe, clownish boy with face paint and espadrilles.

'I love him,' Antonio says suddenly. 'More than anyone in the world. I wish I could take him with me. I wish he wasn't staying here.'

Antonio steers her into Via Garibaldi. A group runs past them. Squeals of laughter, threads of conversation, snag on the music. When he kisses her, Angela is surprised at how warm his skin is, how his lips move over hers as if they belong there. He has one hand on the small of her back. The other cradles her head. She reaches for his shoulders and thinks he tastes of something. Grappa. Cherries. He stops and looks at her, his fingers laced through her hair.

'Butcher's Daughter,' he says, tracing his thumb down her forehead, and across the tip of her nose. 'Come with me, to the Montagnola.'

The people in the street are nothing but dark shapes. They let out barks of laughter, stumble, and clutch each other, their silhouettes lit by the shop windows. The Montagnola is on the ramparts, at the far corner of the walls, beyond the Angels' Gate. A high mound, grass-sloped and furred with undergrowth, it looks down over the Certosa and the darkness of the cemetery. Angela has heard the joke that is probably not really a joke, has heard Signora Ravalli say more than once that half the babies born in Ferrara are conceived there. Antonio runs his thumb down to her chin. He leans forward, his lips dabbing at the gloss that smells of peaches. She tastes him again. Then kisses the soft hollow of his neck.

'Don't you want to come with me?' he whispers. 'Don't you?'

'Yes.' The word comes out as barely more than a breath, barely more than a single beat of her heart. Angela lifts her head away and looks at him. 'Yes,' she says, louder this time. 'Yes, I want to come with you.'

*　　　*　　　*

180

Later, her mind would keep skittering back to the bicycle. To the way its wheels bumped over the cobbles. To how its mudguard rattled as he pedalled across the bridge, leaving the castle and the lights and the dancers and music behind them.

Angela sat on the crossbar, holding her dress up so it wouldn't get caught in the spokes. She felt the faint grit of the summer night brushing her cheeks. On the Corso d'Este, the palazzos stood, pale and still. No lights burned in their windows and there were no street lamps, but in the soft blackness ahead Angela could sense the shapes of trees, and the house with the glossy front door where she looked for the memory of her mother. The bike tyres whooshed and chirped as the cobbles eddied into broken pavement and all at once the Angels' Gate loomed up. Seeing it, Angela wanted to let go of the crossbar and stretch her arms out. She wanted to reach for the huge locked doors and give them a mighty shove—break the rusted chains, and push them open, so she and Antonio could ride like this forever into the emptiness that lay beyond.

*   *   *

The bike judders onto the grass that tufts between patches of rubble, and Angela jumps down. She wobbles on her sandals and Antonio laughs, and catches her, and offers her the flask. The grappa does taste of cherries. It makes her cough. He pats her on the back, then slips his arm around her and guides her up the track onto the ramparts where the wide path runs through the avenue of trees that leads to the Montagnola.

At the base of the hill, he hides the bike in a thicket. On the path, twigs snatch at Angela's dress, reach for strands of her hair. She slips once and trips on a root, but Antonio has her arm. He pushes a bush aside, and guides her down the slope a few steps until they are standing on a patch of grass.

The clearing is barely big enough for the two of them. They are up so high that above the feathered tops of the trees Angela can see the square tower of the Certosa guarding its field of the dead. A mile away, coloured lights shimmer above the Castello. The band is playing a tune she can't quite make out. Music floats on distant beams of pink and green. Antonio's lips brush her ear. His arms are around her waist.

'You don't have to,' he whispers. 'You don't have to, if you don't want to.'

She can feel his hips. The heat of his chest against her back.

'I want to.'

She turns round and looks at him, as sure of this as she has ever been of anything. Antonio reaches into his pocket. He hands her the flask. This time she takes less. He takes a swallow of his own, then lays it on the grass and reaches up and pushes her cardigan off her shoulders.

*   *   *

Afterwards, Antonio's leg is heavy across her. He moves, and slithers down. His lips fastening, teeth smooth against her breast. When he raises himself on his elbow, she can feel his eyes, and follows his fingers, as they walk the pale contours of her body.

182

'Was it?' he asks. 'Was it your first time?' His hand moves across her belly, the jut of her hip. 'It was,' he says. 'Wasn't it?'

Angela nods and closes her eyes. And in this new place where there is nothing in the world except the feel of him, she loses track of time. Her fingers lace through his hair. She cradles his head, back arching, while his mouth feathers her stomach. She folds her legs around him, and feels her breath leave her body as he lifts her up and moves inside her.

Later, he pushes her hair up. She feels his lips on the back of her neck. He kneels between her legs, runs his hands down her back and Angela would like to ask him to stop, but she can't. In the next second her eyes tear. She bites down and tastes dirt. Earth under grass. Her hand clutches at the rolled ball of her cardigan. At a stone. At Antonio, as he reaches for her hand and their fingers twine and lock.

'*Ti possiedo*,' I own you, he whispers. '*Ora, tu sei mia. Per sempre.*' Now, you're mine. Forever.

*   *   *

The next morning when she wakes up, Angela is dizzy. It takes her a moment to realize where she is. Not on the Montagnola, but in her own room. Turning her head on the pillow, she sees slats of sun coming through the shutters. The bright bars wobble and tilt. The room feels unbearably hot. And close, as if the walls are inching inwards and will crush her. She moves her legs gingerly. Pain rolls up her in waves.

A faint greasy slick of the gloss meets the tip of

her tongue when she runs it across her lips. Saltiness and the taste of copper mixed with the sweet aftertaste of the grappa rises in her throat, and for a moment her head spins. Then she rolls sideways, closing her eyes.

Breathing in the familiar smell of her sheets and pillow, Angela slides her hand between her legs and fingers the bruised, swollen skin and realizes that she's crying. That tears are seeping under her lids and clotting her eyelashes and wetting the pillowcase—not because it hurt, or because it still hurts. But because she's just remembered that it's tomorrow and he's gone.

*   *   *

Barbara came back a week later.

The heat hadn't budged. It pressed down like a hard, bullying hand, threatening to melt the stones and ramparts, push them back down into the marshy delta they had risen from. With no rain and almost no dew at night, the pavements and cobbles were dull in the morning sun. The smell of rubbish hung in the air. Around the city, the fields spread away, flat and green. The harvest workers, pickers who migrated south to north with the crop and slept in barns and tents, started before dawn and stopped just after sunrise, their tiny figures vanishing like mirages as the sun climbed into the solid white of the noontime sky. Standing on the Montagnola, Angela smelled the sour stink of the irrigation ditches and the drying mud of the Po as it lay withering in its banks.

She went almost every day. Walked at sunset like a pilgrim along the path, then climbed the mound

184

and slithered down to the spot where they had lain. At first, she thought she could still see an imprint in the scraggy grass, but little by little it had faded, and after that she had found no sign of Antonio. No hint that he had ever brought her here.

At first, she was sure he'd write, or maybe even telephone. Ask her to come and visit him at the university in Padua, which was hardly far away. Or come home. Show up outside her door on a Sunday morning with a bouquet of flowers. But after the second week, then the third, she knew he wouldn't. By the time she started school again, Angela felt an emptiness so large it became a weight. A leaden nothingness she dragged behind her.

She knew by then that she would not hear from him because he did not love her. Or even want to remember her. Understood that having her had been the same as getting drunk or fulfilling a dare. She tortured herself by wondering if he had thought of it already when he stopped to help her clean the shop sign. If he had planned it that far back. Or if it was just impulse on the night. If he had thought of it, or if Piero had. *Have fun, Little Brother.* For no more than the price of a bracelet.

When, right on time, she got her period, she slid the blue beads off her wrist and buried them in the bottom of a drawer.

*   *   *

'What's the matter with you?'

Barbara peers at her through a veil of cigarette smoke. They have finished classes and are sitting at a table outside a dingy cafe near the market, which

Barbara has chosen because she says her mother, who would have a fit if she saw her smoking, never comes to this side of town.

Smoking is Barbara's new 'thing'. Now, she looks at her friend through the haze that always seems to surround her. Barbara prefers American cigarettes. Marlboros, if she can get them. The smell makes Angela queasy. The taste of the smoke Barbara breathes out through her nose like a dragon makes her mouth dry. It gets in her clothes and in her hair. She can't believe that Barbara's mother is so indifferent that she doesn't even realize she smokes. But Barbara insists it's the case, and Angela doesn't have the energy to argue. She doesn't have the energy for anything any more. She feels like she hasn't been alive since Antonio dropped her off at the top of her street that Sunday morning, smoothed her stained dress and handed her her ruined cardigan, lifted her hair and kissed her on the forehead, then rode away as the first shreds of light snaked across the August sky.

'Nothing,' she says, shaking her head. 'Nothing's wrong with me, I'm just tired.'

Barbara reaches across the small rickety table and touches her friend's hand. She had her hair cut in America, too. Her long braid is gone. Barbara's new fringe falls in her eyes. Sometimes Angela has the disturbing feeling she's someone else.

'Angie.' The tips of her fingers press the back of Angela's hand. 'Angie, come on,' she says. 'Tell me. I'm your friend. Remember? What is it?' Barbara leans forward. 'Is it your father?'

Angela shakes her head again. Then she can't stop shaking it. She goes on and on, as if she can

186

rattle loose the memories that have latched onto her and are sucking her dry. Suds billowing and streaking on glass. Antonio's arms below the rolled up white of his sleeves. His wet footsteps, and the bounce and jolt of his bicycle. The soft dark and the looming shape of the Angels' Gate. The *thwap* of bushes. And distant music, and lights, and Antonio's hands as they untie the knot behind her neck, and rock her backwards, and push her dress up, wadding the slithery nylon into a belt around her naked waist.

Grass. Her legs. The taste of his skin.

Tears streak the eyeliner she is not supposed to wear to school.

'It's him, isn't it?' Barbara's fingers wind around hers. 'It's the factory boy? It's what's his name? Antonio?'

Barbara gets up, leaving her cigarette burning in the coloured tinfoil ashtray. Somehow she circles the rickety table without either tipping it over or letting go of Angela's hand. She puts her arm around her shoulder.

'That bastard!' she says. 'That fucking bastard.'

Barbara squeezes, and Angela feels the silky, expensive cotton of her blouse. She smells the sandalwood oil Barbara has taken to rubbing behind her ears and into the hollows of her collarbones.

'Are you pregnant?' Barbara whispers. 'Is that it?'

Angela shakes her head.

'Are you sure? Because if you are, my sisters can ... there's—'

Angela shakes her head again, vicious and hard this time, her forehead knocking against Barbara's jaw.

'Well, thank God for that!'

Barbara wraps both arms around her and Angela presses her face into her friend's shoulder. She doesn't care that people walking past are looking at them, or turning away and deliberately not looking at them. She grabs and holds on as if Barbara's a raft and she's in danger of slipping off. Of going under and being swept away, drowned in all the pictures she can't get out of her head.

*　　　*　　　*

It was about a week later that Barbara gave Angela her first pair of trainers. When Angela opened the box she actually burst out laughing. Or did the closest she'd come to it in the last six weeks.

'Well,' Barbara said, 'at least I made you smile.'

She sat back on her haunches and blew a thin stream of smoke out of Angela's window. It was a Saturday afternoon. Angela's record player clicked, dropping a new record, and Neil Young went off mining for a heart of gold.

'But I don't run,' Angela protested. 'I don't know how.'

Barbara snorted.

'Yes, you do,' she said. 'Everyone runs. Everyone knows how. Besides, I'll show you. I even got you the right kind of socks. We'll have to go in the morning, before school.' Barbara stood up, stubbed her cigarette out on the sole of her shoe and tossed the butt out of the window. 'That's it,' she said. She looked at Angela and grinned. 'That's my last one.'

'What?'

Barbara nodded.

'I'm giving them up. For the track scholarship.'

This was Barbara's latest plan. She had decided that even Rome or Milan or Turin were not far enough away. She wanted to go to university in America. Her parents weren't thrilled by the idea. Her father said America was a Sinkhole of Capitalist Militarist Corruption, and her mother said there were perfectly good universities right here in Italy. For once they agreed. They were not going to pay for her to go to America even if she got into the Ivy League, whatever that was.

Barbara, being Barbara, had retorted that she'd pay for herself. She'd get a scholarship. There were millions. Her sister in Milan was sending her information. The easiest to get were in athletics, even for women. Especially for women. According to Barbara, American universities were practically giving athletic scholarships away. Since something called Title Nine, schools in the USA were falling over themselves to have women's track teams. The only problem was to decide where you wanted to go.

Angela couldn't help doubting this. But if Barbara was willing to give up the cigarettes, she thought she should do her part by pretending to be enthusiastic. Or at least interested. She'd put on the shoes and go, once or twice, until Barbara got tired of the whole thing.

At first, it was hard, hot, panting work that made her head swim and her legs ache. Then, little by little, as the weather grew chillier and November slid into December, the runs Angela shared with Barbara grew easier. Eventually, they even became pleasant. As January came on, alternating days of

189

low freezing fog with cold, hard sunshine, the two girls ran side by side, saying nothing, their feet falling in time. Breath matching breath.

Then came a weekend when Barbara went with her mother to Padua to visit her sister at the university and, somewhat to her surprise, Angela found she wanted to run by herself. As her father's snores growled behind his bedroom door, she laced up her shoes feeling both guilty and excited, the same way she had felt when she was little and had slipped without his knowledge beyond the confines of the neighbourhood.

The city streets were still with Sunday morning. As she passed the old military barracks the first sun caught the shards of glass on top of the walls, making them glitter like white-tipped fangs. Crossing in front of the Corpus Domini and the Annunziata and the great patterned face of the Schifanoia, her trainers silent on the cobbles, Angela felt herself fading into the city. Becoming transparent—just another ghost rubbing shoulders with the old men in their black coats, and with the d'Este, and with La Borgia herself. All of them mingling like smoke.

At the Punta della Giovecca she climbed onto the ramparts. Beyond the walls, the fields were washed in mist. She could hear but not see a car. Standing suspended between earth and air, Angela felt as if she was on the edge of a precipice. Tension thrummed her arms and legs and back. For a split-second, she had the impulse to turn around, to stop, because what she was doing— coming here to run alone—was a betrayal of Barbara. An infidelity, as surely as the nights Barbara's father had taken to spending with his students were infidelities. Then she gave herself a little shake.

Her first step cracked ice in a puddle. The next left a footprint in frost. Her breath bloomed and trembled on the chilly air as the heat began to throb into her mittened hands. Above her, the white sky was traced with naked trees. Below her, her feet fell, one chasing the other, faster and faster, until she almost believed she was no longer touching the ground.

*   *   *

As the winter deepened, Angela found that she liked running alone even more than running with Barbara. Sensing instinctively that Barbara would feel betrayed by this, she fell into a pattern of deception. Lied by omission, and silence, and stealth. And became convinced that lying made her feet turn faster, made her feel as if she was nothing but a shadow, flying across the frozen ground like the shadows of the crows that dipped and fell above the empty ramparts.

On the mornings she didn't run with Barbara, she went by herself, very early. Other times, she went at dusk. She took to saying she had to work for her father, then changing in the back room of the shop and slipping down the alley past the store room and into Piazza Travaglio, where she climbed up beside the Porta Paola. Then she would run along the top of the walls, past the flat white roofs of the hospital, past the line of trees above the football pitch, past the Montagnola, past each memory and year as if she was running through her life, outpacing herself until she reached the

191

Angels' Gate.

There, chest heaving as her heart slowed, she would come down and pause behind the iron railings of the houses at the top of the Corso d'Este and watch the curtained windows. When she turned away, she would see the castle in the distance, burning at the heart of the city. Sometimes it looked like a fire at the end of a tunnel. Or like the sparkling lure that teases a fish. Other times she imagined its lights must look like the lights birds see when they gaze down from the night sky, silver pinpricks far below where they hover in cold air and silence.

On evenings like that, the walk back along the Corso made Angela feel as if she was drifting back down to earth. Or being reeled in. Every step making her more solid, more prone to the rules of gravity and memory. Until, by the time she got to Via Mazzini, passing the spot where the gates of the ghetto had once been, she would be worrying about her exams, or her father's books, or being late for dinner.

Her father still did most of the cooking, but Angela helped him. Sometimes she did it all herself. And she was thinking about jointing a chicken—about the quick, firm whack with the cleaver and the clean split of bone and cut of skin—and about whether she had remembered to buy enough carrots, and if they might be out of oil, when on the first Thursday in February she came around the corner into Via Vittoria and mounted the steps and put her key in the lock and smelled burning.

Her immediate thought was that something had spilled on the stove and rolled into the gas flame, or been forgotten in the oven. That her father must have turned it on, then gone downstairs to the Ravallis' to borrow salt or butter or the onions she had forgotten to buy and that any second he would reappear, swearing, as if the oven itself was the miscreant.

She ran up the stairs and pushed open the door to the flat. A haze shimmered in the kitchen. Whatever it had been was surely blackened by now.

'Oh, *papà*.'

He had grown more forgetful, preoccupied by the shop and by his diatribes against the supermarket, and—she knew, although they never mentioned it—by the mushroom cloud of debt that refused to shrink no matter how much of her savings account she squirrelled back into the cash trays.

Angela darted through the doorway, eyes fixed on the pan that sat smoking on the stove. She turned the burner off and, pulling her sweatshirt sleeve over her mittened hand, grabbed the handle and tipped it into the sink where it sizzled and hissed like a devil in the *Purgatorio*. The burning oil made her eyes tear, so it was not until she had shoved open the window and was trying to fan the sheet of cold air that she turned and saw her father.

He lay on the far side of the old scarred table. The chopping board he had been working on had tipped up and fallen beside him. Red chunks of tomatoes—the first from Sicily, sold out of a van on Corso Porto Mare—oozed on the tiles. His face was contorted. His mouth open, as if someone had punched him suddenly in the stomach. Flung over

193

his head, his hand still held the coring knife.

* * *

'He's not dead. He's not dead.'

Everyone tells her this. The ambulance people who bring a chaos of bleating sirens and flashing lights. Signora Ravalli who rides with her in a police car to the hospital. The doctor who comes, trying not to look as if he is in a hurry, to tell her that something is very wrong with her father's heart and that they will do the best they can. Even Signor and Signora Pirotti, who have left their supper and come to sit with her in the waiting room.

'He's not dead,' they say, and clutch her hands as if it is supposed to bring some comfort.

Which it does. Even if Angela is not sure what it means. Not really. Because even though everyone tells her that her 'quick thinking' has saved his life—that he had a massive heart attack, and that if she had not returned and found him and called the ambulance, well, things would be very different. Even though everyone tells her this, she is not sure what she is supposed to think about it.

Because he looked dead to her. He felt dead, when she touched him. And he feels dead now, lost somewhere behind those doors she cannot go through, where they are cracking open his chest and reaching in to grasp his heart the way she has seen him crack open the chest and reach in to grasp the heart of a lamb or a cow. Angela closes her eyes and wishes that she did not know what those organs look like. Liver, kidneys, the round and oozing heart. But she does.

194

Sitting in the hard moulded plastic chair, she reaches into the neck of her sweatshirt and feels for her necklace. The gold is warm from the warmth of her body, and as she rubs it she imagines that she is rubbing off the A for Annabeth. That she is freeing it. And that it is breaking apart—swirling into a million tiny pieces that rise and finger their way through the closed doors and fly down the labyrinth halls of this hospital where her mother left the world and she came into it, until they find her father and settle themselves. Nest like birds on his cracked open heart. And form an A. For Annabeth and Angela.

*   *   *

It is almost midnight when the Pirottis take her home. Her father is doing 'as well as can be expected'. She can't see him, can't even glimpse him through a glass window until tomorrow, at visiting time in the afternoon, and perhaps not even then. So there is no point in her sitting here. The nurse says she should have something to eat. That she should get some sleep. She is a nice woman with grey curling hair that escapes from her cap in little horns. When she brings out a pile of forms and asks Angela if she is old enough to sign them, to be legally responsible for decisions about her father's care, the lie skips out like a heartbeat. Deception, Angela thinks, is truly second nature to her now. She swears and signs on the line.

If they notice, which they almost certainly do, the Pirottis say nothing. When they were young, girls got married at her age. During the war, they picked up guns and shot and got shot at. For the poor at least, for those who labour with their hands, childhood is a modern invention. Besides, they've all heard what happens if someone like her father doesn't have a daughter or a wife or son. He could be moved anywhere. Shuffled and forgotten like a pack of worn-out cards. This, after all, is what families are for. To grab your hand in the crowd.

Signora Pirotti offers to spend the night. But Angela shakes her head. After all, she's hardly on her own. In the ghetto no one is on their own. The Ravallis are downstairs. Nonna Franchi is round the corner. Barbara lives five minutes away. She's surrounded. And all she wants is to go back to the flat. Alone. She can't stand the idea of sympathy, or crying, or anyone else's food.

Behind the closed door and freed of the burden of other people's eyes, Angela wonders if she had not gone running, if she had been here, could she have changed this? The doctor said, *No*. More or less. Not that she asked him directly, begged for his absolution as if he were some kind of priest. But he called her father's heart 'a ticking time bomb'. Said that the only miracle, other than the fact that he had not died instantly, was that this had not happened years ago. Angela thinks of that now and wonders if her father knew. If when he held a pig's or an ox's heart in his hand, he understood that there was something wrong with his own—felt it, reluctant in his chest like a clock that has to be coaxed into running.

If he did that, if he urged his heart on day after day, pushing it to one more beat, Angela knows he did it for her. She knows this just as she knows that if he is holding on now, if he is clinging to the fragile web that stops him from joining her mother, he is also doing it for her. The knowledge makes her stop. She stands on the stairs as if his love has turned her to stone.

Angela sleeps on the sofa. She wraps herself in the old maroon blanket that usually lies folded across the foot of her parents' bed and puts her father's slippers on her stockinged feet. During the night they fall off and flap onto the floor as if they're trying to walk back to their place beside his chair.

When Angela wakes up, it's still dark. Stiff from propping her head on the uncomfortable armrest, she smells the stale, woody scent of her father's cigar and thinks, just for a split-second, that she has fallen asleep in front of the TV and had a bad dream and that she can hear him snoring, the grunts and snuffles jumping like puppies at the door of his bedroom down the hall. Then she smells the charcoaly beef smell and the greasy residue of burnt oil and sits up, her clothes tight with sweat, her arms and neck aching.

Through the window she can see that the strip of sky above the roofs is the faded dirty black of winter dawn. The stars, if there were any, will be fading. Angela looks at her watch. It's half past five. She wonders if her father is still on this earth, or if he's gone, if while she was sleeping he slipped away to join her mother, and realizes with a pang that a part of him has probably wanted to do just that for a very long time. She saw him kissing Signora Ravalli that once, but that was years ago. Other than that, as far as she knows, he's never glanced at another woman. He's gone to his shop, and sharpened his knives, and driven out to see the veal calves, and mixed sausage meat, and worked in the cold room without feeling the warm, slick rub of another naked body. The band of someone's arms around him. He's locked the shop and smoked his cigars and walked home to cook dinner, for her. So he could read her a story, lay his hand on the top of her head. Pass her a crumpled envelope and tell her to buy a dress.

Angela sits for a moment on the edge of the sofa. Then she knows what she has to do.

*   *   *

'I don't get it,' Barbara says. 'I mean, I just don't get it. What the fuck are you doing?'

It's the night before Valentine's Day, exactly a week since Angela's father had his heart attack and she started opening the shop by herself. Barbara runs her hands through her hair, digging her fingers into her scalp and pulling at the ends as if Angela's making her crazy.

'It's like you're quitting.'

Her voice rises to something close to a shriek. If the shop was still open, Angela would tell her to calm down, but it isn't, so she doesn't bother.

'It's like you've just decided to be a fucking quitter,' Barbara announces. 'Shit!' She bangs her fist on the cash register, making it ping. 'It's like you're giving up fucking everything!'

In place of smoking, Barbara has taken up swearing. 'Fuck' is now her favourite word, although she knows lots of others, too. Angela's not sure where she's learned them all—from the toilets at the bus station? From her sisters? She has no idea, but she supposes she's lucky not to be

198

called something worse than a 'fucking quitter'.

'I mean.' Barbara takes a deep breath and lowers her voice, trying another tack. 'I mean,' she says, 'I understand, Angie. I do. Really. I do. Shit. But your dad's OK. I mean, he's going to be OK? Right? And you're still telling me you're not coming back to school?'

Angela does not point out that legally she could have left school ages ago. That lots of people do. People who have to do boring things, like working in a factory, or taking care of their parents and paying bills and putting bread on the table. Nor does she point out that her dad, whom she has never called 'Dad' in her life, is anything but OK. That he's OK only if you count being alive and sitting up once and being able to mumble for a few seconds at a time because you can't talk, much less feed yourself, or walk, or go to the bathroom, OK. She doesn't say it. Any of it.

Because she doesn't have to. At least not to Barbara, who knows it already because she has always had the disturbing ability to know Angela—better, it seems sometimes, than Angela knows herself. Which is why they are such good friends. Which is why Angela does not mind her swearing any more than she really minded her smoking. Because Barbara is Barbara, and the luxury of not having to explain to her, or even talk, feels like leaning back into a hot perfumed bath. Feels like closing her eyes and letting her limbs float while the water creeps up to her neck, and chin, and mouth.

For a brief second, Angela remembers the day they watched Antonio playing football from the walls. She remembers how Barbara knew

199

instinctively who she was watching, which exact person, and what it meant. And how, instinctively, she also knew what had happened when she came back from America. How she knew it all, just as she knows now, even before Angela really does herself, that Angela has no intention of going back to school. Or of taking her exams. Or of having any chance of going to university. At this particular moment in time, in fact, she's really only interested in arranging sausages on trays.

Tomorrow is Friday. Sausages are Friday's Special of the Day. Given the occasion, the fact that it is also Valentine's Day, Angela wonders if she should have done something with hearts. Ox. Lamb. Human? Barbara watches as she arranges the last sausage, crimps the white doily she's used to edge the display and carries it back into the cold room.

Before she switches out the light, Angela looks around at the empty shelves. It's lucky the shop isn't very busy because she's used up almost all the stock. There are only a few more chops. Some shoulder of mutton and rag-end necks. Some mince. A side of beef is due to be delivered tomorrow, but the truth is, she has no idea what to do with it. The pigs and lambs, thank God, come in pieces. As for the sausages, she stayed up half last night battling with the mincer, and with the peppercorns and fennel seeds that look like mouse turds, and the slimy casings that feel like exactly what they are.

She closes the heavy white door, fastens the latch, and washes her hands in the big sink, feeling the chalky scrape of the soap that is already toughening her skin, making it red and hard. Then

200

she reaches for the books that are kept below the register so she can close out the day.

'You can't do this.'

Barbara's voice is resigned even as she says it, but Angela loves her for trying. For the fact that she won't quit. This is the third night in a row Barbara has turned up at the shop. She has gone to the hospital with Angela, too. Bought displays of dyed carnations and spiky gladioli and written cards that say things like *'Get Well Soon!'* Now, she's perched on the spare stool beside the register wearing her running clothes, a new set of dark blue leggings and a matching sweatshirt with the logo of some American university in bright yellow on the front. She reaches out and puts her hand over Angela's, stops the pencil that is about to move across columns and will add up nothing more than the growing shadow of the mushroom cloud.

'Your dad wouldn't want you to.' Barbara looks at her. 'You know that, Angie,' she says. 'He's so proud of you. He wants you to go to university. He doesn't want you to do this.' Barbara studies Angela's face. Then her fingers grip Angela's. 'You haven't told him, have you?'

Angela doesn't look at her.

'You haven't told him.' Barbara nods. She almost smiles. 'He thinks the shop is closed. He thinks you're still going to school.' She's like a stonemason who's finally got a chisel in a crack, and she's leaning, hard. Determined to cleave this rock away, split it from the mother cliff.

Angela doesn't say anything, because the truth is, she has no idea what her father thinks. She's not even sure he knows it's her who comes and sits beside him every evening, who watches while the nurse spoons mush into his mouth that opens the way a baby bird's or a kitten's mouth opens. Still, as usual, Barbara's right. Just in case, on the off chance that he does know who she is, she hasn't said a thing.

She's sworn the Pirottis and the Ravallis and Nonna Franchi to silence too. And for now at least, they'll do what she wants because they feel sorry for her, and for her father. And because they agree. Look at all the children who go to university, take up the promise of the New Italy all bright-eyed and come away with a paper that says they know philosophy or economics or all the great English novels and still can't get a job because there are no jobs. What good is that? Besides, unlike Barbara, they know about families. They know what they're for. They understand that until her father comes back, she must keep the door open, and the lights on, and the blades sharpened—and make sure they have something to cut.

Which is why she has accepted the offer. The one made by the cousin who rears the vealers. He called yesterday to say he has heard and that he wants to help. That he'll come in twice a week to do the butchering. For a fee. Which Angela can't afford, but will pay. Because otherwise there will be nothing for her father to come back to.

*   *   *

The cousin's name is Ubaldo, which Angela thinks is both appropriate and unfortunate, because although he isn't that old, a good ten years younger than her father at least, he's losing his hair. It's slid

202

back from his forehead and now hangs, caught like a glasses strap behind his ears.

She has, of course, known Ubaldo all her life. But not well. More like you know a building or a tree you walk past from time to time. She can't, for instance, remember a conversation she's had with him. If Ubaldo has conversations, which, frankly, she doubts. And she hasn't been to the farm for years. Back when she did occasionally go with her father, they didn't stay long. Her father only lingered to play cards and drink Ubaldo's bad wine and worse grappa when he went on his own, when he craved, she supposes, unadulterated male company. Which he certainly got. Ubaldo lives alone with three dogs, rib-thin yellow things, and his herd of dairy cattle, and the vealers—leggy boy calves with sweet wide eyes who suckle and graze and are teased for a few months with the possibility of a future.

It seems cruel, that dangling promise of summer days. But who is Angela to talk? She wears leather. She eats veal. And the calves run and buck on salt-sharp grass and are killed at home, which everyone says is better, and Ubaldo doesn't seem like a cruel man. Rotund, he's the same cylindrical shape as her father, if not quite as tall. They might even look alike, if Ubaldo had her father's mane and his smile, and if there wasn't something wrong with one of his eyes, which wanders, making him appear—admittedly through no fault of his own—both sly and feckless at the same time.

Not that it affects his touch with the knives. Watching him the first evening, Angela has to admit he's good. Fast at slicing muscle and cracking bone. They have agreed that he'll come twice a week, in the evenings after he's finished on the farm. He'll make up enough cuts to stock the cold room, and cut roasts for any special orders, not that they get many these days.

This arrangement makes Ubaldo happy because he says he loves her father like a brother. And besides, he can use the extra money. And it gives him an excuse to come into town. Get off the farm, 'stretch his legs'. He winks at Angela as he says this, his eye veering wildly sideways. She makes a point of not understanding. And of hovering at the cash register. When he goes into the cold room, she locks the till, turning the key surreptitiously and slipping it into her pocket.

Then she watches him. More closely than he knows. It occurs to her that she's been rather stupid, to get herself into this position, to become dependent like this, and that it's because she never really watched her father. So she has resolved that on the evenings when Ubaldo is here, while she sits at the register, the books open in front of her, or wipes the empty glass cases and mops the floor and sprinkles sawdust like powdered sugar, she'll watch what he's doing. Take note of how he separates the rib bones, prising them apart, slowly, almost tenderly, before he raises his arm and brings the cleaver down. Of how he lifts a loin and runs his hand over it, feeling for the grain of the meat. Or trims the fat in one neat long cut from a pork belly.

*   *   *

By the end of the first month, Angela's not surprised her father almost died. It's exhausting. All this serving and smiling and watching, it's much

204

more tiring than she would have guessed. And not in the same way that wrestling with angles and proofs, or even running, is. It doesn't leave her with a virtuous ache. It just leaves her feeling as if she's been drained. In fact, recently she's felt more than once that someone's pulled the plug on her life, that everything that was previously Angela has whirled away.

One night, after visiting her father at the hospital—who was asleep, propped up like a giant doll, his head lolling, tubes running in and out of his arm—she finds she doesn't have the energy to eat. She's tried to keep her strength up, she knows it's important, but she can't be bothered to cook the chop she brought back. Even slicing bread seems too much. She blinks. The blade of the bread knife ripples. She gives up and drops it on the kitchen table, abandons the loaf on the bread board and opens a can of soup and drinks it sitting on the sofa, out of the pan.

The soup tastes like nothing at all, which is oddly comforting, as if flavour might require too much effort. As Angela spoons it towards her mouth, she watches the television with one eye. Afterwards, she takes the pan back to the kitchen and dumps it in the sink beside the other pans and the selection of dishes that seem to have found their way there. Then she goes back into the sitting room and puts on her father's slippers and rolls herself up in the maroon blanket. The news has started. It shows a picture of what looks at first to be a castle or a barracks, but turns itself into a prison, Monferrato in Turin, where they are holding Renato Curcio, one of the leaders of *Brigate Rosse*—they of the five-pointed star—who kidnapped the prosecutor

Mario Sossi two years ago. Or rather, the prison at Monferrato where they *were* holding Renato Curcio. Until four o'clock this afternoon when a woman arrived for visitors' day with a parcel that turned out to be a gun. She is believed, the TV newsreader says excitedly, to be Renato Curcio's wife, another founder of the *Brigate Rosse*. Margherita Cagol.

A picture flashes on the screen as he says this. Margherita Cagol is pretty and has dark hair that falls to her shoulders. The photo is black and white, but the newsreader assures the nation that her eyes are green. She doesn't look all that much older than Angela, or very different from anyone else you'd see in the street. She could walk into the shop and Angela would sell her a pork chop without even thinking about it. But the newsreader insists that would be a mistake. That the public should be vigilant. That anyone who sees her should call the Carabinieri. Immediately. At a special number where operators are standing by. Because Mara, as she prefers to be called, is very dangerous.

Angela feels her eyes closing. The photo on the TV screen wavers as if it's underwater. First Mario Sossi, she thinks, now Mara's own husband. No wonder they're worried. Walls can't stop her. Jails won't keep her out. Mara Cagol makes men disappear like smoke.

*   *   *

Urban guerrilla warfare plays a decisive role in the task of achieving political disorientation of the State. It strikes directly against the enemy and clears the way for the resistance movement. Armed propaganda achieved by means of guerrilla operations is a phase of the class war, the statement in the newspaper says. Then, a bit farther down it adds: *The Christian Democratic Party must be liquidated, destroyed and dispersed. The Christian Democrats are not just a political party, but the black soul of a regime that for thirty years has oppressed the masses and workers of the country.*

These are the latest 'communiqués' from the Red Brigades who, since Mara—as the press now obligingly call her—staged her prison break, have not, as Nonna Franchi would say, Let the Grass Grow Under Their Feet. They haven't Buttoned Their Lips, either. Apparently no one ever told them to be Seen and Not Heard. Or if they did, they weren't listening.

Because these days the *Brigate Rosse* seem to feel the need to announce to the nation their innermost thoughts and desires on a regular basis. When they're not shooting people in the legs. Or kidnapping them. Or both. Last month, a Christian Democrat Party leader was gagged and chained to his desk, along with six office workers. He was 'tried' then and there, found guilty, and '*gambezzati*-ed', shot in the knees. The latest kidnap victim is an industrialist called Vittorio Gancia. No one knows if he's been *gambezzati*-ed or 'tried'. No one knows anything at all, because last week he disappeared like smoke.

Sparito Nel Nulla!

It sounds like a toast. And feels like a rerun of a film. Or, Angela thinks, a sickness that flares up. A fit of epilepsy. An infection that won't die. Someone vanishes. There's a police hunt. One thousand, two thousand, four thousand Carabinieri are mobilized—antibiotics battling a virus in the national blood. Cars are stopped. Doors are knocked on. People cry on television.

This time it's coming from Milan, not Genoa. Not that it makes much difference to Angela. She looks at Vittorio Gancia's picture, half expecting him to be Mario Sossi, then blinks as the words swim across the newspaper. As the letters dance down the page, jigging in time to the snicker and huff of her father's snoring. It's comforting, that sound. If she closes her eyes, just for a minute, she can almost believe she's at home, working at the kitchen table or sprawled on the knobbly rug, and that he's asleep in his chair. But, of course, he isn't. And neither is she.

The infection started the day before. Or two, or three, days ago. It's a little bit like the Red Brigades, nobody knows for sure. What they do know is that it too has announced its intentions.

Her father has been moved back from the recovery ward to a ward with private rooms where all the nurses and doctors wear gloves. All the time. And sometimes even face masks. Angela has to put one on when she comes close to him. Her lips can only brush his skin through paper. Her hand takes his through a film of plastic. His eyes look up at her, and she is not sure who he is seeing. She wonders if she looks enough like her mother. When she bends down to kiss his forehead it smells clammy, like a steak that's been left a little too long in the cold room.

The doctor has reassured Angela that it's not so uncommon with heart patients, for them to get infections. Especially heart patients who are made weak with recovering, who are 'worn down'. Those are the words they use, again and again. 'Worn down', as if her father's a step on a staircase, or one of his own blades. A strip of steel worn to the edge of nothingness from too many years being stropped on a whetstone. That's how he looks, too. Not exactly thinner, but smaller, as if he's retreating inside himself, walking backwards out of the world.

Angela thought dying would be dramatic. But it isn't at all. It's just this walking backwards. Or in her father's case, shuffling. It's just the inside of him getting smaller and smaller, until in one moment that she will not quite be able to put her finger on, he won't be there any more and she'll realize she is alone in the room, and that his carcass is nothing more than that. Just a carcass, like a thousand she's seen before. An old frame of bones. Some worn flesh inside pallid skin. Too much fat. A mane of white hair. Twisted hands chapped and red from a lifetime in a butcher's shop.

*   *   *

It's Wednesday 4 June when Angela's father finally dies and she isn't even there. She's in the shop watching Cousin Ubaldo feather slices of veal, which is not as easy to do as it looks, to make them thin as pieces of pink paper. In the moment her father leaves the world, she's staring, hypnotized by the silver blade. She sorts this out in her head— exactly where she was standing, what she was doing—when she gets to the hospital later that night and finds his bed empty.

209

The hospital staff—the nurses, who have taken off their paper masks and plastic gloves, unveiled themselves like brides—are very kind. They sit with her. They explain about how his heart stopped. How the infection crept through him, skirting the barriers set up by the antibiotics, jumping the walls, stealing into his blood, his lungs, his heart. They tell her that he was in no pain, that he fell asleep and his dreams carried him away.

Angela thinks about that. With the nurses gathered around her, with one of them holding her hand, she imagines her father wandering down halls. Sees him getting smaller and smaller as he pushes open doors, until finally he finds the one her mother stands behind. Angela imagines his voice hushed with anticipation. She hears him whisper, *'Annabeth?'* And sees her mother, turning around and smiling. Reaching for his hand as he takes hers and the years are swept aside like last year's leaves.

She keeps this picture in her mind as she signs the final set of papers, which feels like giving him away.

His body has already gone to the morgue. When they ask if she would like an autopsy, Angela's throat tightens. For a second, she thinks she will be sick, then she shakes her head. When they ask if she would like to see him—to 'say goodbye', or to be certain, presumably, that they are not making this up—her heart stops. Quite suddenly, she feels light-headed, as if her body is no longer subject to the rules of gravity, as if it's left the ground and is rising, like a balloon that might go too high and pop. It is all she can do to ask them to call the Barellis. After that, Angela sits very still, because quite suddenly her insides feel as if they are made of glass, and she is afraid that if she moves they will shatter and she will bleed to death.

*   *   *

'Angie?'

Barbara's face swims in front of her. She is squatting, one of her hands on each of Angela's knees, and Angela wonders if she has been asleep because she didn't hear Barbara arrive, wasn't even aware of her until she spoke. She blinks, pushing away the maze of hallways she has seen her father wandering down.

'Angie?'

Barbara's brown velvet eyes are liquid with tears. One escapes. She lets go of Angela's knee for a second and teeters as she wipes her cheek with the back of her hand.

'Do you want to go home?' she asks. 'Or you can come to our house. *Mamma*'s away but—' Barbara nods. 'We'll get a taxi.'

'No.'

Angela's own voice surprises her. It sounds as if it belongs to someone else. Someone angry. She shakes her head and tries to smile so Barbara won't think she's angry with her.

'No taxi,' she says. Because she knows absolutely that she cannot be inside anything as small as a car.

'I want to walk,' Angela says, but that is not quite true. What she wants to do is run. Climb up onto the ramparts and run round and round and round

211

the city walls. Circle Ferrara so fast she turns back time—swirls her life, and all her past, her father, and even her mother, into a safe pocket of stone. Trapping them there, so they can never escape and she will always know where to find them.

'Come on,' Barbara says. 'Come on, let's get out of here.'

As they step out of the front doors, Barbara stops and looks at Angela, her face creased with concern.

'Are you sure?' she asks. 'I can get a taxi, I can—'

Angela shakes her head. 'I want to walk,' she says, and Barbara nods and reaches for her hand. Together they step out onto the Corso Giovecca.

They take the long way, turning away from the main thoroughfare and winding towards the heart of the old city. The sound of traffic fades. Silence seeps and thickens. They are dwarfed as they pass the Schifanoia, where for a second Angela stops, thinking of the murals of the months—of the dancing women and flying animals. Of the flowers and stars that rest inside its great stone shell like hidden pearls. She has read that the faces in the paintings are the faces of the d'Este mistresses and court ladies, that all the goddesses were modelled on the dead, and she wonders if from now on she will see her father's face. If he will look down at her from carved lintels. Stare out from ornate frames of paintings.

Barbara waits and says nothing. Then they walk on, their footsteps tapping time, measuring the beginning of this new life as they pass Santa Maria in Vado and the blank-faced wall of the Annunziata.

They continue like this, not speaking, holding

212

hands, feeling the layers of the city close around them, until suddenly Angela is aware of something other than their footsteps. A voice, muffled and crackling, it sounds like a radio that's been turned too far up so it distorts, or a huge television set that's been left on.

'What's that?' She stops, unnerved.

Barbara shrugs.

'Probably the vigil.'

'What vigil?'

For an insane moment Angela wonders if the city somehow knows that her father is dead, and if all the old black-dressed ladies, and the fruit-sellers, and the women from the bakery and the laundry, and the man from the kiosk where her father bought his cigars have turned out to make speeches and light candles for him.

'What vigil?' she asks again, and Barbara looks at her.

'For Mara.'

'Mara?' Angela frowns.

'Oh,' Barbara says, as if something has suddenly occurred to her. 'You don't know? I mean, you didn't see the TV tonight?'

Angela shakes her head. Of course she has not seen the TV. She has not seen anything. She has no idea what Barbara is talking about.

'They killed Mara Cagol.'

For a second Angela doesn't know who Mara Cagol is. Or was. Then she remembers. The five-pointed star that looks as if it's leaning backwards. The men who disappear like smoke.

Before she can ask anything, Barbara says, 'This afternoon. They were doing house-to-house searches. You know, looking for that guy, the rich

213

guy who got kidnapped. Gancia. Anyway . . .' She shrugs and starts walking again. Angela falls in beside her.

'Yeah,' Barbara continues. 'They were doing house-to-house searches. I don't know, somewhere outside Milan. And all of a sudden there was a lot of shooting. At least that's what they say. At this one house. Two Carabinieri were killed. And so was Mara. She was inside.' Barbara shrugs. Her eyes slide sideways, meeting Angela's. 'My dad says she was murdered. He heard, when they found the body, that she'd been shot in the back. Other people are saying she was wounded and trying to crawl away and they just shot her. You know, like an animal.'

They have reached the small piazza in front of the Palazzo Paradiso. The noise is coming from a man standing on the steps speaking through a megaphone. It makes his voice so muzzy that Angela can't really make out what he's saying to the two or maybe three hundred people, mostly students, who drift and eddy below him. She looks around. Flyers have been pasted on the walls of the surrounding houses. *Lotta Armata per il Comunismo,* Armed Fight for Communism, the headline reads. The same photograph, the one on the television, stares out from all of them. Over and over, everywhere you turn, there is the pretty dark-haired girl with the five-pointed star leaning backwards behind her. Underneath, the words, *Mara, il tuo assassinio non resterà impunito*—Mara, your assassination will not go unpunished—appear again and again.

Someone moves through the crowd handing out candles. One is thrust into Angela's hand and

214

before she even knows what she is doing, she is holding a flame, raising it above her head. It flickers and glows, one of dozens. Hundreds, which fill the tiny piazza, turning it into a sea of stars. All of them fallen to earth and burning for the memory of Mara Cagol.

*   *   *

Angela's father is buried five days later, his body laid at the foot of the stone angel beside Annabeth's. She has been waiting for him, Angela thinks, for a long time. A lifetime. Hers. Seventeen years, four weeks, and one day.

Bending to put down the white roses she has brought, Angela feels the locket inside her black dress, tapping against her chest like a finger tapping some last tiny message from her parents. She presses her hand against it, wondering if she should have given it back, sent it to be with her father the way she sent his best suit and blue tie and the black shoes Nonna Franchi had come to the house to polish specially.

Leaning in the kitchen doorway, Barbara had watched the old lady, and commented afterwards that it was 'creepy', the way she had rubbed and polished. Spat on the toes, her creased lips puckering a kiss to bring up the shine. But Angela didn't think so. If anything, she wished that there was more, a few favours, a few small kindnesses, that could be done for the dead.

The best she had been able to think of was cleaning the flat. Especially the kitchen. After the funeral, after the lunch the Ravallis insist on hosting—the Pirottis and Nonna Franchi and

Angela and Barbara and even Cousin Ubaldo clustered around their table—it still smells like bleach. Acrid and eye-stinging. Barbara opens the window and stands in front of it, eating a cucumber from the dish on the counter, cutting it into wedges, salting it and chewing it methodically. Angela sits at the table watching her. Outside there are footsteps and the sound of a Vespa. Angela lays her head on her arm and closes her eyes, breathing in the sharp smell and letting her hand wander across the scrubbed wood, reading the map of its scars.

Later, despite the heat, she wraps herself in the maroon blanket and lies on the couch, her father's slippers on her feet. When it gets dark, Barbara makes a nest of cushions and bed pillows on the floor beside her. In the early hours of the morning, as Angela's hand drifts to the floor, she feels the silk of Barbara's hair, then the answering pressure of her fingers. A few moments later, Barbara unwinds the blanket and slips beneath it. Her body is hard and soft at the same time. Her long thighs and muscled back as warm and smooth as sun-touched marble.

*   *   *

Barbara gets her scholarship, to a university in Ohio. She leaves on 12 August. Before that, she goes with her mother to Milan to shop for her new life. When she comes back, Angela goes after work to the Barellis'. She sits on Barbara's bed and watches as Barbara shows off her new clothes, then packs them in her new suitcase, which is pink and has flowers on the side. They talk, make promises,

216

bring food from the Barellis' kitchen and eat it sitting cross-legged, picking crumbs out of the rug. But for all that, their conversations aren't the same. This leaving has built a wall between them. Or rather, Angela thinks, a window. A plate-glass window just like the one at the shop. Standing on either side, they can see each other. Can read each other's lips. Even tell what is behind each other's eyes. But there is no press of flesh.

On the actual day, Angela arranges for Ubaldo to be at the shop and goes with Barbara's mother and sister to the train station. When the train comes, she hugs Barbara. She can smell the sandalwood oil, feel the familiar brush of her hair, but it's like holding a doll. Something inside her friend is already gone. Angela is almost relieved when Barbara finally climbs into the carriage and opens the window and leans out and waves. Angela waves back. As the train begins to move, she keeps waving. She doesn't stop until it has grown small as a toy.

Angela leaves the platform with Barbara's mother and her sister, who has finished university in Padua and is home for a visit before going back again to live with her boyfriend whom everyone hates. When they reach the front of the station they look at her as if she's something they've found and don't know what to do with. Finally, Barbara's mother asks if Angela would like a lift home. She shakes her head and thanks them, then stands and watches as they walk quickly away not looking back, as if they're afraid it might encourage her to follow. After they have driven off, she goes down the steps and turns in the other direction.

It is very hot, and most of the town is already

217

closed for *Ferragosto*, but the supermarket is open. In all these years, Angela has never once been inside it, and only rarely walked past—and then fast and with her head turned, as if whatever's in there might jump out and grab her. Now she stands looking at the big bright green sign above the door and the posters advertising soap powder and discounts on pasta. The rubber mat makes a pinging sound as she pushes open the door. Inside, the air is cold and damp as winter fog.

Angela goes up every aisle, looking at the toothpaste and the shampoo, the plastic bags of oranges and grapefruits, and all the boxes of cereals and different kinds of tea, before she comes to the meat counter. Which isn't really a counter because there are no display cases. Instead, the meat is all piled in a kind of trough. Frost spangles its back, as if the chops and bacon and legs of chicken are guests of an Ice Queen.

Each cut sits on a little polystyrene tray—pink for pork, blue for lamb, green for beef—and is wrapped in layers of see-through film. Two women pushing silver trolleys come around the corner. Angela watches as they stop and pick up items and put them down again and finally don't choose anything. When she leaves she sees them standing in the check-out line with frozen pizzas. She bought one herself. It's pepperoni with double cheese and when she gets home, she puts it in the oven, then eats the whole thing standing at the kitchen window, looking down on the Spanish synagogue where the doors are still padlocked, and still peeling, and that someone really ought to paint.

*　　　*　　　*

On *Ferragosto*, she doesn't go out. Instead, for the first time in a long time she goes into her room and sits on the floor and pulls out the bottom drawer of her chest. For an awful moment, she can't find the blue beads. At first she tells herself she doesn't care, then she realizes she's crying. Her fingers scrabble through a layer of sweaters. She pulls out a handful of old socks and a pair of moth-eaten mittens then, finally, there they are.

They're bluer than Angela remembers. She pushes back the shutter and holds them up to the evening light. The first faint strains of music are coming from the Castello. Closing her eyes, she lets her hand slip between her legs. That night when she lies down on the couch she keeps the bracelet on her wrist.

Seventeen days later, on the first of September, the factory explodes.

*　　　*　　　*

If she hadn't heard it, Angela might not have been aware of it, at least not right away. She isn't aware of much these days, except the shop. Anywhere else—in the flat, walking home—she can barely move. But there, she can't stop. She's taken to cleaning the mincer using an old toothbrush, and to polishing the window. She arrives every morning while the sky is still the colour of pearls and the only sound is the high swooping cheep of the swallows. In the store room she mixes up lemon juice and vinegar in a preserving jar the way Nonna Franchi used to. Then she stands on the street

219

making circle after circle on the glass, tighter and tighter, with wadded-up handfuls of newspaper. At night, she spends extra time washing the floor before sprinkling the sawdust. Watching it fall through her fingers like tiny honey-coloured petals.

Angela had just finished serving a customer, when it happened. It was eleven o'clock in the morning on a Wednesday and August was over, so all the shops were open and everyone was back from holiday and having coffee or eating granita at the pavement bars or wandering between the stalls of the fruit-sellers in the Palazzo Municipale.

Later, during the Official Inquiries and trials that followed, they would read in the newspaper how the factory's management, in an effort to 'streamline and increase efficiency', had, with the consent of the union, cut its maintenance routine. So when a spark flew into an unemptied bin, the resulting fire, which had not been very big or seemed very serious at first, rapidly became both, because the extinguisher the foreman grabbed did not work. After that, they would read that it was, at best, a matter of if not seconds, certainly not more than a minute, before the flames found the pocket of gas that had built up during the holiday due to a leak in the pipe and poor ventilation.

Not that the shoppers and strollers and coffee-drinkers of Ferrara were aware of any of that at the time. They were not aware of much at eleven o'clock that morning, except perhaps that the day was already very hot and that there was a shortage of cucumbers and melons due to the late spring. Until they heard the noise.

It was a combination of a crack and a boom and

220

was followed by a shudder. By a physical rocking of the air. People walking on the walls said they felt them shake. Glass rattled. Bicycles tipped over. At the Duomo a pigeon fell straight down onto the steps. Then, in the Piazza Trieste, the milling crowd, who had turned and looked up, wondering if despite the clear sky they had heard thunder, saw a second sun.

A ball of yellow and red. Some described it as a giant fist—a golden hammer of God descended from the heavens that opened its fingers and hung for one perfect moment like a vast blessing hand. Then snapped closed with a roar. And was swallowed by a shimmering blackness that rose and spread, quivering to the sudden yowl of sirens.

Like everyone else, Angela ran into the street. She stood beside the Pirottis and the man who owned the leather-repair shop and the ladies from the laundry, all of them staring upwards, mouths open, hands slack, until someone ran shouting from Via Volte towards Porta Paola. Others followed seconds later, thundering like a buffalo herd towards the noise. *'Antonio. Antonio's building.'* The words ran through Angela's head, stopping her brain until someone else shouted that it was one of the factories—a fire, an explosion, an attack—and Signora Pirotti, whose bad knee stopped her from running anywhere, pushed Angela onto the pavement because fire engines and ambulances were already screaming up Via Mayr.

Few of the factory workers shopped inside the walls. As a rule, they preferred the newer stores, purpose-built for the blocks of flats. But still the shop grilles came down. All along the street,

Angela heard them, rattling like trains on broken tracks. By afternoon, the word went round that because all the ambulances were busy, bodies were being laid out in the church, that the dead were waiting in the house of God. The blades of the helicopters whump-whumped as they landed on the car park that had been cleared near the Sacra Famiglia then rose again like giant carrion birds, ferrying their bloodied cargo to hospitals bigger and better-equipped than Ferrara's.

It took Angela fifteen minutes to walk to the church. A thousand years ago the Sacra Famiglia had been the site of Ferrara's first cathedral. After the river changed its course and the city centre moved with it, it had been stranded beyond the Darsena and the safety of the walls. Now it sat in exile out near the racecourse.

Cars and ambulances arrived and left. Firemen and Carabinieri and first-aid crews scurried back and forth from a makeshift tent where those who were severely burned waited to be airlifted. The tent had been put here, Angela heard someone say, because it was necessary to get as far away from the factory as possible, since it was still burning and there had already been a couple of smaller explosions, and no one knew how many more pockets of gas the flames might find.

Other people had come, too. Women mostly. Some old, some young. Wives and sisters and mothers. Some ran to and fro, darting from a fireman to a policeman, grabbing sleeves, shouting, begging. Others stood in small knots, blank looks on their faces. One girl, not much older than Angela and heavily pregnant, had tears streaming down her reddened cheeks. No one noticed, or if they did they didn't care, when Angela eased open the huge door of the Sacra Famiglia and slipped inside.

What hit her first was the smell. It always did, on the rare occasions when she went into churches. The strong, sweet, cloying scent of the incense, dense and heavy like a spice cake on the edge of burning, and the familiar odour of damp stone— the smell of centuries she had grown up with, cold marble and the faint mildew of plaster—mingling with the smoke from the votive candles. This time there was something else, too. Something animal. Flesh and blood. Both familiar and different to the smell of the butcher's shop. She baulked like a calf at the door of an abattoir, blinking as her eyes adjusted to the light.

When she finally stepped inside, Angela could feel the cavernous space above her, the high, empty flight of the roof. It was quiet and very still. So much so that it took her a moment to pick out a faint, low, continuous murmuring, and to understand that it was coming from two priests. They moved in concert, up and down, reciting the prayers for the dead. There were other people, too. Several nuns, one of whom had a clipboard and seemed to be trying to identify bodies. And a handful of women doing exactly what she was doing, moving from corpse to corpse, slowly, silently, methodically, looking for a familiar face.

*   *   *

Afterwards, she did not understand how she knew he would be there. But she did. She had known it when she left the shop, padlocked the grille, and

223

instead of turning towards the city and the flat, had gone down across Piazza Travaglio and passed through the walls at Porta Paola, following the route Antonio had taken a thousand times, every night and every morning, the way he had been going that winter night when she saw him all those years ago.

Now she stood looking down at the face that was the reflection of his. A little thinner, the nose not quite as sharp, or the mouth as generous. The eyes would be the same, if he opened them, black as river stones.

She dropped to her knees, aware too late that she was in a slick of blood. Piero's heart could not have been pumping or they would not have brought him here. It was just the last shadow of his life she knelt in. His hair was still wild, or at least half of it. The other half was matted. Her hand came away, sticky and dark, when she smoothed it off his forehead. Face paint, she thought, it's face paint, and saw again the low, sweeping bow, the idiotic half-drunken grin, the way he and Antonio had wrestled, their bodies twining like young, limber snakes. And Antonio. Standing on the ladder above her, looking down, smiling. *'I told my brother, I told Piero, he deserves more than bread. He deserves roses, too.'*

*   *   *

It is two days before she opens the shop again, and even then more than half the shutters on Via Mayr are still locked down. Angela wonders briefly if she should join them. She weighs the keys in her hand. But she's afraid of stock spoiling, and besides she has spent two days in the flat with its dirty dishes and piles of clothes in the sitting room and sounds of the Ravallis snuffling below. She bends to unlock the padlock. The sky is milky and there's still a strange smell in the air. The street is so quiet it might be Sunday. She notices a thin black dusting on the pavement. It's fallen all over the city, wormed its way into the cracks and smeared the windowpanes. The remains of lives.

The shop reveals itself little by little as she pushes up the grille, like a picture developing. She steps inside and feels the coolness and the silence. Her father's white coat still hangs on its peg. The collar is frayed, one pocket ripped and re-stitched. She touches it, her fingers resting on the worn cloth.

'*Buongiorno, papà,*' she says, just like every morning.

By 10 a.m. there have barely been any customers and there is nothing left to clean or polish, so she opens the books. Scarcely a week after her father died, she had a visit from a man at the bank. He had been short, only a little taller than she was, and had worn a grey suit made of fabric that hissed when he reached out to shake her hand.

'Signor Carossi,' he had said. Then he had offered his condolences for her father's death, and asked what she planned to do.

Angela had stared at him, until finally he had chewed his lower lip and assured her that he understood that this was 'a difficult time', and that the bank, presumably in the person of himself, was 'eager to help in any way it could'. When she still had not replied, he had chewed his lip some more, then said perhaps it would be better if he came back in a few weeks. Finally, he had turned to leave, but stopped again, lingering in the doorway, allowing warm dusty air from the street to blow in. There was something, he'd said, that she ought to know. That he felt he ought to tell her. The supermarket 'had expressed an interest' in buying the butcher's shop. The bank man had tried to smile as he said this, then added that he hesitated to mention it just now, and he was sorry if he had upset her. But he thought it might help to know she had 'options'.

A week later, she had received a letter informing her that the interest rate on the loan had been increased 'due to the bank's enhanced risk as a result of the death of the proprietor and subsequent unavoidable changes'.

Now, with the books spread in front of her, all she can see are clouds. Mostly the mushroom cloud, which seems, like the smoke that rose from the factory, to have grown darker and thicker. She closes her eyes, but that is no better. Piero bows and laughs, crimson running down his face. There is a tap on the glass.

Angela starts and looks up. Ubaldo is standing on the pavement. He grins at her and waves, his bad eye veering wildly so he appears to be looking two ways at once. He pushes through the door, his newspaper tucked under his arm.

'Ciao.'

Ubaldo drops his paper on the counter beside the cash register. The front page is still covered in pictures of the fire, of the ruins of the factory, of men with blackened faces, and of what appear to be pieces of twisted metal.

Ubaldo whistles and puts on his apron. Then he

226

crosses the shop, flips the paper open, and runs one of his big hands down the page which lists the day's races.

'There,' he says lovingly. 'There she is. Our fame and fortune.'

His finger with its chipped nail rests under the name of a horse called Delilah. But Angela is not looking at that. Her eyes have slid to the facing page where there is a picture of men in dark suits, union officials coming down the steps of a building in Rome, their faces grim. The caption says it is the headquarters of the Christian Democrat Party where they have been 'holding meetings to ensure the ongoing protection of workers' rights'. Below, in black-lined columns, are the names of the dead.

Ubaldo is saying something—about this horse and how much he has bet on it and what they can do with the money when it wins. Angela blinks. She sees her finger reaching out, touching the name, reading it like braille.

Piero Giovanni Tomaselli, twenty-one, of Ferrara.

She closes her eyes and hears them laugh. She sees Antonio. Feels his hand on the small of her back.

But it isn't Antonio's. It's Ubaldo's.

'*Carina*,' he is saying. '*Carina—*'

Warmth seeps from his huge body, as if he's one of his own cows with their pale wet mouths and soupy eyes. The hot damp of him presses through the thin cotton of her overall, through her blouse and onto her skin. Angela can feel the bulge of his stomach. She can feel his belt buckle, and the hardness below.

'You're tired,' Ubaldo murmurs. 'You work too hard, you should let me—'

227

She jumps backwards. The stool flies sideways. Pinned against the marble counter, Angela spins, reaches up, and grabs.

'Don't!' The blade of the filleting knife flashes. 'Don't ever touch me again!'

For a moment both of them stand, frozen. They watch as the bright line of blood runs down Ubaldo's arm. As it opens in a stream and begins to dribble through the dark hairs on the back of his hand. A drop lands and blossoms on his apron, poppy red against the washed-out stains from cows and pigs and sheep.

Ubaldo stares. For once, both his eyes on the same thing. His mouth opens and closes, like a fish gasping for air. Then he turns and crashes into the stool. Like a terrified animal, he scrabbles over it and around the counter, slipping on the sawdust as he grabs for the door.

The last time Angela ever sees him he is running down the pavement, holding his arm with his free hand, lurching and slipping like an ungainly horse.

*   *   *

She goes to see the man at the bank three days later. They agree that she will keep the butcher's shop open until she has used up all the stock in the cold room. Sold the chops and roasts Ubaldo had prepared. She does it fast. She puts up a SALE poster like the one in the supermarket. And then it's over. On the last day, the day when Signor Carossi comes in his hissing suit and she gives him the keys, he asks her if there is anything she would like to keep. She looks around. What would she do with the mincer or the cash register? Finally, she chooses several knives. She wraps them in her father's apron. Then, at the last moment, she takes his white coat, too.

*   *   *

It wasn't difficult for Angela to find work. The Pirottis were more than happy to pay her to do their books, and their son-in-law was a carpenter and he paid her, too. She insisted on doing them at home because she did not want to walk down Via Mayr. If she had to go to Ripagrande or to Via Settembre, she made certain that she skirted the blocks near the butcher's shop. She only slipped up once, when it was unavoidable, when a woman who had a tailor's shop near Piazza Verdi wanted to hire her. Even then, she waited until sunset, as if somehow that would help, then scurried, trying to keep her head bent although it was a clear evening and wasn't raining or even very windy. It didn't work. Forced to stop when she crossed the street, she had looked up. And seen the shop front, the plate-glass window and even the *macelleria* sign boarded over. The sheets of plywood were pale, almost white in the dusk. Already they had been covered with posters. Green ones, advertising laundry soap and roasting chickens and discounted cooking oil at the supermarket.

*   *   *

Christmas came and went. Angela spent it with the Ravallis. Barbara did not come home, but wrote to say her father was taking her to San Francisco where they would meet her sisters and then go

229

skiing. She sent Angela a tracksuit from her university, and asked how the studying for her exams was going and when she was going to take them.

The answer was never. By December Angela had five or six small shops she did the books for, and in January a pizza parlour up near Piazza Ariostea hired her to come in three afternoons a week. The owner had a bakery and bar too, and had fired his last accountant for stealing. He paid her under the table, in cash. On her birthday they gave her a party, and told her she was still *una bambina piccola*, 'a little kid' at twenty, which was especially true since she was only eighteen. After that first night at the hospital, she had found it complicated to stop lying about her age. So she didn't.

She was dreading 4 June. She watched it inch closer and closer on the calendar, as if it would mean something, this mere fact that her father had been dead for a year. Barbara had telephoned on her birthday. She suggested Angela should come to America in August, for a holiday. Barbara would send her a ticket. She was going to buy a car and they could drive to Yellowstone Park, or maybe even all the way to California. Angela said that sounded nice, but she knew from the sound of Barbara's voice, from how fast she was talking and the high, insistent pitch of her words, that it would never happen. That her father would send her on a trip, or her mother would rent a house somewhere, far away and very expensive, where there was no room for Angela.

During the last week of May it suddenly became very hot. The grass in the centre of Piazza Ariostea turned bright green and the low hedges sprouted faster than they could be clipped. Nasturtiums and pansies tangled out of the window boxes she passed on her way to the pizza parlour. The tubs of little plants, African violets and miniature cyclamen the florist next door set out on the pavement, had to be watered almost every hour, and finally brought in under the canopy.

The second of June was a holiday, but Angela came in anyway. The owner was considering enlarging the place, putting a bigger restaurant room out in the back, and had asked her to look at the numbers. Besides, she did not want to stay at home. For the last three nights she had lain awake on the sofa, watching the shadows from the street move across the sitting-room ceiling, certain she could hear her father snoring down the hall.

She had keys, and opened up the pizzeria. The place had nothing as fancy as air conditioning, so she turned on the fan and got a chair and propped the street door open, hoping there would be some draught, or at least a slight shifting of the hot muggy blanket that had draped itself over the city. The office was behind the bar, so she jammed that door open, too. It was just before noon when she heard someone come in.

'We're closed,' she called, wondering if she should hang the sign over the back of the chair so it could be seen from the street.

There was no reply. Probably it was the owner, come back for something he'd forgotten last night. When no one appeared in the office doorway, she finally got to her feet and went out into the main room.

He was standing with his back to her among the wiped tables with their upturned chairs, his hands in his pockets, sleeves rolled up. His arms were brown, as if summer had imprinted itself forever on his skin. The sunlight from the door caught his hair.

'*Ciao, carina,*' he said as he turned round. '*Da quanto non ci si vede.*'

PART THREE

FLORENCE

2010

SUNDAY 7 FEBRUARY

Enzo Saenz was giving up and going home. The last two days had been an almost total waste of time. He had watched hours of security tape from the cameras at the airport, bus stops, and train station, and seen—precisely nothing. At least nothing that even vaguely resembled Anna Carson, in or out of disguise.

The databases were showing precisely nothing, too. There was no further information on the black BMW. The crime-scene techs had lifted fingerprints from all over Kristen's flat that matched Anna Carson's, whose did, in fact, match Angela Vari's. But so what? She'd been there with her husband the day after she arrived, and left her ID bracelet in plain sight. The only function that had served was to finally introduce into the mind of Kenneth Carson the suspicion that they might not, after all, be making this whole story up as part of some nefarious international conspiracy. Pallioti was dealing with him, thank God. Enzo would have given up days ago, found an excuse to put him in a cell somewhere and thrown away the key. Which was why Pallioti was Pallioti and he wasn't.

Despite the high-level hand-holding—James MacCready and even the Consul were also doing their part—Dr Carson was just barely being persuaded not to 'go public'. Not to rush to the nearest television studio or newspaper office. Just thinking about that made the back of Enzo's neck cold. He could close his eyes and see the bulletproof vests and helicopters and machine guns. No one—not Enzo, nor James MacCready, nor Pallioti nor even His Dickheadness, the Consul—would put any money on which way that would come out for Kristen. Or Anna Carson.

Enzo took a breath and wondered if he'd been wrong. Yet again, he saw her eyes widen as she stared at the tiny screen on the phone, and saw her glare as she denied what she had seen. There was no question she'd been angry. But some niggling part of him now wondered if the anger had come, not from belligerence—a vestigial *Brigate Rosse* instinct telling her that all and any policemen should go fuck themselves—but from fear. If he had reached out, been less aggressive. If he had, for instance, bothered to find out who she was before he had ambushed her, perhaps he might have talked her out of running. Or at least now be able to make an educated guess as to why she had.

He sighed, wondering why he couldn't accept that he knew the answer to that one already. Leopards didn't change their spots. As far as he could see, Angela Vari had been *Brigate Rosse*. And a turncoat with it. When it got too hot she'd got scared, gone running to the police and offered them the one thing she had: Antonio. In short, she'd shopped her lover to save her own neck. Charming. He just wished he could figure out what the hell she was up to now. And why she'd bothered to take the girl's teddy bear.

Enzo slammed the drawer of his desk. The noise made him jump. It was past five on Sunday evening and the building was unusually quiet. Pallioti had gone to his sister's. For the briefest moment, Enzo allowed himself to dwell on Seraphina. Her smile, her laugh. Her beautiful house. And beautiful son.

236

And charming husband. Then he pushed her from his mind. Or, more realistically, put her back in the shadowed corner where he kept his cache of safe, unattainable longings.

He stood up and looked at the USB drive that had been dropped on his desk an hour earlier. It held the logs he had requested from across the country—every identity card that had been reported stolen since Thursday by anyone, male or female, who might conceivably bear any physical resemblance to Anna Carson. There had been daily updates, but so far, like everything else, they'd led nowhere. He picked it up and shoved it into his jacket pocket.

*   *   *

The cat, feeling hard done by and ignored, didn't speak when he opened the door, just swished her tail and gave him the evil eye.

'There's no point in looking like that,' he said. 'I've told you I'm sorry.'

She glanced in the other direction, as if he might conceivably be talking to some other cat, then hopped down off the sofa arm and sauntered into the kitchen, ignoring him. Buying her fresh fish was ridiculous. Feeling like a supplicant, Enzo picked up her bowl and opened the bag without even taking his jacket off. He told himself that he'd only stopped at the supermarket because he fancied something that wasn't out of a can.

'*Ciao* to you too,' he muttered as he put the bowl on the floor. Then he took off his shoes, shrugged out of his jacket and went to stand under a hot shower.

*   *   *

Dinner was a fat speckled river trout. A glass of wine. Buttery yellow potatoes barely bigger than his thumb. When he'd finished it, donating the bones to the cat bowl, Enzo poured himself a second glass and felt more human. He hit the button that raised the blinds and stood for a moment, swilling the deep almost purple wine in the globe of the glass and staring out at the city.

The clouds and sleet of the last few days had finally been driven away by a sharp, biting wind that swept down from the mountains, rattling the grey empty branches of the trees and chasing the last dead leaves from the gutters. It had rippled the water of the Arno until the customary placid brown was spittled with white caps, then whipped into the piazzas, snatching at newspapers and bus schedules and discarded paper cups. Then it had fled, leaving a night sky spangled with stars.

Enzo felt the cat brush his legs, as close as she ever got to thanks, then heard her patter away and make a soft *whump* as she jumped back onto the sofa. He thought of his grandparents, and wondered if the old man had his telescope out—if he was taking advantage of this rare night to climb up onto the roof terrace in his winter coat and trace Orion's Belt. Pick out the Bear, and the Twins, and the Bull. He wondered about his mother, if she was in her studio, lost in her strange world of colours, or if she had gone out to walk her boundaries as she sometimes did on winter nights, moving through the pale twisted trunks of the olive trees. He should give up this job, he thought

238

suddenly. He knew too many policemen who had spent too long walking the boundary of what was decent, what was bearable to humankind. Pallioti was the exception. And he was rare. Many more reached forty, then fifty, with something dead behind their eyes. It wasn't too late to have a family: a wife, children, something more than fantasies and a cat to come home to. Medical school was probably out of the question by now, but he wasn't stupid and there were plenty of other jobs he could do. He rolled the glass in his hand, raised it, and let the wine slide across his tongue. Then he turned and looked at the USB drive that sat on the counter. Five minutes later he'd booted up the computer and was scrolling through the entries.

Enzo's first instinct had been to ignore the south, then he thought he'd better not ignore anywhere. Still, he betted on Rome. That had been Angela Vari's last stomping ground, the place in Italy that would be freshest in her mind, even if it was thirty years ago. If she had contacts, they were likely to be there.

After forty minutes of sifting through reports of stolen purses, pick-pocketed wallets, and mysteriously vanished passports and identity cards, he felt his certainty ebb. A few cases were remotely likely, but nothing stood out. He moved on to Milan. There, he noted two names, both of them young men. It was possible, but difficult, and on the whole he didn't see why she'd take the hardest option. He made a note of the names to follow up in the morning nonetheless. Then found himself yawning, and was contemplating finishing the bottle and taking up the task over breakfast, when he saw that it had been an unusually quiet weekend in Reggio. Parma, Modena, and Bologna between them had only a handful of missing cards. He glanced at his watch. It wasn't exactly late. He might as well finish the province before he called it a night. Five minutes later, Enzo sat up. Then he leaned forward and squinted at the screen.

*   *   *

'The description fits. It's Bologna. Close to Ferrara.'

Pallioti felt himself smile, out of nostalgia as much as anything else. He recognized the edge in Enzo's voice for what it was—the desperation that passed for hope in policemen. The need to believe you'd found something, anything, that might crack a case gone dead. Which, let's face it, this one had. He'd spent the afternoon at his sister's playing with his nephew, not talking about it and thinking of nothing else.

'So you think that's where she's going, Ferrara?'

'Why not? Don't you?'

Pallioti nodded. He supposed he did. Whether it is good for us or not, we go back to what we know. A thin snow had begun to fall. He had parked his car, tipped the garage attendant, lingered to discuss the likelihood of Italy retaining her World Cup title, and was walking home. Light slanted through closed shutters, picking up the snow, making it almost fluorescent against the dark.

'In any case.' Enzo sounded testy now, not unlike his nephew when he stayed up too late. 'I've spoken to Bologna. They're going to try to get this woman, the one whose wallet was lifted, to come in tomorrow morning. So I'll be leaving early. I just wanted to let you know.'

Pallioti murmured something about being in touch, then the phone went dead and the only sound in the street was his footsteps. His fingers tapped the smooth metal case. He did it without being aware of it, the way some people pulled their ears or fiddled with their tie. Morse code, more than one person had told him it sounded like. His private little SOS. Or, in this case, Angela Vari's name. He turned the corner, heard a bell begin to toll from across the river, a faint hollow sound, and stopped and fished in another pocket for his keys.

The sense of unease he had been feeling all day had not been chased away by his nephew, or his sister, or his brother-in-law, whom he actually liked. Instead it had followed him, like a waif tugging at his sleeve. Enzo's voice, for a reason he could not quite put his finger on, had made the urchin bolder. Pallioti had been to Ferrara only once, quite a long time ago. Flat as a pancake and very windy, it was supposed to be beautiful. But he had found it rather sinister—a time warp enclosed by walls, the great brooding castle with its moats and dungeons looming over the centre of town, looking down on abandoned cannons and a statue of the screaming Savonarola. The waif dogged him across the empty lobby. It hung about as he waited for the lift. Pallioti didn't like flat places. All the shadows were wrong.

*   *   *

'Alessandro. How good of you to call.'

The voice was exactly as he remembered it: thin,

241

smooth, and cold. Like surgical thread, Pallioti thought, that had been stored in a freezer. It was incongruous, in one who had grown quite so large. All fat men were expected to sound like Santa Claus. Not in this case. The whippet still lurked inside the flesh.

'I'm sorry I didn't have the time, earlier. I wanted to thank you. For your help.'

'Not at all. I take it you got what you needed.'

'Yes.' Pallioti thought of the dog-eared files he had handed Enzo Saenz two days ago. 'Thank you,' he added. 'I'm sure your help expedited things.'

There was a sound on the other end of the phone that was something between a chuckle and a 'humph'. A general acknowledgement of the man's importance. Pallioti smiled. It wasn't something his friend had ever been exactly shy about, even in the old days, when they had first known each other, when the man on the end of the phone had taken Pallioti under his wing, offered him his patronage, much as he now gave his to Enzo.

Pallioti swirled the grappa he had poured. He'd thought twice about making this call at all. Asking for a little help in getting a sensitive file sent quickly was one thing. What he was about to ask for now, on the other hand—dirt, intuition, the squishy viscera at the heart of history—was something else altogether.

'I'd been meaning to say . . .' Pallioti examined the neatly clipped edges of his nails, wondering how best to get what he wanted, and decided on flattery. 'I want to congratulate you, truly, on the latest initiative. With the Americans,' he continued. 'Deeply impressive. I was going to write. But, well.' He coughed self-deprecatingly, suggesting he knew full well that the quality of his letter paper, never mind the words written on it, could never really come up to scratch. 'In any case,' he oiled on, 'it's very good of you. And on a Sunday night, to take the time to talk. I appreciate it. Deeply. I wouldn't impose unless it was important. I know I can count on your . . . discretion.'

What a load of rubbish, he thought. Hogwash of the first order. Since being elevated to his present great height, the fat man was known to spend most of his time farting around on golf courses. And as for the new 'Transatlantic Intelligence Sharing Initiative', anyone with half a brain knew it was gobbledygook. 'Intelligence sharing' with Uncle Sam, if it wasn't an oxymoron in the first place, only went one way. Not yours. And if by any chance anything remotely impressive had been done, with the Americans or anyone else, it had been done not by the man himself, but by minions. Who would then have been banished, sent scurrying away with their tails between their legs and their lips buttoned so their master could step up and take the credit. The only bit of what he'd said so far that was true was the last bit. Or rather, the last two bits. He suspected what he was asking for really was important. Crucial, in fact. And the fat man was discreet. At a price. He'll make me pay for this, Pallioti thought. He'll make me pay, extravagantly, and at the time and place of his choosing.

The silence on the other end of the line caused him to wonder if he'd gone too far. Slathered it on with too big a paddle, if such a thing was possible. Apparently not.

243

'Of course,' his friend said finally. 'Anything at all. What can I do for you, Alessandro?'

'Tell me about Angela Vari.'

There was a pause.

'Angela Vari?'

'Yes. That's right. Angela Vari.'

Pallioti rolled his eyes. They hadn't actually spoken when he'd asked for help obtaining the file; he'd gone through a minion. But surely the fat man had known what, or rather who, was in it.

'Angela Vari.' This time, her name was followed by a faint humming sound.

'Yes.'

The humming stopped.

'She was the girl. In the flat, where they held Aldo Moro. At the risk of being impertinent, may I ask, Alessandro, why you're suddenly so interested in her?'

Pallioti took a breath and started to open his mouth, then stopped when the humming started again. He waited.

'She was a strange girl,' the fat man said suddenly. 'I do remember that. I wasn't certain, you know. Even at the time.'

So his friend had been one of the doubters. Pallioti didn't know if this surprised him or not. He put his glass down.

'You weren't certain?' he asked. 'That what she was telling you was good?'

'No.' The word came out slowly. 'No. Not so much that. No,' his friend said again. 'The information she gave us was good.' He laughed, this time it was a sour, tight little sound. Miles away Pallioti heard ice clink in a glass. 'The proof was in the pudding, so to speak.' There was a

244

splash of liquid, the tap of a bottle being put down. Single malt, if Pallioti remembered correctly.

'We'd never have got Tomaselli, it wouldn't have happened,' the fat man said. 'At least not for a long time, probably, without her. So, no. It wasn't that.'

There was another pause. Pallioti could see him, sniffing his drink and weighing what he would tell. And what he wouldn't. A slurping followed, and finally, a sigh.

'It was just,' his friend said, 'well, Moro, really. Did you ever meet him?'

'Aldo Moro?'

Pallioti shook his head. He refrained from pointing out that Aldo Moro had been dead for over thirty years, and that although his own career had generally been acknowledged as stellar, he had hardly, as a very junior policeman, been invited to Rome on a regular basis.

'No,' he said, 'I never met him.' And left it at that.

'Well,' the fat man said, 'I liked him. A lot of people didn't. Found him a cold fish. Inscrutable. All that. Very private. People say they respect it, but actually they resent that sort of thing. Reminds them that at heart we're all peeping Toms. And he was bright, of course,' he added. There was another slurp and clink. 'Moro. Very bright. People resent that, too. On the whole. They say they don't, but they do. But he was quiet. And, well, something more than that. Made people uncomfortable.'

'Something more than the fact that he was intelligent and modest about it?'

It was a feeble attempt at humour, but his friend was right. Lots of people, certain types of men

245

especially, were more comfortable with a good dose of braying and back-slapping.

His friend had the good grace to laugh.

'Well, yes,' he said. 'Actually. It was more than that. There was something, well, unearthly about him.'

'Unearthly?' This was such an uncharacteristic statement that Pallioti wondered how much whisky, exactly, had been consumed down in Rome. 'Something "unearthly" about Aldo Moro?'

'Yes. And not Down. Up. You know what I mean? There are certain people, well—you wouldn't be surprised if they grew wings.'

Pallioti felt himself go still. He had heard plenty of politicians described as Satan's henchmen, or even the Big Guy himself. But the other—and coming from this source. That was a first. He remembered the posters after the body was found, Moro's soft, sad face. What else was his friend going to suggest? he wondered. That during his fifty-four days in purgatory Aldo Moro got holes in his feet and the palms of his hands?

'She was the same,' his friend added.

'Angela Vari?'

Pallioti reached for his grappa bottle.

'Yes. She was a very strange girl.'

'Strange how?'

'Well . . .' Pallioti heard his friend take a sip of his drink. 'Born martyr. Kept sticking her hand in the flames, for a start. Went on and on about some smashed synagogue and how silence was as deadly as bullets. That kind of stuff. You know, she said she killed him, Moro. At first.'

'Aldo Moro? Angela Vari said she killed him?' Pallioti sat up. This was news. And would kick

246

things into a whole different league. 'Was it true?'

'Well, who knows what was true? We couldn't exactly pinpoint the time of death. But my instinct? No. I thought it was garbage. What evidence we could find said so, too. But Angie was strange.' Pallioti could almost hear the fat man shrug. 'Perhaps that's why they liked each other.'

'Liked each other?'

'Yes. Alessandro, are you having trouble hearing? Is that why you're repeating everything?' His friend chuckled. 'Moro and the Vari girl. Yes. They were, apparently, well, according to her anyway—we didn't exactly have a chance to ask him—friends. They used to talk.'

'Talk?'

'Yes, Alessandro. Talk. So she said. Whisper, actually, if you want to be pedantic.' He had the good grace not to add, 'which you apparently do'. 'About, well, things,' he continued. 'Philosophy. Religion. Love. Good. Evil. You do remember? It's called a conversation.'

Pallioti didn't know which unnerved him more, the idea that he might appear to have forgotten what it was to indulge in abstract discourse with another human being, or the idea that the blonde American doctor's wife who had been sitting across a conference table from him less than a week ago had discussed love, religion, and evil with Italy's most famous murdered politician.

'How very Mary Magdalene,' he murmured.

A bark of laughter issued down the phone.

'Well, I wouldn't go that far. But somewhere along those lines, in her version anyway. She said he reminded her of her father.'

'Her father? Aldo Moro?'

'I know. I know,' his friend said. 'Her father was a butcher from Ferrara. The resemblance wasn't immediately obvious to me, either. But she wasn't making it up, Angela. She meant it. I believed her. I think Moro became a sort of surrogate *papà* to her. During all those days in that ghastly little cell. A sort of reverse Stockholm Syndrome or something. She cooked for him, you know. That was her job. Nourishing him. Body and soul.'

'You don't mean . . . ?'

The grappa choked on the back of his tongue. But then again, why not? The rumour had always been that, starved of seeing each other for months, couples had managed to have sex in the cages in the courtroom during the Red Brigade trials. It was probably utter nonsense, of course. There was almost as much rubbish written about the BR as there was about Mary Magdalene. On the other hand, if he'd been locked in a tiny room for days and days and suspected he was about to be killed and a young girl had—

'No, no!' His friend, who had obviously been thinking along the same lines, barked. 'No. No. No, there was none of that. This was a purely platonic affair. Angela and Aldo. A meeting of minds. I'm quite sure of it.'

Both of them were silent for a moment. Chastened as schoolboys.

'Not so surprising, I suppose,' his friend went on a moment later. 'The meeting of minds, I mean. They were idealists after all, the *Brigate Rosse*. And so was Moro, in his way. No,' he said. 'That was all it was. I'm sure. Certain, in fact. She was Tomaselli's. Body if, in the final analysis, apparently not soul. Moro might have won that

248

round.' The ice clinked again. 'Some of her money was used, you know,' he added, 'to buy the flat, the one they kept him in, on Via Montalcini. Angela always claimed she didn't know. That she handed it over to Tomaselli and believed him when he said he'd put it in the bank for her.'

Pallioti could see his friend's head shaking, either because the girl had been so incredibly naive, or because the lie was so preposterous.

'Blind love, literally. If you believe in it. Or her,' his friend said. 'But she did care for Moro. I do believe that. Loved him even, I think.'

Pallioti stared at the clear liquid in his own glass. He could feel himself frowning. 'I don't understand,' he said. 'If she, if Angela Vari cared so much for Aldo Moro . . . If he reminded her so much of her beloved father—I assume he was beloved?'

'Oh yes. Yes, as far as I know. Very beloved. She was apparently devastated when he died.'

'Well . . .' Pallioti hesitated. 'If that was the case then, if—'

'If she loved Aldo Moro, why did she wait until the day of his funeral? Why didn't Angela Vari save his life? Why didn't she come to us before he was killed?'

There was a silence.

'Yes,' his friend said a moment later. 'That's the problem. My question, too. That was what I never understood about the Butcher's Daughter.'

'Did you ask her?'

'Of course. We all asked her.'

'And you never got an answer?'

There was a pause, and for a moment Pallioti thought he might lie. Might not be able to resist

249

the temptation to play the Know-It-All, provide the answers even if he didn't have them, just to make himself look good. But he didn't. When he spoke again, for the first time his friend sounded old.

'No. Not really. Tomaselli promised her it wouldn't happen and she believed him. Love. That great catch-all. They didn't kill Mario Sossi. I don't know. Of course,' he added, 'some people thought they did. Get an answer. Or, rather, some people—quite a few, if you want the truth—thought they knew.'

'Knew?'

'That she was a bald-faced liar. As guilty as the rest of them. Worse really, since she used Moro's memory. Made up stories about how much she cared for him. How much he reminded her of her father. At least the others didn't stoop to that.' He sighed. 'There were plenty of people, Alessandro, who thought she might as well have pulled the trigger. Or that, despite evidence to the contrary, she did. At least once. There were ten shots after all. Plenty to go round.'

Silence throbbed down the phone as they both remembered the photograph that had been splashed across front pages around the world. Aldo Moro wrapped in a blanket and curled like a baby in the boot of a car, one white hand cupped to his chest.

'And you?' Pallioti asked finally.

'I don't know.'

Pallioti could see his friend, running his hand over his eyes that had once been bright and hard.

'I honestly don't know,' he said. 'I never did. And yes, I asked. But no, my friend, I never did get the

250

answer. Perhaps you will. I take it that's what all this is about. That she's come back.'

It wasn't really a question so Pallioti didn't answer. There was another sigh from the other end of the phone.

'I confess, I'm not surprised,' his friend said. 'I wondered, when they let Tomaselli out of jail. If she'd turn up. He went to her funeral, you know.'

'Tomaselli?' That did surprise Pallioti. From what he remembered of the time, no one was going out of their way to do favours for the BR. 'Antonio Tomaselli?' he said again. 'You let him out for Angela Vari's funeral?'

'I'll send you the photos. You can see for yourself. Come along, Sandro,' his friend said a few seconds later. 'Don't sound quite so surprised. We're not completely inhuman. He went in a prison van, had armed guards with him and stayed all of fifteen minutes. Just long enough to be convinced she was dead.'

'Even so. If the BR had got wind of it, they might have tried—'

'Another of their famous *Brigate Rosse* stunts? Like Mara Cagol busting her husband out of jail? Yes, the thought crossed our minds, too. We didn't exactly send out invitations, but . . .' He let the words linger. Then added, 'Sadly, nothing happened. The place was as quiet as a grave. So to speak.'

The unease that had lingered like stale smoke began to solidify in Pallioti's mind, shift into discernible shapes. All of them ugly.

'Are you saying?'

'Come, come, Sandro,' the fat man said quickly. 'I'm not saying anything.'

251

No, Pallioti thought. But he had heard it. Loud and clear. They had staked Tomaselli like a goat. Dangled him beside Angela Vari's empty tomb. A little vengeance on the hoof. Pallioti could hear it now. *Tut tut, terrible tragedy, but if dangerous criminals will try to make a run for it, if their outlaw compatriots will go about shooting at the police, trying to free terrorist prisoners—well, really, what can you expect?*

'Alas,' his friend murmured, 'as I said. It was a non-event. Little Angela was buried and everyone went safely home to prison. Do you have any idea,' he asked abruptly, 'by the way, why she's come back? I mean specifically?'

From the dead, or to Italy? Pallioti was tempted to ask. He thought about adding something about them being one and the same, but the joke went dry in his mouth.

'Not really,' he lied, and knew as he said it that it sounded like what it was.

'Hmmm,' his friend said. 'Interesting.' And then added, 'Well, lovely to hear from you, Alessandro.' His voice became almost jovial. 'I'll get you those photos. Just to prove we do have a heart.' He laughed. 'But, old friend . . .'

'I'm listening.'

There was a pause. Pallioti heard a wheeze of breath.

'There were people who never believed her,' the fat man said quietly. 'Intelligent people. Remember that. And there were those who believed her and never forgave her. Didn't really feel, as our American cousins say, like "letting bygones be bygones". So, it's worth remembering that the fact is, no matter what Angela Vari's

252

reasons, she knew where Aldo Moro was. She knew what was happening to him. And she did nothing.' Pallioti heard the clink of ice. 'When the deal was done with the Americans it was suggested to *piccola* Signorina Vari—possibly even by me— that she make her departure and not return.'

'I see,' Pallioti said slowly, wondering if he did.

'All I'm saying, Sandro, is that if by any chance little Angela has happened to grace our shores again, well—if it were me, I'd keep an eye on her. And on Tomaselli. In fact, especially on Tomaselli. It might be awkward if they attracted, how shall we say? The wrong kind of attention? I don't need to tell you about long memories in certain quarters. And, well, salt in the wound, that kind of thing. It can get nasty.'

Pallioti felt the hair begin to rise on the back of his neck.

'Call it what you want,' his friend said quietly. 'Some people might use the word Justice.'

*   *   *

It was almost midnight. Anna Carson stood in one of the tunnels in Via Volte, her back against a damp stone wall, and watched the snow fall between the arches. Flakes drifted down, languid as feathers, and melted on the dark cobbles. There was a handful of new restaurants in the street, all of them closed now, lights still glowing over their brightly painted signs. The effort at gentrification had only gone so far, though. The arches were still as dank and sinister and smelling of piss as they'd always been.

These days Via Volte was apparently touted as a

local highlight. *The Middle Ages Come to Life!* the tourist brochure she'd seen had said. Although why exactly anyone thought that might be a good thing was always slightly mysterious to her. Rats, plague, shit, darkness, and fleas. The flyer had been selective when describing the street's history, too. Until the war, Via Volte had belonged to the prostitutes. When the Fascists came to power they'd turned a blind eye until they hadn't, then it had become a tunnel of running footsteps punctuated by the occasional shot and scream. By the time she'd walked home at nights with her father—by the time she'd stood hanging on his hand watching Antonio in his canvas shoes, pushing his bicycle on a night not unlike this—it had been nothing more than a dark alley. A boundary between the ghetto and Via Mayr, the strange little bridge houses spanning it like tired hands. Probably those had been gentrified now, too. At least on the inside. From the outside, their windows were still tiny and multi-paned, their doors as narrow and dark as the doors children should not pass through in fairy tales.

Anna looked at the vault above her, at the pitted stone, the cracks, and white rimes of lime, and was not sure why it hadn't collapsed. Why all the rooms hadn't fallen down into the street. She rolled her shoulders, flexed her hands to stop them from freezing and shifted the pack at her feet and the two shopping bags piled on top of it. She was cold and tired. Spoilt from the last three nights she'd spent in the relative comfort of hotels.

On Thursday, she'd taken the first train north. Jumped on as soon as she'd reached Santa Maria Novella, not picky about the destination as long as

254

she got clear of Florence. She'd ended up in Reggio, which had been all she'd wanted—a medium-large town with a fair selection of hotels. The one she'd chosen, just behind the Duomo, had been a bit down-at-heel with a full dining room and family run, which virtually guaranteed not enough staff at dinner time when she'd made sure to ask for a room. She shouldn't have been able to check in without an identity card or passport. But when the harried girl behind the desk had asked for it, she'd faffed with the backpack, pulling half the contents out, strewing them across the lobby floor until she was handed a set of keys and told to bring her ID down later. On Friday morning, she'd made sure someone else was on duty, then paid in cash and vanished during the breakfast rush.

Thanks to Graziella Farelli, no such antics had been necessary in Bologna. Anna had stayed there two nights and left early this morning, hoping that the reports to whatever database kept the details of where everyone stayed and when wouldn't be updated until Monday. She was betting that, on that score at least, Italy was still more Catholic Church than Brave New World, that bureaucracy still shut down for the weekend.

Now, however, things were different. Using Graziella's identity card to register at another hotel would be too risky. She had dodged and weaved, changed her appearance as best she could, but tomorrow was Monday. It would only be a matter of time. If Graziella Farelli had not realized already, she would surely understand by tomorrow morning that her wallet really was missing rather than just misplaced. Then, if she had not already done so, she would report the loss of her ID card

255

and wallet first thing. By which time a description of Anna Carson would also be turning up on whatever databases descriptions of missing women turned up on.

Despite the fact that they had been basically on the verge of splitting up, arguing more or less non-stop—about Kristen and everything else—Anna had no doubt that Ken would have reported her missing. And sooner rather than later. She suspected, in fact, that he had gone demented. It would be a matter of control, she thought acidly, as much as passion. She'd found that comforting once. The God Complex, so well documented in doctors and especially surgeons, had made her feel secure. Then it just drove her crazy. They'd almost split, she couldn't count how many times. At the eleventh hour, he'd always talked her into staying, not because he loved her, but because he needed to win. And over and over again, she'd given in, although she wasn't sure why. Habit? Inertia? She smiled bitterly. The irony was, up to a few years ago, she'd stayed for Kristen. Told herself that no matter how much the kid acted out, she'd lost one mother and couldn't lose another. She'd told herself Kristen 'needed her'.

A tremor of guilt, a physical shiver, passed through her as she thought again of Kristen's room. The still air, fuggy with loneliness. The bare walls. Anna reached into her pocket and felt the scratchy balding head of the little white bear. Her finger pressed his bright black eye.

A bell began to toll. Seconds later it was joined by another. Midnight. The Witching Hour. Time for the dead and undead to walk. Anna picked up the pack and fitted it onto her shoulders. Then she took a shopping bag in each hand. She looked both ways. No windows were lit and no one was moving. A street lamp glowed at the mouth of Via Carbone, highlighting the black skeleton of a bicycle, blue plastic shopping bag tied over its seat. She stepped out from under the arch, Kristen's boots leaving dark footsteps in the snow.

*   *   *

She had arrived in Ferrara just after noon, and been immediately struck by how ordinary and how surreal it felt at the same time. Like one of those dreams when you meet yourself as a child. The castle had seemed, not smaller, as memory required, but bigger and uglier. Cannons had been placed at the entrance, cannonballs stacked beside them as if the town expected to be attacked. The moat was fetid and green and laced with ice. The row of shops cowered in the opposite buildings.

Anna had turned away, heading automatically for the Corso d'Este, where the grey palazzos still faced each other, tears of damp running from their shutter latches. The fat legs of the little boys still dangled from the portico of the Prosperi Sacrati. Winter fog, so cold it felt splintered with ice, drifted across the afternoon, thick enough that, as she neared the end of the street, she had not been able to see the Angels' Gate, and had the panicked thought that it might not be there. Then, all at once, it had loomed before her, the crumbling pillars and great wooden panels with their giant padlock still sealing in the past.

Laughter had come from the top of the walls as a bicycle rattled down the path, the boy standing up and pedalling hard, his girlfriend on the seat behind him clutching his waist. Anna had watched them disappear. Then she'd turned around. The line of houses still stood behind their iron railings. The doors had been repainted and the gravel of a few of the drives replaced by fancy herringbone paving. But winter branches still laced above the frost-white lawns. Stone steps still led to front doors.

The cemetery had not changed much, either. She'd been half-afraid, as she wove her way between the crypts, her fingers brushing the monuments as if she was blind, that her parents' grave might have disappeared. Or been moved to make room for the more recently departed. Or those who at least had someone left to remember them. But the stone angel still hovered near the wall of the little courtyard, hanging back as if she was shy, her wings half-spread, one hand raised.

Anna hadn't understood as a child that her father probably hadn't been able to afford the statue. That part of the mushroom cloud that had haunted her and helped to kill him had probably begun with its pitted marble cheek and folded gown. The angel had looked so exactly the same, down to the chip on her sandalled foot and the wilting bouquet that lay on her pedestal, that at first Anna hadn't even noticed the new line of engraving that had been added below her parents'.

Angela Vari, Daughter, 1958–1980.

When she finally caught her breath, she'd asked herself what she'd expected. Then wondered if she'd had a funeral, and if so, if anyone had bothered to come.

The bouquet had answered at least part of the

258

question. The flowers were real, not plastic or fabric, like some she'd stepped over. Livid blues and reds whose dye had leaked off, speckling the gravel. Curious, she'd lifted the blooms. The card was stuffed down in the stems. *Annabeth, Marco, Angela—Forever in my prayers, Renata.*

The smell of chicken soup. The sound of kitchen shutters banging open, a voice scolding. The warmth of a hand slipping her a coin for the collection at Easter Mass. The sight of her father, one drunken summer night, holding a woman in his arms, kissing her in the shadowed halo of a street lamp. Renata Ravalli, who all these years later kept them in her prayers. Anna found herself grateful. But the fact that the Ravallis, or at least one of them, were obviously still alive and might still live in Via Vittoria made her wary. After leaving the cemetery, she'd taken her time, circling like a hungry cur dog. It had been more than an hour before she crossed the Corso Giovecca and slipped into the ghetto, then sidled like a thief into Via Mayr.

What she'd found made her stop in her tracks. Although, she didn't know what she'd expected. A minimarket? The delicatessen of her mother's dreams? Anything but what she saw.

There was a hole in the sign. MACEL—IA it read, the letters chipped and barely legible above the sheets of plywood that had been nailed across the front of her father's shop. *Fuck Berlosconi!* someone had spraypainted. Three *Avatar* posters were pasted below, suggesting the Prime Minister might be bright blue and have a tail. Anna was not sure, but she thought a small squeak escaped her, a twinge of outrage from the Angela who still

259

dwelled inside her.

'Fuckers,' she had found herself muttering, then darted across the street like her younger self, dodging between a rattling grey van and a new Mercedes whose driver had honked and raised his fist. Glancing down the block she'd seen that the Pirottis' shop had somehow survived and was still open. Mindful that if Renata Ravalli was still alive, Signor and Signora Pirotti might be too, Anna had ducked round the corner, where a van that looked suspiciously like their old one was parked, and seen the door to the store room.

It had been easy. The lock had been damaged, part of the hinge pulled away, either deliberately or by mistake. She'd eased it open, telling herself she only wanted to look. Inside, leaves and bits of newspaper littered the floor. Rust marked the old porcelain sink. A work bench along the far wall where the buckets had once been stacked was piled with old crates and what looked to be bits of a vacuum cleaner. A big ladder, possibly the same one she and Antonio had used, hung on cobwebbed brackets on the wall, half its rungs missing. The place was obviously abandoned. Anna had stood, staring. Then, under the grime, she'd noticed the outline of the hatch—the little door her mother had insisted on putting in to hand buckets and sponges and soap and bags of sawdust through.

Now, she stood holding the fruits of her afternoon shopping spree, and felt her stomach sink. There was just enough light from the street lamp on the corner to see that someone had come along and closed the door. Anna hesitated, then put the bags down, and felt along the rotting sill.

Relief flooded through her. It wasn't locked. It had just been pushed, or had blown to, and was jammed. She got her fingers in a crack, and pulled.

Inside, it was pitch dark. Anna closed the door and dug in one of the bags for the torch she'd bought. It was a big one, a Maglite, the same kind the police carried at home in the States, equally useful for lighting dark corners and bashing people over the head. The bright white beam made the little room seem even smaller. She ferried her bags to the far wall beyond the ladder, then took the pack off, rested it at her feet, and began to feel with her free hand around the edge of the hatch.

It had occurred to her that they might have sealed it up from inside. She had no idea what they'd done in there. Perhaps the whole interior of the butcher's shop had been turned to rubble, just out of spite. Just to finally see off the threat of her father's veal rolls and Friday Special sausages. The wooden panel didn't budge. Anna huffed in frustration. Then her fingers found the little slip lock. She tried to pull it back, but it stuck. She put the torch between her feet, pointing up at the cobwebby roof, and used both hands. It still wouldn't move. She was beginning to wonder if it had been nailed or super-glued, when finally, she picked up the Maglite and put it to its other intended use. One good whack and the lock gave. The hinges on the little door creaked as she pushed. She hoped they hadn't rusted out, wouldn't snap so the whole thing came off in her hand. Whining, the hatch finally swung back. Anna took a deep breath, then shone the Maglite through the opening.

The first thing it caught was the marble counter,

thick with dust, then beyond, darkness, and a weird shine, the window made black by the boards nailed over it. Threads of light zigged and zagged in a silver spider's web, a black hole at its heart where someone had thrown a rock at the glass. The name, VARI, was gone, replaced by two lines of red lettering: *Carne in Fretta!* Anna read backwards. *Sette Giorni alla Settimana! Dalle Sette alle Sette!* Meat Fast! Seven Days a Week! Seven to Seven!

So, the supermarket hadn't let it go derelict after all. They'd merely tried to beat her at her own game. And failed. The Angela inside her felt a spurt of satisfaction. She swung the light up and caught white tiles, half expecting to see them cracked too, attacked out of sheer spite. But, no. Her grandmother's pig and cow were still there, smiling down on her.

Anna set down the torch, reached for the pack and shoved it through the hatch. Next, she lowered each of the shopping bags, trying not to tip them over, or at least not to break anything, then she dropped the Maglite, the beam canting wildly as it hit one of the paper bags. Finally, she took a deep breath, put both hands on the ledge, and hoisted herself up.

MONDAY 8 FEBRUARY 2010

The first thing Pallioti saw when he walked into his office was the parcel lying on his desk. He stood, his overcoat on his shoulders, and looked at it as if it might contain a bomb. His friend had been as good as he promised, but now, in the cold light of day and after a good night's sleep, Pallioti felt a bit of an ass, running up red flags, grovelling for favours, and talking himself into a minor state of panic over—what? A missing girl who was probably fine. Probably holed up in some five-star resort having the time of her life. And a middle-aged woman who had probably walked out on her husband.

Having just endured breakfast with Kenneth Carson—listened politely while he harangued the police, the government, and all Italians for the better part of two hours—Pallioti thought that if he was married to him, he'd probably walk out, too. No, he'd run. Bolt like a jack-rabbit and never look back. He had reached the point in life where he was no longer surprised by where love struck, and frequently amazed by whom otherwise perfectly rational people decided to marry.

As far as Anna Carson herself was concerned, he had to admit that, no matter who she had been in the past, there was no real evidence that the poor woman had done anything wrong in the present. He had heard from Enzo, who had arrived in Bologna at the crack of dawn and already spoken to one Graziella Farelli who'd had her bag rifled in church and who did bear a passing resemblance to Anna Carson, if she'd cut and dyed her hair. But then again, so did a lot of women. Tallish, good-looking-ish, and darkish wasn't exactly unusual.

No. The long and the short of it was, the woman who had once been Angela Vari might or might not have stolen a wallet, and might or might not be looking for her stepdaughter—something that might be inconvenient, since she hadn't bothered

263

to inform anyone, but was hardly against the law. And that was about it. All in all, it was a pretty paltry excuse to work himself into a state of existential angst over some adolescent, late-night, ludicrous—not to mention drunken—suggestion that the police had taken to stalking and killing citizens they held a grudge against. Next he'd be insisting the CIA planned 9/11 and the moon landings took place in a warehouse outside Houston.

He shook his head, wondering what was wrong with him. Perhaps it was age. Perhaps this was the police version of a mid-life crisis—sending Enzo off on wild-goose chases. Allowing, even encouraging, both of them to wallow in what he was beginning to think of as BR Syndrome. A highly communicable state in which anyone even vaguely involved in law enforcement became completely hysterical at the mention of the words *Brigate* and *Rosse*.

He sighed, took off his coat and hung it in his cupboard, smoothing the arm and flicking a speck of icy grit from the cuff. Such, he thought, was the legacy of guilt. *Every Police Officer in Italy Shall be Haunted by the Ghost of Aldo Moro Now and Forever, Amen.*

Turning around, he rather hoped the packet might have vanished. But it was still on his desk. Pallioti reached for the silver letter opener he kept in his top drawer. The thing was thirty centimetres long and sharp as a shiv. As handy for opening throats as letters, it had been given to him by a woman he had once, very briefly and a long time ago, thought he might marry. Apart from a vague memory of her voice—which had been low and almost obscenely beautiful—it was the only relic of the affair. Weighing it in his hand, seeing his engraved initials on the blade, he thought it was actually a far more appropriate gift than it had seemed at the time. He wondered if he'd given her the obligatory coin for it. Probably not, otherwise they'd have been married happily ever after. He shrugged, slipped the point under the flap and slit the envelope in one clean cut.

The photographs were eight by tens, black and white, glossy and slightly cracked, and old-fashioned looking. Pallioti spread them on his desk, wondering when it was that things created in his own lifetime had come to feel like antiques. There was no note, no billet-doux from his whippet friend trapped in the fat man's body. Yellowing paper tabs were taped to the bottom of each shot, giving the names of the unwitting subjects. High-tech for the time.

Surveillance photos always gave Pallioti the creeps, partly because he found them so interesting. There was something horribly irresistible about gazing on people who did not know they were being watched, a nasty little jolt every bit as satisfying as a grappa.

His friend had sent perhaps twenty photos in all. Which meant there were almost certainly more where these came from. Jesus, Pallioti thought, fanning them across his blotter, didn't they have anything better to do than document the burying of an urn filled with sand? He wondered how many photographers had been crouched behind monuments and lurking in mausoleums. Tomaselli himself certainly appeared, on first glance anyway, to be completely unaware of his starring role. He

265

wasn't in chains, either. Nor were there five minders—only two that Pallioti could pick out, standing respectfully far back. His estimation of the prison services went up a few notches. The fat man hadn't been joking after all. They did have hearts. He pulled out his glasses and slipped them on.

Even through a telephoto lens, even in black and white and over the space of three decades, it was obvious that chains were hardly necessary. And would have been obscene. Because Antonio Tomaselli was devastated. His handsome face appeared empty and slightly crumpled, like a piece of paper that had been screwed up and only partially smoothed out. He stared at the hole at the foot of a stone angel as if he wished he might somehow be sucked into it. In one photograph, he stood with his hand over his mouth, his shoulders hunched in grief.

He had loved her.

Pallioti straightened up, ashamed of himself for being surprised. He drummed his fingers on the edge of his desk. Then he leaned down and examined the prints more closely.

Almost all the shots showed a priest and five mourners. The death had been reported in the papers—that was the point after all, for everyone, or at least certain people, to 'know' Angela Vari was dead. But only after the fake internment. So the mourners here would have been those who had been previously notified, her equivalent of family.

Three of them were clearly older. Probably they were friends of her parents, or distant relatives of some kind. He had barely skimmed the file before handing it over to Enzo, but he didn't think Angela

266

Vari had any close relatives. The two women and a man stood together in their baggy black coats. The man wore an old-fashioned black hat of the type Pallioti remembered their gardener wearing to his mother's funeral when he was ten. The women wore headscarves and no gloves. Wound in their pale fingers he could make out what looked like lengths of string. Rosary beads. Heads bent, they intoned their prayers for the dead. Pallioti could almost hear the words, smell the faint sickening waft of incense drifting down the years.

As if by mutual agreement, the three black-clad figures stood on one side of the grave while Antonio Tomaselli stood on the other. He wore no overcoat, just a dark suit and tie. The prison service, or someone, had been generous. The clothes appeared to fit. They even made him look a halfway suitable partner for the woman who stood beside him. She was tall. Her dark hair was pulled back, accentuating the strong bones of her face. She appeared to be about Antonio's age, but something in the way she stood suggested that she was at least twice the man he was. Possibly twice the man any man was. She wore a black overcoat, not unlike Pallioti's own, black heels, black gloves. Even from thirty years away, Pallioti could tell they were expensive. She reminded him of those statues he'd seen in picture books of Pallas Athena. He wouldn't have been the least bit surprised if in the next photo she'd been holding a spear or had an owl emerging from her forehead.

No such luck, although one of the photographers did catch her putting her hand on Antonio Tomaselli's shoulder, speaking to him much the way a parent would speak to a distressed child.

267

In another picture, she had stepped into the background and was holding her arms out, fending off the two minders, her mouth open, obviously telling them to leave Antonio alone as he stood in tears, his hand on the outstretched arm of the angel.

Pallioti straightened up and frowned. If this woman was part of the prison service, all he could say was that it had sure gone to hell in the last thirty years. He squinted down at the faded little yellow strips of paper. The old people were named as Alda Pirotti, Tommaso Pirotti, and Renata Ravalli. Antonio Tomaselli was Antonio Tomaselli. The woman, unsuprisingly, was not Pallas Athena. Her name was Barbara Barelli.

*   *   *

The train left right on time. It was old and dented and unglamorous, but prompt. Anna lifted the bike she had stolen into the luggage van. There had been at least two dozen pig-piled outside the library in Piazza Paradiso. Some had been shoved close enough to be chained to the metal rack. Others were chained to other bikes, or to themselves, back wheel to front, hobbled like cowboys' horses, so it had taken her a while to find one that wasn't locked.

She had almost been undone by a pair of old ladies who had walked by, slowly as turtles. They hadn't seemed to notice her, but Anna knew better. Nonna Franchi had had eyes not just in the back but probably in the sides and top of her head as well. Watching them, she had missed Nonna with a pang so sudden it felt like a cramp—a vicious little stab of loss. When she was sure they'd turned the corner, she'd grabbed the handlebars and lifted the unlocked bike out of the tangle with what she hoped was the confidence of ownership. Moments later, she was pedalling through Piazza Trieste, thinking that the fact the thing had gears at all made up, almost, for the spectacularly uncomfortable seat.

Now she climbed into the carriage, which was all but empty, settled herself by the window, and watched as Ferrara slipped into a wasteland of railway yards and industrial estates. Silver fencing topped with razor wire guarded the car parks that stretched around huge blocks of business parks that had expanded like ink blots, seeping into the flat featureless countryside. There was no sign any more of the factory that had exploded. It would have been pulled down years ago. Somewhere there would be a plaque, an obligatory listing of the names of the dead. Beside an entrance door or in a lobby. Next to a dribbling fountain whose bottom was lined with pennies and waterlogged cigarette butts.

Leaning back in the seat, Anna drew her new jacket around her. She'd replaced her whole wardrobe yesterday, with cheaper and certainly less fashionable substitutes, and had been sorely tempted to keep Kristen's beautiful, and very warm, down parka if only to layer under her new sleeping bag. Even with a pad, the shelf of the cold room left a lot to be desired. Then she'd told herself not to be stupid. So it had gone, along with everything else—the pack that was so obvious she might as well be waving a flag, and, of course, Graziella's wallet. She couldn't use the ID card again. Although, she still had well over a thousand euros of her own left, she'd taken what cash there was, then zipped the wallet into the deep inner pocket of Kristen's coat, and pushed the whole lot through the panel of the Caritas box. There had been almost nothing in the box, which was why she had chosen it. Not because some poor unfortunate would have the chance to be outfitted by Barney's, but because, unlike city dumpsters, it would only be emptied when it was full. Which could be weeks away. *Grazie a Dio*, Thanks be to God, the swaying letters had said as Anna walked quickly away.

*   *   *

It was the better part of an hour later when the train jerked and slowed. Anna had been standing between the carriages for the last ten minutes, worried the station was so small and would be so empty that she would not have time to jump out and get the bike from the luggage van before the train pulled out again. Then she would have to walk, and that would take a very long time.

She bent and peered through the grimy window, watching as the platform slunk into view, nothing but a concrete terrace and a shelter sided with perspex like a bus stop, two slatted benches inside and a sign with the name hanging above. There wasn't a house in sight, or even another building. It was just a train stop, barely even a place. In the middle of nowhere.

A guard stuck his head out of one of the forward carriages, watching as she ran back to the luggage van. The moment she'd lifted the bike down, he raised his hand. The train was moving again by the time she slammed the door. Its grey rump rattled past, then grew smaller and smaller until it finally shrank to nothing, swallowed by the empty stretches of the fields. Anna turned round. There was only one road. A blast of wind, smelling of mud, hit her in the face, making her eyes tear as she got on the bike and began to pedal.

After forty minutes, her calves burned. She stopped, bent and massaged her legs, fingers easing the knotted muscles. It was not true that you could flip from one sport to another. That legs could run, pump, and kick equally happily. At least not at her age. Not any more. She hadn't been on a bike in years and the seat of this one was so fiendish that she found it more comfortable to stand up. Anna licked her lips and tasted salt. She'd stopped once to consult the map she'd bought yesterday. It had been reassuring, a check on her nerves, but the truth was, it hadn't been necessary. The sea marshes wouldn't be more than nine or ten kilometres away now, as the crow flew. She knew exactly where she was.

*   *   *

Tucked into the passenger seat of Antonio's tiny rattling Fiat, her hand on his thigh, her elbow hitting his as he searched for the gears that were so loose it was hard to tell first from third, she'd felt her hair blown back in the draught from the open window as she'd watched the fields and the rows of the orchards, green and dense with summer.

'I've never brought anyone here before,' he'd said suddenly. He'd smiled, not taking his eyes off the thin greyed strip of road.

271

'To the abbey?'

She'd turned to him as she asked, and found herself still amazed that he was here. Or that she was here with him. Or both. Although, in the week since he had walked into the pizzeria, they had barely been out of each other's sight.

Angela had taken him home, to her den of dirty pots and pans and clothes and memories. They had climbed the stairs and shut the door and fumbled, barely speaking, into the sitting room, to the sofa, to the worn rug, for . . . she wasn't even sure how long for. The rest of the day. The night. The next day. She had called and told the pizza man she was sick, forgotten several of the small jobs she was supposed to do, and hadn't cared. She hadn't even asked where he'd got the car, or why he wasn't going back to the university at Padua, or what he was going to do in Rome, which was where he said he was going. He could tell her, or not. All she had cared about was that she could touch him. Feel him inside her like the beating of her own heart.

He shook his head.

'Not the abbey,' he'd said. 'Not Pomposa. We'll go there after. We're going to the farm. My grandpa's farm. I told you, remember?'

Anna wiped her eyes with the back of her hand. The fields around her were flat and featureless as the sea. The past ought to have markers. Way signs. A pile of rocks or a forked stick. Something at least to tell you how far you had to go. And let you know when you arrived. She pedalled on.

Forty minutes later, she saw the pillars, rising out of nowhere. Two abandoned columns, they fronted the ghostly outline of a track. Now well past noon, fog was creeping in, hazing the already weak sun.

By tomorrow morning, the whole world would be sugared in frost.

Anna got off the bicycle. She was aware of her heart hammering, suddenly frantic, as if it was trying to escape. Scrabble through her breastbone and take flight. Or run. Bound ahead on its own.

'*Ciao, carina.* Long time.'

'Where are you?' she'd demanded, standing in the breakfast room at the Excelsior, and he'd laughed.

'Where do you think?' he'd asked, and if she'd allowed herself to, she could have felt his breath seeping through the tiny phone she'd held clamped to her ear. Now she almost thought she heard him, his voice hanging in the still, chilly air.

'Where do you think I am, *carina*?' he'd asked again. And then, 'Last time, I came and found you. Now it's your turn.'

*　　*　　*

Anna stepped through the pillars, half expecting the ground to give way. Or to find that, like something out of a children's book, she'd stepped through a slit in time. That all around her the fields would billow and roll into green, and she would look up and see the Fiat parked on the pale packed gravel, see Antonio leaning against the door. Hear him say, 'This is where I grew up. This is my *nonno*'s farm.'

She hadn't been able to see the house and barns then, and she couldn't see them now. The fields looked flat, but the landscape was not as empty or as dead as it appeared. The track, rutted and frozen and all but impassable, ran on for some way

273

before it fell down into a slight dip, almost a hollow, that the buildings nestled in. She propped the bike against the crumbling brick.

Anna felt in her pocket for the knife. It was a filleting blade, mid-length. She had found it last night in the butcher's shop. Or rather it had found her. Backing out of the cold room, she had felt something finger her hair. Spinning around and resisting the impulse to scream she had realized it was nothing but some old utensils, abandoned on a cobwebbed hanging rack. The knife had not been as sharp as she would have liked and, unable to find a whetstone in the litter of the shop, she'd used the underside of the marble counter instead. Which had done well enough. Then, for lack of anything better, she'd wrapped the blade in a sock. The point had stuck through, jabbing her in the thigh as she pedalled.

Sweat rolled down her chest and her hands were itchy in the cheap wool. She could see the track dropping ahead, disappearing as if it went over the edge of the world. When she reached the lip of the hill she stopped, letting her eyes roam down the shallow slope. Then she began to run.

But even as she did, even as she pulled her hands from her pockets, flailing, tripping on a tuft of weeds and regaining her balance, she knew she had come to the right place. She recognized the little pond. And the stand of poplar trees. And the well in what had been the front yard where Antonio had been so happy to find the bucket still attached to the winch even if it leaked and the water was brackish. Anna gathered speed, hit loose gravel, scrambled and let out a cry, not caring now who saw or heard her—and knowing that there was no

274

one to see or hear. That there hadn't been for a long time.

The fire must have happened years ago. Earth had blown and packed over the rubble. Spikes of dead grass poked up, furring the yard like an old man's cheek. The house had been derelict, but still standing, still with all its doors and windows, when Antonio had brought her here. He'd gone around to the back, and pushed open the door. Led her into the cool stone-floored kitchen, showed her where the table had stood, and where his mother and grandmother had cut notches on the inside of the pantry wall, marking each birthday he and Piero had passed. They stopped when they were not much higher than his waist.

She had watched as he pressed his finger into the last shallow indent that had marked the top of his brother's head, seen how he pushed against it, as if he could make the wood splinter and somehow release Piero's ghost. Finally, Antonio had wiped his eyes with the back of his arm. Then he had taken her hand, and they'd climbed the stairs, stepping on every creaking board.

In the room under the eaves there had been the stuffy smell of bats and the thin skitter of mice. Antonio had put his arms around her. He had whispered in her ear. He had leaned down, and with the elbow of his shirt had made a circle on the dusty pane so she could see what he had seen every morning from the bed he shared with his brother, the sea of fields that spread around them, lapping the island of his grandfather's farm.

*   *   *

A shard of glass glinted in the weakling sun. Faint char marks were still visible on some of the pale square stones. Anna wondered how it had started. If someone had been living here and had been careless, left the stove on or let an electrical box short out. Then she thought of the boarded-up front of her father's shop, the spider's web in the plate glass, and wondered if that was what had happened here. If they had come with torches down the slope bearing petrol cans and rags the way centuries before they had sacked the houses of traitors and burned the hovels of witches.

On the far side of the yard, the barn was still standing. But the roof had fallen in, taking half the walls with it. For a crazed moment, Anna had the idea that she might not be wrong after all—that Antonio had set up some kind of camp in the ruins and any second now she would spot the rear bumper of a car sticking out from under a tarpaulin or pile of brush. She skirted around and peered through a broken window, but the only thing she saw was the sagging skeleton of a tractor.

Anna turned around. She had been so sure, so absolutely certain when he said 'find me' that this was where he meant. That this was where he would have gone.

'Antonio!'

She cupped her hands to her mouth and shouted, then jumped at the clatter as an egret rose, startled from a thatch of bullrushes at the edge of the pond, and flapped towards the sun.

'Antonio,' she whispered.

Then she screamed his name again, so loud her lungs scorched.

Enzo Saenz watched the blurry figure scuttling through the tunnel that connected the platforms of the Bologna train station. It moved out of one security camera's range and into the field of the next, dodging passengers coming in the other direction, the pack making it hunchbacked. At the top of platform three it came up the steps and stood, disoriented for a moment in the daylight. Then it turned abruptly, walked towards a bench, and stopped to study a vending machine. Enzo leaned forward as it reached into a pocket and found a coin.

Come on, he thought, come on.

Slowly, a pale, ungloved hand reached out and pushed a button.

'Bingo,' he said out loud, and froze the tape.

*   *   *

The junior detective who had been sent to Bologna train station and returned with the trophy of the CCTV tapes grinned, trying to suppress the excitement—the thrill of being part of what was obviously a major investigation, even if he didn't know what it was. Rumour in the cafeteria said the woman they were looking for had murdered her husband, who was a mafioso who had abused her for years, and was now on the run, and possibly in possession of a series of secret bank numbers leading to accounts in the Cayman Islands that she planned to use as bargaining chips. A rival story circulating through the gym showers said she was a courier and drugs mule for a trafficking ring based

277

in Bari who'd 'gone rogue'. In the course of the last few hours, Enzo had heard each told in increasingly elaborate detail and had done nothing to refute either. He'd stood by the coffee machine tearing open sugar packets and nodding in a way he hoped might suggest both were true.

He glanced at his watch. It was past two o'clock in the afternoon. They'd been at it all day and were still running Graziella Farelli's name through the database that covered hotel stays. Now he was sure they'd get a hit, and probably sooner rather than later. Probably from somewhere large, business-oriented, and not more than a few blocks from the station. If they could get to the room before the cleaning crews—and let's face it, probably after them, too—they'd almost definitely pull some fingerprints. Maybe they'd get a visual ID from the desk or a room-service guy. Any and all of which would be interesting, but Enzo didn't care any more. He started the tape again, watched as the blurry person peeled a wrapper off something, then wandered away and vanished behind a pillar. It was Anna Carson. He knew it. He could feel it right down in the bottom of his gut.

'Gotcha,' he muttered to himself, then turned round and asked if they could get a team to the station, preferably yesterday. If they could seal the vending machine, see if they could lift a print that matched Angela Vari's. They should try the rubbish too, if the bins hadn't been emptied and she'd thrown the wrapper away. And everybody who'd worked yesterday morning would need to be questioned. Thanks to Graziella Farelli they had a photofit and a sketch. Someone—a conductor, a ticket salesman, a platform guard—would remember something. Sunday mornings were quiet, and cherry red was a memorable colour.

He shook his head and wondered if she'd ever get smart enough to throw that rucksack away. Then he wound back the tape, slowed it down and watched the figure again. The ice-cracking feeling grew. Enzo held out his hand. Someone gave him the train schedule. He ran his eye down the lines of tiny print, and resisted the temptation to yip.

The date/time stamp from the CCTV picture in front of him read Sunday 7 February, 10.14 a.m. The next train had been the 10.20 to Ferrara.

*   *   *

Not twenty miles away from where Enzo was sitting, Pallioti slumped down in the front seat of an unmarked police car and wondered if he was losing his mind. Common wisdom said people got more sensible as they got older. He had the distinct impression he'd been getting rapidly crazier.

Right this second, for instance, he was supposed to be having lunch with the Mayor, then yet another meeting with Kenneth Carson, during which he was supposed to reassure the poor man, yet again, that the entire force of the Italian State was working on his behalf and to hint, without saying anything at all, that there was every reason to expect the happy family would be reunited, possibly within hours. He was supposed, in short, to be doing his job—leaving this whole mess in Enzo Saenz's more-than-capable hands while he sat behind his desk like some po-faced coot, keeping his hand firmly on the tiller. Steering the Good Ship Law Enforcement through waters deep

279

and turbulent. Instead, he was behaving like a half-baked psychic receiving messages from old photographs. Next he'd probably start demanding pieces of Kristen Carson's clothes, closing his eyes and making whirring sounds and talking in broken sentences about auras and bodies of dark water. Sad, but it couldn't be helped. Barbara Barelli had stuck to him like a burr.

He'd finally put away the photographs and turned his attention to other matters—Kristen Carson wasn't the only mess they had on their hands. People were still busily stuffing carved giraffes with heroin, laundering money through a chain of hair salons in the Oltrarno, and counterfeiting fashion labels in the basement of a Chinese supermarket out beyond the Fortezza de Basso. In other words, life in Bella Firenze was going on as usual and all those busy little bees had to be attended to. He had chaired a meeting finalizing the details of a raid on a sweatshop making fake handbags and come back and told Guillermo to get him everything he could find on the Barelli woman. Her name was familiar. He thought it was from something he'd seen recently. He wished to hell he could remember what. He read too much. He was getting old. His brain wasn't what it used to be. Possibly it never had been.

An hour later, Pallioti had listened in silence to what his secretary had to say. Then he'd ordered a car from the garage and set off for this fancy private neighbourhood in a suburb of Bologna, where he now lurked like a deranged stalker outside the office-cum-home of Avvocato Barelli. Any second, she would probably call the police and he would get arrested for harassment, or inappropriate parking, or just being a man in a dark overcoat. Because, if what Guillermo had told him was remotely accurate—and Guillermo being Guillermo, it inevitably was—Dottoressa Barelli was not shy about asserting her rights, or those of her clients.

She had begun her career as a lawyer representing sports stars, all women, a number of whom had fought and successfully won the right to be reinstated on national teams after accusing several of the track coaches of sexual harassment. Pretty much a straight choice of *'sleep with me and get a berth on the team, or don't and stay home— your choice.'* The settlements had been large, the publicity embarrassing and the cases had made Barbara Barelli's name.

But she hadn't rested on her laurels. According to Guillermo she specialized in Women's Rights. Female factory workers whose overtime pay was half of men's, a consortium of prostitutes challenging the law that insisted brothels were illegal and thus forced them onto the streets, a lesbian couple who wanted to adopt. All of them and more had found their way to Avvocato Barelli's office. Over the course of the last two decades she'd won some cases and lost some, and become something of an icon in the process. So, given her long history of challenging the paternal establishment, it might not have been much of a surprise that she had acted on behalf of one of the more notorious members of the BR.

Except that it was. Because not only did Barbara Barelli not deal with criminal cases—much less terrorism charges which were a specialist area in

281

themselves—she didn't represent men.

Guillermo had pulled a long interview off the Internet in which she expounded at some length on the thesis that 'men had more than enough representation in society' and therefore she felt it her duty to devote 'what small talent she had' to redressing the balance on behalf of the 'repressed', i.e. 'the millions of women who laboured daily under an iron fist'. A footnote said the talk had been given at a number of Professional Women's Associations across Europe where it was invariably met with thunderous applause. Which had left Pallioti both a little disturbed—the idea of, wittingly or arguably worse, unwittingly, being the 'iron-fisted oppressor' didn't really sit all that well—and puzzled. Because whatever else Antonio Tomaselli might or might not be, he was definitely a man.

Barbara Barelli had first begun representing him shortly after she qualified to practise law, some few years after the photographs had been taken at Angela Vari's funeral, and had stuck with him ever since. He was not only one of her very rare, if not her only, male clients—his was her only criminal case. Which was puzzling on both fronts. Because Tomaselli would almost certainly have been far better off with one of the handful of lawyers who represented the other *Brigate Rosse* members. Who, indeed, had made careers out of it. But he had apparently chosen and stayed with Barbara Barelli, right up to last year, when she had handled the final negotiations for his release.

Pallioti wanted to know why.

Impatience prickled him. It had taken just over an hour to drive up from Florence. Guillermo had checked and found that Barbara was not due to be appearing in court in either Milan or Bologna today. Of course she might be in Rome, or Naples, or anywhere else where the sisterhood was being oppressed by iron fists like his, but Pallioti didn't think so. There were two identical dark blue Mercedes parked on the paved forecourt. One was registered to a Hedwige Aarlheissen, who was listed as living at the same address as Dottoressa Barelli. The other was registered to the Avvocato herself.

Pallioti knew this because Guillermo had told him, and because he had seen her drive in thirty minutes ago and get out of it and walk into the house. He had not called ahead because he was a great believer in the advantage of surprise. So he had lingered around, sitting in the front seat of the highly recognizable unmarked police car for the last half hour in the hope that Hedwige would decide to go shopping or to the gym or somewhere. He didn't know what the relationship between the two women was, but he thought Dottoressa Barelli might be more forthcoming if he spoke to her alone.

*   *   *

'Bar, he's still there.'

Hedwige stood by the window, far enough back so she couldn't be seen, and pointed across the street. Barbara looked up from the kitchen island where she was chopping cherry tomatoes. She diced with a vigour that made Hedwige nervous, the blade flashing so fast that she was convinced Barbara would, one of these days, amputate at

283

least one if not several of her own fingers. Still, she watched, fascinated. When Hedwige was a child her parents had taken her to a Japanese steak house in New York where everything flamed, sizzled, and was slashed. It had been every bit as good as a horror film and was one of her favourite memories. Her parents, on either side of her, had drank Mai Tais and laughed and caught bits of steak thrown through the air in their mouths like circus dogs. Perhaps Barbara could have a new career as a chef in a place like that, if she ever gave up being a lawyer. Which she wouldn't.

'Who?' she said, without looking up.

'The man in the car who's been sitting across the street for the last hour.'

'What?' Barbara frowned.

They were having guests for dinner, some magistrate and a singer she'd taken up with who, for whatever reason, Barbara was hell-bent on impressing. Hedwige had no idea why, and she wasn't jealous—they'd been living together for fifteen years, the green goddess had gone to ground long ago—but she was annoyed. Because when Bar got like this she was like a terrier digging a hole. This particular hole was some kind of fancy marinated concoction involving many small vegetables and things in shells. Obsessive Behaviour 101. It made her a demon on a case, but it was a pain in the ass to live with. Multi-tasking was not, on the other hand, a mystery to Hedwige. Back in the day, she'd been a heptathlete. Barbara had been a sprinter. Big surprise.

'The man,' she said. 'Who I told you about when you came in. He's been sitting across the street, in a car, for the last hour.'

'What does he look like?'

Hedwige shrugged.

'He's in a car. I don't know. Dark hair. Dark coat.'

Barbara finally put down the knife and walked to the window. Unlike Hedwige, she went straight up to the glass.

'Son of a bitch!' she swore, turning towards the front hall.

'What?'

Hedwige followed her.

'It's a cop, for Christ's sake. In an unmarked car. You can tell those things a mile away.'

A blast of cold air hit Hedwige in the face as Barbara yanked the door open. Whoever the policeman was, Hedwige felt sorry for him.

*   *   *

'Dottoressa.'

Pallioti had got out of the car as soon as he saw the front door open. In her early fifties, Barbara Barelli was if anything more impressive in person now than her photographs suggested she had been thirty years ago. His initial impression had been right. She did look like Pallas Athena. An angry Pallas Athena in designer jeans and a red silk blouse.

'What the hell do you think you're doing?' she demanded, and he found himself putting his hands up, like a bad guy in an old Western.

'I have told you,' Barbara Barelli said. 'I have told you, and I have told them. I will not put up with this kind of shit. And I mean it. If you think you can intimidate me just because—'

285

'Dottoressa, please.'

Pallioti began to reach into the inside pocket of his overcoat, then paused, wondering if he should tell her what he was doing in case she shot him. He realized she didn't have anywhere to hide a gun and proceeded, gingerly, holding out his credentials, hoping his hand wasn't shaking.

Barbara Barelli took them. Her hands, he noticed, were long-fingered and fine, tipped with perfectly manicured pink nails. She frowned, lines almost as deep as his own cutting under her dark swept-back hair.

'Florence?' She looked at him as if she thought he might disagree. 'What are you doing here? Who are you?' she asked. 'I don't understand.'

Pallioti refrained from pointing out that that might be because she hadn't given him time to get a word in edgeways.

'Alessandro Pallioti,' he said, extending his hand.

Her grip was as firm as his own.

'So I see.'

She dropped his hand and returned his credentials. Then she cocked her head and asked, 'So, what can I do for you, Dottore?'

'I have to ask, are you Avvocato Barbara Barelli?'

She smiled, either at the idiocy of the question or because he obviously felt so stupid asking it, and for a split-second Pallioti saw a very different woman. Then the avenging goddess was back. She folded her arms and nodded.

'I am,' she replied. 'Should I say it out loud? The whole title? Are we being taped?'

Pallioti smiled and put his credentials away. He liked Barbara Barelli.

'No.' He shook his head, then looked towards the house. 'I just didn't want to make more of an ass of myself than I already have.'

'I'll forgive you,' she said. 'I still don't understand what you want.'

'I want to talk to you about Antonio Tomaselli.'

*   *   *

Looking back on it later, Pallioti thought he might as well have said, 'I want you to have wild sex with me in the back of the car.' Or, 'I want your help kidnapping eight-year-olds and starting a prostitution ring.' Either would have evoked the same reaction.

Avvocato Barelli's face closed as if a steel shutter had been pulled over it. Her black eyes turned hard and cold. Without another word, she turned on her heel and began to walk back to the house.

'Dottoressa!' Pallioti called. 'He's missing. He has a seventeen-year-old girl with him. He may have abducted her.'

She stopped dead, standing in the middle of the road. The heavy silk of her shirt rippled across her back, caught in the breeze that huffed off the mountains he had just driven through.

'She's seventeen,' Pallioti said again. 'The girl. She's a student. An American. Her name is Kristen Carson.'

Barbara Barelli shivered. She turned round.

'What did you say?'

'The girl is a student. In Florence. An American. Her name is Kristen Carson.'

Pallioti stepped forward. He pulled a copy of the photograph of Kristen from his coat pocket and

287

held it out.

'She's from a town called Concord,' he said. 'In Massachusetts. She's taking a year on a programme with an American school. To study art history. Then she wants to go to college.'

Barbara Barelli reached out and took the photo. She studied it, frowning.

'We think he contacted her first on Facebook.'

The frown deepened.

'When?' she asked finally.

'As far as we know, for the first time, about nine months ago.'

She glanced up. 'Just after he was released.'

'Yes.' Pallioti nodded. 'It might have begun even earlier. He suggested that she come to Florence, for the year abroad. He even did the research. Sent her the information. Said it was a "way for them to be together".'

'You're saying he stalked her, on the Internet, lured her here—and now he's abducted her?'

Pallioti nodded.

'She was last seen getting into his car.'

Barbara Barelli closed her eyes. Then she opened them and asked, 'Her parents?'

'They're here. They came over, from the States, for her eighteenth birthday. Last week. They were throwing a party for her. Fancy. A lot of her friends. That's what makes us think she may be being held against her will. Otherwise we might be inclined to think she was just off on a lost weekend. She was seeing Tomaselli. Going out with him. Apparently she was smitten.'

'Oh, yes.' Barbara smiled. There was no warmth in it at all. 'He can be very charming.'

'Apparently. But Kristen was looking forward to

288

her party. She was, by all accounts, excited about it. Had bought a dress. Been fussy about the food. The cake. As I said, we know she went off with Tomaselli on the Wednesday. She hasn't come back. Do you have any idea at all where he might be? Or how we could contact him?'

She shook her head. 'No,' she said. 'No, I don't.' Barbara Barelli looked down at the photo in her hand again. 'And you say no one's heard from her? Not at all?'

'As best we know, no.'

She caught the qualification and raised an eyebrow. Pallioti did not elaborate. He thought it best to leave Anna Carson, and who she might or might not have spoken to, out of it for now.

'Messages have been left on her phone,' he added. 'By us, her friends. Her parents. As far as we know, none of them have been answered.'

Barbara Barelli swallowed. She handed him the photograph.

'It's cold out here,' she said. 'Perhaps you'd like to come in.'

*   *   *

The house was large and new and very fancy. Not unlike the matching Mercedes that sat outside, the automotive equivalent of stone lions flanking front doors or griffons perched on gate posts. Barbara Barelli may have devoted her working life to championing admirable causes, but she'd clearly been well paid for it.

'This is Hedwige, my partner.'

The tiled hallway opened onto what Pallioti believed was known in America as a 'family room', a large, airy space containing a number of sofas and armchairs and a glass-topped dining table and vast flat-screen television, which in turn opened onto a 'kitchen area'—a sort of corral of polished granite interspersed with vicious-looking stainless-steel machines.

The woman who was doing something with one of them looked up at Pallioti and smiled. She was as fair as Barbara was dark, and as tall, and, obviously, even under a sweatshirt and pair of tracksuit bottoms, as well-toned and muscled. They reminded Pallioti of a pair of very fit horses. But where Barbara's dark eyes were still and flinty, this woman's were as round and dewy as a doe's. When he shook her hand he half-expected her to whinny.

'I'm making a smoothie,' she said. 'Do you want one?'

Pallioti had no idea if she was talking to him or to Barbara Barelli. He had no idea what a 'smoothie' was, either. In certain circumstances it might have sounded obscene. He was not reassured by the stainless-steel machine or by the pile of vegetation that lay beside it. Barbara Barelli rescued him.

'I think we need something stronger.'

She opened a refrigerator that was as large as most people's wardrobes. Pallioti watched as she lifted out a bottle of white wine. He shook his head as she reached for a couple of glasses, then wished he hadn't. Eating or drinking anything offered—even smoothies—pretty much guaranteed that you'd get thrown out later rather than sooner. No matter how much they wanted you to go, most people wouldn't show you the door while you had a glass or a plate in your hand. Hedwige had stopped what she was doing and was watching Barbara.

'Perhaps I'll change my mind,' Pallioti murmured, but Barbara didn't seem to hear him

'That son of a bitch,' she said suddenly. 'That fucking son of a bitch. I trusted him.' Her hand shook, slopping wine onto the counter. Hedwige took a towel from a rail by the stove and mopped it up.

'Have a seat.' Barbara waved vaguely towards the sofas and chairs. Then she said, 'Oh, sorry,' and poured Pallioti's wine.

This time it went in the glass. He took it, sipped, and put it down and thanked her. She nodded, but she wasn't paying attention to him. Her eyes narrowed as she stared towards the television, which was turned off. Finally, she looked at Pallioti again.

'The parents,' she said. 'The girl's parents?' As if she had forgotten what he told her in the street.

Perhaps she had. The news that a client she had worked to get released might have abducted a teenager was likely to be as startling as it was unwelcome. Pallioti had the feeling that Dottoressa Barelli did not like being surprised and did not take well to being wrong. And given her attachment to women's causes, this would be something of a double, if not triple, blow.

'I never liked him,' she said suddenly. 'Not from day one. The first time I saw him. Son of a bitch.'

Pallioti waited. When she said nothing more, he frowned.

'Then, Dottoressa, if I may ask—'

'Oh, ask away.' She put down her glass and he noticed it was almost empty. 'I did it because I

291

believe that even if you don't agree with what someone's done—even if you think they're despicable—it's my job. I did it for the system, because otherwise it cannot function and we're all screwed.' She threw back her head and laughed. 'There,' she said. 'That's the high-minded explanation. The good Law School answer. The truth?' She reached for her glass and looked at Pallioti. 'I did it,' she said, 'for a friend. Because I knew she'd, they'd, want me to. Love.' She shrugged. 'It's why we make all the biggest screw-ups in our lives, isn't it? I even tried to like him,' she added. 'I did. I tried to like him because . . .' She waved her hand again and let the words go. 'The parents?' Barbara Barelli asked, looking at him. 'I'm sorry. You were saying?'

Actually, Pallioti had not been saying anything. He slid his own glass, almost untouched, a little farther away.

'They're in Florence. They're very worried. Naturally. I have to ask you, Dottoressa, and I understand it puts you in an awkward position—' Barbara Barelli made a huffing sound, as if there was nothing he could tell her about awkward positions. 'Once more, given the circumstances, you'll understand why I have to ask: have you heard from Antonio Tomaselli? Or have you any idea, any idea at all, where he might be?'

At that, Barbara smiled.

'And once more, I have to tell you—privilege, Ispettore. I may have just said I don't care for him, and I don't. But I am Antonio's lawyer.'

Pallioti nodded. He had not really expected more, but he realized he had hoped for it. He was aware of Hedwige, silently watching both of them.

292

'For the record,' Barbara added, 'and in the spirit of goodwill, given the circumstances, I will say that the last time I saw him was . . . I don't know? Three months ago.' She waved a hand. An obviously expensive watch caught the light and glittered. Pallioti wondered if there was a matching one on Hedwige's wrist.

'Do you have any idea where he is?' Barbara Barelli asked.

Pallioti shook his head.

'We've checked known addresses,' he said. 'Known associates. Of course.'

'Which led you to me?'

'More or less.' He thought of the pictures.

'But nothing?'

She didn't sound surprised. But then again, Pallioti thought, why would she be? Why should any of them be? Tomaselli'd been *Brigate Rosse*. And that's what they did. Went underground. Disappeared. Melted away like smoke. A few gunshots and, *Poof!* Now you see them. Now you don't.

'I was hoping I might ask you—' Pallioti paused, then pressed on. 'Is there any family property, for instance? Anything, any place, from his childhood perhaps, that he might have mentioned?'

She shook her head.

'No. Not that I know of. Of course, he was in prison almost thirty years. So . . .' She shrugged as if this explained anything.

'Think, Dottoressa.' Pallioti watched her closely. In his experience prison gave people more time to remember than to forget. 'It could be very important. If he has this girl—'

Barbara looked at him sharply.

293

'And you really believe he does? Honestly? You aren't just fastening on him because he used to be BR?'

Pallioti looked at her for a moment.

'We can't prove it,' he said finally. 'But yes, I believe that she is with Antonio Tomaselli and whether or not it began that way, or he intended it, I believe that he is now holding her against her will.'

'Why? Why would he do that? Has there been a ransom demand?'

Pallioti shook his head.

'No. As I said—'

'Then why?' Barbara cut him off. 'Why would Antonio abduct, or kidnap, or whatever you want to call it, a seventeen-year-old American? I can't see what's in it for him?'

It was the lawyer's question—and Pallioti had no intention of providing an answer. Even if he had one. Which he didn't, although he thought he saw a glimmer. Of what? Revenge? Love? Punishment for the woman who'd betrayed him? A desire to reel her in? Hook her using her stepdaughter like a bright lure dangled in front of a wary fish? He looked at Barbara Barelli. And reminded himself that whether he liked her or not, she was playing for the other side.

'Kristen was last seen,' he said carefully, 'getting into Antonio Tomaselli's car. Since then, she's vanished. No, I know it's not proof. And you're right, there's been no ransom demand. Nothing like that. In point of fact there's been nothing at all. But, yes we do believe he has her. As I said, I do.'

Barbara crossed her arms and nodded.

'So, I ask again,' she said. 'Why?'

'Why do fucked-up creeps take girls?'

It was Hedwige who spoke. Pallioti had almost forgotten she was in the room. She pushed herself off from the counter where she'd been leaning.

'It's what sickos do,' she said, her tone of voice suggesting strongly that she'd proffered this opinion of Antonio Tomaselli before. More than once. 'He fucking killed Aldo Moro, or . . .' Hedwige looked at Barbara and shrugged. 'OK. OK. Or he stood there while somebody else did it. Who knows? And frankly, who cares? What's the fucking difference? You're part of it, you own it. You don't get to choose.'

Barbara sighed. 'Hedwige—'

'No.' Hedwige glared at her. 'No. I mean, what the fuck do you expect from a guy like that? That he's going to change? Jesus Christ, Bar. In your dreams. The Red Brigades ran around shooting people in the legs. And that's when they were being nice. They weren't fucking heroes. They weren't anything but self-righteous little killers. And don't give me "why",' she snapped. 'You know "why" isn't worth shit when you start going around shooting people.'

Hedwige's chest was heaving. The argument had clearly raged between them, and more than once. And as interesting as it might be to hear its ins and outs for the umpteenth hundred time—like most people of a certain age in Italy, Pallioti had had this discussion himself—he didn't feel inclined just now. Hedwige's words echoed the tiny voice inside him that he half thought he'd managed to stifle. She was right. They all knew it. Antonio Tomaselli, like everyone else who had been involved, everyone else who had done nothing to stop it, was nothing but a cold-blooded killer.

Pallioti glanced at his watch, and thought again of Kristen Carson. And of her increasingly distraught father, who held his phone like a man with his finger on the trigger. James MacCready was babysitting him this afternoon. But nobody could keep the genie in the bottle forever. Sooner or later Dr Carson would stop listening to them and start making calls. To television stations. To newspapers and bloggers. To friends in Washington.

And if they could do nothing, couldn't find hide nor hair of his missing child, why should they blame him? Wouldn't Pallioti himself do the same? Wouldn't any parent? Yes. Even if all hell broke loose. Which it would. Armed searches and SWAT teams, and bullets. Lots of bullets.

One way or another, every day Kristen Carson was missing, every hour they didn't find her, her chances of surviving—if she was still alive—grew smaller.

What little complacency Pallioti had felt this morning went up in a puff of stale, ugly-smelling smoke. He took a card from his inside pocket and laid it on the counter.

'If you think of anything,' he said, looking from Hedwige to Barbara then back again. 'Anything at all that might help us, please call me. It's confidential,' he added. 'No one ever needs to know.'

*　　　*　　　*

Barbara followed him into the hallway.

'It wasn't all rubbish, what I said earlier, about why I do this.'

Pallioti smiled as he buttoned his coat. 'I know.'

'We both have our jobs.' She held out her hand. 'I'm sorry I couldn't be of more help to you, Ispettore. But I take mine as seriously as you take yours. I also don't lie,' she added. 'I haven't seen Antonio in the last three months.'

Her grip was as firm as her gaze, and again Pallioti realized he liked her. You could do worse, he thought, much worse, than have this woman stand up in court for you.

'You should know,' he said, groping for the words—not sure even what he was trying to say, or if he even believed what the fat man had told him last night, if it was more than just childish nonsense, the sort of macho toughness ageing policemen like to think they might once have been capable of. 'You should know, Antonio Tomaselli has . . .' He tried again, then failed, and shrugged. It sounded too ridiculous.

'Enemies?' Barbara was still holding his hand. Again, the not-very-nice smile played over her face. 'People who'd like him dead?' she said. 'Who find the fact that he's out of prison an affront, and would use any excuse? You don't want to believe that, do you, Ispettore?' She cocked her head, her dark eyes reading his face. 'You couldn't survive if you really thought that the State, that your beloved Polizia even, might go around "eliminating" those they find inconvenient. Or just plain don't like. That they might do a little "correcting" when they think the courts have got it wrong? No,' she said. 'You couldn't. Because then there would be no difference between You and Them. Both judges.

297

Both executioners.' She shrugged. 'I've heard of you, read about you. You'd never serve in a force that did that.'

'No.' Pallioti shook his head. 'No,' he said. 'I wouldn't.'

Barbara dropped his hand.

'Well,' she said. 'To answer your question. Yes, I have told him. Believe me, Ispettore, I have told him.'

'And did he believe you?'

Barbara crossed her arms, hugging the red silk shirt.

'To be honest,' she said, 'I have no idea. I wasn't lying about that, either. Yes, I've represented him a long time. But I don't know Antonio all that well. I doubt anyone does. On the other hand, he's not stupid. And I doubt anyone in jail forgot Ulrike.'

In May 1976, Ulrike Meinhof, the co-founder of Germany's Red Army Faction, otherwise known as the Baader-Meinhof Group, had been found hanging in her maximum-security cell. Her death had raised a certain number of uncomfortable questions, such as how had someone whose possessions were monitored and who was kept under twenty-four-hour observation managed to commit suicide by rigging a noose and hanging herself?

'That was Germany,' Pallioti said, and stepped out onto the gravel.

Barbara followed him, standing on the top step.

'Of course,' she said. 'You're right. That was Germany.'

The weak winter sun caught her red silk blouse, the band of her expensive watch, the dark gleam of her hair.

298

'I saw it, you know.'

Pallioti turned. He was aware of the cold, the fact that it was late in the day.

'Saw what, Dottoressa?'

Barbara Barelli blinked. She was holding her arms tight across her chest.

'Mara Cagol's autopsy report.'

He frowned.

'Not the one that was released to the press,' she said. 'There are always two. But surely you know that. I saw the real one.'

Barbara Barelli looked at him for a moment.

'Mara was shot in the back,' she said. Then she swung the door closed, leaving him standing alone in the drive.

*   *   *

'Ispettore Saenz?'

Enzo jumped. He'd finally left Bologna an hour earlier—they'd found the hotel, a box of hair dye and two ruined towels in a laundry chute and, most importantly, lifted a fingerprint off the vending machine—and he'd driven like a bat out of hell to Ferrara, half high on the idea that he might even find Anna Carson and get home in time to sleep in his own bed.

'I am Carla Rossetti,' the woman said.

Her outstretched hand and grey tailored suit made him suddenly aware that not only had he not shaved, but after two frantic drives and a long day in the Bologna police station, he looked like a tramp. His habitual uniform of jeans, trainers and leather jacket felt as if he'd slept in them. His shirt was rumpled. He had no luggage. The fact that he outranked Ispettore Rossetti by some considerable distance did nothing to mitigate the fact that if she had not been standing beside him, the receptionist at the unexpectedly chic Ferrara hotel where Guillermo had booked him a room 'just in case' would undoubtably have taken one look at him and thrown him out.

Guillermo, who had spoken with the Ferrara police, had given Enzo the name of his contact. Too late, Enzo realized he had assumed—for no particularly good reason, and probably quite a few bad ones—that 'Ispettore Rossetti' was a man, not the mahogany-haired Amazon he was facing.

'Shall we?' She gestured towards the tables and chairs scattered around the lobby. 'I have what you asked for. Or would you rather—' she hesitated and smiled—'unpack? I'm happy to wait,' she added.

For a bald-faced liar, she wasn't bad. Enzo wondered what it was—kid, lover, husband? All of the above? A cold splash of loneliness hit him, so real he almost shook himself like a dog. He had nothing to unpack. And still held out the hope that he would not need the room at all and would be heading back over the Apennines in a matter of hours, dragging Anna Carson like some bounty hunter's prize so he could sleep alone with his cat. It must have shown on his face, because Carla Rossetti looked sympathetic.

'I'm afraid the news isn't very good,' she said. 'Perhaps we ought to order a coffee.' She was nice enough not to say that he looked like he needed one.

A double espresso later, Enzo was forced to agree. The news was not very good. He didn't know what story Guillermo had cooked up when

300

he'd called Ferrara and asked for their help, but it didn't really matter. The net result was the same. 'Graziella Farelli' had not checked into a hotel, or a B&B, or a guest house, or rented a tourist apartment. Not last night, or the night before, or any time in the last week.

'I ran it backwards a few days, just to be certain,' Ispettore Rossetti explained.

Enzo took the printout she handed him, refrained from telling her that she'd wasted her time, and thanked her instead. He made a mental note to write a citation and make sure it got to the right person. More women needed to be promoted and she had been nothing if not thorough. She'd even checked the city's homeless shelter.

But not only had 'Graziella Farelli' apparently not slept anywhere in the city, she also hadn't booked any kind of transportation, train, bus, or boat—there was a tour company that ran down the river even in this frigid weather, bird-watchers mostly, according to the Ispettore—in order to try to leave it. Nor had she rented a car. Or bicycle. Ferrara apparently had a higher density of bicycles per capita than any other town in Europe, except for some place in Belgium. Carla Rossetti informed him of this with no small measure of pride. Enzo was tempted to ask if she'd checked roller blades and skateboards too, but decided against it.

The second sheet of paper Rossetti pulled out of her briefcase did not make him any happier than the first had. Only two handbags and one man's wallet had been reported missing or stolen in Ferrara during the last forty-eight hours. One belonged to a sixty-year-old bald day-labourer who weighed ninety kilos. One to a student with blue eyes and blonde hair who stood just over a metre and a half, and the last to a seventy-five-year-old who was in a wheelchair in an old folks' home. When Rossetti asked if she ought to check any of these out in person, Enzo told her not to bother. No red backpacks or green quilted down jackets from somewhere called Barney's had turned up at left-luggage in the bus or train stations, either. And no cars had been stolen. The long and the short of it was, if Kristen's stepmother was in Ferrara, she was either sleeping rough or staying with someone.

Or she had led them a very pretty dance. Been even cleverer than he'd given her credit for—a mistake he vowed then and there not to repeat, even if he had to write *Brigate Rosse* one hundred times on the pad in the hotel room where he was now almost certain he'd be staying.

Realizing they would trace her to Bologna, he thought, and to the wallet and hotel, Anna Carson had bought herself some time to do he-didn't-even-want-to-think-what by making certain she was seen getting on the Ferrara train—which was, after all, where they would expect her to go—and then either getting off before she got here, or immediately catching another train to God knows where. Or she'd arrived, trotted to the bus station and paid cash on a local puddle jumper. Or she'd ducked off the station in Bologna, somehow avoiding the cameras, and never left at all. The possibilities were virtually endless.

Enzo knew Guillermo had not told Ferrara any more about the mystery woman they were searching for than he had told Bologna. Probably the same stories would circulate here soon enough,

302

maybe even better ones. Although, he thought, it would be hard to come up with something much better than the truth. That the *Brigate Rosse*, now in their fifties, were back. And still winning. He groaned inwardly. Or perhaps he only thought it was inward, because Carla Rossetti was looking at him with something like concern on her face.

He thanked her, then he told her what he needed. She listened without taking notes and said she would go herself, immediately, to the train station. She would send someone else to the bus station. They would get the CCTV tapes for him and hold them at the Questura. She showed him where it was on a little green and red tourist map and told him a room would be at his disposal for as long as he needed it, beginning with all night tonight.

If he could not spot Anna Carson getting off a train or onto a bus in Ferrara, Enzo would have to go back to Bologna and pick up the trail where it had gone cold. The thought made him sick with frustration. He thanked Carla Rossetti again and waited until she left. Then he went to the front desk and asked the clerk where he could find a store that sold underwear and socks.

*   *   *

It was past 7 p.m. when, showered and shaved, Enzo left the hotel. Coin, God bless it, had not only been open and willing and able to supply socks, underwear and shirts, but had even stretched to a new pair of jeans, two very warm rolled-neck sweaters, and gloves, which Enzo usually disdained. Not tonight. There was a damp chill hanging in the air that threatened to turn his very breath to ice. Before it left his lungs. Ferrara was not only flat, it was freezing.

Before venturing out, Enzo had taken time, not only to call his grandmother and ask her to feed the cat, but also to feed himself, and go back over his file on Angela Vari while he ate. After finishing with room service, he had taken a pen and marked up the tourist map Carla Rossetti had given him. Made little Xs on the old Spanish synagogue, and on the corner of Via Mayr where her father had had his shop. He doubted, frankly, that she'd do anything that obvious—and since she was supposed to be dead he could hardly go knocking on doors and asking if anyone had seen her. But there was no harm in looking. He figured the detour would only take him a few minutes before being locked up all night in the Questura.

Enzo walked along the walls of the Castello and passed under the arch that led out to Corso Libertà. The Duomo shimmered under the gaze of its floodlights. People thronged in front of it, their shadows dancing on the piazza. The market stalls were still open and doing brisk business. The scene looked almost medieval. It was the silence, as much as anything else, Enzo realized, that gave the town its slightly unreal air. Closed to traffic, the only noises that echoed off the buildings of the old city were human—laughter and snatches of conversation or arguments, punctuated by the whirr and rattle of bicycles and the sharp ding of bells as they coasted over the cobbles.

There was no way to tell any more where the ghetto had begun. No plaque or statue marked the place where the giant gates had once swung shut, locking away half the inhabitants from dusk to dawn. Enzo stopped in front of the newer synagogue where Bassani had worshipped, and where, in the Garden of the Finzi-Continis—which he had been disappointed to read in the hotel brochure didn't actually exist—Micòl had sat in blonde splendour looking down on all the broken-hearted young men. There was a plaque by the door listing name after name, entire families who had been swept up during the German occupation and shipped east in cattle cars, towards sunrise and death. The street where Angela Vari had lived was opposite. Enzo turned down it and felt the past close around him.

The houses were not that tall, three storeys most of them. Jammed together, they blocked out what light there was, reducing the sky to nothing but a darkened strip. There weren't many street lights. As a result, he missed the Spanish synagogue, got to the end of the street before he realized his mistake, and doubled back. When he finally found it, he discovered that the door of the mangy brick building was padlocked, the paint peeling. There was a plaque here, too. Something about the d'Este dukes, and then *Distrutta nel 1944 per mano dei Nazifacisti*. Destroyed in 1944 at the hands of Nazi Fascists. He could barely make out the words. Someone passed on a bicycle, nothing more than a dark shape teetering down towards the corner. A pigeon rustled its feathers against the cold. A block away, footsteps and laughter rose and died. Enzo turned and looked across the street.

The house where Angela Vari had grown up was no different from the others. If anything, it was a little smaller. Narrow, brick, only two storeys high.

There was a light over the front door, which looked to be newly painted. There were four windows on each floor, shutters closed over all of them. Light snuck through the slats in the lower ones. The second storey was dark. Enzo knew that during the war displaced families had sometimes moved into the ghettos and taken over whole houses and flats. After the Jews had been rounded up and taken away, others had simply stepped into their lives. Sometimes, literally, into their shoes. He wondered if that had happened here. If that was how Angela Vari's family had come to call this place home, and standing in the street, looking at the house, he thought of the girl whose father had died, who had laboured on here alone in what must have been her own kind of hell, a void of loneliness, and wondered where she was now. Had she survived all these years only to find the past repeating itself? Had she come back and found someone living her old life? Or had she found no one and moved in herself, a ghost reclaiming its safe haven?

For a moment, the idea gripped him, and he became convinced that that was exactly what she had done. That somehow she had got inside, found a key, gone up the stairs, and was there now in the dark behind those closed shutters. So close that if he called her name she'd hear him.

Enzo started to cross the street. Then he heard a phone. A young couple carrying grocery bags emerged out of the dark. He watched as in the light from the door lamp the woman dug her mobile out of her handbag with her free hand, shifting a bulging bag to the other. The man laughed and fished in the pocket of her jacket as

306

she talked, pulling out a set of keys. They smiled at Enzo as they went up the steps to Angela Vari's house. A minute later the upstairs lights went on, and Enzo turned and walked away.

The Questura was in the opposite direction. It was cold and felt like it might snow and he needed to watch what would probably be dozens of hours of CCTV tapes. But he didn't care. He found what he was sure had to be Via Ragno, and then a damp tunnel lit by a few neon bistro signs that was the supposedly famous Via Volte. A shorter tunnel took him to Via Mayr. A line of cars moved slowly down it. He jerked to a halt as abruptly as if he had come to the banks of a river and stood watching as their lights caught the shuttered fronts of shops. Then he saw the one on the corner that was boarded up, felt the familiar prickle, and walked down the opposite pavement, resisting the urge to hurry. When he stopped and looked up, he saw the sign above the graffitied boards had been vandalized and half of the letters were missing. But there was no question about it. It had once read *MACELLERIA*. Butcher's. Beside it, the narrow mouth of an alley opened into darkness.

Enzo stood very still, watching the front of the deserted shop for perhaps five minutes. Then he slipped across the street and into the alley. Pausing to let his eyes adjust to the dark, he saw a van pulled towards the back, taking up almost the entire space. From the way it listed he could tell that it had at least one flat tyre, if not a missing wheel. Either way, it hadn't moved recently and wasn't going anywhere soon. He edged forward, feeling down the wall, until he found it. The door was sodden, half-rotten, and unlocked.

307

Barbara Barelli leaned back in the driver's seat of the Mercedes and indulged herself in the luxury of pure rage. She had parked on the road and called Antonio, realizing almost as soon as she'd done it that it was pointless. At least she'd had the wit not to leave him a message, tick him off like some outraged schoolmarm. As if that would do any good. Finally, she'd decided to walk in. Sniff the lie of the land. The light had been falling out of the sky fast, and by the time she got halfway down the drive and saw the buildings they looked black and white, as if not only life, but colour, had leached out of them.

Standing there, she'd remembered everything Antonio had told her. Every heartrending detail. About his grandparents. And his childhood. And how much the countryside meant to him. He'd been good. He'd sensed the dregs of sympathy and guilt, legacy of her nice middle-class upbringing. The vague, uneasy suspicion that people like her, and her parents, and the State, and possibly all of Italy, had not only been responsible for what the BR had done, but in some dark place had willed them to it—had sent them out to rob and kidnap, kneecap and murder, by proxy. And then, of course, there was Angela. The stiffening corpse of love and obligation they'd stepped carefully around for almost thirty years.

Barbara closed her eyes and heard herself laugh. She supposed, really, she had to hand it to him. Antonio had played her well and truly. And she hadn't even seen it coming. Not until it was way too late. Until he had her right where he wanted her. Ironic that, in the end, she and Angie should have that in common.

There'd been no sign of life at the so-called farm, but that didn't mean anything. He'd hardly hang out a WELCOME sign. The car was probably behind the house, or in the barn, which sat to the left and was long and low and made of stone. Barbara remembered it from the property description. 'Outbuilding—possible use for conversion as holiday cottage'. In some other universe, maybe. Holidaying here defied imagination. Just before she'd turned away, she'd thought she might have seen something, a movement in an upstairs window. But when she'd looked again, she'd realized it had been a mistake, nothing but the last reflection of daylight playing on the glass. And yet, for all that, she was sure he was there. She could smell him, huddling in the dark. Waiting like a spider beside his baited web. Barbara was not given to histrionics, but as she walked back to the car she'd felt the hair stand up on the back of her neck.

After that, she'd driven away, found a ratty little tourist bar on the road to Pomposa, and gone inside and sat at a table nursing a coffee and grappa watching the sunset, such as it was, and wondering what the hell she should do. Her first instinct had been to wait until morning. The cops always did things at dawn, usually around 4 a.m., when the mind and body were least present, floating happily between life and the ether, and thus unlikely to respond well to loud bangs and lights. To screaming and guns. She'd always considered that stuff a bit cowardly to be honest.

Sort of cheating. All those big men with their combat gear eking out the last little advantage of surprise, doing everything they could to stack the odds. Not that she was necessarily averse to a little odds-stacking. A win was a win, and she could certainly eke out twelve hours.

She'd just about decided to do that, take a page out of their book and wait at least until first light before she confronted him, when she'd thought of the girl. Seventeen. Blonde. He'd known her name. He'd tracked her and stalked her on Facebook.

'Fucker,' Barbara had said out loud, causing the bartender to jerk awake. Then she'd stood, paid the bill, and gone out and got in the car and driven back.

*   *   *

Now she hovered at the head of the drive, engine purring, foot on the brake. Night had dropped over this nowhere Antonio had chosen. The car's headlights spread into the dark, then wavered and gave up when they found nothing to hang on to. Barbara thought of the card nestled in her pocket. Sitting in the bar, she'd taken it out, run her finger over its sharp edges and the discreet raised letters of its engraving. Alessandro Pallioti. The idea was deeply tempting—to call the number and shove all this into his elegant lap. Lean back like a fainting heroine and let him catch her. It was his job after all, and he was reputed to be good at it. She'd even liked him. But she couldn't do it. It wasn't her style. You reap what you sow.

The big Mercedes bounced in the deep ruts of the drive. If she got stuck or messed up the undercarriage, Hedwige would frigging kill her. She loved these cars like they were babies. Rounding the curve, Barbara saw a faint glow in the lower windows of the house—in what must be the kitchen and sitting room. She reached the yard and swung around so she was facing outwards, then opened the door. The wind swept in, blowing salt, chasing a handful of dead leaves and corralling them between the single bent tree and a broken stone trough.

When she finally got out of the car, Barbara heard the distant echo of a bell and realized it had to be coming from Pomposa. It would be an electric carillon now, or maybe even a recording, tolling the memory of the faithful. She closed the car door and took a breath. A feeling she didn't want to name skittered up her back.

'Don't be a baby,' she muttered.

She'd done things that were harder. Lots of them. In prisons. And courtrooms. In police stations. So, what was the big deal? All she had to do was walk up, knock on the door, and tell him the truth.

*   *   *

Hearing Antonio's name fade to nothingness, Anna had nearly given up. It had crossed her mind that she had to be insane. That all of this—stealing Kristen's clothes and that poor woman's wallet, dyeing her hair, coming here—all of it was crazy. She should have taken the policechild's offer. Let him help her. Talked to him. Told him who she was. And what she knew.

Walking back up the hill and along the track,

311

getting on the bicycle and beginning the long ride back to the train station, she'd decided. She'd even stopped and turned on her phone. She'd turned it on twice a day, at 7 a.m. and again at 7 p.m., exactly as Antonio had told her, but there had been nothing from him, no text or email. Only a series of calls from Ken. Now, there was not even a signal, but still her mind was made up. She would call Ken as soon as she was on the train. She would go straight to the Questura when she reached Ferrara. This time, she would tell everyone everything. Then, standing on the little platform as the light bled from the sky, waiting for the thin grey line of the train to come slowly into sight, Anna had remembered Antonio's voice. Remembered exactly what he'd said as she stood there in the Excelsior, the perfectly ordinary sounds of people eating breakfast clattering around her. *'This is between you and me, carina. No one else. Just us. Do you understand? Do you believe me?'* And she thanked God that there had been no signal, no possibility of a call.

*   *   *

It was dark by the time the train pulled into Ferrara. Anna abandoned the bicycle at the station, left it in one of the racks outside the ticket office. Its owner, if he or she cared, would find it soon enough. Unchained bikes had been pilfered for rides to the train even in her day. She walked back to town on aching legs, cold rippling through her. The bells tolled eight as she reached Piazza Trieste.

Crowds were wandering through the night

market, milling around the outside heaters and gathering under the porticos of the tiny shops that huddled below the southern wall of the Duomo. The smell of food made her almost desperate. She bought a sausage in a roll, and then another with cheese melting across it and *rucola*, bitter and chalky on her teeth. She ate them walking among stalls, watching the vendors who stood wrapped in sweaters and scarves and overcoats. Lettuces and peppers were piled with livid orange carrots. There were pyramids of tomatoes and swollen bulbs of aubergines, their skins purple and glistening. For a moment she felt as if she had not seen colour, or tasted food, for thirty years.

She bought a coffee and sat on the steps of the Palazzo Municipale, watched people drift back and forth under the arch, and thought of nothing. As exhaustion washed over her, she felt the same odd, familiar sense she had sometimes had as a child— that time had slipped away, past and present mingling like the water of muddy streams. Drifting, she let go. Felt herself spinning and turning, and feeling any moment she might nudge a bank, and climb off her little raft of memory, and walk home to find her father waiting for her. See Nonna Franchi sweeping the steps. Signora Ravalli gossiping at the corner. Hear Barbara on the phone, shouting about schoolwork.

She started, spilling the dregs of the coffee. Cold bit into her. Getting up, Anna crumpled the cup and threw it away. Then, after using the Ladies in the bus station, she threaded her way through the shadows, and crept down the alley, and slipped like a stray cat through the broken door of the store room.

Anna Carson was stronger than she looked. She bucked, bit, kicked, and tried to elbow him in the stomach. Enzo gave her an A for effort, but he was better, faster, and twenty years younger. He had her face-down on the floor with her hands cuffed behind her back in considerably less than a minute. He'd have had no problem doing it in the dark, but the flashlight helped. Especially when he found the blade. Stuffed into her pocket, it was damn near thirty centimetres, and sharp.

He set it on the counter along with the light and wondered why he didn't feel more triumphant. But here in the weird shadowed light of a derelict butcher's shop it hardly seemed like a big victory— more the tawdry end to a shabby little story of revenge and betrayal that he didn't even understand. It was hard to look down on this woman and think of her as an 'enemy of the State'. But maybe that had always been the advantage people like this had—the fact that they looked so ordinary.

She didn't swear or call him names or threaten to sue him, which surprised him a little, especially since she'd lived in America. She didn't spit at him, either, which was virtually de rigueur. Instead she just lay there. His own very small pen light had given him just the briefest glimpse of the den she'd made for herself—the sleeping bag, the camping lantern, the tins of food, the opener and single spoon and bottle of water. The tiny little heater. The bucket and pack of wipes. It might have been the enviable nest of any homeless person or, even

314

more likely, an illegal immigrant. Nothing but the little white bear had given her away. He'd found it tucked on a shelf under the counter in the cold room in what had obviously been an effort to at least conceal if not hide it, and for some reason hadn't been able to put it back. Instead, he'd sat it on her sleeping bag, then gone into the main shop and switched out his light and stood so still beside the hatch that he might have been dead himself while he waited for her.

'Angela Vari, also known as Anna Carson, I'm arresting you for theft and trespass. I will be transporting you back to Florence, in custody, where you will be questioned in the presence of personnel from the US Consulate.'

The announcement was as much courtesy as anything else, and drew no response at all. In fact, Anna Carson didn't make a sound until he took out his phone. Then she found her voice.

'What are you doing?'

The question was so bizarre that Enzo actually paused. What did she think he was doing, ordering Chinese food?

'I'm calling for back-up. From the police,' he said, 'to get us out of here, because I don't think you'll get through that hole with your hands cuffed and I want to get back to Florence before dawn.'

'Don't.'

She had twisted round and was staring up at him.

'What?'

'Don't,' Anna Carson said. 'Please. Please, whatever you do, don't call the police.'

He had addressed her in English, but when she spoke it was in fluent Italian, and sounded so panicked that Enzo crouched down beside her.

Her eyes were wide, enough of the whites showing that he was afraid they were about to roll back in her head, that she was going to have a seizure. It was probably the influence of the place, but Enzo couldn't help thinking of an animal just before it was about to be slaughtered. An uncomfortable feeling ran through him.

'Why don't you let me help you get up?' He started to apologize in case he'd hurt her, then brought himself up short. She had, after all, been about to knife him. 'Here.' He took her arms and hoisted her to her feet, trying to be gentle. Or at least not rough.

'Don't,' she said again, as soon as she was standing up. 'Don't. Please. Please don't call the police.'

'I am the police.'

Enzo looked at her. Had she forgotten who he was? Had she lost it completely? Regressed in some weird way? Or did she think she was going to get tortured? Beaten up? After thirty years of living in the States was she still really convinced that those kind of things happened in European police stations? The expression on her face certainly seemed to suggest it. The woman was terrified.

'I won't let anything happen to you, Signora Carson,' he said. 'You're safe. I promise you.'

'No.' She shook her head, panic rising in her voice. 'No. No. No!' she wailed. 'You don't understand.'

'What don't I understand?'

Enzo, who had taken his phone out again, lowered it.

'It isn't me. It's Kristen.'

'Kristen? What about Kristen?'

'He'll kill her.'

Even in the weird low light he could see that her face was white. That high red patches had blossomed on her cheeks, making her look as if she had a fever.

'He'll kill her,' Anna Carson said again. 'Antonio will kill her. He will. He promised me.'

Enzo tried to keep the urgency—the desire to grab her and shake her—out of his voice.

'You've spoken to him?'

She nodded.

'Since he took Kristen?'

She nodded again.

'When? How recently? How many times?'

'Once. I called her phone. That day, after I saw him in that picture the girl took. I left a message on Kristen's phone and he called me back. He told me that it was just between us—that I had to come for her, find him, and that if I told anyone anything, or went to the police, he'd kill her.'

The words came out so fast she was panting. Enzo looked at the phone in his hand.

'You have to believe me,' she said. 'You have to. I know him. I promise you, I know him. He isn't lying. He's done it before.'

*   *   *

Enzo had turned the phone off. It was against his better judgement, but he did it.

After that, they'd stood for a good minute or two there in the butcher's shop, he and Angela Vari, or Anna Carson, or whatever he was supposed to call the woman who now sat across from him on the

317

opposite bed in his hotel room. Then, finally, she'd said, 'At least, please, please, let me explain.'

Enzo hadn't answered.

'You said once, you said in the hotel that day,' she'd added, 'you saw. You knew that I'd recognized him—and you said if I talked to you, you'd help me. Please,' she'd said. She'd been watching him, reading his mind. 'Please just let me at least talk to you. Just let me do that. Then, if you don't believe me, you can do whatever you want.' She shook her head. 'It's not like I can stop you. But just hear me out first. Please. Do it for Kristen.'

So he had.

He'd gathered up all the knives, the ones hanging above them and the one she'd had in her pocket, and tossed them through the hatch. Then he'd refastened the handcuffs in front of her so she could climb through. When he'd told her that if she tried anything, anything at all, not only was the deal off, but he'd hog-tie her and call every cop in Ferrara, she'd nodded. Then at the last moment she'd said, 'Wait!' And gone back and picked up the little white bear. Enzo took it from her and tucked it in his pocket.

In the alley, he'd taken off his jacket, draping it around her shoulders, holding her close as they started down Via Mayr, hopefully looking more like a courting couple than a guy with a woman in handcuffs. Force of habit dictated that he'd already checked out the side entrance to the hotel lobby, which was fortunate. Enzo brought her in that way, avoiding the desk, counting on the fact that the drinkers in the bar would be too absorbed in their own conversations to notice the man and woman huddled with cold and lust who scuttled towards the lifts and promptly disappeared.

*   *   *

Now they sat facing each other on the matching queen-sized beds, Anna Carson with her hands cuffed in front of her, and Enzo looking at his watch and thinking he'd give her exactly one hour. He'd be able to explain that if he had to.

He glanced up. Even in the softly lit room, she looked ragged. The sleek blonde woman he had met a week ago was gone. Grubby and exhausted, her cheeks were still white and blotched an unhealthy red. Enzo stood up and undid the handcuffs. A voice in his head reminded him that she was still Angela Vari, that he could still end up writing *Brigate Rosse* a hundred times on the pad. He gave it a nod. He was twenty years younger and a cop and he had no intention of letting her out of his sight. She rubbed her wrists and tried to smile.

'Thanks.'

'Are you hungry?'

She shook her head, diffident, almost shy, like a child trying to behave. Enzo felt a pang of shame, then told himself not to be stupid. He was just doing his job. Or rather, he wasn't. And it wasn't too late to correct that. One call to Carla Rossetti would have Anna Carson safely in a holding cell, a second would have Pallioti on the way.

'Bathroom?'

She shook her head, then said, 'Well, yes actually. I'd kill to wash my hands and face, with soap. And if you had a towel.'

He helped her take her jacket off. She moved

319

stiffly, like someone who'd been beaten up. Enzo gestured towards the bathroom, then followed, stood in the door and watched her. The crest of her back, her shoulders as she bent over the sink were narrow, fragile, even under the heavy, cheap sweater she was wearing. He couldn't help noticing that the dyed hair, which was probably closer to her natural colour, was actually more flattering than the fake blonde. Even dirty, a few stray curls caught the back of her neck. When she looked up into the mirror after drying her face, he realized again that her eyes were more green than brown. They met his in the glass and he looked away, suddenly embarrassed that he was standing there.

'OK,' she said, and tried to smile again. 'Thank you.'

They went back into the bedroom. Anna sat on the opposite bed again. She picked up the little white bear, then put him down, propping him against the pillow. Enzo retrieved a bottle of fizzy water from the minibar and poured them both a glass. She took hers, sipped it and nodded.

'I don't know how to explain to you.' She looked at him. 'I don't know.'

She ran a hand over her eyes. Enzo noticed the ringless fingers and remembered the boxes in the safe. He'd thought then that she'd abandoned them because she didn't want to be recognized. Now he realized it wasn't that at all. Stripping them off her fingers had been her way of re-entering the past.

'You see, it all goes back.'

Her voice was so tired it was wavering. Watching her, Enzo wondered what it must have been like, how exhausting it must have been to shove aside one self and grow accustomed to another—to put lives on as if they were layers of clothing, then be condemned to wear them forever.

'It's as if it never stopped.' She looked up and gave a half-hearted smile, as if she'd been able to hear what he'd just been thinking. 'Not really,' she said. 'I mean, I tried to fool myself sometimes, that it was gone. But it wasn't. It never is. It just gets put aside for a while, and now it's happening all over again.'

'What is?'

The beds were so close their knees were almost touching. Enzo shook his head. A minute ticked by, then another. If she wouldn't or couldn't talk to him, there was no point. He was about to say that this was a bad idea, that he had changed his mind and was taking her back to Florence, when she said, 'Rome.'

'Rome?'

Anna Carson nodded.

'Rome. Rome is happening all over again.'

Enzo reached out and took her hand. It was cold. He held it for a moment in both of his. Then he said, 'Tell me.'

PART FOUR

ROME

1978

The man sat on the narrow bed, elbows resting on his knees. He wore a white shirt with the sleeves rolled up and collar open, and suit trousers of a navy blue so dark it might have been black. The matching waistcoat and jacket were hung neatly over the back of the chair in the corner, which together with the bed and a desk, were the only pieces of furniture in the room. Overhead, the light bulb buzzed like a trapped fly.

Angela stood, staring. She could feel Antonio behind her, standing just outside the open door with his back turned, like a sentinel. The plate was warm in her hands. *Manicotti*, a recipe of her father's. She had made it this morning and carried it here on the bus, changing three times, lugging the basket like Little Red Riding Hood.

'Ah. You've brought me lunch.'

The man's face was long and creased. His features, the wide mouth and rounded nose, were soft and sagged slightly, as if he might be melting. Which was certainly possible. The room was tiny— no more than a big utility cupboard tucked between the kitchen and bathroom—and very hot.

'Thank you,' he said, and smiled.

Angela started and stepped back, clutching the plate as if he'd growled. She'd been told he was angry, that she had to come because perhaps he would take food from her, since he wouldn't take it from anyone else. The description had made him sound like an enraged animal. So the smile threw her off.

She took a breath and put the plate down on the desk beside a pad and a pen, then opened her

325

mouth, started to say, 'I hope you like it,' before she remembered she wasn't supposed to talk to him. Or even acknowledge him. Or look at him any more than she had to. Mostly, she wasn't supposed to tell him her name. All she was supposed to do was feed him and pretend he wasn't there.

*   *   *

Later, they would ask her, and ask her, and ask her, how she hadn't known. And she would tell them, and tell them, and tell them again, all the while knowing that most of them did not believe it, and finally wondering if somewhere, deep down in the well of herself, she did not believe it either.

Sometimes, when they accused her of lying, she was tempted to agree with them—to say that she had lied as surely as Antonio had lied when he told her that he was enrolled at the university in Rome, when he left their tiny flat every morning at eight, and came back every evening at six, and talked about his classes and his friends and what he had done during the day. That it was no different at all, except that the lies she had told had been to herself.

Then, she would almost agree. Would be tempted to say that of course she had known— from the start. From the moment Antonio walked into the pizzeria. From the moment he turned round. That all through that long, hot summer, every time he held her in his arms, or kissed her, or moved inside her, she had known.

She'd been tempted to say it not only because it was what so many of them—the police and the magistrates and prosecutors and psychiatrists—

326

already believed, because it would make them happy, and would be easier, but also because it would be reassuring. Much more so than the truth. Which was so simple, and so terrifying. That she had had no idea at all. That she had slept, and lived, and eaten, and made love, under the shadow of that sickening tilted five-pointed star, and never even known it was there.

Because she loved him. Because when he told her something, she believed him. Because it is not normal to look into the face of the human being you expect to spend your life with and suspect that they are living another life. That every time they walk out of the door, or around the corner, or are away from you, even for a minute, they become someone you do not know.

It was a myth that love encompassed everything. In fact, she had finally understood, it encompassed very little. And only what you wanted it to. Only what protected it. Like everything struggling to survive, love was selfish, and narrow, and fanatical. That was why it made so many people kill for it.

So, no. When Antonio had finally suggested, after they had been in Rome for several months, after they had sat on the scratchy old sofa in the flat in Trastevere and watched on television as the body of the German industrialist, Hanns-Martin Schleyer, had been removed from the boot of the car where the Red Army Faction had deposited it after kidnapping and eventually shooting him, when about a week after that, he had suggested one evening that perhaps she should sell the flat in Ferrara to the Ravallis after all, since surely they would never be going back there, she had not thought much of it. Certainly she had not

327

suspected any connection between the two things. Any more than she had suspected, after the sale, that he had not put the money in the bank. Locked it, as he promised, into a savings account 'for their future'. For the flat they would one day buy. For the children they would one day have. Certainly, she hadn't looked at him across their rickety little table, her bare foot resting on his as they drank coffee in the mornings, and thought it was being used to construct a box, a windowless cell, a cage to keep a man in in a utility room on Via Montalcini. That while she was keeping the books at a trattoria down the street and at the dry cleaner's around the corner, Antonio was not taking classes at all, but building a 'People's Prison'.

To look into his eyes and think that would have been crazy. As crazy as she was later told looking into his eyes and not seeing it had been.

Love was just love, she had snapped at them then. It didn't come with a crystal ball. And it didn't promise not to lie.

*   *   *

He had finally told her on 20 March, four days after the kidnapping. And even then, he had not really told her. Or she had not really heard. It was hard, later, to remember which.

What she does remember is that it was a Monday, and that the trattoria was closed so she had been able to work in peace all afternoon and with the television in the stuffy little office turned off. Which was a blessed relief, because by then she is sick, sick to death, of hearing about the

328

kidnapping of Aldo Moro. And even more than that, she is sick of the Red Brigades. She cannot read or hear one of their stupid, long-winded communiqués without being back in the hospital, without feeling the hard moulded plastic of the chair. Without hearing the laboured wheezing breaths of her father's dying. It's not that she blames the BR for his death, exactly. But she can't separate them from it, either. The same way you cannot separate the taste of the food that is in your mouth from the moment when someone tells you they no longer love you, or the song that is playing on the radio when they raise their hand and hit you.

So she is happy to have the television off. And when she walks home, carrying the bunch of tulips she has bought and thinking that soon she will be able to wear sandals again, she looks away from the newspaper kiosk that is still displaying the picture from two days ago, the one the *Brigate Rosse* issued of their latest prisoner, the most recent 'enemy of the people' who is *Sparito Nel Nulla*. Aldo Moro, the sweet-looking, sad-faced man, who smiles quizzically from under a five-pointed star.

Being one of the people herself, Angela finds it hard to feel much enmity for him. She doesn't see why she should, but mainly, she doesn't care. What she cares about is that the owner of the trattoria is going to give her more hours after Easter, which will mean more money, which may mean they can begin to think about moving to a slightly bigger flat. Antonio does not want to touch the proceeds of the sale of Via Vittoria—he says that should be a 'lock box' for their children, and she agrees. But

329

it would be nice to rent something where the kitchen was not a closet and where the bathroom was separated from the bedroom by more than a curtain. Not that she doesn't love where they live. She does. The building is on the side of a small piazza. There are mews where the carriage horses that work up in the tourist sites are stabled on the other side. She likes the smell of them, and the sound of their hooves on the cobbles when they leave in the early morning, and the soft shuffling they make as they settle themselves in the dark. It is warm enough now to leave the window open, so she can hear them and imagine that they reach Antonio in his dreams and take him back to his *nonno*'s farm, and the dogs that slept by the well, and the warmth of his brother, Piero, huddled against his back on a winter night.

She keeps a mint in her pocket and gives it to one of the older horses that is looking out over the stable door before she goes into the building and runs up the stairs and is surprised to find Antonio, home early and sitting on the sofa, waiting for her.

When she bends to kiss him, he pulls her down, but she waves the tulips at him, and laughs and skips towards the little kitchen where the window faces west and is open, spilling sunlight into the scratched porcelain sink. She runs water in a vase and feels his hand on her back.

'What are you cooking?' he asks. 'Tonight?'

Angela shrugs. She takes a knife and begins to strip the leaves and cut the stems of the tulips.

'Can you make *manicotti*? The kind your father used to.'

'I don't have what we need. I'd have to go to the shop and—'

330

'I bought it.'

She turns around and looks at him. Antonio is never picky about food. If anything, he doesn't care. And although he makes the bed and even, occasionally, washes things, she has never known him to buy groceries. Not even an apple. If the milk goes sour it sits in the fridge until she notices. He is watching her carefully.

'Can you?' he asks, and Angela feels something inside her. A glitter of cold. As if she has swallowed an ice chip.

She picks up the vase of tulips, edges past him, and places it on the table.

'It's not for me,' Antonio says. 'It's for someone special. He has low blood pressure. He isn't eating.'

For a second, they stand there looking at each other, with the table and the tulips, which are yellow, between them.

Then Angela says, 'Someone special?'

After he tells her, she sits down hard on the wobbly chair.

'You . . . ?'

She can't finish the question, but he shakes his head anyway. He is leaning against the little kitchen counter now, the sun catching his hair.

'I didn't have anything to do with that,' he says. 'With Via Fani. I don't even know the people who did. Our job is just to run the prison. That's how we do it,' he adds. 'We don't tell. Only what people need to know. That way it's safer for everyone. I don't even know their real names and they don't know mine. That's why I didn't tell you. To keep you safe.'

And to keep you safe, she will think later. But she

331

doesn't think it now. Now she just stares at him. Her stomach is doing something strange. It's falling, in slow motion. Sinking like a sack of kittens through dark water. She reaches out and grabs the edge of the table, as if it will hold her up.

'How long?' she asks finally. She is trying to remember. Something happened in Padua, something bad. But when? Before he went to the university? After? And then she realizes. That isn't it. That doesn't matter. This isn't about that. This is about the hand of God in the sky. The unions, and cost-cutting, and maintenance. And mostly, Piero. This is about bread and roses.

Antonio nods.

'Someone has to do something,' he says. 'We can't just do nothing. The Communists won't do it, they've sold out. The unions won't do it. The Christian Democrats are rotten. They're all rotten. No one stands up. No one fights.'

Angela doesn't say anything. She closes her eyes and sees a field of flickering stars. She feels hot wax on her hand, and the warm stickiness on her fingers as she touches Piero's forehead, his eyelids, his lips.

'We're going to put him on trial,' Antonio says. 'We're going to make him answer for what's happened. We're finally going to make them listen.'

Angela thinks of Mario Sossi, of his white collar and prosecutor's robes. She remembers his wife. The letters to the Pope. The letters to the President. Aldo Moro was going to be President, all the papers agreed. She has not seen his wife. She doesn't know if Signora Moro too is pleading and crying. But she has seen the police. The

332

newspapers, the TV. The radio says there are fifty thousand. Police, Carabinieri, army. There are roadblocks all around Rome. They are stopping cars on the highways. They are opening boots, pointing machine guns. It is the biggest manhunt in Italy's history.

She opens her eyes and meets Antonio's. Black as wet stones.

'The police,' she whispers.

He shrugs.

'If no one says anything, they won't find him.' He pulls out the other chair and sits down. 'If someone does, say anything, they'll kill us. All of us. We know that. They'll shoot us the way they shot Mara.'

Angela remembers this, how the night her father died, Barbara said something. Something about Professor Barelli insisting Mara Cagol had been shot in the back, 'like an animal', as she tried to crawl away after being wounded. *Mara, il tuo assassinio non resterà impunito.* She looks at Antonio and shudders.

In the next moment, he has his arms around her.

'I'll be all right,' he says. 'We'll all be all right. This will make things better. They'll have to listen now. They'll have to change. You'll see. For the future. For our children's future.' She pushes her face into his shoulder, into the warm, familiar, soapy smell of his shirt. 'I need your help, Angie.' He strokes her hair. He rests his chin on the top of her head. 'It will all be all right. Nothing is going to happen to me. No one is going to talk. But I need your help. We don't want to hurt him. We just want him to own up, admit what he's done, and make them change. But if he won't eat, if we can't get him to eat, we can't take care of him. Do you see? Will you help me?'

Angela nods. She keeps her eyes closed. But she nods.

*　　　*　　　*

The *manicotti* lasts two days, during which the trial of fifteen *Brigate Rosse* members begins in Turin. One of them is Renato Curcio, the husband of Mara Cagol. Now that she is gone, Angela thinks, he has no chance of disappearing. There is no one to arrive on visitors' day with a gun in a chocolate box. If he is even allowed visitors, which she doubts. No matter what Antonio says, the police are not stupid.

Angela considers this as she starts the *cacciatora*. Antonio said 'no bones' in the chicken. Angela doesn't know if this is a precaution against choking, or in case one might be secreted away. Sharpened in the dark after they turn out the light in the little room, then used as a weapon. She finds it hard to imagine. How many people could you stab with a chicken bone? And surely they have guns? At least the rest of them—Antonio hates the things. Not that she would know. Because so far she has only been to the flat on Via Montalcini the once, and she didn't see anyone except Antonio, and him. But the others were there. She heard them, in another room, scuffling like mice while she lifted the baking dish out of the basket.

Angela has always been a quick learner, so she understands this already. She would have even if Antonio hadn't told her. It isn't exactly, as the Americans say, rocket science. But it is crucial.

The most important part of what she already thinks of as the BR's—she doesn't like to use their whole name, even to herself—Litany. Of the prayers from their private little book of hours.

Each shall see and hear according only to his
  need.
You cannot betray,
Or be betrayed,
By what you do not know.

The words sizzle as she throws the tiny dice of green pepper and chunks of tomato into the burning oil. Then she turns her attention to the chicken.

Her father's knives, along with some of his clothes, his cap and his slippers, his white coat with its frayed collar, and the old maroon blanket from the end of her parents' bed, and a few other things—one of his cigar boxes she hides in the back of a cupboard and stores lire in, and a music box that is broken but belonged to her mother—have come with them to Trastevere. She sharpens the knives herself, but only when Antonio is not there because he can't stand the chalky scrape of the blade on the whetstone. He doesn't like the points, either. He turns his face away when she tests the tips, bouncing them on the pad of her thumb. He winces when she runs the blade against her finger to make sure the cut will come clean.

It's strange in him, she thinks, this squeamishness, this distaste for blood. Because it bothers her not at all. Angela brings the cleaver down with a cool smack, relieving the chicken of first one leg and then the next before she splits the

335

breast wide open.

*   *   *

This time, he stands and makes a little bow as she comes in.

He's been working at his desk. The pad is open. He flips it closed, but not before she sees the words running across the page. *My darling, I think of you. Kiss the children for me.* There's a book, too. Something about Marx. He picks it up and places it on the bed.

'My homework,' he says, smiling at her. And then, 'Thank you for this. The last was delicious. Your mother taught you well.'

'Father.'

The word is out before she even realizes she's said it. Angela feels the horrid familiar flush creeping up her neck and into her cheeks. She glances over her shoulder. Antonio is outside the door again, but she can't see him because this time, without thinking, she pulled it halfway closed behind her.

'Your father?' His voice is a whisper. He's watching her as she puts the plate on the desk. 'Your father taught you to cook?'

Angela nods. Without meaning to, her hand feels for the locket where there is now a tiny photo of him opposite her mother's. She drops it, then takes the plastic fork and spoon rolled in a paper napkin out of her pocket.

'I have daughters.' The words are not much more than a breath. 'I love them very much.'

Angela feels her hand hesitate. She places the implements beside the plate.

336

'I hope you enjoy the food,' she murmurs, then she turns and leaves.

Outside, Antonio locks the door and drives the bolt home.

'What did he say to you?' he asks.

Angela shakes her head. She even manages to smile.

'That he liked my food.'

She brushes past him and picks up the basket, mutters something about not wanting to miss the bus. She has come by herself and is leaving alone this time. Antonio kisses her and smiles at her and lets her out of the flat. She rides down in the lift and walks across the lobby. When she gets to the street, she can't stop shaking.

*   *   *

'*Ciao, carina*,' he says when he comes home a few hours later.

Angela smiles.

'*Da quanto non ci si vede*,' she replies.

Hey baby, long time. They sound like a bad American film. The one they saw last month. Or maybe the month before that. They love films. They love sitting in the back, in the dark, watching the story loom over them. Antonio puts his arms around her, he pushes her towards the little kitchen. She's wearing a skirt. When he lifts her onto the counter, she wraps her legs around him.

'I need you to do something,' he says. He runs his finger across her lips and down to the top button of her blouse. 'I need you because I know I can trust you.' He reaches for his belt buckle. Then he asks her to deliver the first letter.

The envelope is absolutely plain. There is nothing written on it at all. But it feels as if it's made of lead, as if it's going to fall through the bottom of her handbag.

'You get off the bus. You walk three blocks. There's a phone box, on the corner. Go into it, but not until ten o'clock. Don't be early, don't be late. Lift up the receiver, look like you're making a call. Then hang up and leave the envelope on the top of the telephone. Come out and walk away. Don't look back.'

Antonio's voice throbs in her head. He's with her while she rides on the bus and gets off and walks alone through the dark streets.

When she sees the phone box, she feels a pang of relief. She's been here almost seven months now, but Rome is huge. She only knows her own little pockets of it, and although she followed his instructions exactly, she was afraid she might have made a mistake—got on the wrong bus, walked the wrong way without realizing it. Antonio has never been angry with her. Not once. He's never even raised his voice. But there is part of her, some tiny sliver, that knows what it would taste like. Earth on her tongue.

The door of the phone box is cold to the touch. Inside, it smells of mould and old leaves. Angela lifts the receiver and feels the damp, slightly sticky plastic, the memory of other people's words. She pretends to drop a token in and dial a number, then waits and looks out of the scratched perspex window. There's no one walking on the street, which is wide and quiet. Lights shine from the

338

houses and blocks of flats. There are trees, not as big as the ones by the Angels' Gate, and not with ruby leaves, but nice enough. This is an expensive neighbourhood.

She finishes her make-believe call and puts the receiver back. Then she reaches into her bag and takes out the envelope and places it on top of the phone, making sure it is tucked in the little crack where the casing is bolted to the wall so it won't fall on the dirty floor.

She leaves and closes the door carefully. She can see the envelope quite clearly, an oblong of white, and for a second she's gripped by panic. Antonio didn't say anything about that, about whether she should try to hide it. But in a phone box, where? Her watch says three minutes past ten. Angela looks at the letter one last time, then turns away and starts up the pavement, her footsteps sounding too loud as she passes under a street light. Half a block later, she checks her watch again. Four minutes past. For a reason she can't explain, she stops.

There's a cluster of trees just here, and a gate pillar, and the edge of a wall. Angela steps into their shadow, then turns and looks back. The phone box hangs on the edge of the street lamp's halo. Her hands are cold. She shoves them into her pockets, and is suddenly aware of the hard pattering race of her heart. The wall is rough and snags her coat and hair. She has no idea why she is doing this. She knows she should go, should keep walking, do as she's told. She knows Antonio would be angry, even furious, if he knew. She feels his breath on the back of her neck. *Ti possiedo, per sempre.* I own you, forever. But she can't help herself. She waits.

The woman comes from the opposite direction, her shape emerging out of the dark. Angela is too far away to see her face, but from the way she walks, from her build, she guesses they're about the same age. Angela can tell, too, that she's trying to walk slowly—trying to look 'normal', whatever normal is supposed to look like when your father has been made to disappear like smoke. She stops on the kerb opposite the phone box. Silhouetted in the street light, Angela sees the bulge of her stomach as she turns sideways and realizes she is pregnant. Unconsciously her own hand goes to her belly, which is flat and hard. There is no traffic. The woman looks both ways before she crosses the street.

Her first steps are tentative. Then, like an animal that's broken loose, she dashes, legs whirring under the mound of her belly. She's wearing a dark coat and a green scarf that catches the light as she almost falls against the phone-box door, shoving it open with both hands. Even from this distance Angela can see her arm reaching out through the blur of the perspex, snatching for her father's letter, for the words he has sent from nowhere.

*　　　*　　　*

It's very late when Angela finally gets home, almost midnight. Antonio is waiting for her. He puts his arms around her. Runs his warm hands under her sweater and up her back.

'Did you deliver it?' he asks.

'Yes,' she says. She lays her head against his chest. 'Yes.'

Later she lies in his arms and feels him anchoring her into the world. On the way home on the bus, it started to rain. In their cramped little bedroom, Angela closes her eyes and feels herself rocked on the muffled noise from the streets below. On the whoosh of tyres and the stamp of the horses. And finally on the slow huff of Antonio's sleeping breath and her waking one as they mingle and rise and fall like the tide.

I have daughters.
I have daughters.
I have daughters.

*   *   *

Aldo Moro's interrogation has begun.

Its purpose is to clarify the imperialist and antiproletarian politics of the Christian Democratic Party and to ascertain the direct responsibility of Aldo Moro . . .

The communiqué, which had been sent to newspapers in Genoa and Milan and Rome, flies like a banner across all the front pages. It ripples from kiosks and corner shops. And it isn't alone. There are other headlines, too. Dozens of them, not dictated by the BR.

Terrorists' Demands Rejected. Parties Agree, No Negotiations. Moro Letter Appeals to Government.

The words dog Angela as she walks from the dry cleaner's to the florist's where she has recently picked up a third job. And then from the florist's to the trattoria.

The letter to the government, which was addressed *'Caro Francesco'* and signed *'Most Affectionate Greetings, Aldo Moro'*, had confused her at first. She knew it hadn't been the one she delivered because the papers said it had been in the same packet as the communiqué, which had appeared in all three cities at 8 p.m. It shouldn't have come as a surprise, but it was the first time it occurred to her that she was not the only one taking buses, walking in the dark, pulling envelopes out of her bag. She wondered how many there were, and felt strange thinking of herself as part of a secret army, a brigade who acted and worked in concert but never saw one another or even knew for sure that they existed. That the other soldiers were not more than mice in a neighbouring room.

You cannot betray,
Or be betrayed,
By what you do not know.

Then she reminded herself that she was not one of them. That all she did was cook meals. Walk to a phone box. Deliver the words, *'kiss the children for me'*. And then only because Antonio asked her to. Only because he beat inside her like a second heart.

*   *   *

Surrounded by large tin buckets, and piles of stripped leaves and the sweet fecund smell of two-day-old lilies, Angela opens the books and adds up numbers and sees that the florist is going, and probably sooner rather than later, the same way as her father's shop. Without really meaning to, she finds herself trying to think up ways to stave off yet another mushroom cloud. Could they have 'specials' on day-old carnations? Or overgrown pots of African violets? Could they offer two-for-one deals the way the supermarkets do, but on dying lilies instead?

She likes the florist's, but of her three jobs, the one at the trattoria is her favourite. Usually she is there alone except for the owner, a tall man with stooped shoulders who hums as he lays the tables and argues with the greengrocer about the menu. In the dark back office where she sits with the TV turned off, she can pretend the world really is about the availability of asparagus. Or the supply of the first small, pungent melons. Or about arguments over the price of *rucola* and the firmness of tomatoes.

Outside, on the streets, walking to and fro, or even at her other jobs, or at home when the television is on, it's not so easy. The bodyguards bother her most.

Oreste Leonardi. Domenico Ricci. Giulio Rivera. Raffaele Iozzino. Francesco Zizzi.

Their names appear in the papers and on posters, in boxes ringed in black. On the day of their funerals, both the dry cleaner's and trattoria closed 'out of respect'.

'They were just men doing their jobs. And for that, they're dead. They had wives. Children. Those bastards can keep their revolution.'

The dry cleaner shook his head, pulling the shutter down over his shop.

At the florist's they sold more flowers than in the whole week before. Bouquets were tied to railings, and left by fountains and on the steps of churches even though they had not been frequented, or

343

perhaps ever even visited, by any of the five men. And that was nothing, nothing at all, compared to the drifts of blossoms and ribbons and gifts that were left on Via Fani.

Angela sees it on television—a tide of flowers surging across the pavement, spilling down to the bus stop and climbing the iron railings opposite the intersection where Aldo Moro's car stopped and the shooting began.

His driver, the papers said, had kept driving even after he was shot. Had been trying to manoeuvre, twisting the wheel and stamping on the pedals, when the fatal bullet hit him. The guard beside him had thrown himself over the seat and onto Moro. Had shoved him down, covering Aldo Moro with his own body as he died. The three men in the following car never had a chance. They were hit by a barrage of bullets, semi-automatic fire. Two had been killed instantly. The third died moments after arriving at the hospital.

A cross has been set up, a worn beret tied to it, medals pinned to the brim. Two students from Foggia stand hand in hand and tell the television reporter that they have come to Rome specially to see the spot where the five policemen died. Where they were murdered for doing their duty. A woman calls them heroes. Another woman stands with her child, who is fingering the big bows on the bouquets, pulling petals off the occasional flower and shifting from foot to foot as his mother tells the reporter that she has brought him here 'because we have to learn something.'

*　　　*　　　*

344

The next time Angela sees him, he doesn't look well. The collar of his shirt is grubby. A button is missing, and he hasn't shaved. Or been allowed to shave. She really doesn't know. There is a toilet in a sort of closet behind a screen at the back of the room—she'd noticed it and looked away, embarrassed—but no sink.

She stands just inside the door holding the plate. It's lamb, with peas and the first baby carrots, and she realizes that she wants him to say something, or at least smile at her. His smile is soft and although his eyes are dark and her father's were blue, there's something about them that is similar. There's a new pad on the desk, and several more books about Marx and Lenin.

'I have to read them,' he says when he sees her looking at them.

He is sitting on the edge of the bed, his hands dangling between his knees as if he is too tired to do anything else with them.

'I have to read them to understand what I have done. For my trial.' He looks up at her, and it seems as if his face has sagged even more. As if the lines have deepened so they might cut into his flesh, carve his features away. 'Did they teach you Lenin in school?' he asks.

Angela shakes her head. They didn't, although she can remember Barbara's father talking about him over Sunday lunch. 'That which advances the revolution is moral!' he had shouted from the head of the table. His words had slurred slightly, and Barbara's mother had rolled her eyes. They had been eating beef and Angela can remember the spots of gravy that dotted the starched linen cloth as Professor Barelli waved his fork. 'That which

345

does not advance the revolution is immoral. Elegant!' Barbara's father had thumped the table, making the glasses rattle. 'The truth is always elegant!' he had announced, reaching for the bottle. The wine had spilled, dribbling down the side of his glass. Barbara kicked Angela under the table.

The plate is hot. Angela pushes the books aside, knocking one onto the floor, and puts it down abruptly. She bends to retrieve the dog-eared paperback. Her hand closes over it, but all she can see is the old beret, the faded ribbons of the medals, the too-big bows and surging tide of flowers.

That evening, when she gets home, she tries hard to remember. She stands by the calendar that hangs on the kitchen wall and puts her finger on the box that is 16 March. She presses hard, digging with her nail so it leaves a tiny sickle moon. But it's no good. Time has both slowed down and speeded up, jammed altogether, and she can't sort out the days. Or maybe she can. She tells herself she remembers. On that Thursday, she and Antonio had breakfast together. They sat at the little table and she rested her bare foot on his while they watched the sun finger the thyme and rosemary she is growing in the window box. She's sure of it.

*   *   *

The next letter isn't a letter, it's a box. Quite a big one. Wrapped in brown paper, it will barely fit in her bag.

Several days have gone by. She has made meals on almost every one, but Antonio has taken them himself, so she has not had to go to Via Montalcini, which honestly is a relief. If she does not have to go into the flat, if she does not have to wait while Antonio unlocks the door and then step inside that little room, which, although it has a fan of some kind, is hot and smells sour and close—if she doesn't have to do that, she can almost forget why she is making extra food. Why Antonio has asked her to go out and buy a razor, and a toothbrush, and a comb.

This time, she is to arrive at 11 p.m. And although she's only done it once before, the bus ride seems almost familiar. She gets off with two other people, a couple. For a moment she's terrified that they will walk in the same direction, that they will live in the house opposite the phone box and stand and watch her, or worse, want to use the phone. But they don't. Holding each other's arms, they laugh and run across the street.

Everything looks just the same. Even so, Angela slows down. She finds herself looking either way, peering into the gaps between the buildings and the shadows thrown by the trees. There are fifty thousand policemen and soldiers and Carabinieri looking for Aldo Moro. She pulls her bag closer to her, as if a hand might reach out and snatch it. But nothing moves, and there's no sound except her footsteps and the faint rustle of the spring night in new leaves.

Angela makes her pretend call. The phone box smells the same. The only thing that's different is that someone's written 'Laura' and a phone number in blue magic marker on the back wall. She hangs up and places the box on the top of the telephone. Then she walks quickly away up the street, eager to put as much distance between her and it as possible, telling herself that whatever else she does, tonight she will not stop. She will not look back.

But she does. As she reaches the pillar and the edge of the wall, she can almost feel the shadows of the trees pulling her in, reaching out to wrap her in their darkness. She hesitates, then turns and rests her back against the wall again, feeling the stones stroke her jacket and her hair.

It's five, or maybe seven or eight, minutes before the woman comes. This time, she's walking faster, as if she doesn't give a damn any more about trying to look 'normal'. She doesn't even pause, never mind look both ways, before she crosses the street. Instead, she walks diagonally. There's a desperation in her step, a slight stagger. A moment later, when she's halfway across the road and caught in the glare of the street light, she reaches up and wipes her face with the back of her hand.

It's warmer tonight. She isn't wearing her green scarf, and her coat is unbuttoned, and Angela is certain, although it has not been very long, that she is bigger, that even in this short time the baby she carries inside her has grown. The woman pauses for a moment as she steps up onto the pavement. Then she shoves open the door and grabs the box on the top of the telephone with both hands. But this time she doesn't whirl away. Instead, very slowly, she lifts the box and holds it against her face.

*   *   *

'In Twenty Days They Killed A Leader', La

Repubblica cries. '*The Destruction of a Man*', writes *Corriere della Sera*. 'If they had killed him, I could have understood more easily,' one of Aldo Moro's colleagues says. 'But not this.'

Yet again, packets have been left in Genoa and Milan and Rome. Yet again, newspapers have received telephone calls telling them where to find the latest communiqué, and the most recent letter. In this one, Aldo Moro begs the government to bargain for his life—to exchange him for other 'political prisoners'. Everyone knows that by this he means Renato Curcio and the others standing trial in Turin. '*I am a political prisoner and am being subjected to a difficult political trial with a political outcome,*' Aldo Moro writes. '*Time passes fast. Any moment,*' he warns, '*could be too late.*'

Angela tries not to read the headlines, or anything else, on her way to the flat on Via Montalcini. And fails. She knows now that the box she delivered was a tape, a recorded message from Aldo Moro to his family. All the papers say so, although they will not say what it said. Not that it matters. It isn't the words, she thinks, it's the timbre and touch of his voice. The caress of that familiar sound. That's what his wife and children crave.

Standing in the street, holding her basket, looking at the little printed words on the newspapers, she hears her father's whistle. The aimless scattered pebbles of his tune that was not a tune at all, just the sound he made in the world. She never heard her mother's voice. Or if she did, if there was a split-second when Annabeth spoke to her, she cannot, of course, remember it. But she is certain, nonetheless, that she would know it.

349

That it is lodged in her soul like a splinter. Finally, she pulls herself away and walks on. But all the way to Via Montalcini she feels a weight, the palm of her father's hand, resting on the crown of her head.

Antonio has not said so in so many words, but Angela knows he's worried. The police have knocked on either fifteen, or twenty, or fifty thousand doors in Rome, depending on which report you want to believe. As time goes on the chances can only get greater that they will knock on one that will somehow lead them to Via Montalcini, and what the papers are now calling 'the People's Prison'. Last night, Antonio told her to be careful of what she wears. That it should be as drab and as ordinary as possible. *Don't stand out.* No pretty summer dress for the sudden surge of spring weather. Nothing bright-coloured. Nothing memorable. If she meets anyone in the lobby or the street, she should be pleasant and smile. She should not walk too fast, or move too slowly.

Be ordinary.

Be one of many.

That is the best way to disappear.

He also told her not to take the same route, that she must do something slightly different every time she makes the trip. So it takes her longer to get to Via Montalcini than it should, and by the time she does get there the food is cold. There are no mouse sounds from the other room. The flat feels abandoned. Antonio looks tired when he opens the door, and for an awful moment, as she steps inside, she thinks: Something terrible has happened. He's choked, or had a heart attack. He's dead. But it

350

isn't that. As she goes into the stuffy little room carrying the plate, the plastic knife and spoon shoved in her pocket, Angela sees that it isn't that at all. Although a part of her thinks it might as well have been.

She hasn't seen him for quite a while and his colour is pallid. Horrible. Aldo Moro's cheeks have stretched downward, and he's grey. His face is grey and his hands are grey and his shirt is dirty. His hair is dishevelled, as if he's been running his hands through it over and over, and although she knows they have allowed him a razor, he hasn't shaved. But for all that, it's his eyes that upset her most. The last time she was here, his smile didn't reach his mouth. Now it doesn't reach his eyes either. They are as dull and still as stagnant water.

She glances over her shoulder. The door is ajar as usual, but she can't see Antonio. She senses that he's not standing guard out in the hall, but has gone somewhere else in the flat. For the first time, she and Aldo Moro are alone together.

'I've brought *parmigiana*,' she says. 'The first aubergines are in.' And she tries to smile, the way she's seen people smile when they are tempting children. But she has never had a child. It strikes her quite suddenly, standing there, that she has never had anyone, not really. Except her father and Antonio.

'If there's something special? Something you'd like me to make?'

She's afraid her voice is shaking. He looks up at her, dully. There are papers scattered across the bed and on the floor. There's no sign of the Lenin books. There are no books at all, just pages and pages of scrawled writing. He's barefoot, and the

351

room is closer and smells worse than usual, as if there might be something wrong with the toilet behind the makeshift screen.

'You have to keep your strength up,' she says. 'You have to eat.'

He stands up, like a child obeying an order, and sways slightly, then looks at her, as if he's just realized that he knows who she is, or has at least seen her before.

'I love my country,' he says suddenly. 'But it, apparently, does not love me.'

'They love you.'

The words are out of Angela's mouth before she even realizes she's said them. He shakes his head. The smile plays around his mouth now, but it's different, like a reflection, as if he's angled a mirror down inside himself.

Angela glances at the door. It's still ajar, and there's still no sign of Antonio. She puts the plate on the table, rustling the papers, pushing a pad aside to cover her words.

'They love you,' she mutters. 'Your family loves you.'

His face sharpens.

'You've seen them?' The question is a hiss, nothing more.

Angela takes the plastic knife and fork out of her pocket.

'Your daughter,' she breathes as she puts them down. 'Your daughter loves you.'

Then she backs out of the room, her heart hammering as if she has just run the fastest mile of her life.

*   *   *

352

That night, Antonio brings his shirt home. Angela washes it, standing at the kitchen sink, rubbing a bar of soap up and down the collar and the cuffs. She rinses it in the plastic bowl and watches the water swirl down the drain. Then she fills the bowl again and does it once more. Finally, the water runs clean, and she finds a hanger and hangs the shirt up in the little bathroom. When she steps out, Antonio is sitting on the rattly old sofa they got in the market for nothing because someone was going to throw it away. He sticks out a foot, in a mock gesture to trip her. She is supposed to stumble and land in his lap, but she doesn't. Instead, she stops and looks at him. He's exhausted. His eyes are red-rimmed.

'Why are you doing this?'

She can hardly believe that the words are coming out of her mouth, but they are, and once they start they don't stop. 'What good is this? What is it for? And you? I don't care about the others. But you. Why? What is it for?'

Antonio looks up at her, and for a second she thinks he isn't going to answer. *Ask me no questions, I'll tell you no lies.* Or that he's going to spout some revolutionary nonsense at her, quote one of the endless statements about the proletariat that the *Brigate Rosse* has been blurting and babbling and hammering everyone with for years. Or perhaps he'll be like Professor Barelli and shout, and thump his hand to make himself right.

But he doesn't. Instead he says, 'You know why.' And Angela feels something inside her crack.

'You can't believe,' she shouts. 'You can't believe that doing this will bring him back.'

353

Antonio is looking at the television, but he isn't seeing it. She knows that. She understands that instead of the endless parade of images— something about car racing and a fire—he's seeing the building out beyond the Darsena with its narrow balcony and the laundry flying like flags from the rails. He's seeing the view from the window of his *nonno*'s farm where the fields are now fallow and the pond overgrown with bullrushes. He's hearing his father's voice, telling him that university is pointless. And Piero's telling him it isn't. And his own voice telling them that they must ask not only for bread, but also for roses.

His hand is clutching and letting go, and clutching again at the old maroon blanket that she keeps folded over the arm of the sofa. Angela kneels on the cushion beside him. Teetering, trying to keep her balance, she puts her arms around him. She holds his head against her shoulder. She presses her fingers into his beautiful black curls and whispers something that is nothing at all, just a sound in the little room.

*   *   *

There Will Be No Secret Negotiations. The Trial of Aldo Moro Has Begun.

It's badly printed and blurry and lying face-up on the desk, but he doesn't seem to care. Today, he is very angry. His voice quavers. Spittle hangs at the edge of his lips.

'They are saying,' he gestures at the newspaper page, 'the government—my friends!—are saying that I was against negotiating for the release of Mario Sossi. They are saying that I didn't agree,

354

and that I wouldn't agree now. It's a lie!' He looks at her, his dark eyes swimming as his voice drops. 'It's a lie. I told them we have to have a heart. We have to compromise. We have to learn to talk to one another or we are lost. It isn't just bullets that kill people. It's silence. Refusing to speak. Sossi's life . . .' His voice drivels off. 'A man's life,' he says a moment later, 'is sacred. It's God's to give and take away. We have no power if we do not have humanity.'

He turns his back on her. Leaves her standing there, holding the plate.

'That's what I told them,' he mutters. 'Anything else is a lie.'

Antonio took his shirt the morning after she washed it. He's wearing it now. Standing this close in the tiny room she can smell the soap, the same bar she used this morning. His shoulders heave, in anger or resignation, she's not sure.

'My family,' he says, and Angela feels her stomach tighten.

As usual, the door isn't quite closed, and also, as usual now, Antonio is not standing right outside. He seems to have decided she doesn't need his protection, that she can be trusted to walk into a space the size of a broom cupboard and give a sixty-year-old man who has no shoes or belt or anything but a pen and papers a plate of food. She can see why. The mention of Mario Sossi's name reminds her of the photographs she saw of him, of how small and inconsequential he looked in his prison. The same thing is happening to Aldo Moro. Once, she had thought that Mara Cagol, the Red Brigades, made people disappear like smoke. *Sparito Nel Nulla!* Now, she understands that it is

355

not that simple. That they do not vanish all at once. Instead, in the shadow of the five-pointed star, they shrink. Shrivel like dying flowers until nothing is left but petals and dust.

'Have you seen them?' The whisper is desperate. As faint as the hiss of air seeping out of a balloon.

Angela shakes her head. She pushes aside a pen, a pad of paper, unlined and unmarked, its pages blank and white and empty, and sets down the plate. She has brought him a blue cloth napkin from the linen she packed up and carried away from Via Vittoria, and she is folding it, and laying out the plastic spoon and fork and knife the same way they do in the trattoria, when his hand closes over hers.

It takes her a moment to understand. He is pushing a scrap of paper into her palm. She doesn't look up. She doesn't meet his eyes as she shoves her hand into her pocket and backs out of the room.

*   *   *

Via del Forte Trionfale 71. Angela is not sure what she expects it to look like, but she understood at once, as soon as she got on the bus home and pulled the smudged tiny scrap out of her pocket, what it was. This is where Aldo Moro lived. This is where his family waits for him.

She had stared at the cramped handwriting, the five words of the address, as the bus lurched along, feeling something like panic, as if he had given her a bomb. A tiny incendiary device that could explode at any moment and ruin her entire life. She'd crumpled it up and held it, balled in her palm until she got off. Then she'd dropped it in the first litter bin she passed and vowed to forget it.

But it was not that simple. The next morning, the words were beaten in the tattoo of her feet as she walked to the dry cleaner's. She heard them in the clink of glasses and the rattle of plates as the tables were cleared at the trattoria after lunch. At the florist's they whispered as the cellophane was wrapped around blooms. *Have you seen my family? Have you seen my family?*

And then, two days later, walking home, there is the newspaper, a special late edition. People are lining up to buy it at the kiosk on the corner. They turn away and open it there on the pavement, read, their heads bent as the pages flutter in the April evening wind.

Angela stops. There was a time when she paid little attention to the papers, when they were a backdrop on the far horizon of her life, removed from everything that counted—her father, the shop, Antonio, Barbara, how fast she could run a mile. Not any more. Now she feels they are written to her. Personal messages that might as well carry her name. She sidles around a large man in a jacket and flat cap until she can see the poster pasted to the kiosk's sign-board, read the ugly black letters:

Red Brigade Communiqué Number 9
The Interrogation of the Prisoner Aldo Moro Has
Been Completed.
There Are No Doubts, Aldo Moro Is Guilty and
Therefore Is Condemned to Death.

When she gets back to the flat, Antonio is not

home. The little flat closes around her, its walls collapsing until it feels no bigger than a broom cupboard. A utility room. One more People's Prison.

Finally, at seven o'clock, Angela snatches her jacket and her purse and runs down the stairs. In the bus shelter, she studies the map. Via Trionfale snakes high above the city, and there, off it, is Via del Forte. She has no idea how long it will take her to get there, or when she will get back.

In the end, she walks what seems a long way. A few times, she stops and looks down at the lights of Rome burning in the spring night. The neighbourhood is unlike anywhere she has ever lived. It is as different from Ferrara and the ghetto and even the Corso d'Este as it is possible to imagine. None of the buildings are old. They look like the shoe boxes out at Darsena, except they are bigger, and set back from the street and most of them have balconies. Greenery flows over the railings and drops like Rapunzel's hair.

Lights glint through the tresses of ivy. Trees cast shadows against the concrete walls. Angela knows when she finally finds the right street because there is a crowd, a blob of people in the soft dark. She can hear them murmuring and shifting, stamping like anxious horses. A line of policemen stands facing them. Several more stand on the pale stone steps of the building. One turns towards the glass door and Angela sees the outline of the gun he carries.

As she sidles into the crowd it becomes clear that most of them are journalists. They rustle and twitter among themselves and strain at the fact that they are not allowed to surge across the street and into the building, ride the lift up and storm the doors of the penthouse flat where someone has muttered that the Moro family is hiding. Angela leans back, cranes upwards. But there is nothing to see, just tiny glints of light escaping through closed shutters.

When a few minutes later a car comes down the street and is waved to the door and a woman gets out, the crowd trembles, taut as hunting dogs. A couple of the journalists shout questions. 'Have you spoken to your mother?' 'Has she had word from your father?' 'Has there been another letter?' The woman runs up the steps, her head bent, and Angela finds herself leaning forward, standing on tiptoe, straining to see her face, and her belly. She is consumed by the idea that if the woman will only look this way, will only stare for a moment into the crowd, their eyes will meet and they will know each other. But when the woman turns at the top of the steps, it is clear she is not pregnant.

She raises a hand. Stillness falls as quickly and completely as if she was the Pope. She doesn't even have to raise her voice.

'Pray for my father,' she says.

*   *   *

It is four days before Angela goes to Via Montalcini again, and in the meantime things become very strange. The President of Italy pleads for Aldo Moro's life. 'A sense of humanity may induce them to a gesture of repentance,' he says. Aldo Moro's wife, Eleonora, goes to a special Mass and kneels side by side with the political leaders she has attacked because they will not bargain,

359

dice and deal with the Red Brigades for the life of her husband.

Watching on TV, Angela studies Signora Moro as she comes out of the church. She has read enough of the papers to gather that it was Agnese she saw on the steps, his daughter who is not pregnant. But other than that, she doesn't know what she's going to say. How she is going to tell him that she saw nothing but a building, a crowd in the dark, some policemen and a woman begging them to pray. Then, it appears she may not get the chance even to do that, because two days after her trip to Via del Forte Trionfale, a reporter at the newspaper *Il Messaggero* receives a telephone call telling him to look in a rubbish bin where he finds a statement entitled *The Trial of Aldo Moro*. The text is intoned on the radio, flashed across the television screen, and printed on front pages, not only in Italy, but around the world.

We announce that we have carried out the execution by suicide of Aldo Moro, President of the Christian Democrats. We consent to the recovery of his body by making known the precise place where it rests. The body of Aldo Moro is immersed on the slimy bottom of Lake Duchessa.

There is footage of helicopters taking off and of commandos standing beside them in the snow of the high Abruzzi, which stretches white and untouched save for the footprints of boar and wolves. Frogmen crack the ice both of Lake Duchessa and of a smaller lake in a neighbouring valley, but the bottoms, though undoubtedly slimy,

360

yield nothing.

*   *   *

'Is it true?' Angela's voice sounds very small, even to her.

Antonio is sitting on the sofa staring at their television, which is always on now, as if the only way they can be sure of what is happening is to see it on the screen. He looks up at her as she speaks and shakes his head. Then, a little to her surprise, he gets up from the sofa and comes and puts his arms around her. It's the first time since the night she shouted at him.

'No, *carina*,' he says. 'It's not true. We don't even know who sent it. It's a fake.'

He smoothes her hair. His hand on her cheek, the feel of his chest and shoulders, his chin as it nudges her forehead is like air. She has been slowly suffocating without it.

'We're not barbarians,' Antonio says. 'No one is going to kill him.'

Angela looks up at him.

'I promise you.' Antonio's lips brush the top of her head. He takes her face in his hands. 'No one is going to kill him. I promise you, *carina*. I promise. But we have to make the threat—to force them. To be recognized. To get their attention. They'll give in,' he says. 'They'll take us seriously. You'll see. They'll give in.'

'And if they don't?'

'They will.' He kisses her. 'They will,' he says. 'We're not the killers. They are.'

*   *   *

361

The next day, when she arrives at the flat, there are the usual mouse sounds, scrabbling and rustling from behind the closed door, as if whoever is in there is burrowing away, afraid of Angela's eyes. Afraid that if she so much as glimpses them they will go up in flames, or fly apart in tiny pieces.

As usual, Antonio is waiting for her. And, as usual, after she has unpacked the basket, he packs it again, loading in two of her baking dishes from previous meals. He goes to the cupboard for a plate and plastic utensils, and she lifts the lid off the top dish and sees that, also as usual, it has not been washed. Lentils in tomato sauce line the bottom, and there are still chunks of onion and pork. Angela lifts one out and eats it absently, watching Antonio as he searches through drawers for the box of plastic spoons.

The taste brings her father back with a jolt. Suddenly she is standing again in the kitchen in Via Vittoria, dicing carrots, the knife rising and falling above the old chopping board while he stands swirling oil in the cast-iron pan, seasoning it with pepper. She eats the remaining two pieces, making sure to catch some of the lentil sauce, wipes her hands, and puts the lid back on the baking dish, which she will have to scrub and scour after she's lugged it home on the bus. So much for proletarian equality. She's half tempted to march over and bang on the closed door. Shout through the keyhole that doing dishes is moral, and thus good for the revolution.

After the plastic spoons are finally located, Angela takes the meal. She watches as Antonio unlocks the door, then steps into the tiny room.

362

The first thing she sees is the front page of the newspaper, carefully clipped and lying on the desk. In the centre of it is a photo of Aldo Moro. Wearing the same white shirt, and freshly shaven, he sits in front of the five-pointed star, holding a copy of the morning edition of *La Repubblica*, which bears the banner headline, *Moro Assassinato*. Moro assassinated. His head is tilted. He has his quizzical little smile on his face, the same one he has now as he sits on his bed watching Angela.

He looks much better than when she saw him last, as if the anger has left him and he has even found this last episode—the slimy lake, the frogmen and helicopters and reports of his 'suicide'—almost funny.

'What have you brought me?' he asks, and it takes her a moment to realize that he is not talking about the bowl of risotto she holds in her hands.

He stands up in his stockinged feet as Angela bends over to put down the bowl. They are so close they are almost touching. The door is ajar. She can hear Antonio in the main room, talking in low tones, presumably to one of the mice who has emerged now she is safely out of sight.

'Agnese,' she whispers, and his hand reaches out and closes over hers.

Angela looks down at the pale, soft nails, the long, elegant fingers and narrow bones so unlike her own father's, and doesn't have the heart to tell him that that's all. That she took the bus and walked up the street and stood in a crowd, and saw nothing except a glimpse of one of his daughters and tiny slats of light escaping through the penthouse shutters.

'And your wife,' she murmurs.

'Noretta?'

The hand tightens. Angela nods. Then she lies. She whispers everything she can remember about Signora Moro from the television. What she was wearing. Her silver hair. Her glasses.

When she stops, his eyes are shiny and far away.

'Your grandchild,' she whispers. 'He's getting bigger and bigger. He's waiting for you to come home.'

'Anna.'

Angela has no idea if this is the pregnant woman's name, but she nods anyway.

'She was wearing a green scarf.'

'Maria Fida, Anna, Agnese, Giovanni,' he whispers.

The names of Aldo Moro's children flutter in the fetid air. Angela nods. He turns away, and she reaches into her pocket and takes out another linen napkin, and a twist of salt that she lays carefully beside the bowl.

'What is your name?'

She looks up. He's watching her. Angela swallows. Part of her would like to, but she can't look away from him.

'Angela,' she whispers.

He nods.

The voices beyond the door have stopped. Angela glances behind her, but before she can turn to leave, he reaches out. His thumb presses her forehead. He makes a small cramped cross, and whispers, 'Don't let them take your heart, Angela.'

*　　　*　　　*

364

The sickness hits her like a punch. By the time she gets home, she is doubled over, can barely creep up the stairs and let herself into the flat. With very few exceptions, Angela had been blessed with rude good health. While other children succumbed to flu, tonsillitis, winter colds, and even things more serious, Angela barely ever spent a day in bed. Once, when she was eight, she had been pushed over playing in Piazza Lampronti and had skinned both knees, got a bloody nose and sprained her wrist, necessitating a week's worth of wearing a brace and much attention from Nonna Franchi, but that was about it. So she is wholly unprepared for the waves of nausea punctuated by pains in her stomach as sharp as knife jabs.

When Antonio comes home and finds her curled up on the sofa, her face pale and sweating, he calls the doctor, a round, smooth-faced man in a suit whose shoes make squeaking sounds and who comes right away and pronounces that she is neither pregnant nor has appendicitis, but has probably 'eaten something that doesn't agree with her', and will almost certainly feel better by morning.

She does, but not much. Antonio goes to explain to the dry cleaner's and the trattoria, which sends him home with a jar of soup, and the florist's, who adds a bouquet of day-old lilies. When he comes back, he holds her hand and smoothes her hair and tells her to sleep and leaves her tucked up on the sofa in the old maroon blanket.

Angela does sleep. Almost as soon as she hears the door close and his footsteps echoing on the stairs, she feels herself sinking, being pulled down into some place so dark and empty it feels like death. She is not alone in this well of dreams. Voices flutter around her—her father's, her mother's, their words fingering her cheeks. She hears the shuffle of worn shoes on cobbles and the rustling of prayers. Once, the darkness parts and she finds herself on Via Vittoria. It is night. The street lamp is hazy and the familiar houses rise on either side of her, cradling her in the deep womb of the ghetto. She stands at the corner and watches while ahead a figure moves away from her, a man whose footsteps ring words she can hear but not make out, and whose shadow looms in a five-pointed star.

She wakes up sweating, and pushes the blanket aside and realizes that it is dark, that the spring night has dropped over Rome. When she sits up, her head swims a little, but not too much. Antonio is not in the flat. Her mouth is dry and her tongue feels swollen. Her bare feet are strange on the floor and unreliable, but she goes into the kitchen nonetheless and makes herself a cup of tea, and opens the window and listens to the horses shuffling in their stables while the last shreds of cloud fade in the sky.

Feeling better, she rinses the tea mug and goes back into the sitting room and turns on the television. A crowd is gathered at St Peter's, a vast dark sea of heads and shoulders sparked by the candles some of them are holding. The Pope has made an appeal.

'I beg you on my knees, free the honourable Aldo Moro, simply, without any conditions, not so much because of my humble and loving intercession, as by virtue of his dignity as a common brother of humanity.'

366

Despite the warm evening, Angela pulls the blanket back over her. This time she is not sure if she sleeps or not. She seems to drift on the noise from the television. Words form and break before she can get hold of them. When Antonio finally comes home, she keeps her eyes closed, her face buried in the cushion. She feels him bend down, brush her hair aside, put his hand on the hot, damp back of her neck. He kisses her shoulder, then turns off the television and goes to sleep in the bedroom.

The Pope's appeal does seem to have some effect. The next day, the Red Brigades issue a specific demand for the first time. They will free Aldo Moro in exchange for thirteen prisoners, among them Mara Cagol's husband and another man who was one of the kidnappers of Mario Sossi.

Aldo Moro writes another letter begging the government to agree. It is delivered in what is now a regular pattern, to Milan, Rome, and Genoa. Angela dreams of this. Of people who look no different to herself dropping his words into dustbins. Slipping them through the open windows of cars. Tucking them into the cracks of phone boxes and shutters of shops.

Let the will of God be done, Aldo Moro writes. *We are almost at Zero Hour, it is more a matter of seconds than minutes from the end. We are at the moment of slaughter.*

*   *   *

It is a few days later when Angela forces herself into the kitchen, when she takes down her knives

367

and strops them on the whetstone and begins to dice the veal that she has asked Antonio to buy.

She is doing this, not because Antonio asked her, but because he has told her that Aldo Moro is refusing to eat anything they bring him. He has accused them of drugging him and trying to poison him, when he will speak to them at all, which is not often now. The government has refused to release any prisoners, and the *Brigate Rosse* are refusing to speak to the Catholic organization Caritas, which has offered to negotiate. Neither side will 'recognize' the other. Neither side will speak to the other. And Aldo Moro's words do nothing. He is caught in the middle, stranded in silence.

Let the will of God be done, his latest letter said. Angela who, unlike him, does not believe in God— or at least a God who, as far as she can see, has any discernible will—considers what this might mean as she adds the tenderest baby carrots, the newest peas, the soft furred shells of tiny artichokes to the oil that is spitting in the pan.

*　　　*　　　*

Via Montalcini feels different from the moment she walks through the door. There is a palpable sense of disarray. Usually, the entrance, the kitchen, which are really all she ever sees, are neat to the point of barren. Now there are books and papers lying about. A huge wicker basket sits by the table. There are glasses and knives and forks and plates in the sink. Antonio has to wash one before she can dish out the veal.

The sauce is heavy and velvety and pale, exactly the way her father taught her to make it, and as a treat she has brought rice too, the thick kind more usually used for risotto that she has steamed so it sticks together. She makes a well of it, and suddenly wishes she had remembered to bring parsley, to sprig the edge and sprinkle across the top.

Angela picks up the plate. Antonio unlocks the door to the little room then turns away and goes back into the kitchen, letting her step inside alone.

He is sitting on his bed, his hands between his knees again, almost exactly the way he was the first time she saw him. She doesn't know if they've taken the razor away or if he has just decided to stop shaving. And possibly stop washing. That's how it smells. She tries not to let this register on her face as she sets down the plate.

'I've brought you veal,' she says. But he doesn't say anything. He doesn't even look at her, or seem to be aware that she is in the same tiny space, that she is standing less than a metre from him.

'I cooked it myself. There's nothing in it.' When he doesn't reply to this, she adds, 'I made it specially. For you.'

Angela lays out the plastic utensils, the napkin, another twist of salt, and still he doesn't look at her. There is no sound from beyond the door. She has no idea where Antonio is, or what he is doing. A pall of helplessness descends over her, thickening the air, making it hard to breathe or move. Finally, she steps around the desk and sits down on the narrow bed beside him. The mattress is thin, and she thinks it must be uncomfortable to lie on for one night, never mind the seven weeks they have kept him here. The fan set high up in the wall has developed a whine.

369

'Your grandchild.' She reaches out and takes his hand, which is limp and alarmingly cool. 'Anna's child,' she says. 'You'll hold him soon. You have to stay strong enough to hold him.'

He shakes his head.

'I'll never hold him. They're going to kill me.'

'They won't kill you. I promise.' Her words are urgent. Sharp, as if she is spitting them. Slapping them into his face the way you slap someone who is fainting. 'They've told me they won't. They won't kill you. I know. I promise. You will go home.'

Something in this seems to touch him. Very slowly, his head swivels. When he looks at her, she realizes he has become familiar, the soft mouth, the folds of skin, the eyes that are black but not like river stones, black instead like midnight.

'You have to try. You have to eat. Please.' Her pleading melds with the high-pitched mew of the fan. 'You have to try. What is your favourite? What do you eat at home, with your family? Tell me, and I'll make it. I'll bring it to you. No one else will touch it. I promise.'

'Do you know what I miss?' he asks, and when she shakes her head she is sure he is going to say his children, or his wife, or all of them—his family. But he doesn't. Instead, he says, 'The sky. It has been forty-eight days since I have seen the sky.' He smiles. 'Angela.' She feels a slight, returning pressure on her hand. 'Tell me,' he says. 'Tell me what the sky looks like today.'

So she does.

She whispers that it is very blue, because there are no clouds at all. That in the morning it was as pale as the veins that run under a child's skin, and that now it is darker, more like the breast of a bird,

370

the kind you see in paintings, and that at sunset it will turn the colour of the inside of shells.

When she stops talking, he nods.

'Thank you,' he says, and she realizes he is crying, that thin glassy tears are running down into the folds of his whiskered cheeks. 'Come to my funeral, Angela,' he whispers. 'I only want people who love me to come to my funeral.'

*   *   *

When Angela leaves the room, she is shaking. She feels weak and sick again, and it takes her a moment to realize that no one is there. That Antonio is not sitting at the kitchen table. That he doesn't get up and come to the little room and turn the battery of locks.

She stands, confused for a moment, then she notices that the door to the room off the kitchen is open too, and that there is no noise coming from inside. She tiptoes over and peers in, her heart banging as if she expects a giant hand to reach out and grab her. Inside, she sees mattresses and stacks of books and clothes hung over chairs. She turns back to the kitchen. Sun is pouring through the huge window over the sink and spilling onto the unswept floor.

Angela whirls around. Before she knows what she is doing, she is back in the horrid, stuffy utility room. She is taking his hand. She is pulling him up off the little bed, and dragging him past the desk to the open door.

He comes with her obediently, shuffling in his stockinged feet. Angela pauses, listens. But there's nothing. So she leads him out, and into the kitchen, where they stand there like children, holding hands and staring out of the window.

There's a park across the street. They can see the feathery tops of the trees and a single puff of cloud, the kind Nonna Franchi used to tell her were angel's kisses. He turns his face towards the sunlight that hits the dirty dishes and the rimes of food and the glasses that have lip marks on them, and as he does Angela looks behind them towards the entry hall and the front door, which she realizes is ajar.

She has no idea where Antonio has gone, but she knows the way out of here. She knows the lift—she could push the button in her sleep. She knows how many steps it is to freedom.

Without quite being sure of what she is doing, she walks into the hallway. She can see a sliver of the landing. No shadows fall across the floor. The only sound is her breath, and the scrabble of her heart.

She has begun to turn around, begun to go back, and grab his hand, and lead him to the lift, when footsteps sound on the stairs.

*　　　*　　　*

The door flies open and a man Angela has never seen before strides in. He is shorter than Antonio and has dark hair and glasses and is wearing a striped shirt with a linen jacket over it and is walking so fast he almost slams into her. For a moment, they stand paralysed, staring at each other. Then he shoves past her into the kitchen, swearing as he bangs against the wicker basket.

Angela feels her head spin. People say that, but

372

this time it's true. She will say . . . she will say—she has no idea what she will say. Then it flicks across her mind that there are two of them and one of him, and if they are quick, if they can find a knife or—

But the kitchen is empty. The spot in front of the sink where Aldo Moro had been standing, his face bathed in sunlight, his eyes fixed on the trees and the puff of cloud, is filled only by dust motes that dance and drift and land on the floor beside a smattering of crumbs and a crumpled ball of paper.

The man she doesn't know is already round the corner. She follows him in time to see, even before he reaches for the handle, that the utility room door is closed.

When he opens it, Aldo Moro is sitting at the desk. He has a plastic fork in his hand, has speared a piece of veal, and looks up, head tilted, smile quizzical. His eyes meet Angela's. Then the door is slammed and the locks are turned.

*   *   *

'God damn it!' the man explodes at Antonio as he walks into the hallway. 'Where the hell were you?'

Antonio shrugs.

'An alarm went off, in the garage. I went down to check.' He takes a gun out of his pocket and places it on the table. 'It's OK,' he says, nodding towards Angela. 'You can trust her. I told you. Nothing happened, right?'

'She didn't lock the door.'

Both of them are talking about her as if she isn't there, as if she isn't standing near them. Antonio shrugs again.

373

'I'm sure she was about to.' He comes and puts his arm round her. 'Weren't you?' he says, and from the pressure of his hand, from the rigid way he is standing, she realizes that whoever this man is, Antonio hates him.

She nods. Antonio leans down and kisses the top of her head.

'You can trust her,' he says again. 'I told you.'

*   *   *

She leaves a few minutes later, carrying the basket, the cloth folded over the top of it. As soon as she gets into the lobby, even that feels heavy. It must show on her face, because Antonio, who has come down in the lift with her, says, 'Don't mind him. He's an asshole.'

She nods. She wants to ask about the gun. She wants to know how long he has been carrying it, and if he always sat out there with it, if the trigger was unlocked and his finger was on it while she was laying out plastic knives and forks and whispering the names of Aldo Moro's children. She wants to ask what he would have done if . . .

But she doesn't. Instead, she smiles and lets him kiss her and tell her he'll see her tonight, before she walks back out onto the street where the sun hits her like a slap and makes her eyes water and where she starts to shake so badly that as soon as she gets round the corner she has to cross to a bus stop and sit down on the bench and put her head between her knees.

*   *   *

374

April is over. Angela's twentieth birthday is coming up. Four days before it, on Sunday morning, Antonio says he has a surprise. He is going to take her to Ostia.

'But we have no car.'

The little Fiat broke down some time ago, shortly after they arrived in Rome. They sold it to a junk dealer because they couldn't afford to fix it and, as Antonio said, you don't need a car in the city anyway. He beams at her across their rickety table that even putting coins under the legs won't fix.

'Yes, we do,' he says. 'For today.'

It is a red Renault, and Antonio has already put everything they will need into it. Her basket that he has packed with a bottle of wine and glasses and food for a picnic. Their swimming things, rolled in towels. He has even bought her a new pair of sunglasses, fancy ones she admired once in a magazine. They are in a case on the passenger seat with a ribbon tied around them. At the last minute, as he is starting the car, Angela shouts, 'Wait, there's something we've forgotten!' And runs back inside and upstairs and grabs the old maroon blanket so they will have something to sit on at the beach.

The road to Ostia is straight and feels as if it runs slightly downhill, unspooling like a long grey ribbon. They turn on the radio and sing along. Antonio reaches out and takes her hand and squeezes it, and for the first time in a long while they feel as if they are themselves again. As they drive away from Rome, the last fifty days melt. Flake away. Angela leans back in the seat and thinks that this is how she used to feel when she ran.

At the ancient port, which is now not very near the sea in much the same way that Ferrara's Darsena is not very near the Po, they park under the pine trees and wander among the ruins of the Roman city. They walk into houses, step over crumbled walls into people's kitchens and bedrooms and store rooms. They lean down and trace the outlines of mosaics of dolphins and sea monsters and ships and climb up the steps and sit on the warm stone seats of the amphitheatre. Then they get back in the car, and follow the river to the sea.

The blanket is spread on the soft loamy earth where the pines meet the sand. They change behind their towels and run holding hands into the soft sloppy waves. Antonio swims and dives, while Angela only paddles up to her waist, until he attacks her from behind and pulls her under, sucking her down like a sea creature. Later they drink the wine, and stretch out on the blanket feeling the sun dapple their wet skin. Antonio rolls over lazily and licks the inside of her arm and the well of her collarbone. His tongue is warm and smooth and when he kisses her, his lips are salty.

'I love you, Angela,' he says. And a little later he takes her hand, and presses her palm to his mouth. Then he reaches back into the basket and pulls out a tiny box.

The ring is gold, a very thin band with a tiny emerald, her birthstone, set into it. Antonio slides it onto her left hand. Then he folds her fingers around it and says, 'Marry me.'

And Angela says, 'Yes.'

And despite everything that has happened in the last weeks, she thinks she has never been more happy in her life.

*　　　*　　　*

There's traffic, and the drive home takes longer than they would like. So by the time they get back to Trastevere it feels like it has been forever since they last felt each other's skin, disappeared inside each other's taste and touch. When they finally find a parking place and get back to their building they are so impatient that they run inside and upstairs, and it is only late at night, after Angela has fallen asleep and woken up and they have made love again, that she remembers that although they grabbed the basket and the beach towels, they have left the blanket, covered in sand, in the back of the red Renault. She means to fetch it the next morning. But when she wakes up, Antonio is already gone and the car is gone with him.

*　　　*　　　*

Monday passes in a blur. Angela has time to make up at her jobs from when she was sick. Antonio has said he will take her ring, some time next week, and have it engraved with the date, 7 May 1978, and she decides that she will not tell anyone they are getting married—not that she has anyone to tell except the dry cleaner and the florist and the man who owns the restaurant—until after. Until she can put it on her finger and never take it off.

Somewhere in the back of her head, she knows that what she really means by this is, 'until after all of this is over'. Until the mice decide they have tortured the country and extracted their pound of

377

flesh from Aldo Moro and they let him go and dismantle the People's Prison, and the flat on Via Montalcini is no more. She senses that this will be soon—that that is why Antonio has asked her to marry him now. That it's his way of telling her that any day they will have their own lives back, their own future, and that all of this, whatever it was, will be nothing but a bad dream. In the meantime, she threads the ring onto her gold chain and wears it with her locket, next to her heart.

That night, Antonio brings her a bouquet. Pink roses. She knows they are a few days old—this is the bad side of working at the florist's, she understands which blooms get discounted and when and will never look at bouquets with the same eye again—but she doesn't care. They are the first flowers he has ever brought her. She puts them in water with a crushed-up aspirin—another recently acquired nugget of wisdom, along with how to fold clothes and napkins—and makes him a special dinner. They share a bottle of wine and talk about when they will go to Mestre to tell his parents, and do not even turn on the television. The next morning, Tuesday 9 May, Antonio gets up very early. Angela looks at the clock, and sees that it is just after six. Half-asleep, she hears him in the kitchen. Before he leaves, he comes back to the bedroom and kisses her, and holds her face in his hands, and whispers, 'I love you, Angela Vari.'

*   *   *

It is seven hours later, just after half past one that afternoon, and Angela is sitting in the back room at the florist's trying to understand how things

378

could possibly have got so out of control, how this mushroom cloud could have grown quite so fast and under her very nose, when a woman screams.

The sound is high and shrill, and by the time Angela and the florist have rushed out of the shop and into the tiny piazza that fronts it, it has wound down to a kind of keening wail. A crowd is bunched around the fountain, and within seconds the wailing grows as if it is being passed from person to person.

'What? What?' people are asking.

A man turns away, his face ashen, his hands twisting.

'They've done it,' he says. He stares blankly at Angela and the florist, who is now clutching Angela's sleeve. 'They've done it,' he says again. 'They've murdered Aldo Moro.'

*   *   *

Angela can't move. At first, she hadn't believed it. She found herself shaking her head, saying first to herself, and then out loud and over and over again, 'No, it's not true. It's not true. No, it's not true.'

But it is. And now she knows it because she is standing in front of an electronics shop with a clutch of other people watching the television footage from Via Caetani, where at one o'clock this afternoon the body of Aldo Moro was found.

There is footage of the street, which is clogged with people and policemen and Carabinieri. There is a blurred shot of an ambulance flying by, and the high *whoo-whoo* of sirens. And then, there is a colour photograph. It was taken by a photographer called Gianni Giansanti, who looks no older than

379

Angela is and caught the break of his life when he happened to be around the corner at 1 p.m.

Gianni Giansanti is still talking about this, describing how he had his camera and turned and sprinted, when the photograph he took fills the screen.

Aldo Moro lies in the boot of a car, his head twisted on his shoulder. He is unshaven and wearing his navy blue three-piece suit, the trousers he always had on and the jacket and waistcoat Angela saw that first day draped neatly over the back of his chair. He has been shot ten times in the chest. One of his hands is curled like a baby's over his heart. Several policemen are trying to stop people getting too close to the open back of the red Renault. A Carabinieri officer is reaching for the edge of the maroon blanket that Aldo Moro is lying on, and that has obviously been his shroud.

*   *   *

The street tilts. Angela reaches for the wall of the shop, but she doesn't feel the rough brick beneath her hand. Instead she feels the worn wool that all her life was folded at the foot of her parents' bed. That she slept coddled in for the weeks and months after her father died. That Antonio covered her with when she was sick. That he lay her on while he licked the sea from her skin, and kissed her. That she felt rough and sandy against the back of her legs as he opened the little box and slid the ring onto her finger and asked her to marry him. The maroon blanket that, in her fever for him, she forgot to bring in from the back of the red Renault they drove to Ostia.

There's a dustbin a few steps away. Angela's lucky to get to it in time. When she does, she's sick. Once. Twice. And again.

*   *   *

Via del Forte Trionfale is a river of light. A thousand flames, perhaps more, flicker from the candles that the silent crowd stands holding. Stars, fallen to earth and burning for the memory of Aldo Moro.

Already, posters are tied to railings and the backs of benches and the sides of rubbish bins. Some have flowers looped through the strings and ribbons that hold them in place. Aldo Moro's face stares out from them. Underneath are printed the words, *Egli Vivrà Nei Nostri Cuori.* He will live in our hearts.

The family have issued only one statement: that they do not wish for any officials, any members of political parties to be present at his funeral. In the early hours of the morning, it begins to rain. People tent the candles with their hands trying to keep them from going out. Some sputter and die anyway. Some people melt away. But many stay, standing mute and wet, their mere presence the strongest rejection of the proletarian revolution— of the communiqués, and '*gambezzati*-ing', and ranting, and bullets—that they can think of. Angela looks at their faces and feels his thumb on her forehead.

Near dawn, as it begins to rain harder, a ripple runs through the crowd. The funeral has been moved forward. He will be buried today in Torrita Tiberina, where the family has a country house.

Angela has no idea where this is, but she knows she is going there. She takes one last look at the closed shutters of the top-floor flat. They are shiny in the first grey light. Today the sky will not be the colour of a baby's veins, or of a bird's breast, or of shells. Rain pours off the balconies, tangling the long strands of ivy, and tips into the street, and flows like a river to Rome.

*   *   *

Angela finds an open bar, buys herself a coffee and a roll and sits at a table by the window looking at nothing. When the kiosk next door opens, she gets a map and a bus plan. Torrita Tiberina is not so easy to get to. It takes her almost three hours. When she arrives, she realizes she is not alone. His family has said they do not want any outpourings, any national demonstrations of grief. Even so, bunches of people stand outside the church. They watch as the pale wood coffin is carried inside, and follow at a distance like wary sheep as it makes its way to the cemetery. Later, Angela will read that crowds gathered at crossroads and threw hydrangeas into the path of the funeral cortege. That when it stopped at a light, a truck driver climbed down from his lorry, and hurried across three lanes of traffic to press his lips to the side of the hearse.

After the prayers have been said and the coffin has been placed in the vault, there is nothing left to do. Angela doesn't even have any flowers to leave and she knows she has missed the last bus. In no particular hurry to begin the long walk, she stands in the cemetery and watches as the family files away—Anna, Agnese, Giovanni, Maria Fida. The names that fluttered in that tiny awful room, their wings beating the stagnant air.

*　　*　　*

Monica Ghirri stopped at a bar after the funeral. She had thought Giovanni would say she was crazy, last night when she insisted on going and standing outside the building on Via del Forte Trionfale, but he didn't. Ever since that terrible March morning he has been quieter, and more understanding. She knows that he has always loved her, just as she has always loved him, even if the spark between them died some time ago. Two children, jobs, bills, schools, in-laws, will do that for a couple. But since the kidnapping, since that morning she stood on the pavement and watched five men die and another vanish, something new has flowed between them. An unspoken anguish. A sadness that dwells somewhere beyond the realm or remedy of words. It's like an underground river they find themselves in, side by side up to their knees, steadying each other, and that Monica suspects may, in fact, be nothing more than the underpinning of life. So, when she said she needed to go to Via del Forte, and then this morning announced that she was taking the car and driving to Torrita, her husband didn't argue or ask why. He just said he'd take care of the children.

She closes her eyes and remembers that the first thing she thought was, *Fireworks*. Then she realized fireworks didn't go off on Thursday mornings in March in the middle of Rome.

She opens her eyes, but she can still see it.

Sometimes, she's afraid she'll never stop seeing it—the driver sprawling into the road, his hands flying up, as the car's back door is yanked open and a man wearing a black suit and clutching papers is dragged out. Then, as they pull him forward, his head jerks up, and his eyes meet hers.

Monica dreams of those eyes. They are still and dark as night, and in her dreams he looks at her and silence ticks like a clock and she realizes that his suit was not black, but dark blue, and that his hair is a crinkly iron-grey touched with silver. And that his lips are moving. That, as they drag him away, he is speaking. To her.

Then she wakes. She bolts upright, her hands wound in the sheets, lips cottony and tongue swollen and tears running down her face because he was trying to tell her something. But between the breaking glass and the bullets and the screaming, she couldn't hear him.

She knocks back the brandy that came with her coffee, and wonders what she's going to do. Not in the next ten minutes, or half hour, or hour after that—that's simple. She'll get in the car and drive home. Make dinner. Tuck in her kids, maybe read them a story. No, what she means is what is she going to do in the next day, and week, and day after that? Because since the moment she saw Aldo Moro dragged from his car, since the second he looked up at her, and their eyes met, and his lips moved, since then she has felt his heart beat inside her.

Sometimes she was sure she heard his voice. Felt his hunger, or anguish, or exhaustion. She marked the days on a calendar. Every one. All fifty-four of them. She read every word that was printed, all the letters in the newspapers.

I am a prisoner.
I kiss you for the last time.
Give a kiss to the children.
We are almost at Zero Hour.

And now he's dead. And there is nothing but a dull, reverberating emptiness.

Monica stands and takes her bag off the table. She brushes spilled sugar from the strap. She pushes the door open and hears the voices in the small fuggy bar cut off as it snaps closed. Her umbrella wasn't much use at the cemetery; the shoulders of her coat and her blouse are soaked. There doesn't seem much point in hurrying as she makes her way to the car.

The heater fogs up the windscreen. Waiting for it to clear, Monica turns on the radio. Then she can't stand it and turns it off again. She isn't sure what they are having for dinner. Perhaps she ought to stop and get something. She can't remember what's in the refrigerator. The wipers snap back and forth. If anything, it's raining harder now. She turns the defroster up to a roar and watches as the little puddle of clear glass spreads slowly upwards. When she can see, she pulls out and winds her way through the narrow streets. She's gone a few miles when she sees the girl.

Hunched, hands in pockets, plodding along the side of the road, she's so wet that her dark hair is plastered to her skull. She doesn't even look up when Monica pulls out to pass her. All the same, Monica recognizes her. She saw her last night at Via Forte, and again outside the church. A fellow pilgrim.

Monica pulls into the side of the road, stops, and

385

watches the blurred figure get larger and larger in the rearview mirror. The girl doesn't run, or even look up, or seem to care that the car is there. Finally, Monica has to roll down the window and call out to her, or else, she'd walk right by.

'*Ciao! Ciao*, hello!' she calls. 'I was at the funeral. Can I give you a lift?'

*   *   *

The voice startles Angela. She slips on the muddy verge and puts her hand on the car to steady herself. The Mercedes is warm and steaming, as if it's alive.

'I'm sorry?'

The window is half open, rain spattering in, and the woman is talking to her, maybe asking directions. She's small and doll-like and blonde, with curly hair not unlike Angela's own.

'A lift,' the woman says. 'I'm going back to Rome. I saw you, last night. And at the funeral. Can I give you a lift?'

Angela is about to shake her head, to say no, she's fine, even if she isn't, or if she doesn't know what she is, when she hears something in the woman's voice. The offer is less a question than a plea. Angela frowns. Her brain doesn't seem to be working correctly. *Don't let them take your heart, Angela*. She hears his voice all the time now.

'I'm very wet.'

She looks beyond the woman to the car's leather seats, to its fancy interior, with wood on the dashboard. She has never ridden in a car like this, and surely, soaked as she is, she'll ruin it. The woman shakes her head, she actually lets out a

386

little laugh that seems almost relieved.

'Well, it's raining,' she says. 'It would be strange if you weren't.' Then she leans over and opens the passenger door. 'Come on, get in.'

So Angela does. The seat cradles her like a hand. She places her muddy, squidgy shoes carefully on the navy-blue carpet and puts her soaking bag beside them, which seems like the best place for it. When she closes the door, the car surges forward without a sound.

At first, Angela doesn't dare lean back against the padded headrest but then, little by little, as the heat courses through her, she can't help herself. Rain streams down the windows. The clack and slap of the wipers pushes time away. Angela closes her eyes and feels like she's melting. She is almost asleep when the woman says, 'I saw it.'

Angela looks at her.

'I saw it,' the woman says again. She glances at Angela, then back to the road where a truck is putting on its lights, slowing for a puddle that has spread like a lake across the tarmac.

'When they took him. I was there. On the pavement, beside the bus stop. I'd just taken my kids to school.' She shakes her head and laughs, then reaches up and wipes her cheek with one of her tiny hands, and Angela realizes she's crying.

'I was just standing there, you know, waiting to cross the street—we live right opposite—and I saw the cars, the accident. When they stopped and made his car run into them. And I remember, I just thought, Oh, how stupid. Bad drivers are so careless. Then there was shooting.'

They've slowed to a crawl, are nosing their way through the grey sheets of rain, following the red wolf eyes of the truck.

'I'd never heard a gun go off before,' the woman says a second later. 'I thought it was fireworks. Isn't that stupid? Isn't that the stupidest thing you've ever heard? Fireworks at nine in the morning. But now, I hear them all the time. Every bang. Even if it's just a door slamming, I think it's a gun. And I see it, those men dying. I see it every day. Isn't that crazy?' She glances at Angela again. 'That's crazy, isn't it?' she repeats. 'That's what crazy people do. Play films in their heads like that. Over and over and over.' Damp curls bounce and cling to her cheek. 'They didn't even have time to get out of the cars. Those men. Only one. He fell, and lay there in the road. His blood . . .'

Tears are streaming down her face now. They hit the high collar of the silk blouse that pokes above the neck of her coat. Ahead of them, the truck has cleared the lake puddle. As they drive through, Angela feels the Mercedes' tyres slip, then take. A fin of spray rises up.

'They just reached in and took him,' the woman says. 'As though they had the right. Just to take him like that. Pull him off the face of the earth because they wanted to. And, you know the strangest thing? He didn't even fight. Or try to get away. He didn't do anything. Except look at me.'

They have come into a town. There is a sign Angela can't read, partly because it's graffitied and partly because of the rain. Grimy buildings, their windows black and slick, slide by.

'He looked at me,' the woman says. 'And since then, nothing's been right. Nothing. Because he said something to me. And I keep thinking, I'm certain, that he was asking, begging me, to stop it.

388

To save him. But I couldn't.' She takes a breath and her voice drops. 'I couldn't,' she says. 'I was standing right there, but I couldn't do anything. Nothing. Nothing at all. And now they've killed him. I'm sorry.'

She reaches out and touches Angela's thigh, her jeans that are so wet they're a second skin.

'I'm sorry,' she says again, looking back at the road. 'It's just, you were there. You know? Like me. Last night. And at the funeral. It's good to talk to someone who . . .' She shakes her head. 'I'm forty years old. I have a husband and two children, and I can't stop. I dream about it, every night.' She puts both hands on the wheel and frowns as her voice breaks again. 'I couldn't hear him. I couldn't do anything. I couldn't do anything at all, to stop it.'

'No one could have stopped it.'

Angela's voice sounds strange and far away. Hollow, as if it's coming from a tunnel somewhere deep inside her. 'No one could have stopped it,' she says again. 'No one could have saved him.'

'What kind of people?' The woman shakes her head. 'What kind of people do that?'

Her voice chokes off, replaced by ragged breathing, as though she's been held underwater.

'I'm sorry,' she says again. 'I'm sorry.' Then she pushes her hand through her hair and makes an effort to smile. 'Where would you like to go?'

They have reached the outskirts of Rome. Torrita is only thirty-five miles north of the city, nothing in a car. What took hours this morning, changing buses and waiting for new ones, has flashed by in barely thirty minutes. Angela looks at her and almost laughs. Then she realizes she can't

389

say 'nowhere', and feels a faint nudge of panic.

'Anywhere,' she says. 'Anywhere is fine.' The woman looks as if this is the wrong answer.

'I can get a bus,' Angela adds. 'Now I'm back in the city.'

'But, I can drive you. Really. It's not a problem.'

'No.' Angela shakes her head. 'I'd like to be alone for a while,' she adds. 'You know, before I go home.'

The woman nods, but even as she says it, Angela knows it isn't possible. That she no longer has a home. She wonders if she ever did. Or if the last few months have just been borrowed, weren't really ever part of her life at all. Is that what Antonio planned, somehow, from the very beginning? From that day in the orchard? That it would always be like this? She reaches into her jacket and feels through the soaked cotton of her shirt, her fingers finding the hard nub of the ring that hangs around her neck, no date engraved inside the band. She wonders when he bought it. Or if it was borrowed too, like the red Renault.

They have come into the city and are winding through the modern expensive suburbs with their balconies and concrete walls and trees. Looking out of the window, Angela half expects the phone box to flash by. To see a woman wearing a green scarf, life swelling inside her as she hurries down the pavement, clutching a box of words.

'I'm sorry?'

The woman has said something to her, but she has no idea what it was.

'I live just here. Up the street. Look.' They have stopped at a light. 'If you'd like to come in?' The woman looks at her, her blue eyes searching

Angela's face. 'If you'd like to get dry, have a meal. Or, if I can help you. I could . . .'

Angela looks out and sees a sign that says Via Stresa. Another says Via Fani. Across the street a triangular neon light spelling *Bar, Tavola Calda,* sparkles in the rain.

'This is fine.' She picks up her sodden bag. 'Here is fine. Anywhere.' Angela looks across at the shelter. 'I can get a bus.'

The woman nods, reluctantly.

'Well, OK,' she says. 'If you're sure.'

Angela opens the Mercedes' door.

'Thank you.' She gets out, feeling her shoes squelch with rain. Then, before she closes the door, she leans back into the car. 'The men?' Angela asks. She can feel traffic behind them, sense the light about to change. 'The men who took him, that day. Did you see them?'

The woman nods. The look in her eyes suggests she has seen them every day and probably most nights since.

'They were dressed as Alitalia stewards,' she says. 'You know, in the uniform. One had a moustache and glasses. The other was taller. Quite a lot taller. Dark hair.'

'Was it curly?'

The light has changed. A scooter shoots by. A car hoots.

'I'm sorry.' The woman leans towards the open door. 'I didn't hear—'

'I asked—' Angela smiles. 'It doesn't matter,' she says, and closes the car door.

The woman is staring at her through the window. She is saying something. Then another car hoots, and another, and finally she is forced to move off.

Angela watches the Mercedes turn into Via Fani, and then turn again, and slide into the mouth of the garage below the building on the corner.

She stands there for some time, on the far side of the stream of traffic, looking at the last things he saw before he was pulled out of the world and dropped into the People's Prison. The buildings are tall and dull. There are some magnolia trees in bloom. Oleander leaves drip beside the bus stop. A few ragged fingers of late Forsythia reach through a fence. She seems to remember reading somewhere, in a magazine or the newspaper, that on the morning of 16 March the sun was shining. She might be making that up, but she hopes it's true.

The light changes and changes again before she finally crosses the street and stops at the memorial to the five bodyguards. She is a little surprised that she can recite their names: *Oreste Leonardi, Domenico Ricci, Giulio Rivera, Raffaele Iozzino, Francesco Zizzi.* The tide of flowers has receded, but the cross she saw on TV is still there. And the beret, the medals with their faded ribbons pinned to its brim. A few remaining bouquets are piled on the pavement, some newer than others. Rain beads on their cellophane wrapping. The flashing neon sign from the bar across the street catches the drops and makes them glitter. Red. Pink. Green. Red. Pink. Green.

*   *   *

Angela doesn't know how long she sits at the bus stop. Later, when they ask her—because they ask her every tiny thing, even the most embarrassing,

392

even the most intimate things—she can't tell them. Just as she can't tell them what time, exactly, it is when she gets up and walks down the street. It is certainly after dark, certainly after the time when Antonio will be back in the little flat, will be turning on the television and wondering where she is and what has become of her. Or perhaps he already knows, and the flat is empty, and after he kissed her and held her face in his hands and told her he loved her, he never planned on coming back there again. She doesn't know. Any more than she knows if he stood at the bus stop in a stolen airline uniform, or if he pulled a trigger, and if so, which one. Which bullet he fired. All of them? Any of them? None of them? It doesn't matter. Any more than it matters that she believed him when he promised her Aldo Moro wouldn't die.

The rain has eased. It falls in showers now, bursting and splatting as the wind picks up. Angela reaches inside her collar. She feels for the clasp her father's fingers could not manage and undoes the gold chain. The locket is soft. She slides the ring over it, feeling the sharp edges of the stone, then reclasps the necklace and tucks it away.

The tiny emerald winks in the light of a passing car.

I couldn't stop it, the woman with the blue eyes said. I couldn't save him. And Angela had replied from far away, No one could have stopped it. No one could have saved him.

But that was a lie.

It isn't just bullets that kill people. It's silence.

All it would have taken was a phone call. An anonymous note. *Via Montalcini.* Two words for a man's life.

Angela leans forward and drops the ring into the gutter. For a split-second, the gold glints. Then it is sucked into the thin dark torrent that runs down the storm drain.

*   *   *

The officer on desk duty looks up as the door swings open. It's been a long, bad day in a string of what now seem to be endless long, bad days, and he hopes, he really hopes, that this woman isn't another nutcase who has come down here to tell him she's had a dream and knows where the kidnappers' prison is, or that Aldo Moro is sending her secret messages spelled out in the hairs in her curlers, or that she's always thought that jerk Guido her sister married was strange and there's something they should know. It's happened in police stations all over the city, but especially here, so close to Via Fani. Then, with something that feels like a punch, he remembers that it probably won't happen much any more. And if anything, that's worse.

She's very young, this one, and soaked to the skin, and looks confused, standing there clutching her bag.

'Can I help you?' he asks, and she looks at him as though she's surprised he's here. 'Signorina?' he asks again, and begins to wonder if something really bad has happened to her. Or if this is one for the city bin—not that they're mutually exclusive.

'Signorina?'

She steps across to the desk, still clutching the bag, places her free hand, her left one, flat on the wooden surface and studies her fingers, which are bare—no rings—and look cold and white. When she finally looks up, the expression in her eyes is enough to make him reach down and feel for the butt of his gun.

'Can I help you?' he asks again.

And he's about to push the button under the counter, get some help for himself, when, finally, she nods, and says, 'I killed Aldo Moro.'

PART FIVE

FERRARA

2010

TUESDAY 9 FEBRUARY

Anna woke with a start. Her head was on a pillow, her hands underneath it. There was the garish blue and green stripe of a quilt, a piece of blue carpet. For a moment, she didn't understand. Then she remembered, and sat up.

Enzo Saenz was sitting on the opposite bed, watching her. Something told her he'd been sitting there all night.

'Are you hungry?'

Anna ran her hands through her hair, catching the tangles in the ends, looked at the red chafe marks on her wrists, and nodded.

'I think so. I'm not sure.'

It was tempting to add, 'I'm not sure of anything.' Shards of dreams—of the inside of her father's ruined shop, of the bicycle with the tortuous seat, of the long, pale road stretching through nothingness and the *crack-crack* of bullrushes as the bird rose out of them—glittered around her. She heard her own voice calling for Antonio, then winding through the dark as she sat here on this bed, telling everything to this man she didn't even know. Letting it spill through her as if a dam had finally given way.

She felt dizzy. And must have looked it, because he was off the bed, shoving her head between her knees, the palm of his hand on the back of her neck.

'Breathe,' he said. 'Just breathe.'

And she did. But not fast enough to stop the tears.

'It's going to happen again, isn't it?'

'No. No, it isn't.' He crouched in front of her. His hands were on her shoulders now, bracing her the way you might brace a wall or a fence that's about to tip over on top of you. 'We can stop it,' he said. 'This time we can stop it.' She looked at him. 'Listen to me,' Enzo Saenz said. 'You have to tell me about the phone call. From Antonio. You have to tell me everything about it. Everything. There's only been one, is that right?'

She nodded. 'At the Excelsior. During breakfast. After I left the message on Kristen's phone.'

'Tell me,' Enzo said. 'Tell me exactly what he said.'

Anna closed her eyes, felt the phone in her hand. She heard the chink of silver and glasses, the tap of footsteps on the marble floor.

'I'll kill her, carina. *If you say a word, just one, this time, to anyone, I'll kill her. Do you believe me?'* he'd asked. *'Do you think I'm lying?'* And she'd said, *'No.'* No, she didn't think he was lying. *'Good. Then come and find me. Because I love you. I have always loved you.* Per sempre, carina. *And you owe me. You owe me a life.'*

'He wouldn't let me talk to Kristen.' Anna took a breath. 'He said I had to believe him, that she was alive. He said it was just between us, him and me this time, and that if I said anything to anyone, he'd kill her. He said I should turn my phone on twice a day, at seven and seven, to see if I had a message from him. Then he'd laughed, and said he'd come to find me when he left Padua, and now I had to come and find him.' She opened her eyes. 'When I asked him how Kristen was, if she was all right, he said she wanted her teddy bear. That's

400

why—'

Enzo reached up and blotted the tears that were running down her cheek. He no longer thought she was lying. About anything. He had already called Pallioti and told him as much while she had been asleep.

'It's all right,' he said. 'That's why you brought the bear. OK. What else?' He studied her face. 'Antonio said something else, didn't he?'

She nodded.

'He said he loved me, and that I owed him a life.'

'And?'

Anna's eyes slid away. Enzo could feel it, this last, crucial thing, stuck in her throat like a bone.

'Anna, I can't help you if you don't tell me.'

She looked back at him.

'He asked me if this time I believed him, because he lied to me, about killing Moro, and I said "yes". And then he said to punish me for what I'd done, to make sure I worked hard, I had a deadline.'

'A deadline?'

She nodded.

'They were always doing that. In their stupid communiqués. They were always setting deadlines. If something didn't happen by such and such a time, they'd kill Sossi, or they'd kill Moro or—'

'He'll kill Kristen?'

Anna nodded. Enzo felt himself go cold.

'When, Anna?' he asked. 'When is the deadline?'

'A week. Antonio said it was a gift, that it was that long. He said I had a week, then he'd kill her.'

*   *   *

While Anna Carson took a shower, Enzo called

401

Pallioti again. Then, after he had brought him up to date and Pallioti had announced he was on his way to Ferrara, Enzo called room service and ordered breakfast, and tried not to think about Anna Carson's naked body behind the flimsy door barely a metre from him.

He was not a tactile person—even with his nearest and dearest. He did not much like being touched, and he did not make a habit of dispensing physical reassurance, the pat on the hand or arm around the shoulder that came so easily to the James MacCreadys of this world. So the fact that, after she had spat out the words 'a week' and burst into tears, he had gathered Anna Carson into his arms like—well, he wasn't sure like what, disturbed him. The fact that he had enjoyed it—the weight of her against him, the smell of her hair and skin, even the damp soaking on his shoulder—disturbed him even more. He was exhausted, he thought. Both of them were. That explained it. What they needed was food. And coffee. And a table. Something large and solid between them.

Behind the door, the shower stopped. She would be stepping out of the tub, skin blushed with heat. Kristen, he thought, and pulled his hair back so hard it hurt. Concentrate on Kristen.

'A week' was Thursday. The day after tomorrow.

*   *   *

Sixty miles to the west, Hedwige Aarlheissen reached across the bed, felt her hand meet empty air, and snapped her eyes open. She had not even undressed, had allowed herself to fall asleep last night after the nightmarish dinner party, convinced

402

that she was only taking a nap and would wake up either to find Barbara beside her or hear her downstairs, banging about, searching for enough leftovers to make a meal from.

A glance at the undented pillows and a split-second of listening told her neither was true. Hedwige could feel the emptiness, the undisturbed air. She swung her legs over the side of the bed. She didn't need to patrol the kitchen or the study, or the library or Bar's office, to know she was alone. And had been all night.

Downstairs the kitchen clock told her it was barely 7 a.m. She made herself a double espresso, then carried the cup as she patrolled the house—checked the locks and back entry and office, confirming what she already knew. Not only was Barbara not here now, she had not been here. She had not come and gone in the night, gathering papers and leaving hastily scrawled notes, as she sometimes did in the middle of a case, or when she had to get to a prison or police station at some ungodly hour.

Her patrol completed, Hedwige put the cup down on the kitchen counter then she pulled her phone out of her trouser pocket where it had nestled all night like a baby possum.

She'd left the ringer on, and turned up loud, so she knew there were no messages before she even checked. All that was in the log were the four calls she'd made to Barbara. Two yesterday evening before the party, and two afterwards, all unanswered. She tapped the speed dial again. This time Barbara's number didn't even ring before her voice cut in, demanding that she be left a message. Hedwige didn't bother. The phone was turned off.

Barbara would see her number and know what she wanted—*Where the hell are you? Are you all right? Has that son of a bitch laid a finger on you?*—when she turned it on again. If she ever turned it on again.

The thought bloomed like a sick black flower in Hedwige's head before she could even begin to stop it. Its smell, fetid and sweet, filled her nostrils and made her stomach heave. She dropped the phone and gripped the edge of the counter, hanging on until her eyes watered. Then she gave in. Hedwige Aarlheissen did not cry. Despite appearances to the contrary, she was the tough one. The strong one. The one who was hard as nails. So the sound that came from her throat was unfamiliar. It took her a moment to even understand what it was.

*   *   *

After hearing from Enzo, Pallioti had been tempted to grab the first car he could find in the police garage and drive like a bat out of hell. Then he'd realized he'd probably be more effective if he got his ducks in a row first. The primary duck was James MacCready, to whom would now fall the unenviable job of convincing Dr Kenneth Carson, yet again, that the very best thing he could do was stay put and shut up. Give them just another few hours. Another day.

Enzo believed what Anna Carson had told him. She had been very young and very much in love, trapped between needing to believe Antonio and betraying him, and in the end, perhaps inevitably, had done both. Aldo Moro had died anyway. And

404

Antonio Tomaselli had spent half his life in jail. And now he was having his revenge. And on Thursday, the day after tomorrow, if he hadn't already, he'd kill Anna Carson's stepdaughter and, Pallioti suspected, probably himself as well, and make that all her fault too.

Unless they found him.

Pallioti liked James, not least because he didn't have to waste breath explaining exactly how delicate this was. They had brought Anna Carson, like some renegade spy, 'in from the cold'. Now, nothing must be done to either upset or distract her. Or to break the fragile bond she'd established with Enzo Saenz. Pallioti didn't know where Antonio Tomaselli was, but he was fairly certain, from what Enzo had told him, that Angela Vari did. Even if Anna Carson didn't realize it.

It was still early. He ought to be in Ferrara by lunchtime. When he finally stepped out of the lift into the police garage, he saw the car Guillermo had ordered waiting for him, and already running, as if the officer on duty expected him to leap in and fly up the ramp like something out of *The French Connection*. The young man scurried to take the overnight bag he kept packed in his office. He placed it carefully on the back seat, then jumped to open the door, standing so straight Pallioti felt he ought to salute. He thanked him instead, slid into the driver's seat, and had just finished adjusting the mirrors when his phone rang.

*　　　*　　　*

Anna leaned against the cold glass of the car's

405

window and watched the countryside she had ridden through at such cost yesterday fly by. The same way she had watched it all those years ago from Antonio's Fiat. The same way she had watched the sodden green of Torrita give way to the outskirts of Rome from Monica Ghirri's car. All of them other lifetimes, shuffled and falling back out of order like a badly played card trick.

'This may be a stupid idea.'

She said it without looking at him.

'It's not.'

They had talked more over breakfast. Anna wasn't certain how she felt about the fact that he'd called his boss, the long-faced man in the black suit who looked like a well-dressed member of the Inquisition, but she supposed it was inevitable. It was only in films that the daring guy and gal went renegade and caught the dastardly villain against the odds and all on their own. In real life, you reported in, and did as you were told.

Pallioti had said Florence would square things with Ferrara—thank them for their help and tell them they no longer needed the CCTV tapes, giving the distinct impression that everything was 'cleared up'—and that he would come straight to the hotel where they should expect him around lunchtime. He had not said what they would do then. Or, at least specifically, that in the meantime they should sit in the hotel room waiting for him. So, when Enzo had asked her what she had planned next to find Antonio—beyond waiting for him to call or send a message so she could beg him to let her know where he was—she'd told him. Then reached for her coat as he picked up the car keys.

406

'Are we sure it's open? That we can get in? Today? In the winter?'

Anna knew the answer. She'd been sitting right across from Enzo at the breakfast table when he'd made the arrangements. The words were just something to say. Something to stop Angela Vari creeping into the car. Not that she'd stay away. Pomposa had always been one of her favourite places.

* * *

They saw the campanile first. The tallest thing for miles around, it rose like a slender needle from the gridwork of winter fields, a beacon to the weary and the faithful, to pilgrims and robbers and those simply in need of succour, material or otherwise. The day Antonio brought Angela, it had seemed to waver in the thick summer sun. Now it shimmered, the pale stone almost pink. Glowing in the crystalline winter air as if a giant mirror had been placed at its foot, gathering light from the sea.

The caretaker was waiting for them. One of the perks of those credentials Enzo carried seemed to be that when he said 'jump' the only answer was 'how high?' Anna glanced at him as they got out of the car. He didn't look or feel like a policechild now. They shook hands quickly. The small man in his padded coat was obviously both eager to know what this was about, and determined to keep his dignity intact by not asking. When it became clear that Enzo wasn't going to say anything, he led them to a side gate and they entered the compound.

Arches rose around them as they stepped into

407

the long cloister. Anna remembered the library, and the refectory painted by the students of Giotto who had wandered down from Padua, and the mosaics. The colours that had still been bright after a millennium, or perhaps had only seemed that way because it had been summer and she had been with Antonio and everything had been bright. The caretaker paused, produced more keys, and opened the door that let them into the base of the bell tower.

Light fell through the narrow casements, but between them it was dark and the steps were worn. Anna, never fond of heights to start with, kept her eyes on the caretaker's back. His feet moved quickly, his small ungloved hand barely touching the guide rope. He could probably navigate these steps in the dark, and perhaps he did—climb up on full-moon nights and gaze down over the fields that melted into a network of canals.

It was probably some kind of miracle that the abbey itself was still standing. Some divine hand must have guided the builders to this piece of solid ground. The area was a notorious marsh, inhabited largely by sea birds and the few remaining fishermen who netted for eels in the brackish muddy water. Their shacks, nothing but rush walls and roofs, were almost impossible to get to if you didn't know the paths and causeways. They had been used by the Partisans, providing perfect and unreachable cover. Antonio had held her around the waist at the top of the tower and pointed them out, whispering in her ear the stories his *nonno* had told him.

She stopped. The idea hadn't occurred to her before, but it did now. If Antonio had gone there,

408

out to one of the huts, they would never find him. They could look forever, but Kristen would die. Which might be what he intended all along—that there was no more possibility of her finding him than there had ever been a possibility of the BR finding Aldo Moro innocent. They had liked to talk a lot, she thought sourly, the Red Brigades, about the unfairness of the Establishment, the State, whoever it was they'd been so damned oppressed by. But it hadn't stopped them from making sure they played with a stacked deck.

In order to come out here, to hole up in one of the eel fishers' huts, Antonio would have had to have brought in supplies, probably used a boat. Which would have been possible, but far too risky and exposed once he had Kristen. And he would have had to stash the car somewhere. Enzo said there had been no sign of it. It hadn't been found at a station or airport or burned out or abandoned. So he must still have it, and have chosen somewhere where he could hide it on site. Somewhere with a barn or an outbuilding. And reasonable access to a road, an escape route.

Or perhaps not. Perhaps she'd understood from the very beginning, from the second she'd seen the photo on the girl's phone, that this time he did not plan on escaping. That there would be no more disappearing like smoke. For either of them.

'Va tutto bene?'

Enzo's hand was on the small of her back. He asked again if she was OK. The temptation to say 'no' was almost overwhelming. Instead, she nodded, and started climbing again.

A breeze was kicking when they came out onto the top of the campanile. Enzo pulled off a glove, reached into his pocket for the binoculars that the car had come equipped with, and handed them to Anna. She took them without saying anything, looped the strap over her head and pushed her hair out of her face. The light was clear and harsh, and for the first time Enzo noticed the lines at the corners of her eyes and mouth. Half a century had left its mark on her, after all. It wasn't unbecoming, just a blueprint of her life. He resisted the temptation to reach out and touch the crease of her cheek, or put his arm round her, steady her as she moved to the stone balustrade and began to scan the landscape laid out like a map below.

The abbey itself was surrounded by what, in the summertime, must be a lush windbreak of trees. But beyond that, the land was barren. When Anna suggested coming here, Enzo had honestly thought that it was probably pointless, and had only agreed—told her it wasn't stupid—because he hadn't had a better idea, and couldn't stand the thought of just sitting around and waiting for Pallioti. Now he realized that she had been right. From up here, you could see for miles. In any other season the occasional lines of trees that ran along drives or tracks or back roads might provide a screen. At this time of year, they were nothing but thin grey fretwork against the faded greens and duns of the fields. To the east, canals spread in broken veins into the marshes. Anna held the glasses in that direction for a minute or two, then swung around and looked inland.

The caretaker had gone back to the staircase. They could hear him fiddling with something, the bannister ties or a bolt on the door, scrabbling like a mouse. Enzo moved to the balustrade beside Anna, trying to understand what it was, exactly, she was looking for, and even as he thought it, knew what her answer would be. That she had no real idea—just something, anything, that might feel like Antonio.

'Pomposa,' she'd said this morning, putting down her coffee cup. 'His grandfather used to take him there when he was a boy. They could hear the bells, on the farm. Antonio thought it was the most beautiful place in the world.'

His *nonno* had been right, Enzo thought. Perhaps it wasn't superlative, but it was extraordinary. A lightship built, not for boats, but for souls. A calling to God here in this empty no man's land between earth and sea. For the first time, he wondered if Antonio Tomaselli had a soul after all, and if so, what had happened to it.

'There.'

Without lowering the glasses, Anna reached out and touched his sleeve.

'What?'

She was looking due south-west over a particularly barren stretch of fields beyond the road they had come in on. Enzo could only see a few tracks, a black lace of trees against the silver sky, the metallic line of a stream or small river threading its way through the irrigation ditches. Anna was pointing towards a cluster of buildings, just visible, low and pale, and nearly lost in the greys of winter.

When he took the binoculars, the buildings jumped like pop-up cards. He could see the cube of a farmhouse, and an outbuilding that stretched beside it. There was a single large tree. No sign of any cars. Or for that matter, any life at all. He followed the track back. It curved and almost disappeared, lost in the dead uncut grass before it met a one-lane secondary road that ambled towards nowhere.

There were no telegraph poles near the property, which meant no power. Which meant the farm was not in use—at least not much. Enzo couldn't see well enough to tell whether the buildings were in good repair or not, if there were holes in the roofs or shutters hanging from the windows. He lowered the glasses.

'What makes you think so?'

Anna shrugged. She was staring intently towards the tiny fading outlines.

'Abandoned,' she said. 'The outbuilding—for the car. Close enough to a road that he could get in and out without too much trouble. The drive's long, and there's nothing else around. Look.'

She was right. There wasn't another building within what had to be two kilometres.

'There are a couple of other possible places. Over there.'

She pointed north towards a bigger road they could see in the distance. The roofs of several cars flashed in the hard light. A village, probably not more than a cluster of houses and a post office, squatted off towards the sea.

'Maybe,' Enzo agreed. 'But a bigger road, too many cars. And houses. Too many places to run to if you got away.'

Anna looked at him and nodded.

'Would Kristen fight?'

Enzo dropped his voice to a murmur. The caretaker hadn't come out, but he'd stopped scrabbling, which meant he'd either left, or was hovering just inside the stairwell, desperate to know why it was that the police had called on a Tuesday morning in February demanding access to the campanile and were now standing scanning the surrounding countryside like bad caricatures of spies. Anna nodded again.

'If she can,' she said. 'Once she realizes what's going on.'

Both of them knew she meant, 'once Kristen realizes this is no lovers' bolt hole'. 'Once he stops sleeping with her', or at least 'making love' to her. Or even being nice. But neither of them said it. Enzo saw a flicker of pain cross Anna's face, and was amazed all over again at how impervious love, and lust, were to reason. And time. And even self preservation—all the parameters of what was generally considered 'life'. He told himself it was none of his business. Then wondered why he was annoyed by it, and raised the binoculars and took one last swing across the empty landscape.

'I think it's the place,' Anna muttered. 'It's just a feeling.' She shrugged. 'It's not more than a couple of miles away from his grandparents', as the crow flies.'

'Is that important?'

'I think so.'

Enzo didn't look at her as she spoke, kept scanning for buildings, tracks they might have missed.

'I told you, he used to . . . Antonio, when he was little,' Anna said. 'He and his grandpa used to walk up to the top of the hill at sunset, where you could see the campanile and listen for the bells.' Enzo could feel her looking at him. 'I think he'd want to

413

hear them again,' she said finally. 'I think that would be important.'

Enzo stared through the glasses for a few more minutes. Then he dropped them onto his chest and zipped up his coat.

'Come on,' he said. 'Let's go.'

*   *   *

They drove north first, following the bigger road they had come in on, branching down single lanes and inevitably dead-ending at well-kept, or not so well-kept, groups of buildings. A barn, a house, a shed. Sometimes a barking dog and curtains at the windows, all obviously inhabited. And not by Antonio. There wasn't so much as a whiff of a black BMW, and since the car hadn't turned up anywhere, Enzo, like Anna, figured he still had it. If he didn't, he'd had to have got hold of a new one, and that probably meant he had an accomplice—somebody supplying him, covering for him, planning with him. And what that meant—Enzo didn't even want to think about what that meant. *Il passato scompare e viene poi di nuovo, come la luna.* The past disappears and comes again, like the moon.

He did think they might have got lucky once, when the track they were following crested a rise and wound up in a semi-circle of abandoned sheds with an old cottage crouched behind them. But a second look revealed holes in the roofs, collapsed walls, and no sign of habitation beyond the snow-dampened remains of a bonfire and a pile of rusting beer cans. Finally, they turned around and went south.

414

The first road they found themselves on was small and narrow enough. The one they branched off on was barely one lane, little more than a track, the tarmac cracked and falling away at the sides so severely that in a few years it would be gone altogether. If Enzo had needed more proof than the lack of power lines that the farm was abandoned, this was it. It probably wasn't even used for storage. Tractors, trailers, all the paraphernalia that went with growing and harvesting, had not been coming up and down here with any regularity. They wouldn't have tyres left if they did. He swerved for a pot hole and nearly went into a ditch.

Neither of them had spoken since coming back past Pomposa. Anna was staring straight ahead, hands clutched in her lap, chewing at her lower lip that was already chapped. Enzo watched the side of the road, looking for the entrance of the track that served as a drive, and for anything else. When he saw it, he braked so hard she jerked against the seat belt.

*　　　*　　　*

'What? What is it?'

Anna was hovering behind his shoulder. Enzo waved her back.

'Please don't come any closer. Get back in the car.'

She stopped moving but ignored the second part of the order, standing in the road, watching as he crouched on the edge of the crumbling pavement, staring at what looked, on first glance, like an empty frozen verge. Then she saw what he'd seen.

415

Tyre tracks, wide, from a fairly big car. And deep, meaning it had been parked there for some time.

'When did it last snow?' He looked back at her. 'Has it snowed since you've been here?'

She nodded.

'The first night. Sunday. But out here, I don't know. It can be different.'

Enzo stood up. He walked a wide circle around where the car had been parked. The tracks were recent. There had been slight melt, some sun when the car had parked here, and the wind had not yet broken down the ridges. If he knew more, if he was a real petrol head, he might even have been able to tell what kind of tyres they were—Pirellis or Firestones or whatever. He would take a bet on the car, though. Something very heavy and probably four-door. Like a big black BMW. Enzo frowned.

He walked down the road slowly, got about thirty metres before he found the entrance to the track, then stopped. It was rutted and deep and had recently thawed enough to get muddy. Which might prove there was a God after all. Because the footprints were dead clear. Someone had walked down here.

He crouched and looked, then stood up again. There were tyre tracks, too. Recent ones. He'd put money on the fact that they were the same tyres, from the same car. He reached for his mobile phone, then stopped.

'Let me see your shoes.'

'What?' Anna was standing behind him.

'Let me see your shoes!'

She looked at him, confused, almost started to laugh, then registered the look in his eye and put her foot out. They were trainers, expensive

416

American ones. Enzo didn't even need to lift them up to know that the tread was completely different from the boots that had made the prints on the drive. He tried to remember if she had been wearing them last night. She had been. She'd dropped almost silently through the hatch in the butcher's shop, and when she'd kicked him, catching him just once in the shin before he got her on the ground, it hadn't hurt. The realization that she hadn't lied about where she'd been yesterday brought a pang of relief, then something else.

'How big are Kristen's feet?' he asked. 'Are they bigger than yours?'

Still watching him, Anna shook her head.

'No. They're smaller. Why?'

Enzo didn't answer her. He was looking at the drive again, at the tyre tracks and the footprints, which were definitely smaller than his own but larger than Anna Carson's. He turned round and took her by the shoulder.

'Get in the car,' he said, hustling her down the road. 'Get back in the car. Now.'

*   *   *

They made the drive back to Ferrara in record time. Enzo figured he broke just about every speed limit in Reggio. Anna said nothing the whole way. Once or twice, he glimpsed her studying her shoes, trying to figure out what he'd seen.

At the hotel, Enzo parked abruptly, and was surprised to feel relieved at the sight of another set of Florence plates on another immediately recognizable unmarked police car. Taking Anna by the arm more roughly than he intended to, he

417

trotted up the hotel steps, and pushed the sleek glass door into the lobby, causing it to jam because he was too impatient to wait for it to open automatically.

Pallioti saw them as they came up the steps. It took Enzo a moment to realize that he, too, had a woman with him—a tall, statuesque blonde wearing jeans and a bright red down coat with a fur collar who looked as if she had recently been crying. He had no idea who she was, and right now he didn't care. Enzo dropped Anna's arm, took Pallioti's, and led him away.

'I think we've found it,' he said, when he was certain they couldn't be overheard. 'A farmhouse out towards Pomposa. We need to check it out, see who owns the property, how it's registered. There's no power. If he's out there, he may have a generator. And there's a problem.'

Pallioti said nothing, stood with his head bowed, listening.

'A car drove in. Recently. Just one. Something fairly big, probably some time after noon on Monday when it was warmer—thawed enough to leave tracks. Whoever it was sat and waited by the road before. For some time, by the looks of it, so I doubt it was Tomaselli. I think the driver walked in first, probably looking around. Doing a recce. There were footprints. Either a small man's or a large woman's. Then they went back to the car and drove in. Only one set of tracks, so whoever it was is still in there. Meaning either Signor Tomaselli has a friend. Or we have another hostage.'

'Yes,' Pallioti said quietly. 'I know.'

* * *

Hedwige Aarlheissen had flung open the front door the moment he pulled into the drive, causing him to wonder if she'd been standing behind it since she'd called and told him Barbara Barelli was missing.

Getting out of his car, Pallioti had seen at once that the serene doe-eyed Amazon he'd met less than twenty-four hours earlier had vanished. In her place was a haggard, teary woman who had obviously slept—or, he suspected, not slept—in the clothes she was wearing. Her black trousers were badly creased. Smudges of something, make-up probably, darkened the collar and shoulder of her cream silk shirt. She'd turned and led him into the family room without speaking.

The dinner party had obviously taken place, and been only marginally cleared away. Serving plates with bits of food clinging to them were piled by the sink. Place mats, coasters, and scrunched-up napkins littered five of the places set at the glass dining table. The sixth, at the head, was untouched, the napkin still rolled in a silver ring. Tears welled in Hedwige's huge eyes. She wiped her nose with the back of her hand.

'Like I told you on the phone,' she said, 'she went off yesterday. About half an hour after you left. I thought she'd be back. I didn't know what else to do. You said to call if—'

Pallioti nodded.

'I think, perhaps,' he said, 'I had better make us some coffee. Then you can tell me exactly what happened.'

*   *   *

419

Pallioti, who was not good with things mechanical at the best of times, had approached the gigantic Nespresso machine that crouched on the counter top with genuine trepidation. Hedwige had murmured something about 'changing out of these things' and taken herself upstairs, leaving him to peruse the terrifying display of dials and levers. He'd finally pushed and pulled several of them, then found a bottle of grappa in the glass-fronted bar behind the dining table as he listened to the sounds of running water and footsteps overhead. He'd been quite proud of the fact that by the time she came back down in jeans and sweater, her face as scrubbed as a schoolgirl's, he'd produced two decent cups of espresso. A hefty shot glass of grappa accompanied hers.

Hedwige had looked at him gratefully, then sunk down on the sofa, cradling her cup. Pallioti sat opposite her in a leather armchair so large and squashy it threatened to swallow him whole.

'Now, Signora Aarlheissen,' he said.

'Hedwige. Please. Signora Aarlheissen is my mother. I haven't spoken to her in twenty years.' She glanced at Pallioti over the rim of her cup. 'She didn't take well to having a gay daughter.'

Pallioti nodded.

'All right, Hedwige. I would appreciate it if you would simply tell me the truth. Or at least as much of it as you know. It will save us a lot of time, which, just now, is one of the things we don't have.'

She bowed her head. Blonde hair fell over her eyes. Hedwige pushed it away with her free hand, then said, 'If she knew, Barbara would kill me.'

Pallioti had wondered if he really needed to

420

point out that Barbara Barelli did not know—at least for now—and that if Hedwige did not tell him, the chances were fair to good that Antonio Tomaselli would kill her. Apparently not, because Hedwige looked at him and nodded.

'All right,' she said. 'It all began, I don't know, about four years ago, I suppose.'

Pallioti frowned.

'What began, Signora?'

'This—' She was agitated enough to overlook the 'Signora'. 'This whatever it is that scumbag has on her.'

The words had taken Pallioti by surprise. He put his cup on the coffee table and leaned forward.

'You are telling me that Antonio Tomaselli "has something" on Dottoressa Barelli, his lawyer?'

Hedwige nodded.

'And what makes you think this?' he asked.

'I don't think it,' she snapped. 'I know it.'

'Yes,' he murmured. 'Of course. I'm sorry. Please go on.'

'Well, the way she treated him changed. It became almost as if, I don't know. Almost as if she was afraid of him. Besides, if it hadn't been true, she'd never have agreed about the farm. Never. Although that was later. About two years—I don't know—maybe eighteen months ago. And the weird thing is . . .' Hedwige looked at him and blinked, her eyes welling up again. 'She hates him. I mean, I knew she never liked him. But she had a thing. Guilt, whatever the fuck. About the Red Brigades. She bought into that crap about what they did being "society's fault", whatever the fuck that means. So, yes—she defended him. But she never liked him. And now she hates him. I mean really hates him. I kept saying to her, "drop him, then. Find someone else to represent him." But she wouldn't.'

Wouldn't or couldn't? Pallioti wondered. And what on earth, he asked himself, could Antonio Tomaselli 'have' on Barbara Barelli? And how— given that in prison she would have been his main conduit to the outside world—had he got it? He'd ask her, if he ever got the chance. For now, the other titbit Hedwige had dropped interested him more.

'The farm, Hedwige?' he'd asked. 'What are you talking about when you say "the farm"?'

She'd picked up the glass and downed half of the grappa. Then uncurled herself from the couch. 'Come on,' she said. 'I'll show you.'

Launching himself, with some difficulty, out of the chair, Pallioti had followed her across the hall to a closed door where she'd pushed a series of numbers on a security pad.

'Bar's never, officially, given me the passcode to her office.' Hedwige glanced over her shoulder. 'But for a really smart woman, she can be remarkably dumb. It's the date plus the distance of the first international race she ever won.'

'Dotoressa Barelli?'

Hedwige nodded as she stepped inside and turned on the lights.

'Sprinter. Bar represented her country for three years, right after she came back from college in the States.' She shrugged. 'No reason why you'd know. She messed up at the Olympic trials, then quit when she started practising law. But she was good,' Hedwige added. 'Almost very good.'

Pallioti had the idea that 'almost very good'

422

would probably not have been anywhere near good enough for Barbara Barelli. And in some ways, worse than bad.

*　　　*　　　*

The room Hedwige showed him into was lined with bookcases and cabinets. A large desk sat in the centre of it. A screen filled half the opposite wall.

'Video conferencing.' Hedwige waved at the screen. 'Without it Bar would have to traipse up and down the country and God knows where.' She'd dropped to a squat and began fiddling with the combination lock on the front of one of the cabinets. 'She didn't take a briefcase or anything like that, yesterday. Just her handbag and her coat. That's why I was so sure she'd be back. I mean, she does have to go quickly sometimes. She keeps a bag packed—if someone's arrested or something. I just hope the damn papers are still here.'

Watching her, Pallioti wondered exactly how much time she spent breaking into her partner's world, and if Barbara knew about it and tolerated it, or was simply clueless when it came to what was obviously one of her lover's favourite pastimes. He would have used Hedwige as a safe-cracker any day. She was almost as good as Enzo Saenz.

At the thought of Enzo he pulled his phone out and glanced at it, but there was no message. Pallioti didn't know whether to be reassured by that or not. He slipped it back into his pocket. When he looked up, Hedwige had the door open and was rifling through a series of manila files.

'Oh, thank God,' she said. 'It's still here. I was afraid she might have taken it with her.'

423

She lifted out a file, crossed to the desk, which was as barren as Pallioti's own, and spread the contents in front of him. They appeared, on first glance, to be the deeds, sales, and purchase papers of a property. Pallioti glanced at Hedwige.

'Two years ago,' she said, nodding, 'when it started to look as though he really might get out, he called Bar and asked her to come and see him.' She waved at the empty screen on the wall. 'Usually she'd just talk to him through that, save her the drive. But he insisted she actually go to him. So she did.' Hedwige shrugged. 'I told you, she'd changed. At least as far as Antonio was concerned. Before, she would have put her foot down, told him he could talk to her here. Not any more. He says "jump" and she says "how high?". That's how I know,' she added. 'I told you. He has something on her. I can't think of any other reason.'

'Did he call her, or did she call him, yesterday, after I left?'

Hedwige shrugged.

'How the hell should I know? She locked herself in here. Then she just left. She barely even spoke to me.'

'But you think she's gone to find him?'

Hedwige looked at him as if he was stupid.

'Don't you?'

Pallioti had nodded. He did. Whatever she might have felt or not felt about the Red Brigades, Barbara Barelli had been upset when she'd heard about Kristen Carson. He was very much afraid she had gone off to be an avenging angel.

'Anyway,' Hedwige said, 'about two years ago, she came back after that visit. Upset.'

424

'Upset, as in angry?'

Hedwige had thought about that for a moment.

'Yes,' she'd said. 'But not really. I mean, underneath, it was almost more as if she was—depressed. Resigned. As you can imagine, Barbara's not passive, but—in any case,' she went on, 'it was a couple of months later when I finally wheedled it out of her. Antonio had asked her to buy a house for him.'

Pallioti raised his eyebrows. He knew many lawyers who were deeply committed to representing their clients—but there were requests and requests.

'And this is it?' He turned and looked more closely at the papers, at the plan and photographs attached.

Hedwige nodded.

'She set up a dummy company. She didn't want her name on it. I don't think it was expensive; it looks—I mean it's apparently almost derelict. A farmhouse left when the family couldn't make it any more, and for sale when they couldn't pay the taxes on the land. I think it's somewhere outside Ferrara.'

*   *   *

Now the photos were spread across the hotel-room desk. Hastily shot and slightly blurry, they showed a solid cube of a house and a long outbuilding fronting a yard shaded by a single tree. Overgrown fields stretched on either side. The photographer seemed to have been standing in the drive, which looked little more than a thin broken track. Both Enzo and Anna were quite certain it

425

was the same property they'd seen from the top of the campanile at Pomposa.

When she heard about the tyre tracks and the footprints, Hedwige's eyes welled. Her voice sank to little more than a whisper.

'Do you think he's killed her?'

She was sitting in the ugly armchair by the window, still wearing the red parka, which Pallioti guessed was Barbara's. Looking at her, Pallioti saw the girl underneath—a big, raw-boned teenager, too good at sports, at odds with her family and perhaps even with herself. He wondered what meeting Barbara Barelli must have meant for her, and realized he knew the answer.

'No,' he said firmly. 'He has no reason to kill her,' although he could think of plenty. 'No,' he repeated, and didn't add *'He's pencilled that in for the day after tomorrow.'*

*   *   *

An hour later, Anna Carson held the phone to her ear and listened to her stepdaughter's voice.

'Ciao,' Kristen said. 'Tell me everything.'

The first time Anna had heard it, barely a week ago, she had found the message annoying— its fake coyness; its little-girl sexuality. Now it broke her heart.

After talking it over, they had decided not to wait until seven, that they couldn't leave it up to Antonio to contact her. Or not. He would have to be prodded. They had to know if he really was there, and what he wanted. Other than to torture her. Get some measure of revenge. Not, Anna was convinced, as much for the twenty-eight years—

426

Antonio would always have known that was a potential stop on the route he'd chosen, might almost have been proud of it—but for the betrayal. And the fact that she had left him.

She saw the wink of the emerald, a flash of gold in dirty water, and heard his voice. *'Ti possiedo. Ora, tu sei mia. Per sempre.'* I own you. Now you're mine. Forever. It was a whisper, so close and tangible that for a second his body was on hers. Weight and heat. The taste of earth.

Looking up, Anna met Enzo Saenz's eyes. They were watching her intently—Enzo, the woman Barbara loved, and the man in the black coat whose name Anna had trouble remembering. She nodded. Then, as the beep of Kristen's voicemail sounded, she felt the room waver and fade, become as insubstantial as this ghost of herself she kept coming face to face with.

'Antonio,' she said. *'Ho sentito le campane da Pomposa.'*

I've heard the bells from Pomposa.

*   *   *

After she cut the connection, the room felt somehow more crowded. They had come up because they could hardly discuss Antonio and Barbara Barelli and Kristen standing downstairs while half of Ferrara's business world passed through the marbled lobby and drifted like pilot fish to the bar, and at first the conversation had been confused. Pallioti had not had time to do more than skim the file on Angela Vari, and as a result had gone to see Barbara Barelli thinking she was merely Antonio's lawyer. That fact alone had

427

been surprise enough for Anna. But on hearing it, she had known at once why Barbara had done it. Had seen her leaning in the kitchen doorway, watching Nonna Franchi polish the shoes her father would be buried in, learning the favours you did for the dead. In this case, her.

The shock had obviously been the same for Hedwige, who now looked at Anna with barely concealed dislike, as if she was the unwelcome piece of a puzzle that had finally slotted into place.

Anna had wanted to ask how Barbara was. Had wanted to ask if Hedwige had a photo in her wallet—so she could see the woman, and look for any trace of the girl she'd known. Barbara Barelli, with her long braid and her crooked teeth. And later, her braces and her swearing and her smile.

But she hadn't. Because she had no right to. She'd surrendered that long ago. Shed it like a skin when she walked into the police station off Via Fani. And shed it again almost a year and half later when, having exhausted Angela Vari, having hollowed her out—mined her life and heart and soul and bartered them for her own salvation— Anna had discarded her like a husk. And stepped between two Federal Marshals onto a plane at Ciampino, and watched out of the little window as first Rome, and then Italy, grew smaller and smaller and finally melted into the sea.

She got up abruptly and went into the bathroom. Locked the door and ran the taps, both of them, and looked into the mirror, almost expecting to see nothing there.

*   *   *

Forty minutes later when her phone rings, Anna is sitting on the bed holding Kristen's bear. She feels Pallioti's hand on her elbow as she stands up. He still looks less to her like a policeman than an undertaker. Or a priest. With gold cufflinks. And a grey tie, flecked with silver, as if he's going to a wedding, or is in mourning.

'Remember,' he says. And she nods.

As if he has to tell her. As if she doesn't know, have it running like rats through her head—along with all the other little verses from the book of hours.

The best lie is almost the truth. Just trimmed—to change the shadow it throws.

'*Si, sono sola,*' she says after she pushes the green button on her phone. '*Certo che sono sola, Antonio. Non ti ho mai mentito.*'

Yes, I'm alone. Of course I'm alone. I've never lied to you.

*   *   *

Pallioti is surprised at how untouched her accent is, as if her own language has been sleeping inside her all these years. He watches Anna Carson as she bends her head, holding the phone. As she tells Antonio that she understands. That she's sorry. That she has thought about what he said, and knows she owes him. That she will do anything.

It's not just her voice. Her face changes too, and he realizes that who he's seeing is Angela Vari. Surfacing like a drowned body. That has rocked, and chafed, and finally slipped the weights that held it down.

'What do you want me to do?' she asks. 'Just tell

429

me. Just tell me, Antonio, and I'll do it.'

There is a silence, and Pallioti feels his heart shrink. He does not need to hear what she says next. He already knows, they all know, what the price will be.

'Yes,' Anna Carson says, finally. 'Yes, I promise. I'll come. I'll be there, tomorrow. Alone.'

*   *   *

'I can't do it. You do know that?'

It was a question, but didn't sound like it. Enzo looked at Pallioti and said nothing.

He was right, of course. They could no more let Anna Carson walk down that farm track than fly. Even if they did believe Antonio would do as he said—send Kristen out of the house, set her free as a bird the second Anna reached the front door. The second, he'd said, that she came close enough to kiss.

Anna had not been able to ask about Barbara without giving herself away, and Antonio had said nothing about her one way or the other. Neither Pallioti nor Enzo seriously thought Barbara Barelli was an accomplice, but the truth was, they didn't know. Any more than they knew whether she was alive or dead. Or even there. Technically, the same could be said of Kristen. Anna's request for 'proof of life' had been laughed off. 'Don't you trust me, carina?' Antonio had asked.

Pallioti sighed. This was the very scenario he had hoped somehow to avoid. Hoped he could twist and turn his way out of. But it was no good. He and Enzo had come to the end, and both of them knew it. The irony was that they would be congratulated.

430

They'd located Kenneth Carson's wife and his daughter. They'd established contact with the probable abductor and determined his price. In short, they had set the game in motion. Now it was time—and perhaps, to be honest, well past time—for them to step back and let the professionals do their job.

DIGOS, the special intelligence police, would be alerted. There would be a SWAT team and, because television expected it and it would cover their asses afterwards, a hostage negotiator. There would probably be helicopters. And combat uniforms. And night-vision goggles. And stun grenades. And then, just before dawn, there would be silence.

Followed by a lot of noise. Most of which would be shooting.

*   *   *

'Are you going to call Rome directly?' The words felt sticky on Enzo's tongue.

Pallioti gave a sour little smile.

'*Certo.*' He shrugged, his shoulders jumping under the black coat that was so attached to him it was a sort of second skin. 'They'll know in five minutes anyway.' He began to punch in the number. 'And insist on taking over. So,' he asked, putting his phone to his ear, 'what's the point in wasting time?'

*   *   *

In the end, Pallioti was able to arrange for them to be there. His clout, it seemed, extended that far.

431

Having Anna Carson on site might be necessary in any case, and he had argued that it was inhumane to make Hedwige sit by herself in a hotel room waiting to hear whether Barbara Barelli was dead or alive. Inhumane and not very intelligent. Barring locking her in a cell in the Ferrara Questura—an option the fat man seemed to have considered—it was better to have her where they could at least control her. Make certain, for instance, that she was not using the hotel switchboard—Pallioti had politely but firmly confiscated her mobile phone—to wake any number of Barbara's legal colleagues, or the local television correspondents. The fat man had made his humming sound, and Pallioti suspected it was the logic of this argument rather than any appeal to the human heart that triumphed.

'We get in, we get out. We get it done before anyone knows it's happened. And then it never did,' he announced.

That was how it was going to work. The farmhouse would be taken just before first light. Even Kenneth Carson would not know what was going on until shortly after breakfast, when his wife and daughter were returned to him and the happy family reunited. As for himself and Enzo, they would be observers only. Privileged to answer the questions asked of them, then shut up and step back and watch how it was done in the big, wide, real world.

Hearing that, Pallioti had barely suppressed a snort. Holding his tongue had been too much to ask.

'Well, old friend,' he'd snapped, 'in that case let's just hope it all runs tick tock, like clockwork. No

432

"salt in the wounds".'

'Don't be petulant, Sandro,' the fat man had replied. 'It doesn't suit you.'

*   *   *

Anna and Hedwige now had their own rooms. Pallioti had been given some sort of penthouse flat on the roof, either because of the sheer impressiveness of his credentials or the cut of his suit. Enzo figured it was fifty-fifty either way, but was leaning towards the latter. The more banal truth was they probably just had nowhere else to stick him. The hotel wasn't as big as it looked and there seemed to be some kind of mini-convention going on. When they finally went downstairs, the bar was so crowded that Pallioti took one look at it, shied like a nervous horse, and announced he was 'taking a walk'. Enzo watched him through the glass doors. A freezing fog had lowered over the city. The fur coats scurried back and forth. Pallioti passed through the castle floodlights, black as a crow, and disappeared towards the cathedral.

Enzo had not been tempted to join him. He couldn't in any case. Someone had to keep an eye on Anna Carson. There was, after all, no guarantee that Antonio Tomaselli wouldn't decide not to wait until '*domani*', but would simply come to Ferrara and fetch her. That he hadn't sensed a trap, and would move first. He might have some trouble finding her, but he wouldn't have much. Especially if she called Kristen's phone and left a message telling him where she was.

The thought turned Enzo towards the lift, and made him fidget on the ride up. He'd checked on

Hedwige an hour earlier. She had ordered dinner and said she just wanted to watch TV. Propped against the headboard with the remote in her hand, the meal untouched on the desk, she'd looked at him with a vacant stare that suggested she wouldn't be seeing much of anything, except the films that ran in her own head. He'd opened his mouth to say he was sure 'everything would be fine', then had thought better of it and backed quietly out of the room. Now he stopped outside Anna's door and listened. Then he raised his hand. And dropped it. And raised it again.

*   *   *

Anna heard the knock, and wondered if she'd been waiting for it. It didn't occur to her for a moment that it was anyone but Enzo Saenz. She hadn't ordered room service.

He stood with his hands dug into the pockets of his jacket. She had seen him without it, but he looked more like himself with it on. As if it was attached to him, the way some people's sunglasses were attached to them, propped on their heads even when it was raining or dark. She undid the chain, and stood back to let him in.

As she did, she caught a glimpse of herself in the big mirror over the dressing table. Ferrara's damp had turned her hair curly again and the dye had made not only it, but also her eyes, a different colour. Darker. Greener. For the first time in thirty years, an older version of Angela looked back at her. Anna reached inside the neck of her sweater and felt for the warm lozenge of gold. She rubbed her finger across it and closed the door.

434

'Have you called him? You might as well tell me.'

Enzo didn't need to add, 'because I'll find out anyway'. He'd taken her phone but there was a perfectly good land line sitting on the desk. Anna shook her head. It was pointless to admit she'd thought about it. He watched her as she sat down on the bed. He'd had a shower, his hair was still damp. But he hadn't shaved. The shadow of a twenty-four-hour beard made his strange-coloured eyes even stranger.

'Where do you get them from?' she asked suddenly. 'Your eyes? I've never seen that colour before. From your mother?'

'Father.'

Enzo turned to the window, pulling the heavy curtains that were already closed tighter, then pulled at the edges, overlapping them as if he was afraid the fog might creep in like a vampire.

'Your nose, too?'

He nodded, his back still to her.

'Are they going to kill him?'

Enzo's hands stopped moving. She hadn't meant to say it out loud. The words had just happened. Enzo shook his head. The lamp caught faint blondish streaks in his hair.

'No,' he said. 'Not unless he forces them to. They're not the BR. They don't carry out executions. All they want to do is get Kristen out.'

'And Barbara.'

'Yes, and Barbara. If she's there.'

'She's there.'

He turned round.

'How do you know? Did he say something? Something you didn't tell us? Think. It's important. It could—'

'Save people's lives?' She smiled, looking up at him. 'Are you telling me my speaking up could save someone's life? Is that what you mean?'

'No.' He crossed the room and sat down beside her on the bed. 'No,' he said. Enzo reached out and brushed a strand of hair off her forehead. 'No. I'm sorry. That's not what I meant.'

'He didn't say anything. I just know. I don't want him to die,' she added a second later. Enzo's finger blotted the tears that seeped and rolled from the corner of her eye. 'I never wanted anyone to die.' The words felt like bubbles of glass. 'I'm so goddamn scared.'

Anna felt the softness of his sweater as he put his arms around her, felt his fingers on her back. The hard ridge of his collarbone. His hair smelled of the hotel's cheap shampoo and his skin of the now almost familiar earthiness, shadowed and cool and deep. His thigh moved against hers. She felt his mouth as her hands found his hair and unwound the elastic. She knew that what she ought to say was, 'We shouldn't do this.' 'I am married.' 'I am old enough to be your mother.'

But she didn't. Instead she said, 'Stay with me.'

WEDNESDAY 10 FEBRUARY 2010

Darkness hung across the fields and rose from the bend of the stream. Shreds of fog wavered at the edge of the headlights.

It was just after half past three in the morning. They had passed barricades as soon as they left the larger two-lane highway—a series of saw horses

436

bearing the neon logos of an electricity company, and signs announcing *Night Work Road Closed,* pointing the way towards a diversion, and apologizing for any inconvenience. There was even a phone number in case of complaints. Pallioti imagined an ancient black phone somewhere in the bowels of Rome ringing unanswered into the dark.

The men who waved them through wore overalls and jackets bearing the same logo, their faces barely visible under the hard hats, the earpieces they muttered into almost certainly not connected to a work crew. Or at least not the sort one might expect.

A helicopter fly-by had taken place half an hour earlier. It had been calculated that they could risk one, and was generally agreed it had been worth it. There were no lights visible in the farmhouse, but the infra-red picked up bodies. Three of them in separate rooms. Two upstairs, one down. Which meant Barbara Barelli was alive. They already knew she was there. Casts had been taken just before midnight from the verge of the road. The tracks matched her tyres.

Half a mile inside the barricades Pallioti, Enzo, Anna, and Hedwige left their car and were ushered into an electricity van. It rumbled down the road for five minutes before stopping. When the door opened, the man who climbed in did not introduce himself. He shook hands with Pallioti and Enzo, nodded at the two women, moved to a control panel with a series of screens on it, and flipped a switch. A picture faded in, blurry and greened. They could see the house, its bottom row of windows shuttered, the top ones staring down onto

437

the empty yard. A single tree stood to one side, its naked branches resting on the roof of the long, low building to the left. The man tapped it with his finger.

'Here,' he said. 'The barn. That's where we assume the cars are. From the plans we were able to get hold of—they date back twenty years to when it was last lived in—there's no access from the house. So unless he's busted a hole in the wall, Tomaselli will have to come out of the front door if he tries to get to a car.'

'What about the back?'

The man nodded at Pallioti and flipped another switch, bringing up a second screen that showed the back of the house.

'There's a door into what we assume is still the kitchen,' he said. 'There's no record of any work being done, so unless he's turned himself into a master builder, the plans we have are basically good. The stairs run up from the kitchen. The front door leads to a hallway between the two main rooms, kitchen right, sitting room left. We're guessing the women are upstairs. So we go in both doors at once. Three men each. Assuming the downstairs body is Tomaselli, the back team goes straight up and gets the women out, while the front team subdues our friend. Or vice versa.' He shrugged. 'Doesn't matter much. We have someone on the roof of the barn. Another two guys on the hill in front of the house, and two more below the berm of the stream behind.' He turned round. 'So it should be neat and clean. Everyone's getting into place about now. It's a little tricky because there's not much cover, but believe me, these guys know what they're doing. Ten minutes,

438

ladies,' he said, smiling at Hedwige and Anna, 'and we'll have your loved ones safe and sound.'

He stood, gave a little bow, and ducked out of the back of the truck. The driver slid from the front and took his place at the screens. Hedwige moved over beside him, mesmerized by the wavering green images that made the farmhouse and the tree and the barn look as though they were in outer space, or part of one of those villages flooded by reservoirs. As if water or sci-fi goo swirled around them instead of air. Pallioti followed the man out of the door. A moment later, Enzo Saenz followed him.

*   *   *

The cold was refreshing after the stuffy interiors of the car and the van. Pallioti was standing on the narrow road. Ahead of them, two more vans were pulled up, both bearing the electricity company's logo. Enzo wondered if they used it for all of these 'situations', or if they had others. Plumbing companies or perhaps pest removal firms. He hoped there was a power line around here somewhere, in case anyone did come by. Or at least an underground cable.

Pallioti shivered inside his coat, flexed his gloved hands and started down the road, heading for what was obviously the command vehicle. Enzo started to follow, then thought better of it. Pallioti had not called his mobile phone, but he had no idea if he had knocked on his door last night; if, prowling the halls, Lorenzo had come to his room and found it empty. Anna came back to him with a jolt. The touch and taste of her. The feel of her curled against him. Enzo turned back and opened the van door.

Hedwige was still sitting beside the driver, watching the screens intently, as if she could pull Barbara out of the house by sheer willpower. Anna sat on the hard bench that ran along the opposite side. She glanced at Enzo as he sidled past. He had his back to her, was between Hedwige and the driver, watching the screen over their shoulders, when all at once the pictures flared white, the yard, farmhouse and twisted outline of the tree jumping suddenly like startled animals. A swarm of dark figures, ant men, appeared on both screens, running.

Then, as the second team hit the back door and went through it, the front door burst open, and a man pushed a girl out. He shouted, his mouth moving silently, and the front team of ant men stopped dead. Even from inside the van, they could see he was holding a gun to her head.

'Antonio.'

Enzo heard the whisper behind him. At the same moment, on the other screen, he saw Barbara Barelli being hustled out of the back of the house, held by both arms and half-dragged towards the edge of the picture. Hedwige started, gripped the driver's arm and clapped her hand to her mouth. Enzo felt a blast of cold air. He spun round, but the van door was already open. Anna Carson was gone.

*   *   *

At first, he couldn't find her. He looked left and right. Then let his eyes sweep over the rutted

440

darkness of the overgrown field that stretched towards the farm. She was already halfway across it, running hard. Enzo leapt the irrigation ditch. He was fit and twenty years younger, but she was fast.

Anna could feel her blood pumping, feel her heart and her arms, her back and legs in every stride. The earth was frozen and stubbled. Her feet hit and cracked ice, imprinted frost, but she kept her eyes ahead, focused on the fading dark, and in the thrumming of her breath heard his name over and over again—*Antonio, Antonio, Antonio.* And knew she was running the race of her life.

Enzo started to call, then decided not to waste the breath. She was hardly going to stop and he had no idea how many people were really creeping around these godforsaken fields carrying who knew what kind of weapons and grudges. He put on an extra burst and felt it pay off. Her figure was silhouetted now against the glow of lights trained on the farmhouse. Enzo pushed himself again, forced his feet to turn over faster. And thanked God, because she stumbled.

He caught her around the waist. Lifted her off her feet. Then slapped a hand over her mouth.

'For Christ's sake,' he hissed in her ear, 'what the hell are you doing?'

Anna twisted like a snake, but Enzo held on. When she stilled, he lowered her feet to the ground but didn't let go.

In front of and slightly below them, they could see the farm lit up like some sort of bizarre film set. The men in black, there appeared to be four of them now, had stopped at the tree. Antonio was standing with his back to the wall of the house, far enough away from the front door and windows that he couldn't be reached from inside. He had Kristen in front of him. She was gagged, what looked like a piece of gaffer tape over her mouth. Her arms appeared to be tied behind her back. Antonio had one arm around her neck and held a gun to her temple.

Anna let out a small moan.

'Sssh.'

'Let her go, Signor Tomaselli, and no one gets hurt.'

The call came from a megaphone somewhere beyond the tree. Antonio didn't move.

'Let Kristen go, and we can talk this out.'

Enzo thought he saw Tomaselli smile at that one. He was sure he saw him shake his head.

'Where is she?' he shouted back.

'Where is who?' the megaphone asked.

'Angela!' Antonio bellowed into the dark. He grabbed Kristen tighter. 'Angela!' he screamed. 'You promised!'

Anna thrashed and kicked, and Enzo felt his hand fall away from her mouth.

'Antonio!' she screamed. 'Antonio! I'm here!'

At the sound of her voice, Antonio's head whipped round.

'You can let her go!' Anna shouted. 'I'm here!'

As he peered into the dark, searching for Anna beyond the wall of lights, Antonio's arm loosened, and Kristen staggered forward. She stumbled, then fell to her knees on the cobbles. Antonio didn't seem to care. He dropped the gun and turned away from her.

'Angie!' he cried, stepping towards her voice. 'Angela! Where are you?'

'I'm here,' Enzo heard her say.

Then Anna began to walk forward, and in that moment, he saw it.

Antonio had moved away from the farmhouse. He was peering into the darkness as the sniper rose from the barn roof.

Enzo threw himself forward. He caught Anna by the shoulders and spun her around as the shot went off.

*   *   *

Anna hears herself scream. Then she hears Enzo Saenz's voice. And feels his hands, pressing her head, hard, into his shoulder.

'Don't,' he is saying. 'Don't.' It's a murmur in her ear, an instruction straight to her heart. 'Don't look. Don't look.'

He is holding her neck, cradling the back of her head, pushing her into his own body so she cannot see what is in front of them in the dead white circle of light.

'Remember him. Do it,' Enzo Saenz says. 'Do it now. For Antonio. Remember him the way you loved him.'

And so she does.

She closes her eyes, screws them tight, and clings to the shoulders of his jacket, her fingers digging hard into the soft leather, and feels herself flying. Back past the beach at Ostia. Past the sand and the taste of salt, past *Marry me, Angela,* to the tiny cramped kitchen in Trastevere where sun spills into the scratched sink and they sit across from each other, her bare foot on his. While Enzo Saenz holds her, while he presses his chin to the top of

443

her head, she flies past the campanile at Pomposa where she stands with all the summer world below her and Antonio's arms around her. She flies past the bedroom under the eaves, and the cleared pane of glass that bears the imprint of his hand. Past the Montagnola, and the Angels' Gate, and the ghosts of the old men under the street lamp in Via Vittoria, to August. To the prickle of orchard grass and the mingled buzz of bees and laughter and the tight, bursting skin of an apple that Antonio holds in his hand and stretches towards her as he smiles, dappled with light.

EPILOGUE

Pallioti allowed Valentine's Day, that most gruesome and unlikely celebration of lovers, to pass before he returned to Bologna. It only seemed fair. Although, he had to admit, he was finding fairness a stretch these days. It didn't interest him much, or at least as much as he suspected it should. This, for instance, was essentially an ambush. Or perhaps, he thought, as he got out of the car and crunched across the expensive gravel, it wasn't. He found it hard to believe that a woman as intelligent as Barbara Barelli would be surprised to see him.

Antonio Tomaselli had held her against her will in the house. He had threatened her with a gun and locked her in an upstairs room. That much was true. But it was also true that she had gone there of her own free will, and that when Antonio opened the door and let her in, she had stepped over the threshold announcing not only that she knew Kristen Carson was there, but also that she refused to leave without her.

Pallioti doubted that when it came to it, Antonio would have killed her, or Kristen. He was almost certain he didn't want to. But then again, perhaps he hadn't really wanted to kill Aldo Moro, either. It was hard to know, exactly, what went on in people's hearts. Or what they would do when they could not get what they craved—whether it was political recognition, thirteen comrades freed from jail, or one last chance with the woman they loved. In his heart, Pallioti was sure Antonio Tomaselli had wanted that. The past returned, and Angela Vari with it.

Like all attempts to unwind time, and every love

story ever written, it was, he thought, that simple. And that complicated.

*   *   *

This time, the bells ran through their full chime before anyone opened the door. When she did, Hedwige Aarlheissen was barefoot and, somewhat disconcertingly, wearing purple fuzzy leggings and a very long and equally fuzzy purple sweater. To Pallioti's eye, she looked like a large mouldy grape. As he stepped into the hallway, he heard Barbara call from the family room.

'Is it the wine order?'

'Sadly not.'

She looked up at the sound of his voice. Barbara was stretched on the couch, a book in her hand. Giorgio Bassani. Very fitting. *The Garden of the Finzi-Continis.* Pallioti wondered if she was merely suffering from a fit of nostalgia, or if the text held a deeper and more immediate resonance for her. He smiled.

'Dottoressa.'

Barbara nodded and said nothing, her eyes following him as he came into the room and turned down the coffee Hedwige offered. The truth was, he would have loved an espresso, but this wasn't that kind of visit.

'I was wondering,' he said to Barbara, 'if we might talk?'

She dropped her eyes, as if she was hoping he might go away, or might have come for something else. When she looked up and saw him still standing there, she put the book down and nodded.

448

Barbara Barelli swung her legs off the sofa slowly. She was barefoot. A thin gold chain glittered around her left ankle.

'I think,' she said, 'it might be better if we went into my office.'

Pallioti felt Hedwige's eyes as he followed Barbara across the hallway and into the locked room.

Barbara Barelli looked around her office as if it was slightly unfamiliar to her—the big desk, the wall-mounted screen, the rows of cabinets and shelves. The blind over the window was half lowered. She didn't raise it. Instead, she gestured Pallioti to what was obviously 'the client chair'.

'Please, Ispettore,' she said, and sat down behind her desk.

A few seconds of silence passed while she gathered herself. Then Barbara Barelli folded her hands on her blotter.

'How did you know?' she asked.

'The magazine article.'

She nodded.

'The publication,' he said, remembering the files he had picked apart over the weekend. 'The American one, what is it called—'

'*Runner's World*. April 2006.' Barbara swallowed. 'Yes,' she said. 'You see, I went to college, in the United States, on a track scholarship. So I still get the American edition. You know, to keep up.'

Pallioti nodded.

'It was . . .' Barbara cleared her throat. 'There was an article. Because New York was coming up, the marathon, and one of the contenders had been operated on by a Dr Kenneth Carson. He does miracles, apparently. On a routine basis. So, they

449

did a profile on him. And there she was.'

Pallioti folded his hands and leaned back in his chair.

'There she was,' he said.

The conversations he had had with Anna and with the US Federal Marshals in the course of the weekend had yielded differing results. For their part, the Marshals insisted—and their statistics agreed—that they had never lost a member of the Witness Protection Program, provided the witness in question obeyed the rules. The cardinal one was No Contact. No anonymous postcards, or wordless phone calls. No backward glance. No last look. If the break with the past was clean, they kept people safe. If, on the other hand, there was the tiniest chink of light, the tiniest tipping of the hat to the past, all bets were off. So, according to them, since Antonio Tomaselli had clearly known all about Anna Carson, it must have been her fault. She must have done something, however unwittingly, to alert him to who and where she was.

But she hadn't. In the last five days Anna had not wanted to say much to anyone, even Enzo Saenz, but she insisted on that. She had kept her locket, with the picture of her parents in it, and she had kept running. But that was all. And in the end, Pallioti thought, it had been enough.

'Go on,' he said.

Barbara shook her head. She passed a hand over her eyes and looked up at him.

'I couldn't believe it, when I saw it. Her. Or, I don't know. Maybe I could. I never really felt that handful of sand, or whatever it was we buried that day, was Angie. I know it sounds strange, but I never felt her leave. You know?'

450

Pallioti nodded. He did know. He remembered quite clearly the moment his mother died. He had not been allowed upstairs into her room, but had been sent out into the garden and told to 'play'. Standing on the clipped grass, his toy army dutifully arranged at his feet, he had felt suddenly as if a vacuum had been attached to his stomach, as if all of his blood and heart and organs had been sucked out, leaving him so weightless that nothing held him to the earth.

'But Antonio,' Barbara shook her head. 'Antonio did believe it. And it devastated him. He was angry of course, or disappointed—I don't know—about what she did. About what he called "her betrayal". At least at first. Later, I think he almost found it a relief. To stop. Tell the story. Pay his dues. Whatever. I'm not sure he ever knew what he was doing, really, back then, or why, exactly. He kept talking about "bread and roses", but when I asked him, he could never tell me what it meant. I think perhaps he wanted to explain that to Angela, or hoped someday he'd have the chance. I don't know.' She shook her head. 'But I do know that he loved her. I don't even like him. I never did.' Barbara looked down at her hands, still folded on the blotter. 'But I will give him that. He loved Angela. I think perhaps she was the only thing he ever did truly love, except for his grandparents, and his brother—and in some warped way he thought the future would be better for them, I don't know, if Aldo Moro was made to stand trial. That it would be some kind of correction. Justice.'

Pallioti grimaced. There was that word again.

Barbara sighed.

'Yes. Whatever the hell that is,' she agreed. 'In

any case, when he heard that Angie had been killed, it broke his heart. I saw him first at the funeral. My parents, well, my father, was still living in Ferrara then, so I heard and I went and I felt sorry for him.' She looked up at Pallioti. 'And eventually I represented him, yes, because in some way I suppose I did understand what they'd done, even if I didn't agree with it. And because someone had to. But I did it mostly because I thought Angie would have wanted me to. That somehow it kept me close to her. I loved her too, you know.'

Pallioti nodded.

Barbara smiled. 'Odd, isn't it? That Antonio and I should have that in common.' She looked down at her hands. 'Anyway,' she went on when she looked up again, 'I suppose I wanted to be near him because he was the last living trace of her on this earth. Or so I thought.'

'Until you saw the magazine?'

'Until I saw the magazine.'

'And you showed it to Antonio?'

She nodded.

'Yes,' she said. 'I showed it to Antonio.'

Barbara Barelli put her face in her hands.

'I don't know if I wanted to share it with someone,' she said. 'Or if I did it for him. Or if I thought I was doing it for her. I honestly don't know.' She dropped her hands and looked at Pallioti. 'I do know I didn't think anything like this would happen. You have to believe that. I just thought, in his place, I would have wanted to know. No. I would have needed to know.' She shook her head. 'And I thought . . .'

Thought, what? Pallioti leaned forward. 'Dottoressa,' he said. 'You are a lawyer. And as

452

such, your first duty is to the court. You must have understood, surely, what had happened? That Angela Vari had been made a protected witness? And what that meant?'

Barbara Barelli nodded. She opened a drawer, pulled out a tissue, wiped her eyes and nodded again.

'I told him he couldn't tell anyone. Couldn't even whisper. That I was only telling him so he'd know she was all right. I thought Angie would have wanted me to.'

Pallioti stared at her. It always amazed and often terrified him, that highly intelligent people could be so stupid. Especially when it came to love. The heart was a great leveller after all.

'I think—' Barbara ran her hand through her hair—'I didn't understand at the time—it didn't even occur to me, but I think it made him even more angry with her. That when he found out she was still alive, had been alive all this time, he felt doubly betrayed somehow, wanted to punish her, not for Moro, but because she never let him know. That she was still alive—that even if they never saw each other again, he wasn't alone in the world. That she was out there somewhere. And that loving him hadn't got her killed. He'd felt so guilty about that. As if he'd killed her himself.'

Barbara looked at him and shook her head.

'I just didn't understand,' she said. 'Not really. I felt sorry for him, but I never tried to know him. He was my client and I didn't even talk to him. Not really. Then, of course, when you showed up and told me, I understood at once. How he knew the girl's name, and about her mother. It was all in the article, even about how she'd been killed in an accident. I can only imagine,' she bit her lip, 'how he must have used that.'

Pallioti nodded. A sour feeling twisted in his stomach at the memory of the emails, how the hook that reeled Kristen in had been baited and set with her mother's death.

'How is Kristen?'

Pallioti was tempted not to answer the question, to snap *Why should you deserve to know?* then told himself not to be petty.

'Fine,' he said.

And it was true. The young were resilient. With help they would bend and not break. So far, Kristen had bent admirably, and she would have plenty of help, mostly from her father whom she had reclaimed her relationship with. It was hard not to think that was all the easier, all this newfound understanding between father and daughter, because Anna Carson, or Angela Vari, as he suspected she would now prefer to be called, had never had much help—and was no longer resilient, but in a military hospital outside Prato being treated for 'advanced shock and exhaustion'. Which was apparently the current lingo for a broken heart.

After a brief meeting with her husband, she had chosen to stay in Italy, not return to the United States 'until she was better'. Whatever that meant. Pallioti had watched Kristen and Kenneth Carson board a plane hand in hand on Friday morning. Neither father nor daughter had looked back. He suspected strongly that from now on the Carson family would be composed of two.

Barbara Barelli opened her mouth and closed it again. Both of them knew she had been about to

454

ask about Angela, and both of them knew he would not have told her.

He had been present during her 'debriefing' over the weekend, and had visited her yesterday with Enzo Saenz, who had taken some long-overdue time off. Pallioti was almost as worried about him as he was about Angela. Enzo had fallen in love late and hard and his self-contained world was pierced. He did not know it yet, but Pallioti understood that he would never know solitude again now that he had been introduced to loneliness.

He looked at Barbara Barelli.

'The car,' he said. 'I take it you won't make me waste the time tracing the holding company that owns it?'

'No.' She shook her head. 'He asked me to buy the house. That was his price, for staying quiet about what I'd told him. And then the car. When he got out. I set up another dummy company.' She waved her hand. 'It's all perfectly legal but . . .'

Perhaps, Pallioti thought. In the strictly practical sense of the word. At least as far as the purchases went. But the court of public opinion would be something else altogether. Not to mention the fact that knowingly compromising a witness would, at the very least, mean she was suspended while she was investigated before being stripped of her right to practise. There might well be additional charges—for lying to the police, not co-operating in an ongoing investigation—depending on who was feeling vindictive. It was a fair guess, given the causes she had chosen to defend, that Barbara Barelli had enemies. Probably powerful ones who would be all too happy to have a dig at her. And

455

none of that even began to touch on her moral obligation to her client, and his safety. To say it had been compromised was something of a sick joke.

Pallioti stood up. What he was about to say gave him no pleasure. Barbara Barelli was a gifted lawyer. The causes she fought for had been the right ones.

'Will you write the letter?' he asked. 'Or would you like me to?'

She looked at him for a moment, then folded her hands on the blotter again and shook her head.

'I'll do it,' she said. 'This afternoon. I'll submit myself for judicial investigation, and relinquish my licence. Immediately. Regardless of the outcome.'

Pallioti nodded. Then he turned on his heel and started towards the door. He was about to turn the handle when she said, 'Ispettore?'

He turned round. Barbara Barelli had stood up. Her fingertips rested on the blotter. The cloud of her dark hair drifted on her shoulders. Looking at her, he remembered again how much he had liked and even admired her.

'I wondered,' she asked, 'of course, I wasn't there, but—have you seen the autopsy report?'

Pallioti smiled. There was no humour in it at all.

'The real one?'

She nodded.

A piece had come out in the papers, barely more than a paragraph, telling yet another pathetic story about the end of the Red Brigades. Detailing how, after his release from prison, Antonio Tomaselli had been 'unable to adjust'. Had struggled first to find a job and then to build a life, and had finally given up on both when he retreated to an isolated

456

farmhouse outside Ferrara where he had 'died in an accident involving a gun'.

Pallioti looked at his watch. 'It should be on my desk,' he said, 'when I get back to the office.'

'Will you tell me what it says? Just for the record?'

His mouth twitched in an unpleasant smile. He nodded. 'Just for the record.'

*   *   *

Once again, the fat man had been as good as his word. It was strange, Pallioti thought, but there really was a code of honour among thieves. Or perhaps it was something less admirable even than that. And more dangerous. An irreducible part of the arrogance that led to the crime in the first place. He had read once that the spy Kim Philby had kept a framed photograph of a mountain in Russia on the wall of his office the entire time he worked for British Intelligence. The idea made him smile. It was a known fact that people never really looked at photographs.

He had, though. All last night. The pictures of Angela Vari's funeral had worried him from the beginning. It was only just before dawn that he finally understood what he was seeing.

Now, he tipped them out and spread them across his desk. As everyone knew, the early hours of the morning were notoriously unreliable. He wanted to be certain, in the cold light of day.

*   *   *

It was not just the number of photos, it was the

angles they had been taken from. Far too many. He had realized at once that there had been more than one police photographer in the cemetery. Now he understood why. They were not merely keeping a record. They were setting up evidence. He couldn't spot the 'shooter' crouched behind the crypt. Or shooters—there would surely have been more than one. Or the shoulder holsters worn by the prison guards—who he doubted were prison guards at all—but he understood now that they had stayed so well back, had taken Antonio Tomaselli's chains off, had not even had him handcuffed—not out of respect, but because they had hoped he would run.

No one had taken the bait and come to try and set him free. Mara was dead, and the others were locked up, or were too smart, or simply didn't care enough. During the war it had been a point of pride among the Partisans that they rescued their own, never handed them over to the enemy. But, as Barbara said, Antonio had never quite been one of them, had never quite belonged. To anyone. Except Angela Vari.

Which didn't mean he wouldn't do something very stupid. Take the opportunity of her funeral, for instance, to bolt. Make a dash, conveniently relieved of all restraints, through the crypts and monuments, and vanish into the city he knew so well.

If he had, he would have been dead. And the whole thing would have been caught on film. All asses amply covered.

Notorious Terrorist Attempts to Flee—Tragic Shooting Assures Safety of Population.

They must have been crushed when he was too

458

busy grieving.

Pallioti wondered if they would have shot Barbara Barelli, too. Possibly, if she got in the way. What did they call it these days? Collateral damage. He pushed the photos away in disgust. Then he turned to the envelope.

He didn't know if this was a second autopsy report. He suspected not. Antonio was not Mara. He wasn't a founder of the BR, or a beautiful young woman who had busted her husband out of jail. And he did not have a wife or lover to be outraged, to organize vigils and light candles and call for 'vengeance' for his 'assassination'. He was just a two-bit conspirator, probably a killer. A dried-up terrorist reduced to manipulating teenagers. So Pallioti doubted they'd bothered. Antonio Tomaselli wasn't worth a fake report. Pallioti found himself half surprised they'd bothered with an autopsy at all. But they had. That was another puzzling thing about pictures. How often killers took them of their victims. He thought of all the film footage, all the photographs, from the camps.

There weren't as many of the autopsy as there were of Angela's funeral. He'd seen hundreds of death reports with more. But there were enough.

The ones shot from the front were ugly. But not as bad as the ones taken from the back, when they'd rolled him over. Pallioti gave a slight shudder. Snipers' bullets made one hell of a mess. Which was more or less the point. If you lined up a good shot, you didn't want to have to take it twice.

As the brief autopsy notes confirmed, Antonio had been hit squarely in the back of the head. Pallioti wasn't too surprised to read that he'd been hit again just below the left shoulder, probably as he went down. Just for good measure. Just to show off. See if you can rupture the heart while you're at it. Not that it was necessary. The first shot was a beauty. It had essentially blown off the top of his skull.

There were a few scene photos showing the diameter of the spatter marks, which were impressive. Antonio's head had all but exploded. From the looks of the body, he had been lifted off his feet, thrown forward, and had landed face down on the rutted cobbles, his hands outstretched. The gun, the one he'd dropped on hearing Angela Vari's voice, had been so far behind him it wasn't even in the photograph. No second weapon had been found on his body or in the house.

Pallioti had expected to feel sick. He had expected to need a drink, or fly into a rage. Had thought perhaps he would pick things up and hurl them against the wall, indulge in what his mother had called 'throwing his toys about'. But he didn't. He didn't even feel the compulsion to call Rome, shriek down the phone at the fat man, who, either before or after he told him again that petulance didn't suit him, would doubtless remind him that they were all fighting the War on Terror.

Instead, he walked to the window and stared down at the familiar view of the piazza, realizing that he ought to be tired. Or at least a little surprised. Barbara Barelli's words came back to him. *You couldn't survive if you really thought that the State, that your beloved Polizia even, might go around 'eliminating' those they find inconvenient. Or just plain don't like. That they might do a little*

460

'correcting' when they think the courts have got it wrong. But of course he could. He had. Because, he thought, looking at the flags, the lily of Florence, the Italian tricolour that flew in front of the fancy new police building, we lie about what we love. To ourselves and to others. But mostly to ourselves. We lie about it because we are selfish and cowardly and human. And because, sometimes, when we are forced to see what we love for what it really is, we have to give it up.

He walked back to his desk, sat down, and unscrewed his favourite pen.

Fifteen minutes later, when he had finished writing, he made a copy of the single page on the machine in his cupboard. Then he gathered up the papers and photographs the fat man had sent him, and slipped them, together with the copy, into a large manila envelope that he addressed to Barbara Barelli. The original page, he folded carefully, then sealed into one of his own envelopes and addressed it to the Mayor.

*   *   *

In the outer office, Guillermo was bent over his computer. He glanced at his watch, then reached out without looking up and pushed the intercom button to Pallioti's office.

'Just to remind you,' he said, 'you have a meeting at three with—'

'Cancel it.'

Pallioti's voice was not much more than a murmur, but the tone caused Guillermo to sit up. He was about to ask if he'd heard correctly when the line went dead. Guillermo looked at the closed door to the inner office and felt his mouth go dry. A moment later when it opened and Pallioti came out carrying a large envelope and wearing his overcoat, Guillermo, without being quite sure why, stood as he left the office.

*   *   *

The day had turned windy and bitterly cold. Pallioti pulled on his gloves as he came down the steps.

I am resigning my position because I will not serve a State that kills people.

I am resigning because of my severe moral reservations.

I am resigning because we've become a murderous, lying, self-righteous shipload of shits whom I wouldn't advise a gerbil to trust and I'm sick of it.

Of all the wording he'd toyed with, he preferred the last, although even in his present state of mind, he realized he couldn't say it. And to be fair, it wasn't entirely accurate. There were many policemen who were neither self-righteous nor liars, and who did their jobs as well as they could. More often than not with bravery and distinction. He just wasn't going to be one of them any more.

The fountain hissed and spat, flinging its silver drops like a child having a tantrum. A few carriages were pulled up near the taxi rank, the horses swaddled in blankets. Behind the glass, the restaurant was full. No one was standing under the loggia or sitting on its steps. Above him, the flags snapped and clicked, keeping time as he crossed towards the flower-seller's kiosk.

The buckets weren't out. It was too cold, and

462

they'd tip over in the wind. Inside the little pavilion, the air was warm and heavy with scent. The flower-seller jumped up from his stool when he saw Pallioti. They had been friends for a long time.

'Dottore.' He clapped his hands together. 'What can I get you? The usual for the Signora?'

The Signora was not Pallioti's wife, he didn't have such a thing, but his sister. He was in the habit of taking Saffy flowers when he had dinner with her once a week, or went to Sunday lunch, or a show or opening at her gallery. She was fond of tulips, in the spring, and generally of roses. He shook his head.

'Something else,' he said. 'Today. Something special. And white. That will get through the night. I'm going to a funeral tomorrow.'

The flower-seller made a face.

'My condolences, Dottore,' he said. 'Not family, I hope?'

Pallioti shook his head.

'No,' he said. 'Not family.'

They were burying Antonio Tomaselli in Ferrara, not far from where they had once buried Angela Vari. He didn't know who would be there, or shed any tears. The man's father, a cripple, had died while he was in prison. His mother, from what Pallioti understood, was blind and frail and had for many years, ever since the death of Aldo Moro whom she had considered a saint, claimed she no longer had a son. He doubted the fat man would show up, and wondered if he'd have the nerve to punch him if he did. Probably not, on both counts. In the end, he thought, it would just be Angela and Enzo and himself, a strange little trio, not one of

463

them believing in God as they stood beside the open grave with a priest and a few DIGOS agents reciting the prayers for the dead.

He watched as the flower-seller prepared the bouquet, his chapped red hands quick and delicate as he chose the blossoms, and trimmed their stems, then crimped and wrapped and tied them with a suitably sombre bow, and thought of what he had said. How, in the end, he had taken a page from the *Brigate Rosse*, a 'prayer' from what Anna Carson had told him she called their 'book of hours'. Kept it simple. Clean and fast. Finally just paraphrasing Barbara Barelli.

I am resigning because when we become judge and executioner, there is no difference between 'Them' and 'Us'.

Pallioti handed a significant number of euro notes to the old man and told him to keep the change. Then he folded the manila envelope carefully into his pocket, and cradled the flowers in his arms as he walked across the piazza, and turned down the alley that led towards the river and home.

AUTHOR'S NOTE

This book is a work of fiction. Although I have tried to stick as closely as possible to the facts surrounding the Aldo Moro kidnapping and other incidents concerning the Red Brigades, it is important to note that Antonio Tomaselli and Angela Vari are products solely of my imagination. Any resemblance they may bear to persons living or dead is completely coincidental.

ACKNOWLEDGEMENTS

With special thanks to Jane Gregory and all of the staff at Gregory and Company.

And to Maria Rejt, Sophie Orme, Eli Dryden, Chloe Healy and all of the others at Macmillan and Mantle who do the 'real' work.

And to David, for putting up with me. And to Joolio, and P, and Cass McGovern, for their good humour, guiding hands, wise advice, and endless patience. Friendship Above and Beyond—